MYTHOMANIA

Copyright © 2024 by Lauren Hope

All rights reserved. No part of this publication may be reproduced, stored or transmitted in any form or by any means, electronic, mechanical, photocopying, recording, scanning, or otherwise without written permission from the publisher. It is illegal to copy this book, post it to a website, or distribute it by any other means without permission.

This novel is entirely a work of fiction. The names, characters and incidents portrayed in it are the work of the author's imagination. Any resemblance to actual persons, living or dead, events or localities is entirely coincidental.

Lauren Hope asserts the moral right to be identified as the author of this work.

Publisher: I.M.L.H Fbg St-Mart 75010 Paris
First edition
Print ISBN: 978-2-9584111-2-1
Ebook ISBN: 978-2-9584111-3-8

Printed in UK by Lghtning Source UK Ltd. - Milton Keynes UK (print on demand)
Cover: PixelshotXCanva
Legal deposit:
British Library, London - October 2024
Bibliothèque Nationale de France, Paris - October 2024

CONTENTS

Dedication

— Author's Note
1

— Introduction
5

1 — Then, here, and now...
9

2 — Escaping the nightmare...
29

3 — Between present and memories...
43

4 — Forrest Hill, 1 year before the tragedy...
73

5 — Then, here, and now...
103

6 – Laura's diary - Y2K
117

7 – Laura's diary: Brandon and Me
129

8 – Laura's diary: Love, glory, lies and betrayal...
139

9 – The night of tragedy, six feet under...
161

10 – Forrest Hill, 8 months before the tragedy...
169

11 – Laura's diary: Battle Plan
179

12 – Six feet under, the night of tragedy...
187

13 – Laura's diary - My life is a long quiet river...
197

14 – Six Feet Under: in the den of vice...
211

15 – Forrest Hill, 8 months before the tragedy...
217

16 – Six feet under, in the den of vice...
231

17 – Forrest Hill, 7 months before the tragedy...
241

18 – Laura's diary: a turning point
251

19 – Laura's diary: a new beginning...
259

20 – Laura's diary: be beaten at one's own game...
273

21 – Forrest Hill, 7 months before the tragedy...
281

22 – Laura's diary: fate and jealousy
321

23 – Laura's diary: My entry into the world
327

24 – Laura's Diary: life change
343

25 – Laura's Diary: so close to the goal...
349

26 – Forrest Hill, the day before the tragedy...
353

27 – Laura's diary: perfect timing
371

28 – Laura's diary: Show time
377

29 – In the den of vice, six feet under...
387

30 – Laura's diary: My last wishes...
403

31 – These days, in the here and now...
409

32 – Downtown Central: First meeting
421

33 – Laura, earlier in the day...
431

34 – Downtown Central, Interrogation Room
439

35 – Laura, earlier in the evening...
445

36 – Downtown Central, crisis unit
449

37 – Laura: in the Palace of the Gods...
463

38 – Tom, journey to the center of the earth...
473

39 – Laura: the other side of the coin...
481

40 – Before the bell tolls, in the den of vice...
489

41 – Tom, in the den of vice...
501

42 – Laura: Checkmate!
507

43 – Meanwhile, on the other side of the mirror...
515

44 – Forrest Hill, a few streets from the clinic...
523

45 – Time for the truth...
533

46 – Epilogue
557

To all survivors.

LAUREN HOPE

MYTHOMANIA

A Tale of Lies, Love and Destruction

First Edition

Author's Note

Mythomania: A Tale of Lies, Love and Destruction is a fiction novel that delves into themes of mental manipulation, cruelty, jealousy, and emotional distress. The plot reveals the sinister schemes a disturbed mind can devise in its pursuit of satisfaction and recognition. This book contains content warnings and may be disturbing, so we advise readers to be aware. If you are a sensitive reader, please proceed with caution.

- Sexual assault / rape
- Mental abuse
- Murder
- Torture
- Kidnapping and abduction
- Blood
- Death
- Violence
- Pornographic content
- Eating disorders, body hatred, and fatphobia
- Swearing or curses
- Nudity
- Drug and substance abuse

"Forgive us for our mistakes as we forgive those who make mistakes against us."

Mt.6.12

INTRODUCTION

―――――――

Somewhere Unreal...

The air feels thick with cold and darkness, shrouding everything in blackness, silence, and oppression. Tom floats, as if his body and mind have been abandoned in an infinite void. He spins with unsettling ease, unable to see anything in this eerie place. No light pierces the surrounding darkness. Is this the end? If that's the case, then this place is anything but a sanctuary. Where are the angels? And where is the compassionate God who embraces his children as they take their final breath?

There is no affection here, only a wavering existence, fused with these cursed surroundings. The energy feels familiar but terrifying. It roams silently, taunting anyone who disturbs its melancholic slumber, daring them to challenge it. It waits, ready to seize its victim and drag them into the depths of despair...

The birds are singing... Once... The freezing wind halts him, sending chills across his body. In the background, soft sobbing reaches his ears—crying born of exhaustion and grief. The miserable woman clings to the little life she has left—but for how long?

The birds are singing... Twice... The presence draws closer, its harmful aura creeping into the space. Tom feels nauseous, and the air becomes unbreathable. Suddenly, the ground gives way beneath him, and what he assumes are his legs are pulled into the chasm. A foul stench rises from the gap, assaulting his nostrils. There is no escape, no place to hide.

The birds are singing... Again... Resigned to his fate? A deep voice suddenly echoes: "Say hello to your wife!" The voice is flat and menacing. The birds keep singing their mournful tune...

"I don't know her!" Tom tries to reply, but no words come out. His lips won't move, no matter how hard he tries... The sobbing in the distance grows louder... The voice returns, now hysterical, annoyed: "Say hello to your fucking wife!"

The birds' song swells... Where are these birds coming from? It's as if their song has no effect on the voice. Is Tom losing his mind? Is he the only one who hears them? Could they be a sign of hope? The sobbing turns into a scream of terror—a final cry, the last breath of the condemned...

"You're finally going to meet your wife! I'm getting impatient!" The entity is beside him now, whispering in his ear. Her tone shifts, playful yet dripping with hatred. A shiver runs down Tom's spine. "Do you want to be like them? Like HER?" She sneers, a wicked grin twisting her voice.

A grey mist forms suddenly, and Tom catches a brief glimpse of what was once a face, now grotesque, swollen. A few blood-stained strands of hair cling to the skull, and empty sockets stare back at him. There is nothing human left in this presence; it embodies madness, hatred, and death. Confident in her control, she presses her face to Tom's and forces a kiss. Like a demon, she thrusts her tongue deep into the mouth of her captured prey.

The birds sing once more before fading away... Tom is pulled into the abyss, his final scream silenced by the explosion. It's too late to struggle... The voice exhales its final words: "You belong to me! Forever!"

CHAP 1

THEN, HERE, AND NOW...

Tom wakes up, sweat pouring down his forehead. Disoriented, he tries to gather his thoughts. The terrifying figure from his recurring nightmare fades as daylight floods the room. For nearly six months, this ritual has played out every morning...At 6:45 a.m., the alarm on his phone goes off, accompanied by a loop of birdsong. Another rude awakening, another shitty day. Irritated, he leaps from the bed and grabs his phone from the nightstand. Shut those damn birds up, quickly! Usually, their twittering soothes him. Closing his eyes, he clings to the memory of her face, trying to push aside the struggles of his nights. He remembers her happy laugh when she set the alarm on his phone...

"You'll see, the birds will take you straight to the countryside."

Her sweet voice, the smell of her skin, her smile... He looked at her with love... He couldn't refuse her anything. So the birds stayed. Stuck in this repetitive moment, they seem to be calling him out of bed, yet also luring him into the torment of his nightmares. Tom isn't sure. He refuses to believe it, refuses to dive deeper. He's just tired. As night falls, he dreads sleep. He often lies awake for hours, fighting the pull of slumber. Sleep means entering a dark place, somewhere between purgatory and the gates of hell.

Before turning off the alarm, he hesitates. If the birds stopped singing, maybe he'd sleep better. But stopping them might mean letting HER go, letting her die. He can't bear the thought of his brain slowly erasing her. She's his reason for living, his only connection to the world... Madee... At the sound of her name, Tom's mood lightens. He looks at the fragile blonde woman still asleep beside him. Melancholy hits him. He leans in to kiss her, to feel the warmth of her body against his. But he stops. He realizes the woman sharing his bed isn't the one in his heart. This woman doesn't care about the birdsong, as long as it doesn't disturb her. She doesn't care about much at all. Laura is Tom's girlfriend. In short, Laura is everywhere. They've only been together for four months. People say opposites attract, and for them, it's true. Tom is quiet and reserved, a homebody, while Laura loves socializing and sharing her life on social medias. Overexposure is her way of seeking approval.

MYTHOMANIA

Laura's breath reeks of alcohol, a sign of last night's indulgence. She collapsed on the bed, still in her dress, suggesting the trip home was rough. Used to these disappointing mornings after her nights out, Tom keeps his thoughts to himself. He looks away from her, his desire to keep his distance growing stronger.

He gets up and heads to the closet. From a pile of "comfort" clothes, he grabs a random pair of track pants and a T-shirt. When emotions overwhelm him, running is his only release. Through sport, he can channel his energy and maintain the composure people admire. No one suspects that Tom, this attractive, calm, and polite guy, struggles with powerful inner turmoil. Dressed in his running gear, unconcerned with his appearance, he moves quietly through the house. It feels like he's escaping something unpleasant, slipping away unnoticed.

At the front door, he takes his trainers out of the wardrobe. He privately laughs at the neat rows of Laura's fancy shoes. Ever since moving in with him, Laura's had a strict rule—no shoes in the house. Anyone who disobeys gets subjected to her boring lecture on cleanliness and hygiene. Yet even drunk, she still takes her shoes off. Tom finds Laura's fear of germs irrational, but he stays quiet to avoid conflict. When upset, Laura becomes rigid, stubborn. She clings to her opinions, treats them as facts, and avoids any discussion. And that's the end.

Tom steps outside and takes a deep breath. His jog is even more enjoyable now that the weather has been fine for a few weeks. After a restless night, his body feels tense, so he starts running briskly. In just five minutes, he can pick up the pace. Tom used to be a smoker. To avoid straining his lungs, he slows down, switching from jogging to walking. Smoking had been a habit for years—it was something that made him feel good, something he couldn't find in daily life. It calmed him, gave him an excuse to isolate himself, a barrier between him and others... Ghosts always have a way of coming back to haunt their victims.

By the time Tom decides to take a break, he's already walked a kilometer. He hasn't noticed the presence silently following him, watching every step, waiting for the right moment...

"Say hello to your wife."

As he catches his breath, the vision of horror flashes before him. The cavernous voice whispers its strange litany... Fatigue must be making him hallucinate—don't panic. It's all just an illusion. Tom isn't superstitious; he's never believed in the supernatural. There's enough misery in the real world without adding to it with ghost stories. His logical mind refuses to accept the idea of things that don't exist. Tom screams, "You're a fucking nightmare!" as if to convince himself he's not losing it. The hysterical voice echoes again, and a cold breeze sweeps through him.

"Say hello to your wife."

Run! Run through the forest, don't stop, don't look back. Don't look back. His lungs burn, his legs scream for relief, but he keeps going. He's out of breath, gasping, but he doesn't stop...

"Say hello to your fucking wife."

MYTHOMANIA

The Presence closes in. His thighs are on fire, his calves ache, the ground feels like it's crumbling beneath him. A sharp pain pierces his chest, and his breath becomes ragged. He screams, unsure if it's from pain or desperation, but it rises from deep inside him. Exhausted, drenched in morning dew, he collapses onto the grass, curling up into a fetal position. With his hands over his ears, he tries to block out the noise. His body shakes uncontrollably, and tears flood his cheeks. Tom rarely lets himself cry; it's his rule, his way of staying sane, of keeping his head clear. What would Madee have done in this situation? Madee... the one who saw the good in everything and everyone. The thought makes him feel even more lost, and the tears come harder.

"Why did you leave me? Why?" He sighs, hoping Madee will appear, hold him in her arms. "Show me the way..." It's a strange request from a man whose fate seems already sealed.

* * *

Tom Collins is the only son of John and Margaretha Collins, magnates of a real estate empire that shares their name. The Collins family is known for living extravagantly, but in their own way. Despite their wealth, this dynamic, hard-working couple break the usual rules of the rich. They are discreet, prefer the company of people they genuinely like, and have little patience for boring social events. They indulge in the fruits of their labor, but never over-spend. The Collins don't flaunt their wealth. To them, it's the result of collective effort, something that wouldn't have been possible without believing in the work of others. This mindset often clashes with a world where flaunting status is the norm.

John Collins hasn't forgotten his humble beginnings. Before he was rich, he worked multiple jobs just to get by. The youngest in a large family that struggled to make ends meet, he left school after high school to start working. No, John didn't always wear a businessman's suit and tie... Now in his sixties, John is tall with a square jaw and grey streaks in his hair. With his fair hair and blue eyes, he looks like a Hollywood actor. His charisma and natural presence leave an impression on everyone, but he isn't arrogant—just painfully shy. For a businessman who should radiate confidence, this is a rare trait. His shyness is often mistaken for pretentiousness, but John has learned to use that to his advantage. Being perceived as a snob allows him to keep people at a distance and avoid wasting time with the media. After a failed interview where he barely said a word, the press dubbed him "Iceberg John."

Among his staff, though, John is known as "The Holy Boss." Every year, he gives significant bonuses to employees at the bottom of the ladder—a rare practice in a large company where top executives usually take the biggest share. His sense of fairness and respect for others guide his business practices. John believes in fair and honest rewards for hard work, which makes him a popular and respected boss, admired for his simplicity and humanity.

MYTHOMANIA

Margaretha, Tom's mother, is vibrant and full of life, nearing 60. Her blonde hair is always perfectly styled in an elegant '80s blow-dry. Margaretha has never been obsessed with makeup, and her face is remarkably free of wrinkles. She has nothing to hide and hasn't tried to fight the passing years, instead wearing them proudly.

A timeless beauty, her bright face, welcoming smile, and laughing eyes make her seem forever youthful. Her slender, graceful figure adds to her air of eternal youth. Margaretha is the Collins family's charming asset. But until she met John, nothing in her life had prepared her for the world of business.

Margaretha was the only daughter of painters. It seemed natural that she would follow in their footsteps, attending art school. She was considered the artist of the future by her mentors. But when fate decides to bring two people together, nothing can stand in its way. It's this mysterious force that sets events in motion, changing lives with clockwork precision.

When John and Margaretha moved into the modest building that would become the scene of their meeting, they were still young and full of dreams. Love awaited them, and the thin wall between their two apartments couldn't keep them apart. It was love at first sight, and they quickly grew close, sharing the same values and ideals. In the evenings, they would talk for hours about changing the world, hoping that one day, they'd be able to help others.

Their poverty wasn't a permanent state but rather a necessary step in their journey, shaping these two vibrant souls.

Margaretha's natural beauty and sensitivity captivated John. Her colorful view of life reminded him of the abstract paintings she adored. For her, life was a mix of light and shadow, a blank canvas where everyone was free to express themselves. For John, who had always carried the weight of responsibility, this artistic interpretation was a breath of fresh air. Margaretha saw greatness in John, even in his youth. Honest, responsible, and protective, she knew from the moment they met that he was her one true love. Their bond, already strong, grew deeper as their complementary natures came to light. They spent every free moment together, unable to imagine life apart. Broke but happy, John and Margaretharadiated a love that transformed everything around them.

But fate had other blessings in store. They had decided to move in together but couldn't agree on which apartment to keep. John loved his tidy home, while Margaretha was attached to her creative chaos. They dreamed of a space where they could create a haven of love, a peaceful refuge where the outside world's problems would disappear once they stepped through the door. Deciding who would move in with the other seemed impossible, as neither wanted to burden the other.

Moving closer to the city and shortening Margaretha's long train rides to art school seemed like the only logical solution. John, who worked in construction, wasn't concerned about where they lived. He was willing to do whatever it took to be with Margaretha. Moving to a bigger apartment meant more expenses, which meant they needed more income. John wanted Margaretha to focus on her art—a gallery had shown interest in her work, and if she could secure an exhibit, she could quit her cashier job and pursue her passion full-time. In the meantime, John took on the responsibility of providing for them. Splitting their income wasn't an option—Margaretha deserved the best, and John was determined to give her a comfortable life.

Days and months passed, but their search for a new place was fruitless. Their spirits began to sink as every apartment that might have suited them was too expensive. Landlords, cautious about their precarious employment, refused to rent to the young couple. Every night, they went to bed feeling like their dream was slipping away. John brooded in silence, taking on the burden alone, shutting Margaretha out. Once again, he carried a responsibility that could have been shared. Conversations became impossible. John would shut down when Margaretha suggested letting go of their search, at least for now. They saw each other less and less, and John began avoiding her. Their love, strong as it was, faced a test. An argument was brewing, and Margaretha couldn't keep her thoughts to herself any longer. She didn't understand why John was shutting her out. She had never been demanding, never given ultimatums, yet he was being so hard on himself. She was tired of watching him struggle alone.

Margaretha knew anger was a poor advisor. She hated violence in all its forms and couldn't bear the thought of saying something hurtful to the man she loved. Sooner or later, she would have regretted it. She just missed him so much. At night, knowing he was home from work, she would press her ear against the partition, just to feel his presence. Sometimes, she'd hear his footsteps and knock three times on the wall. Then, she would start a monologue, telling him how much she loved him, how she saw their relationship, and how she longed to be with him. She'd tell him about her day, about her art lessons, supermarket customers, and even the gallery that had chosen a more famous artist. None of it mattered to her. He was there, and she didn't want to let him go.

On the other side of the wall, John listened, moved, one hand on the partition, the other on his heart. His pride wouldn't let him admit he was failing. He could feel her disappointment when she mentioned the gallery. She had worked so hard... How could they reject Margaretha? So creative, so talented—what a loss!

The weight of it all was too much. Furious, John grabbed a hammer, intending to pound out his frustrations on the wall. Or maybe smash the gallery windows... Angry, he swung with all his might. One blow was enough to send the middle section of the partition crashing to the ground. Margaretha, still behind the wall, burst into laughter at the sight of John standing there, hammer in hand.

Forgetting the frustrations of the past months, the two lovers reunited in each other's arms. As they embraced, they looked around their now connected apartments. With a little work, they could turn the space into the love nest they'd been dreaming of. Beautiful open spaces, endless possibilities for design—all without the wall. Without saying it, the same thought crossed their minds: why not merge the two apartments into one?

It could be done, in theory. But they'd need the landlord's approval. An old widower with little money, their landlord wasn't a practical man. He was a staunch defender of the status quo and unlikely to agree to such a change. It would mean revising the rent, something he wasn't inclined to do. The couple had only one card to play: Margaretha's charm. Their first negotiation failed. The gruff old man waved away their arguments, content with his apartments as they were. Why change anything, he thought? And he didn't have the money to indulge the whims of two young tenants. Their love was touching, but only as long as it didn't affect his wallet.

John insisted, explaining that, as a builder, he would handle both the materials and labor. There would be almost no financial risk for the landlord. The old miser, though tempted by John's offer, wasn't ready to give in just yet. He was the owner, after all, and he planned to let them stew a little longer. He ordered the partition to be repaired immediately and sent John and Margaretha on their way. Satisfied, the old man believed he had won. Youth was fickle, after all, and he figured their enthusiasm would fade. He thought he was doing them a favor—who would want to live here forever?

The neighborhood wasn't a priority for the local council, far removed from downtown, with a population of low-income workers. Politicians didn't care about the problems of the people at the bottom. The area had no access to funds for improvements. Most of the residents were resigned to their fate, just waiting to die. But John and Margaretha refused to let their dream go. They were certain the old man would come around. And when a woman in love sets her mind on something, nothing can stand in her way. Margaretha, with John's blessing, decided to lead the next negotiation. They agreed to the landlord's terms: full payment of both rents during the renovations, with an increase if he wasn't satisfied with the final result.

But that didn't faze them. They started sketching plans, taking measurements, and brainstorming in impromptu evening meetings. Sometimes, they argued over the layout of cupboards or the color of paint. Their budget was tiny, so they had to get creative. Margaretha scoured flea markets and salvaged items left on the pavement, while John hunted for bargains at DIY stores and brought home surplus materials from job sites. More than once, they endured suspicious looks from their neighbors when the work officially began. Ambition wasn't common here, and John and Margaretha stood out. They were young, vibrant, and full of hope—an unfamiliar sight in this place.

They camped out in a corner of their future home, surrounded by tarps, planks, and tools, their lives unfolding amid the chaos. Their belongings, carefully organized into a messy pile, sat at the end of the hall. Occasionally, the old man passed by, pretending to be annoyed. He would remind them of the safety regulations, emphasizing the need to keep exits clear in case of fire. The building wasn't modern, and in an emergency, the only escape was to jump out the windows. The old man knew this, but teasing the young couple amused him. He wasn't much for humor, so he preferred being grumpy.

Six months of hard work, and the apartment was finally done. John and Margaretha could hardly believe it—their first home, transformed. Standing there, ready to embrace their happiness, excitement mixed with anxiety. The landlord's verdict was the last hurdle. When the old man stepped inside, he barely recognized the place. What had once been two small apartments was now a spacious home with a proper bedroom and ensuite bath, a beautiful fitted kitchen, a large living room, a wall-mounted library, and an art studio. Everything was practical, elegant, and built to last. From almost nothing, John and Margaretha had created understated luxury. The apartment had become a gem of architecture. Too bad the neighborhood wasn't for the wealthy, the old man thought. He could rent this place for a fortune...

John and Margaretha watched him cautiously, nervous about the rent he would set. The old man found himself in a dilemma: he admired their hard work and perseverance but had no idea why he was hoarding so much money. He had no children, and when he died, the estate would go to the government. A lifetime of accumulating wealth just to enrich bureaucrats? Never!

Without hesitation, he made them an offer: they would pay rent for only one apartment instead of two. In return, he encouraged them to show their work to professionals. With a bit of publicity, perhaps the area could finally be revitalized. In Margaretha's mind, the idea begins to take shape. The grumpy old man was right: the neighborhood doesn't look great, but its potential is immense. Margaretha writes letters to local newspapers and magazines, taking hundreds of photos of the apartment. She passionately shares her story, introducing herself and John as two young property entrepreneurs. She extols the virtues of modernizing modest neighborhoods and hints at a major renovation project, with the support of their landlord, who owns several buildings in the area. Margaretha has embellished the truth. But she knows that to get the media's attention, you need to offer them either smoke and mirrors or scandal. Bluffing is necessary. The results come quickly. The couple is featured by a top interior design magazine as innovators and visionaries, and soon other newspapers pick up the story.

That's how The Collins Company is born. Investors and the local council, eager to ride the media wave, quickly jump on board. John and Margaretha find themselves stretched thin—one managing the design teams, the other handling negotiations. For a couple who started with nothing, their lives have radically changed. As the money flows in, the Collins name becomes synonymous with success. Slowly but surely, they rise to prominence, sought after for high-profile projects.

MYTHOMANIA

Generous development loans help renovate part of the neighborhood. Trendy newcomers move into the buildings the media raves about. The grumpy old man, proud of his role in the project, is pleased with the economic revival. Privately, he knows none of this would have happened without his consent. He thanks God for his instincts, and in his heart, he believes his late wife, Elisabeth, has guided him to make the right decision.

Despite the pressure, John and Margaretha remain as close and in love as ever. John, finally able to pamper Margaretha, asks her to marry him. Now that money is no longer an issue, he wants to give her the future she deserves. They marry on a beautiful spring morning in an intimate ceremony, surrounded by the people who have been with them before success. They don't dream of a bourgeois wedding filled with their new social circle. John and Margaretha always keep their personal and professional lives separate. Business is too brutal and superficial to compromise their love.

Two years later, after a difficult pregnancy and birth, Tom is born. The Collins family couldn't be more blessed. They had hoped for a child since their financial situation stabilized, but before Tom's birth, Margaretha had suffered three miscarriages. Doctors doubted she could carry a pregnancy to term. For nine months, Margaretha lives in constant fear of losing her baby. Her instincts tell her Tom will be their only child, so she isn't surprised when the doctors say a second pregnancy would be risky, if not impossible.

Nevertheless, John and Margaretha see Tom as a miracle. They never tire of gazing at their beautiful, blue-eyed, curly-haired baby. The young parents always vowed to protect their son from hardship. Life hadn't been kind to them, and they had earned everything through hard work. Now, their mission is to ensure Tom never has to worry about a thing, so he can enjoy life fully. The road ahead will be smooth.

But the sweet utopia of protective parents can't shape a person's character. Despite their best intentions, Tom's life is too easy. From the moment he is born, he has an ideal existence—the kind of life others dream of. The first words he understands are, *"You're perfect, my darling."* Pampered and surrounded by love, Tom grows up bored. Silent, enigmatic, and lonely, he observes the world with sharp eyes, though nothing seems to interest him. Without fully realizing it, he sees the worst in people. Retreating into silence, he spends hours alone in his room. His mind absorbs everything, though his voice is barely heard. To his parents, he is a sweet and tender boy, but to the outside world, his cold demeanor is unsettling. Tom is present without being truly present.

From a young age, Tom knows he holds a special place in a world that offers him nothing. Despite the attention and privilege, he often wonders what life would have been like if he had been ordinary. He isn't like the others, and he knows he doesn't need to work to be somebody. When the time comes, his parents assume he will join their company. As long as John, Margaretha, and their trusted team are there, Tom won't have to worry about anything. His role will be to sign papers.

The prospect of such a future only pushes Tom further into isolation. He isn't good at socializing, and it shows at school. He prefers to read alone rather than interact with other children. His grades are excellent, but his attitude irritates teachers. When asked a question, Tom either refuses to answer or becomes insolent. John and Margaretha are regularly called to the headmaster's office to be told their son is expelled again. The consensus is that Tom has trouble adjusting to school life. One psychologist even diagnoses him with a form of autism, recommending a specialized institution.

The Collins family refuses to accept this. They believe their son isn't troubled—he simply needs the right stimulation. Frustrated by the school system, John and Margaretha hire private tutors. With patience and the right methods, they manage to capture Tom's interest. He thrives in his solitary, unconventional schooling, despite being cut off from other children. He even discovers a passion for running, which he pursues with discipline. John and Margaretha are amazed to see their son's smile break through the silence. Sometimes, Tom speaks passionately about what he is learning. He spends less time alone and seems more interested in life. The couple are overjoyed by the change. They believe the worst is behind them—Tom just needed more time than others. One day, he will be ready for his destiny, and John and Margaretha are confident.

Over the years, Tom becomes a striking young man with a tall, athletic frame. His unkempt hair and growing beard give him the air of an adventurer. He fits easily into the category of "sexy," but he doesn't see himself that way. His appearance is a carefully crafted shield to hide his face. But the first thing people notice are his piercing blue eyes. Tom doesn't want to be seen. He sees himself as a ghost, an anonymous shell waiting to leave one boredom for another. He doesn't want attention—he wants to be untouchable, left alone. He wears the label of the perfect son, but to him, it is a curse he has been condemned to since birth.

* * *

Today, his perfection offers no protection. Curled up, trembling, Tom can't open his eyes. He knows the Presence is still there, watching him. He feels it deep in his gut and kicks the grass with all his might. The shadow is amused by his restlessness, relishing his weakness, his anger at himself. Thoughts race through Tom's mind. He can't take it anymore—the past, the present, the uncertain future. He has nothing to lose, nothing to love. If that shadowy bitch wants him, let her take him. Masks off, comedy's over. Is hell really worse than this? Tom is ready to accept the fate his troubled mind has conjured, but a flicker of life still buried deep within urges him to scream: "You're not real! Fuck you to hell! You're fake! Not real!"

He knows the Presence won't acknowledge him. Moments pass—he's still alive. Five, four, three, two, one... he waits for her to strike back. Nothing happens. Only the icy wind whispers in his ear: "You sold me your soul…" Then, silence. She vanishes without a sound.

CHAP 2

ESCAPING THE NIGHTMARE...

Unaware of how long he's been trapped in a panic attack, Tom struggles to his feet. His knuckles hurt... Blood and dirt are the evidence of his imaginary battle. Fortunately, he jogged in the woods bordering his property, away from people. If anyone had seen him running madly from a creature only he could see, the gossip would have been relentless. He looks like he's come back from a battlefield, with wet grass staining his tracksuit bottoms. To face his fear and this inexplicable terror that grips him by the throat, Tom would have preferred to fight a flesh-and-blood enemy. His legs and back ache, each step a struggle. His head spins, and he stumbles. But he has to go home, even if he doesn't want to. Life always pulls the lost back to where they belong—there's no escaping it for long. But where is his place, really?

Tom has always felt useless. He's the one who wanders aimlessly, the prodigal son who never causes a stir. At least, that's what his parents think... He's not ungrateful, not someone to blame for his life's direction. He's not one of those rich kids who invent problems and spend fortunes on psychiatry. Despite his strange character, his parents have always loved him unconditionally. They've defended, protected, and supported him in his choices, even the ones that crushed their hopes of seeing Tom shine as they had dreamed.

John and Margaretha, so deeply in love... Tom always felt like an outsider to their happiness, a spectator in their perfect world, an accessory to their success. Many times, he wanted to scream at them, to tell them he wasn't their perfect son, not the infallible cog in their machine. But guilt held him back... slowly, it drove him to cut off contact with them. He thought they'd react, that they'd try to pull him back, to understand him... A hundred times he imagined John, the Iceberg, dragging him home by force, or Margaretha crying over the absence of her beloved son. But none of that ever happened. Instead, they kept sending him money and goods, giving him the space he thought he wanted...

At the Collins annual press conference, Tom sees himself again. He hadn't wanted to attend, but he had no choice. By then, his personal life had taken a turn, and he was determined to shake off the burden of his family legacy. It was supposed to be his big day—the inauguration that would mark his official entry into the company...

He stood back, half-listening to John's speech. Tom knew his father hated giving speeches. Every word that left his mouth felt false. It was a formal tirade, carefully crafted by the company's PR team to reassure investors. They had to give the hacks something to chew on, to keep everything politically correct, to maintain the established order. Tom couldn't help but smirk. The hacks would get what they came for...

When his turn came, Tom stepped up to the podium and glanced around the room. The public gaze made him uncomfortable—some eyes beaming with admiration, others hiding hypocrisy. He felt like he might throw up. He could sense them, the vultures waiting for him to slip, ready to pick apart his corpse.

He began with a polite thanks for their presence, the usual line that earned polite applause. Then, with cold indifference, Tom announced that he had no interest in the business world and would never be a part of the company, despite all the hopes placed on him. Silence fell, followed by shock. Then came the camera flashes, scrambling to capture the scandal before the moment passed. Whispers swirled, vultures circled, investors turned pale... John, the Iceberg, shoved his son away from the podium in a fit of rage, demanding calm. Margaretha, stunned, stood just behind her husband. The storm hit—questions fired like bullets, drowning out all reason... Tom doesn't care about small-minded people. Finding Madee soon is his only concern. In her arms he would make love with passion, he would put an end to the man he used to be, and nothing from his old life would matter...

Tom hoped to finally see the disappointment in his parents' eyes by creating a scandal. He wanted them to feel anger, betrayal, and humiliation, to finally see the perfect little boy as just another human being... He dreamed of breaking away from "his world", a world populated by fake idiots who think they're above everyone else... Once again, John and Margaretha said nothing, despite the social unrest. They thought Tom would change his mind one day, so they didn't try to force their will on him. His refusal today was not a final one, he just needed a little more time...

Happy to be free at last, he left the Collins Building with his head held high. Madee's day was not over yet. Tom wanted her, wanted to feel her come and give herself. He could visit her at work, they'd look lovingly at each other, she'd take a break and they'd isolate themselves and make love like two teenagers... Reason overcame passion, Tom didn't want to disturb Madee, his desire could wait, they had long lovemaking nights ahead... Everything would be all right... He went back to his place, tidied up, and packed. Madee had already made room for him in her closets. Tom feels relieved to leave his luxurious downtown loft behind—the soulless bachelor pad that had witnessed his earlier life of debauchery. It is another step in his liberation. There isn't much to move aside from his clothes; nothing in the apartment holds any sentimental value. The magazine-perfect décor has never suited him. He comes home only to sleep, shower, and recharge before heading out to party again.

With some time to spare before seeing Madee, Tom decides to stop by the caterers to pick up dinner. He wants everything to be perfect, as this will be their first real evening together as a couple.

As he strolls down one of the trendy downtown streets, his mind racing, something catches his eye. It's a shop window—one of the many luxury vintage clothing stores that have sprung up since the hipsters took over. Tom stares at the dress in the window, transfixed. A midi pencil dress with white polka dots on black, a sweetheart neckline, and short sleeves with shoulder pads. Simple, sexy, sophisticated. He can picture Madee wearing it, her breasts filling the neckline, her hips curving perfectly against the silk. The dress zips at the back, and he can already see himself helping her undo it, kissing her neck... She is the first woman he has ever wanted to give a gift to. But what if she gets offended?

In that moment, he regrets not discussing relationships more with his mother. He feels torn—he knows Madee will love it, but he is afraid of looking foolish, of being too in love. His doubts are ridiculous. He will buy the dress. Because he wants to, because he loves her, and because he wants to see the happiness in her eyes.

The cars crawled along, lined up in single file. Leaving the city at rush hour required patience, and Tom's was wearing thin. He hated traffic jams, but more importantly, the clock was ticking. He wanted to get there before Madee. Frustrated, he honked his horn, hoping to jolt the other drivers into moving. Why are they so slow? The light is green. Don't they want to go home?

He could feel the anger rising in his veins. He definitely wouldn't miss the city center and all its problems. After thirty minutes, the traffic finally started moving again. Tom drove a little faster to make up for the delay. If the cops caught him, he would pay the fine without thinking twice. But that was unlikely—there were few police officers in the area he was heading to.

As he entered Madee's neighborhood, Tom saw the first houses. Something felt wrong. In the distance, he noticed smoke rising into the sky. He glanced at his phone on the dashboard. He had texted Madee earlier to say he missed her and would be late, but she hadn't replied. That didn't mean much—she was probably still at work and hadn't seen the message. He continued to drive slowly. Crowds were gathering here and there. Something was off.

A local boy banged on his car window two blocks from Madee's flat, waved at him, and then ran off. Tom pulled the handbrake, turned off the engine, and got out. He could walk faster than he could drive in this mess. Once he knew Madeewas safe, he would feel relieved. Inwardly, he prayed she was still at work, that she was far from whatever was happening.

He couldn't wait to hold her in his arms... Then the smell of smoke hit him. As he approached, a security cordon stopped him. Fire trucks blocked his path. His heart sank. Madee's building... her building... engulfed in flames. Tom passes under the cordon, just a few meters away. A firefighter stops him, pulling him back behind the security perimeter. Tom shouts that his girlfriend lives here, that she might still be in the building... The firefighter tells him to calm down. They need to get the fire under control before they can start searching...

Tom spots Madee's boss. He sees the man gesticulating wildly in the distance, surrounded by people trying to calm him down. Fervently hoping Madee is among them, Tom pushes through the crowd. He recognizes her neighbors. There are only five tenants in the building, three of whom have just returned home from work, shocked to have lost everything. The fourth, the old lady who lives in the apartment above Madee's, spent the day at the nursing home... Madee is the only one missing...

Tom taps the boss on the shoulder to let him know he's there. The man, pale as death, turns around. Panic overtakes Tom, and he grabs the old man by the shoulders, shaking him, demanding to know where Madee is. The man stammers, saying she had wanted to leave work early... He thought Tom was with her, but he never imagined something so tragic would happen... Tom feels the weight of dread settling over him. If Madee isn't here... No. He can't believe it. Not Madee. This has to be a mistake. Any moment now, she'll break through the crowd with her light gait and run straight into his arms...

An hour later, the fire is finally out. The firefighters prepare to search the building. Only embers remain of what had once been Tom's sanctuary. Ambulances rush to assist the injured, and the scene is chaotic. In the background, Tom prays with all his might for someone to come with good news. He desperately needs hope... The police are already on the scene, interviewing witnesses before conducting forensic tests. What should have been a night of tenderness has turned into a nightmare.

Tom jumps when he hears the firefighters calling out—they've found something on the second floor. He watches as three men pull a charred, blackened mass from the building and gently place what was once a body on a stretcher. Tom knows exactly who had lived in the second-floor apartment... It's over. Madee has perished in the flames. Paramedics continue their work, but Tom is stunned, in complete denial. Madee can't be dead! Anyone but her!

He doesn't notice the policeman approaching. Tom doesn't even register who he is. But now that the firefighters have found a body, the police are investigating the cause of the fire. The inspector begins asking Tom questions about his relationship with Madee Mitchell. Did she have family? Enemies? Was she hiding something? Was she depressed?

Tom can't handle the questioning. If Madee is just a victim, why does this policeman seem to suspect her?

No, Madee wasn't depressed. She didn't have any secrets. As for her family... Tom doesn't know—she never told him. But everyone in the neighborhood loved her for her kindness and generosity. Nearly collapsing from grief, Tom tells the officer he'll come to the station to make a statement. Tom needs to be alone to process the tragedy that has just shattered his world. Earlier in the day, he was happy. Now, his heart is torn to pieces. In a cruel twist of fate, Madee has died so suddenly, so senselessly...

Tom stumbles back to his car, starts the engine, and drives off. He needs something—anything—to drown his sorrows, but his thoughts are too scattered to form. He flicks on the lights, slams down on the accelerator, and speeds dangerously through the streets. If he crashes the car, maybe that would be for the best. What does he have left to live for now?

He hadn't even managed to die, despite his reckless driving, and now he wasn't far from his loft. He was nothing—just proof that even that bastard God didn't want him. The Creator was too busy sending his fallen angels after Madee, leaving Tom behind. He hadn't had the decency to grant Tom the ultimate mercy of a reunion in the hereafter. Frustrated and miserable, Tom stopped at a grocery store and grabbed as many bottles of alcohol as he could carry. The man at the checkout wished him a good evening with the knowing smile of a seasoned partygoer... If only the bastard knew. Tom felt the urge to punch him in the face but thought better of it. He remembered what Madee had once told him: *"People shouldn't have to pay for my misery..."* This guy was just doing his job. Tom took his bottles and left without a word.

He was ashamed, but he needed to feel wretched. He didn't need something stronger—alcohol was a good compromise. Tom had made a promise to Madee that he would never break. Once he locked himself in, he threw himself onto the sofa, grabbed a bottle of vodka, and started drinking. He drank all night, puking his guts out, only to do it all over again. Abusing his body, hurting himself, gave him an unhealthy pleasure. Tom wanted to die slowly, painfully—nothing could be worse than the vast emptiness in his heart. Without Madee, his life had no meaning. He would stop at nothing to die and join her...

For the first time, Tom saw the dark presence that would never leave him, creeping into the half-sleep of a drunkard. But he didn't stop drinking. Losing Madee was his tragedy, but now he had to face the media frenzy surrounding the Collins family. The press had no qualms about launching a smear campaign against them. The headlines screamed:

"Princes fall, phantom heir abandoned: an empire ends."

"Collins fiasco: property in turmoil."

The slander was rampant, and the journalists were particularly vicious. Some even suggested that Tom's refusal to take over the business was due to bribery. Others speculated that John was a corrupt politician or that the wealthy businessmen had been ruined... The lawyers representing his parents must have had their hands full. If Tom weren't grieving, he'd be kicking himself for throwing his parents to the wolves. He should have spoken to them before the press conference, instead of making a spectacle of himself without considering the consequences.

Consequences... He didn't care anymore. He was just a failure, a piece of crap, a good-for-nothing. Sometimes, he'd kneel in the middle of the living room and ask God to take him. He'd pull out his wallet and toss notes into the air. Everything in this shitty world was for sale, so why not God? How much did the Big Boss want for Tom's life? Tens of thousands? A hundred? A million?

Tom could even make a transfer to the Creator's offshore account at the Bank of Paradise. That's how all the powerful conducted their affairs, and surely, the Father was no exception. This God, worshipped by everyone, was far from a saint, letting his children suffer this way...

Tom waited, ready for negotiations, but the Big Boss deliberately ignored him. He'd give everything he had if only God would listen to him for a moment... To calm his nerves, Tom drank. The dark presence was always waiting to torture him mentally, lurking, and he dreaded each time he opened a bottle. The temptation to escape was too strong. The spiral of destruction had him in its grip, and he was powerless to resist. Before Madee, Tom had known nothing about loss. In fact, he had no idea what life really was. In his comfortable, gilded cage, no one had ever taken anything from him. But now, the wound in his shattered heart deepened with each passing day. The once flamboyant son of a rich man was crushed by the cruelty of life. Madee had been his ray of hope—the light in his search for purpose, the one great love of his life...

Stumbling, Tom begins to climb the aisle. His body moves on autopilot. The memory is too vivid to push away, and he hates when it returns. At that moment, he understood what it felt like to carry a cross. His cross grew heavier all the time, but it was nothing compared to what awaited him at home. Unless Laura hadn't finished her champagne from the night before, she must be awake. If so, he could hope for a few more hours of rest.

Tom feels like a stranger in his own house. Now that Laura has moved in with all her baggage, he barely has a voice. He almost has to ask permission just to piss because she has taken over the house and runs everything. He keeps quiet and stays low. Every day that passes is one day less, he tells himself. With his hand on the doorknob, Tom hesitates. What if he got into his car and just disappeared? Left everything behind on a whim—no money, no papers, gone without a trace? No, he's not brave enough anymore. He paid too high a price for his last act of defiance.

Tom enters the house, trying to be discreet. With the light reflecting off the white walls, the house has a phantasmagorical feel, like the antechamber to heaven. The furniture is minimal; Tom was never good with decorating. That was his mother's job, and she always did her best to furnish her son's home. When he moved in, he threw everything into the attic, keeping only the essentials. The Collins legacy at any cost: deconstructing the established order, finding comfort in his own soulless image.

In the kitchen, he hears music. To the sound of electro, a singer with a soft, remixed voice repeats her chorus over and over. It's the kind of music you'd expect to hear in a trendy bar while spending too much on overpriced cocktails. Laura's racket isn't drowned out by the melody. Tom hears her slamming cupboard doors and swearing. Fortunately, she hasn't noticed him. When she's in a bad mood, nine times out of ten she takes it out on him. Discreetly, he glances into the kitchen. The fragile blonde looks especially upset. She's already playing the role of the girl who's trending on social media, dressed in yoga leggings and a T-shirt carefully tied over her navel to look casual. But her face is far from calm.

Her long blonde hair is slicked back, revealing the attachment points of her extensions. Large dark circles around her eyes, the remnants of long nights of partying, can't be concealed, even under an impressive layer of makeup. She's caked on bronzer and highlighter to try to look good, and the endless false eyelashes complete the sad spectacle of a woman trying to compensate for time with a touch of vulgarity. Thank God she hasn't noticed him. She's too busy opening and closing cupboards like a maniac.

Tom takes the opportunity to slip away. A shower might put him in shape to deal with the nervous breakdown that looms on the horizon. Determined to enjoy this moment of peace, he locks himself in the bathroom. In the huge mirror that dominates the wall, he sees his sad reflection. It's a stark contrast to the multitude of garish cosmetics scattered across this temple of artificial beauty.

Tom looks down, avoiding his reflection. The fear, the shame, the rejection—or maybe all of them at once—can't escape the mirror. It stands as a witness to human vanity and ego. Tom's reflection feels stronger than his fears, and slowly, he raises his head to look at himself. He looks old, but he's only 34...

The last six months have taken their toll. The freshness of his youth is gone. Fine lines have appeared around his eyes, and the shine has disappeared from his sad gaze. His beard has grown, nearly obscuring a face that can no longer smile. He has lost so much weight his shoulders look weak. He barely eats anymore; food isn't a priority. His insides are dead, so what does it matter how he looks on the outside? Tom places a hand on the mirror, trying to cover the face of the stranger he no longer wants to see.

He goes to the shower, turns on the hot water, and lets himself fall to the floor, fully clothed. His clothes form a comforting barrier between his body and the scalding water. He doesn't want to take them off, because that would mean accepting the cleansing of this useless body and his damned soul. Sitting still, soaked, Tom wraps his arms around his knees. He wants Madee inside him, close, at all costs... He wants to relive the warmth of an embrace that now exists only in his memory.

CHAPTER 3

BETWEEN PRESENT AND MEMORIES...

Tom can't always avoid Laura. Sometimes, she terrifies him—especially when she has one of her hysterical outbursts. She tried to hide that part of herself at the beginning of their relationship, playing the perfect partner. But it didn't take long for the cracks to show. After all, no one can suppress their true nature forever. Staying silent during every argument had been Tom's biggest mistake. It was like adding fuel to the fire. Laura interpreted his silence as weakness, as if she had the upper hand... Like those who count sheep or unicorns before falling asleep, Tom counts the steps to the kitchen in his head—one, two, three... It's his way of keeping the anxiety at bay, a ritual he clings to before the inevitable headache strikes. The cupboard doors stop slamming, the music fades, and for a moment, there's only silence. A bad sign.

He steps into the kitchen. Laura is perched on a bar stool, an empty cup in front of her, her head buried in her hands. She looks like a shadow of herself, with a pounding headache and a hangover that makes her nearly unrecognizable. Tom seizes the opportunity to make himself a coffee, the small routine a welcome reprieve before the inevitable hurricane. The espresso machine sputters to life, breaking the silence. Laura stirs, her head slowly lifting. Her eyes, glazed over with exhaustion, scan Tom from top to bottom.

"There you are," she mutters, her tone dripping with disdain.

Tom doesn't reply. This time, he follows the old saying: Speech is silver, silence is gold. His back is to her, but he can feel her gaze burning into him, searching for a weakness, a crack in his composure. Stay calm, he repeats to himself, don't give her what she wants.

Quietly, he picks up his coffee and takes a seat. The room feels tense, charged with the kind of energy that comes before a storm. Laura's voice cuts through the quiet like a knife.

"That's a track I see over there! I've told you a hundred times to take your shoes off when you go outside. Do you have any idea how many germs are on those floors?"

Tom takes a deep breath, letting the words wash over him. He wants to remind her that the house belongs to him, that he can leave tracks wherever he damn well pleases. But he knows better. Laura has a way of twisting even the smallest conflict into a war. And two footprints on the floor are just the warm-up act.

His lack of reaction only fuels her anger. She leans back in her chair, her eyes narrowing, her mind calculating the next move. The air shifts. Her voice softens, her eyes turn to honey, and she looks at him with the same intensity as a predator sizing up its prey.

"You look sloppy..."

Tom doesn't immediately see what Laura is getting at. If that's the best she's got, she's not even close. It's true that he has long since thrown away his youthful, playboy wardrobe. His expensive suits, once symbols of his wild days, now lie forgotten in their covers, never to see the light of day again. They remind him of corpses, buried memories he has no desire to exhume. He doesn't need to wear haute couture just to lounge around the house—a pair of jeans and some worn jogging shorts will do just fine. But Laura isn't finished. She leans in, her voice taking on that familiar, mocking tone.

"I think you should come to parties with me. It would give you a chance to get away from the Neanderthal look!"

Tom doesn't even flinch. "I don't like your parties."

Laura's smirk sharpens. "That's not what they say..."

Red flags shoot up in Tom's mind. He didn't see that coming. For the first time in a long time, his normally impenetrable blue eyes flicker with guilt. The implication in Laura's words is too strong for him to pretend ignorance.

His past has always lurked in the shadows, threatening to resurface. His face had been splashed across newspapers years ago for refusing to work in the family business, and people at these parties had not forgotten. They still whispered about his past indiscretions...

He can't find anything to say. Denial would be pointless; the past is what it is. He had been careful, but he always knew his old, reckless life would catch up with him eventually. And now, Laura's words—casual, yet razor-sharp—are bringing it all back to the surface. Laura's eyes gleam with satisfaction, sensing her small victory.

"Come on, darling, it's a small world at these parties. Everyone has their little juicy anecdotes. You can't imagine what I've been hearing..."

Tom clenches his jaw. "Everyone makes mistakes."

Laura's smile widens, that familiar predator's grin.

"You should realize how lucky you are to have such a beautiful, tolerant woman by your side. Everyone congratulates me on my success where others have failed."

Tom's fists tighten. "I'm not that man anymore!" The words burst out, louder than he intended.

He knows he's overreacted, and that's exactly what Laura wanted. The smile playing on her lips is impossible to hide now, her look of satisfaction unmistakable. She's on the edge of delivering the final blow, and she knows she has all the cards in her hand. Tom wants to stand up, to walk away before she can sink her claws in any deeper. But he can't. Leaving would be admitting defeat. One more victory for Laura, and he's done.

Laura leans forward, her voice low but cutting.

"I know you're not the same man, but you need to learn how to have a normal relationship with your past. No other woman could understand that, except me. You can't go against your nature, Tom. It'll catch up to you if you try."

She pauses, letting the weight of her words hang in the air before delivering the final, gut-wrenching blow.

"You tried... and she died. That's not so bad. She would never have tolerated your antics anyway."

Tom feels the walls of the house closing in on him, the ground falling beneath his feet. How did that bitch know? Madee—his well-kept secret, hidden in the deepest recesses of his heart. He had never spoken of her to anyone.

Laura's gaze pierces him, her eyes gleaming with satisfaction as she watches his torment. She revels in it. Tom can't contain himself; fury surges through him like wildfire. His hand reaches for the coffee cup, and with a swift, violent motion, he hurls it against the wall. The sound of shattering ceramic is drowned by the stool clattering to the floor as Tom pushes it aside and stands inches from Laura's face. He wants to reach out, to wrap his hands around her throat, to feel her struggle for breath beneath his grasp.

But before he can act, Laura grabs the back of his neck and pulls his mouth to hers. She kisses him with force, her breath hot against his skin, her hand already unzipping his trousers, searching for evidence that his rage has ignited something primal in him. She strokes him roughly, whispering in his ear, her voice dripping with mockery and twisted desire.

"Fuck me," she breathes. "Fuck me hard, like you did with the others. Maybe this time you'll make me cum."

Tom jerks backward, violently pushing Laura away from him. He doesn't want her touch. He doesn't want her body. All he wants is to make her pay for everything—for every word, every manipulation, every twisted game. The urge to throw her to the floor and dominate her boils in his blood, but it's not lust—it's hate. He wants her to feel fear. To be silenced.

Laura, dazed for a moment, stands and arches her back, then bursts into cruel, mocking laughter. The sound of it is unbearable, filling the kitchen with her sadistic glee.

"Be a man, Tom, or you'll bury her!" she taunts, her eyes gleaming with satisfaction.

"You make me sick, Laura!" Tom roars, pointing to the door.

Laura's lips curl into a sneer as she retreats, her voice laced with venom.

"You'll pay for this. You'll pay dearly. Trust me."

Tom stands there, breathing hard, minutes ticking by like hours. The adrenaline fades, leaving only a hollow, aching sensation in his chest. What had just happened? How did it escalate so quickly? How had she found out about Madee? And what did she mean by burying her?

Memories of Madee flood back—her funeral, the one he couldn't bring himself to attend. He couldn't face the people who had known her, couldn't stand to hear their hollow condolences. His relationship with her had been too special, too personal. He had convinced himself that only he had the right to grieve her loss. Tom opens a drawer at the bar and finds what he's looking for—a forgotten packet of cigarettes, hidden away for emergencies like this. His hands tremble as he pulls one out. He lights it, hesitating for a moment before taking the first drag. It's harsh, bitter, and it makes him cough, but he doesn't stop. He needs it, just like a cripple needs his crutch. His eyes sting, and he can't tell if it's from the smoke or from the tears that still burn his cheeks. He's weak—he knows it. He's never been able to stand up for himself.

His parents wanted him to have a "normal" childhood, so they enrolled him in a state school. Every morning, the well-dressed little boy would step out of a beautiful car, catching the envious stares of his classmates. They couldn't understand why someone like him wasn't at the rich kids' school. Tom's days dragged on.

The lessons bored him, and none of the other children wanted to play with him. Sometimes, the little girls would hang around, whispering and giggling, dreaming of being whisked away by a Prince Charming in his fancy carriage. But Tom soon realized he was in enemy territory. Recess became a time of solitude, where he would linger in the playground, waiting for the bell to save him.

It didn't take long for the bullying to start. The others began to target him—the outcast, the rich boy. They'd push him, kick at his legs, yank his hair. Lunchtime was no better. Tom would pull his lunchbox from his locker and sit in the refectory, hoping to go unnoticed.

On lucky days, the bullies would mock him from a distance, asking why he didn't have lobster for lunch since all the rich ate lobster, didn't they? On bad days, they'd pin him down, the ringleader dumping his food onto the floor and stomping it underfoot. They'd finish the ritual with a punch to his gut. The laughter of those bastards echoed in his ears long after the bruises formed.

Tom never said a word. Not to his father, not to anyone. The pattern repeated itself in every school they sent him to. When he got home, he'd lock himself in his room, hiding under the covers, his tears eventually drying up. It had to be his fault—how could the whole world be wrong? To them, he was nothing more than the quiet, strange boy.

At night, Tom would cling to his mother, wrapping his small arms around Margaretha's neck as she tucked him in. *"I love you, Mummy,"* he'd whisper, and she would smile softly, stroking his hair, telling him he was her favorite son, the love of her life. In those moments, Tom could almost believe he was normal. Almost. He endured the torment for years. Until he met Mrs. Atkins.

Mrs. Atkins marked the end of Tom's state school days. She hated him from the moment she laid eyes on him—the skinny, red-haired boy with wealth beyond her comprehension. He might appear docile, but she knew better. He was trouble, and worse, he was rich.

Mrs. Atkins wasted no time putting him in his place. She'd call him to the blackboard whenever he faltered in class and force him to write, over and over, *"In my class, the rich get the hard way."* If he wasn't fast enough, her wooden ruler would snap across his fingers. When he finished, Mrs. Atkins would humiliate him further. She'd pull down his trousers and spank him in front of the class. It was a punishment she reserved for "his kind."

Tom never spoke of it. When his parents asked if he liked the new school, he shrugged, his voice silenced by shame. Mrs. Atkins made sure to cover her tracks, planting seeds of doubt in the school psychologist's mind. She hinted that Tom was slow, possibly even autistic—someone who didn't belong in mainstream education. Her lies sealed his fate. The school threw him out like unwanted trash, despite his parents' protests. Tom was nothing more than a contagious germ to them, something that would infect the others if he stayed.

Now, the cigarette between Tom's fingers had burned down to the filter. Only the ash and the butt remained, a bitter reminder of his vice. Smoking had always been his way of ingesting poison, punishing himself for what he was. Mrs. Atkins had been right, after all. He was a bad seed. He needed to be dealt with harshly, or he'd hurt others.

"Be a man, Collins..."

The words echoed in his mind, a cruel mantra from his past. All the love in the world couldn't heal some wounds, and a single good example wasn't enough to repair a broken heart. The negative conditioning clung to him like a second skin—the little girls at school, Mrs. Atkins, everyone who had ever belittled him. He was nothing more than a pawn on life's chessboard, the rotten fruit of pure love that had no place in a lost generation. Perfection was a lie. It was the ugly truth beneath that defined him.

"Be a man, Collins…"

The phrase replayed in his head, over and over. Flashbacks of his past blurred with the present, each one overlapping with the next. Laura hadn't come up with it on her own. Someone had fed her the ammunition, given her the words to destroy him.

"Be a man, Collins…"

It was a joke between schoolboys once, an innocent taunt. But for Tom, it had been the beginning of his descent into hell. Maybe God created man in His image. But Wayne Beckett had created Tom Collins.

* * *

With the acceptance letter in his hand, Tom paced the campus, feeling a mixture of dread and disbelief. Youth and life buzzed all around him—the chatter of students, the energy of a place dedicated to the future. It had been a long time since he'd been in a crowd like this. Near the main auditorium, the new student stands were buzzing with activity. Here, he'd get his timetable and discover which fraternity would claim the next years of his life.

At 18, his solitude was finally coming to an end. With the help of his personal tutor, Tom had excelled academically. But university hadn't been his choice. Tom had naively believed that after high school, he'd have time to figure things out, to find his own path. He'd imagined himself traveling the world, seeking new riches on his own terms. But the Collins empire had other plans.

The day his tutor handed him a stack of application forms, everything changed. His dreams of escape were replaced by cold, hard reality. Each form bore the name of one of the country's top universities. All Tom had to do was choose a course of study, and his tutor would guide him through the process. It all felt so simple, so preordained—and that's exactly what he hated.

None of the options in the brochures appealed to him. Each degree felt like a door closing on the freedom he craved. He had hoped that his indifference would serve as a form of rebellion, but his parents and his tutor were relentless. They were so proud of his academic success, so eager for him to take the next step. Tom didn't want to disappoint them, and their enthusiasm made it even harder to express his own wishes. In the end, he gave in. He asked what course he should study for his future position at the company. His parents, John and Margaretha, brushed off his concerns, insisting that he shouldn't worry. "You're a Collins," they'd said. *"It's in your blood. You'll have a team of experts guiding you every step of the way."* The same old refrain.

Even though Tom wasn't sure what he wanted, they were overflowing with confidence in his abilities. Tom could do anything, they believed—anything but decide for himself. Resigned, Tom let his tutor choose the best course for him. He didn't even bother to complete the paperwork himself. The deciding factor had been the generous donation his parents made to the university. Tom saw the amount on the check his father had signed. He would've preferred to enter on merit alone, even if it meant risking failure. But in his world, money could buy anything—even success.

Money, cars, clothes—everything had been arranged for Tom to succeed without worry. And yet, despite it all, he felt a deep disinterest in his future studies. The campus, however, was impressive. The buildings, a mix of old and new, stood as monuments to the country's elite. This was where the future leaders would be molded, surrounded by a blend of tradition and modernism. The ancient walls had witnessed the rise of brilliant minds, and only the worthy would uncover their secrets. Tom tried to convince himself that he belonged here, that he had a purpose. But deep down, he hated every inch of it. There was something about this prestigious institution that repelled him. Young people across the country would kill to be in his place, but Tom would happily trade places with any of them. He wanted nothing more than to escape.

Lost in his thoughts, Tom realized he had passed the new student stand and quickly stepped back to join the queue. When it was finally his turn, a dark-haired girl with a friendly face greeted him. She blushed slightly, her eyes meeting his as she asked:

"Welcome to Garland. What's your name?"

"Collins, Tom Collins..."

Tom immediately regretted how formal he sounded. He felt like an idiot. The girl, however, didn't seem to notice. She scanned her list, clearly flustered, but unsure how to break the ice with the handsome boy standing in front of her. She babbled nervously, saying it was easier to find him in alphabetical order under C. Tom was about to offer a lighthearted comment to ease the tension, but before he could, her face suddenly stiffened. The warmth drained from her expression, replaced with something colder. She mechanically handed him the schedule without looking up.

"You're staying at Invictus," she said flatly. "Ask for Wayne Beckett when you arrive. The building is near the park, at the end of the path on the left. If you're having trouble finding it, just look for the Lamberi parked outside. Next!"

Tom blinked, a little thrown by the shift in her tone. He hadn't expected much, but he was fairly certain he'd just been dismissed. He thanked her politely and walked away, feeling more unsettled than ever. If the residents of his fraternity were anything like her, he suspected he'd be spending a lot of time alone in his room.

The girl had mentioned the Lamberi, so finding Invictus wasn't hard. The car's metallic gold paint shimmered in the sunlight, and Tom couldn't help but notice the vanity plate: "F$CK."

Seriously? Tom thought. No normal person would drive something like that... at least, no one with an ounce of humility. He wondered if the car was some kind of prank or a mascot meant to show off the fraternity's humor. But if this was their idea of a joke, it wasn't very funny. It reeked of the arrogance of the rich flaunting their wealth for all to see. Tom sighed and adjusted the handle of his bag over his shoulder, bracing himself.

The Invictus residence was as ostentatious as the Ferrari parked outside. White and gold dominated the pristine grounds, and the building looked more like a luxury mansion than a dormitory. It reminded Tom of the homes his parents built for their wealthiest clients—houses designed to impress, to be better than the neighbor's in the endless race for status. Power passed down from one generation to the next. That was the essence of Invictus: power and legacy.

Tom was about to ring the doorbell when it swung open. Two young men, deep in conversation, walked right past him without acknowledging his presence. Not wanting to stand awkwardly outside, Tom slipped through the open door, trying to act as casual as possible.

The interior was even more garish than the exterior—marble floors, gold accents everywhere. The sheer opulence made Tom feel out of place. It was all so tasteless, so over-the-top. He had half a mind to turn around and leave, but before he could, a voice called out from the staircase.

"Collins! There you are, buddy!"

Tom turned to see a young man descending the stairs. His skin was tanned to the point of being almost orange, his blond hair styled perfectly, and his white teeth gleamed like polished pearls. He looked like a human replica of Ken, right down to his designer clothes and the sanctimonious smile plastered across his face.

Before Tom could react, the boy wrapped him in a quick, unwelcome hug.

"I'm Wayne Beckett. Welcome to Invictus, buddy!"

"Tom Collins. Nice to meet you, Wayne..."

"Forget the handshake, man," Wayne said, brushing off Tom's outstretched hand. "That's old-fashioned bullshit. This is a brotherhood, not a retirement home!"

Tom stiffened, uncomfortable with the forced intimacy. He wasn't used to people invading his personal space like this, especially not strangers. Wayne didn't seem to notice Tom's discomfort.

"Good for you, Collins. You look just like you're supposed to. I handpick every brother here, you know. Your parents—John and Margaretha Collins, right?"

"Um... yeah."

"Very rich. That's what we like to see." Wayne's smile widened. "We're very selective at Invictus. Only the best. We—"

"Invictus means 'invincible,' right?" Tom interrupted, hoping to steer the conversation toward something less obnoxious.

Wayne snorted. "Who cares Collins? Let me tell you what really matters. I've got an excellent relationship with the Dean. My friends are the Dean's friends, if you know what I mean."

"Not really," Tom replied, feeling more lost by the second.

"You're an idiot, but you'll learn." Wayne grinned. "Here's the deal: we've already graduated without even bothering to go to class. There's no pressure on us to study. Got it?"

Wayne's laugh was full of contempt, and Tom stared at him, trying to make sense of the situation.

"There are plenty of scholars out there ready to earn cash! One note, and your homework will magically appear! We just need to pass the time until we graduate, and there's plenty to keep us busy… You'll see… C'mon, I'll show you your room. Did you see my car? Got it as a welcome gift when I arrived."

Wayne led Tom down the hallway, still chatting non-stop. He explained that room assignments were based on the wealth of the parents. Those whose families had "acceptable" levels of wealth were downgraded to double rooms, while others—like Tom and himself—were entitled to private accommodations. Wayne leaned in, his voice dropping to a confidential whisper:

"We've earned a few privileges."

Tom stayed silent, skeptical. He couldn't see how paying more made anyone "better off." Wayne's speech was in direct contradiction to everything his parents had taught him. Shifting uncomfortably, Tom nervously shoved his hands in and out of his pockets. He just wanted to be alone, but Wayne was relentless.

"There's an invisible line on campus," Wayne continued. "Don't let them talk to you. You don't mix with other people…"

MYTHOMANIA

Tom frowned. "Which side of the line is the girl from the welcome stand on?"

Wayne snickered. "Lisa Strand? Oh, she's one of the rednecks, sorry to disappoint. Wait... are you trying to flirt with her?"

Tom felt a heat rise in his cheeks. "No, I was just curious."

"Well, that's a relief!" Wayne grinned. "She sucked Dean Carroll's dick, y'know. She's just a great cock sucker. Best blowjob of his life, he told me."

Wayne winked at Tom, as if they were sharing some inside joke. He continued to ramble about the so-called "scholarship girls" and how an Invictus man shouldn't associate with them—unless, of course, he needed a quick fix. Tom's face flushed with embarrassment. He wasn't used to such crude talk, especially about sex. He was still a virgin and had only ever relieved himself with the help of magazines or porn. This was not a conversation he wanted to have with Wayne Beckett. Finally, they reached Tom's room on the second floor, and Tom couldn't have been more grateful to escape Wayne's gossiping. Wayne's monologue had been exhausting, and Tom couldn't wait to get rid of him. Claiming to be tired from the journey, Tom tried to politely end the conversation.

"I think I'm just going to get some rest," he said, inching toward the door.

"Make yourself comfortable, buddy! You know where to find food if you're hungry. Oh, and don't forget, Saturday's the big party for the new arrivals."

Tom hesitated. "I'll probably have to prepare for something... parties aren't really my thing."

Wayne's smile disappeared, his expression hardening.

"Let me stop you right there, Collins. You'd better get used to community life if you're going to stay here. Or else... I could always have the Dean transfer you to the rednecks."

The implied threat hung in the air, and Tom could feel the tension rise. If he refused again, Wayne would make his life difficult. Reluctantly, Tom gave in. "Fine, I'll be there."

Wayne's face lit up once more, his previous enthusiasm returning. He slapped Tom on the back, grinning.

"Good decision, buddy! We're going to have fun. Don't be late—Saturday, 9 p.m.! I'll introduce you to the others. I knew I picked you for a reason. Later."

Tom sighed as Wayne finally left.

There was no pretending that Garland didn't grant privileges to those who could afford them. His room was far too large for one person, more like a small apartment than a dorm. But any sense of comfort was overshadowed by the unease Wayne had left behind. Tom dreaded meeting the other members of the fraternity, assuming they would all be as obnoxious as Wayne.

Though he hadn't admitted it to himself yet, he hated Wayne Beckett from the moment they'd met. Invictus felt like a trap—an inescapable cage, with Wayne as its arrogant warden. Tom had already decided: one semester, then he'd leave. He'd tell his parents that he was motivated to start something new. For now, he would have to survive. And that wouldn't be easy.

All week, Tom avoided his new "brothers." When he did encounter them, it was only for brief, surface-level small talk, punctuated by empty promises to "get to know each other better." He quickly learned why the members of Invictus never attended lectures. On the first day of classes, as Tom took his seat in the lecture hall, the glares from the other students were enough to tell him all he needed to know. They hated him. Elites were despised here.

Not that it mattered much. Tom barely cared about his lessons, but thanks to his photographic memory, he managed to retain enough to impress his teachers. In their eyes, he was already a brilliant student. But it did little to lift his spirits.

The day before the party, Tom called his parents, hoping to find some comfort in their voices. As soon as he heard their excitement, his heart sank. He lied, telling them everything was perfect—his classes were great, he'd made new friends, they'd been right to send him here. He painted a picture of the perfect life for an 18-year-old... even though the reality couldn't have been further from the truth.

Tom's dreaded Saturday evening had finally arrived. At exactly 9 p.m., he stepped into the common room of the residence, feeling a knot form in his stomach. The space had been transformed into a party zone—bottles of alcohol lined the table, pushed against the wall to make room for the festivities. Cushions and benches were scattered across the room, creating an inviting but unsettling atmosphere. There were about twenty people present, some of whom

Tom recognized as members of his fraternity. And, of course, Wayne was there, holding court like a king, flanked by two nearly half-naked girls.

In one corner, Lloyd, the other newcomer, stood awkwardly, sipping a beer. The music was soft, but the tension in the air was palpable. The girls swayed seductively, their bodies moving in rhythm with the slow beat, clearly eager for the party to truly begin. Wayne spotted Tom from across the room and raised his arms exuberantly.

"Buddy! Glad you made it! You're a real brother now!"

He sauntered over, his two companions following closely behind. Both brunettes, one with striking green eyes and the other with deep brown ones. Their long, perfectly straightened hair cascaded down their backs, and their figures were almost unnaturally flawless—Tom couldn't help but suspect plastic surgery, likely from the same surgeon.

"Dude, meet Angela and Beth," Wayne said, gesturing to the girls.

They giggled, licking their lips suggestively as they eyed Tom. Wayne leaned in, his voice loud enough for Tom to hear over the music.

"Angela's dad is a big shot music producer. We met through my parents. Her dad's a client of mine—well, of my father, really. He's one of the top lawyers in the country."

Tom listened politely, but his mind wandered. The usual introductions felt meaningless in a room like this. Wayne, growing bored of the small talk, clapped his hands loudly.

"Alright, everyone, shut up for a second!" he yelled, turning all eyes toward him. "Let me introduce you to my new best friend—Tom Collins!"

The room erupted in cheers, and Tom felt his face flush. He forced a smile, trying to blend in as best he could. The excitement was ramping up, with several of the boys moving closer to the dancing girls, eager to stake their claim. Only Lloyd remained isolated, clearly uncomfortable in the corner, nursing his drink.

Wayne, noticing Lloyd's hesitation, swaggered over to him. He leaned in close and whispered something in Lloyd's ear before pulling a small packet from his pocket. Tom watched as Lloyd's expression changed, his discomfort growing. When Lloyd hesitated, Wayne's mood shifted abruptly. With a scowl, he grabbed Lloyd by the collar and shouted, "We've got a weak link! Say goodbye, Lloyd!"

The room echoed with laughter and cheers as Wayne shoved Lloyd aside. Everyone lifted their glasses in a mocking toast. "Bye, Lloyd!" they chorused, relishing in his embarrassment.

Tom stood frozen, his mind racing. He could already imagine the humiliation that awaited Lloyd. What kind of punishment did Wayne have in store for him? Tom wanted to intervene, to stop the madness, but he knew better than to cross Wayne in front of the others. Instead, he numbly poured himself a drink, hoping it would calm his nerves. Wayne, noticing Tom's compliance, grinned approvingly and joined him at the bar.

"That's the spirit, bro! Just relax."

Wayne led Tom over to a plush sofa and invited him to sit. Tom did as he was told, watching as Wayne leaned over and kissed Angela deeply. Nearby, Tom noticed a tray—its surface lined with several perfectly symmetrical white lines of cocaine, neatly arranged on a pedestal table.

Wayne snapped his fingers, and one of the others eagerly passed him the tray. Without missing a beat, Wayne unrolled a note, bending over to snort two lines in quick succession. Angela and Beth followed suit, giggling as they took their turns. The tray was then handed to Tom.

He froze, the room seeming to slow down around him. He could feel the weight of everyone's gaze on him—especially Wayne's. His heart pounded in his chest as the tray lingered in front of him. He knew he didn't belong here, didn't want to be part of this, but the pressure was unbearable. He hesitated, his hand trembling slightly.

"Have you ever done cocaine, bro?" Wayne's voice was casual, as if he were asking about the weather.

"No..." Tom replied, his voice barely audible.

"Be a man, Collins! Don't be so precious!" Wayne's grin widened, his tone both mocking and commanding.

"I'm not afraid," Tom muttered.

"You're a liar!" Wayne shot back. "Try it then, it's safe. I've been doing it since I was fifteen, and look at me—I'm in top form!"

Tom felt trapped. He knew what Wayne had done to Lloyd, and the thought of being cast out like him made his heart race. His instincts screamed at him to leave, to go back to his room and avoid the chaos unfolding around him. But fear overpowered reason. Tom hesitated only a moment longer before taking the note from Wayne's hand. With shaky fingers, he rolled it and snorted the first line of cocaine.

The burn hit him immediately, frying his brain as his senses blurred. His body seemed to detach from his consciousness, and for the first time, he felt like a spectator in his own life. He wasn't in control anymore. This is it, Tom thought numbly. I'm officially part of Invictus.

Wayne clapped him on the back, pulling him into a tight hug.

"You did it, buddy! You're one of us now!"

Tom barely registered Wayne's voice as his attention drifted to the sofa. Angela and Beth were kissing, their legs slightly parted, moving languidly against each other. Their moans were soft, almost drowned out by the music, but loud enough to catch the attention of everyone in the room. They paused only to snort another line, and Angela laughed as she spoke to Beth.

"Honey, finger my pussy."

Without hesitation, Angela pulled up her mini skirt, discarding her thong as she spread her legs wide, unabashedly displaying herself to Wayne and Tom. Beth wasted no time, sliding her fingers inside Angela, first one, then two, then three. Angela's back arched as she moaned, her hands cupping her breasts as she pushed against Beth's fingers. Wayne, already aroused, pulled down his trousers and began to masturbate.

Tom could feel the cocaine rushing through him, his body reacting despite his confusion. His cock hardened involuntarily, and the sensations were both intense and alien. His instincts were primal, but his mind was fragmented, torn between arousal and horror. He took another line, hoping to push away the dissonance, but it only made things worse. Everything felt out of control.

Angela reached for Wayne's cock, stroking him as Beth continued to pleasure her. But Wayne stopped her, glancing at Tom with a mischievous grin.

"Honor to the new guy," he said with a smirk.

The girls turned their attention to Tom, their hands eagerly unbuttoning his trousers. He felt their fingers on him, felt the heat as they took turns sucking his cock. Their tongues glided over him, and he moaned despite himself, the sound more mechanical than genuine. He was lost in the sensations, his mind too clouded by the drugs to think clearly. When Beth's hand caressed his chest and moved to kiss him, Tom pushed her away, his voice rough. "Just my cock," he muttered.

Beth complied, though there was a brief flash of disappointment in her eyes. Angela, noticing the silent rivalry, moved with more determination, eager to be the first to fuck him. Wayne, ever the orchestrator, decided for them, gesturing for Beth to come to him. Begrudgingly, she obeyed.

Angela, thrilled at her luck, wasted no time. She climbed on top of Tom, her hips grinding against him with fervor. She moaned loudly, her focus solely on her own pleasure.

The crowd gathered around them, watching, some cheering. Tom gasped in response, but the pleasure felt distant, mechanical, as if he were performing a role rather than experiencing anything real. Angela's moans grew louder, more exaggerated, as she relished the attention she was receiving. Tom, however, felt like he was disappearing.

Wayne joined them, moving behind Angela and taking her roughly from behind. Her moans grew even louder, echoing through the room as both men were inside her. Meanwhile, Beth crouched over Tom's face, urging him to lick her. His head pounded, the cocaine sending his thoughts spiraling out of control. He complied, fingering her hard as he sucked on her clit, her wetness dripping onto him.

His body moved automatically, driven by the drugs and the scene unfolding around him. He pulled out from Angela, disoriented, as she moved on to Wayne. Now on all fours on the other couch, she snorted another line while Wayne took over, her moans filling the room.

Tom sat up, his chest heaving as a wave of self-loathing crashed over him. He felt disconnected, like he wasn't even inside his own body anymore. But he continued. He grabbed Beth, pushing her beneath him, and entered her forcefully. A few thrusts, and she came, her body shuddering beneath him. When she caught her breath, she returned to his cock, sucking him off with renewed intensity.

It took him fifteen minutes to finally cum, spilling onto her chin and chest to the sound of thunderous applause. The crowd cheered, their voices distant as the effects of the cocaine began to wear off. Tom felt filthy, his mind clouded with shame and regret. He snorted another line before making his way upstairs, desperate to numb the emotions clawing at him.

On his way out, the people who had cheered for him minutes earlier didn't even notice him leave. His part was over. His initiation had been a success. Now, it was time to survive.

Tom stumbled upstairs, entered his room, and locked the door behind him. He collapsed onto the bed, the weight of the night crushing him. Exhausted, he drifted into sleep, only to be plunged into a dream—a nightmare where his cock was forever hard, and thousands of faceless women passed over him, using him to satisfy their desires, coming in waves, one after the other. He was nothing more than a tool for their pleasure, caught in an endless chain of lust.

When he woke, his mind was blank, a void filled with the inertia of a downward spiral. But as his body stirred, the memories of the previous night came flooding back with brutal clarity. His throat tightened, and a wave of nausea hit him. He was naked. Slowly, he pieced together the events—the cocaine, the sex, the crowd watching.

He had never imagined losing his virginity like this. The weight of it crushed him—he had crossed over, entered the dark side. He had crossed the white line, not just the one made of powder, but the moral line he had always believed he would never pass. His unease turned to panic as the image of his parents flashed before him—John and Margaretha, so in love, their marriage unbreakable. Tom envied them, almost hated them for their simplicity. Their love, their connection, it shielded them from the world's vices. They kissed, they laughed, they understood each other without a word. How could he ever hope to have something like that?

His doubts solidified into a cold certainty: everyone had lied to him. His parents, his teachers, society—everything he had been taught about perfection, about being a good person, was a lie. If he had been perfect, he wouldn't have ended up at an orgy with strangers. The cocaine had revealed the ugly truth—he had no claim to his parents' happiness. No soul mate was waiting for him. The idea of a loving partner was a smokescreen, something that didn't exist in his world.

In the society where appearances meant everything, he was invisible—a piece of meat. His heart beat, but what was it for? He wasn't the prince charming of fairy tales anymore. He was nothing more than a cock to be used. Thanks to the coke, he could hide from the world. No one cared who Tom Collins was. The coke made him into someone they wanted to see—the ladies' man, the one they could idolize for his sexual prowess. But fall in love with an Angela or a Beth? Never. He, the bastard son, had no illusions left. His parents had wanted him to open up, to explore the world, but the Pandora's box he had been given had exploded in his face.

Wayne, of course, was delighted with the party. The very next day, he took Tom under his wing, ensuring they were never apart. He promised Tom that Angela would activate her network of girls, and that the nights ahead would be unforgettable. Tom had two conditions, however: he would use condoms, and he would never see the same girl twice. That included Beth and Angela. He had had enough of them.

Wayne didn't argue. "Once is enough," he said, smirking. "Otherwise, they'll start getting ideas about rings and relationships."

As for the condoms, Wayne argued that sex was better without them, but Tom insisted. It was the last vestige of his control, a matter of principle, and perhaps the only way he could preserve what remained of his integrity. He refused to cum inside any of these girls, no matter what.

Tom also insisted on continuing his studies. He wanted to earn his degree, if only to cling to some semblance of normality. Wayne reluctantly agreed. To avoid withdrawal symptoms from the cocaine, Wayne encouraged Tom to smoke weed instead, reserving the heavier drugs for the parties. The rest of the time, they had to maintain the image of being "good boys" to avoid arousing suspicion from their parents.

Wayne curated Tom's new image, dressing him in designer clothes from luxury boutiques. Veridi, Jeff High, Jean Lamart—Tom traded his old, modest wardrobe for a more sophisticated one. The term passed, and despite everything, Tom never left. Wayne had become his mentor in vice, teaching him all the tricks of the trade. Tom learned how to "shop," which in their world meant stocking up on cocaine. Wayne introduced him to a network of dealers who were more than happy to hook a wealthy new customer. Tom hated everything Wayne stood for. He hated the arrogance, the entitlement, the way they flaunted their privilege as if nothing could touch them. And yet, Tom couldn't escape Wayne's influence. He had become Wayne's "Collins bitch," the leader's lapdog. No matter how much Tom despised him, he was trapped in Wayne's world, and he didn't know how to get out.

The coke flowed freely, one orgy after another, blurring the edges of Tom's reality. He loved the feeling of the powder burning in his nostrils, the way it fried his brain and split his body and soul in two. Sex was just an afterthought. The drugs gave him his hard-on and dulled everything else. For a man who now saw himself as an object, it was the ultimate depersonalization.

He chased girls without knowing their names. Some men would have worn that as a badge of honor, but not Tom. The girls who took him were all the same—the beauty queens, the worldly dolls. They lived for pleasure, for the endless pursuit of excitement. They were the ones who kept plastic surgeons in business, their bodies technically flawless, but their souls rotten beneath the surface.

They wanted to be beautiful, they wanted to be popular. Above all, they wanted to strategize their way into marriage before thirty. But behind the polished exteriors, behind the perfected bodies, there was a hollowness. They exuded an aura of decay—an overused, worn-out energy that no amount of makeup or surgery could hide. They had thousands of miles on their hips and their souls, and it showed.

Fueled by pornography and a desire for validation, they mimicked the actresses they watched on screen. They condemned the very practices they reproduced in the bedroom, always pushing themselves further, always performing. It wasn't about pleasure—it was about being seen, being talked about, being relevant. They needed the attention to remind themselves they still existed. And Tom? He simply used them, sliding them onto his cock, back and forth, an endless rhythm with no meaning. His orgasms were hollow, stripped of any real feeling. The pleasure was mechanical, like everything else in his life.

At this pace, the years passed in a blur. Before he knew it, Tom had his diploma in hand, finally able to return home, relieved to have distanced himself from Wayne. He was no longer Collins' bitch. He had emancipated himself from the toxic grip of his former mentor, and now, he had all the cards to make it on his own.

When he returned, his parents were delighted. To them, Tom looked great—healthier, perhaps more mature. They had no idea of the beast that had awakened within their son, no clue of the transformation he had undergone.

He settled into a loft downtown, using their money to fuel his new lifestyle of parties, drugs, and casual sex. His days became a lazy, uncommitted routine—just having fun, drifting through life, waiting for the inevitable day when he would finally land in the sterile confines of an air-conditioned office.

CHAPTER 4

FORREST HILL, 1 YEAR BEFORE THE TRAGEDY...

Sun Valley is just waking up. The lights in the houses of this wealthy neighborhood are still out, shrouded in the quiet of early morning. Paperboys haven't begun their deliveries, and the household staff won't start work for another hour. The partygoers will sleep until midday at least. Families are nestled in their last moments of sleep before the bourgeois day begins. Tom is driving his convertible through the silent streets, taking his time as he passes the grand homes, trying to catch glimpses of how the other half lives. He isn't interested in the luxury—he can afford to live in a place like this if he wanted to. No, what fascinates him is the illusion of normalcy. He peers at the few decorations visible through a window left dimly lit, indulging in a small, strange indiscretion. He wonders what it's like to live a life where everything has meaning.

As he coasts down the hill toward the motorway, his nostrils are numbed. He sniffles like a man with a cold, though the real cause is the coke he's been riding all night. The high is starting to fade, and Tom knows he should have taken another hit before leaving. This would be his last line of the night before sobriety forces its way back into his veins. His body craves more, but he ignores it.

Despite knowing the route by heart, he switches on the GPS. He's fully aware that driving under the influence is dangerous, but the steady, robotic voice from the GPS helps keep him focused. It's a strange comfort, guiding him home like a faithful companion in the early hours. At least it keeps him grounded.

Tom has been battling with self-doubt for weeks now. Drugs used to be an escape—a way to forget who he was—but now, they've become something else. Something emptier. He wouldn't say he's depressed, exactly, but the artificial highs don't hold the same appeal. Every day, he promises himself he'll take a break, get his life together. But the lure of wild, easy nights is stronger. He wonders what he would become without cocaine. Who would he be?

Tonight was no different from the others. He'd gone to a bar, ordered drinks, and spotted two women—beautiful, sexy, but all too familiar. They always looked the same, the type who came onto him without hesitation. After a few cocktails, the night started to heat up, and Tom ducked out to the bathroom. He sniffed his first line there, and when he came back, it wasn't Tom Collins who saw the women—it was the man who could get hard on command. They left the bar with the more eager of the two leading the way. The rest was a blur. It always was. Fucking, sniffing, fucking, sniffing—Tom went through the motions until they were spent, until they had nothing left to take from him.

He never asked their names, and he never gave his. When they insisted, he called himself John, like his father. It felt like an insult, a slap in the face to the man who had always been faithful and devoted to his wife. Unlike John Collins, Tom couldn't get it up out of love or desire. He needed cocaine to fuel him. And that's the thought that gnawed at him. His body, worn from years of meaningless orgies, was starting to rebel. His mind, fogged by drugs, was beginning to send warning signals, like a machine pushed too far.

Cocaine had always been the drug of the party, the enhancer of pleasure. But now, Tom found himself craving it outside of the usual hours. He wanted to get high alone, locked in his apartment with only the powder and his demons for company. No sex, no distractions. Just the drug and the void it created.

The only thing stopping him from sinking further was fear—fear that he was already too far gone. To compensate, he smoked twice as much weed, convincing himself that it wasn't addiction. He still thought he could stop anytime he wanted. Bullshit. Deep down, he knew the truth. The coke had sunk its claws into him a long time ago.

Tom was lost in thought, barely registering his friend's voice in the background. Distracted, he failed to notice the GPS, and before he knew it, he'd taken the wrong exit off the highway, missing the turn for Winston Road. The GPS insisted he was on the right path, but Tom's gut told him otherwise. He had no idea where he was. The car had led him straight into a trap—or at least that's how it felt. He made a mental note to take the car in for servicing later in the afternoon. The faded sign by the disused railway tracks read "Forrest Hill," but something about the place felt off. He had never heard of this part of town, which wasn't surprising given the state of it.

The road was barely marked, the tarmac cracked and uneven, and one-way signs left him with no option but to continue forward into what seemed like a no-man's-land. Tom surveyed his surroundings with growing unease. The buildings—concrete blocks stacked haphazardly on top of one another—seemed lifeless, but the occasional laundry hanging from a balcony or light flickering inside hinted that people lived here. Further ahead, he saw the remnants of an abandoned construction site, the foundations left to decay because no one had wanted to invest.

He slowed down, careful not to damage his tires on the dilapidated road. The area was nothing like the pristine boulevards downtown, where Tom usually felt at home. Closed storefronts lined the streets, their windows plastered with *"For sale"* signs. Yellowed posters clung to the walls, advertising products that no longer existed or events that had likely never happened. Time had forgotten this place. Tom noticed the absence of graffiti or vandalism—this neighborhood seemed too forgotten for even troublemakers to care.

Amid the decay, a park stood out like an oasis in a desert. It had lush green areas, surprisingly well-maintained, with flowerbeds adding a touch of life to the bleak surroundings. Tom hadn't seen a single person on the streets, which meant he didn't feel immediately threatened, but caution tugged at his instincts. He double-checked the locks on his doors. In a place like this, you were more likely to get mugged than win the lottery. With his flashy sports car and polished, privileged face, he was an easy target. He cursed himself under his breath for getting lost in a place like this. If he were superstitious, he might have taken it as a sign—perhaps a warning to stop using cocaine. But no. This mess was the result of his own absent-mindedness.

His thoughts drifted back to the high he was chasing. He hated how reality came crashing back when the coke wore off, how it forced him to confront the emptiness he lived with. He needed something to calm him down, to cut himself off from the world that disgusted him. Cocaine was his internal GPS, his autopilot. There were a couple of grams stashed in the glove box—just a tiny line wouldn't change anything... He felt as though he had been driving in circles for hours, the streets all blurring into one. His hands trembled on the wheel as he approached a crossroads. Should he turn left or right?

Mechanically, he chose left. The buildings on that side of the road appeared to be in better condition. He figured that meant it was where most of the locals lived. Thirty meters ahead, he spotted a small improvised terrace on the sidewalk. A handful of tables had been set up in the middle of a square surrounded by overgrown bushes and faded artificial flowers. One sign, flickering under the harsh glare of streetlights, caught his attention. The name of the establishment glowed faintly on the wooden sign: Elaine's Cafe. Something about it beckoned him. Breakfast. That's what he needed.

Tom's stomach growled, reminding him that his last proper meal had been long ago. He breathed a sigh of relief—at least it wasn't the drugs this time. He was just hungry. Elaine's Cafe had to be one of those cozy spots, run by a sweet old lady who baked apple pies. Or maybe that was just wishful thinking. More likely, he'd find cockroaches crawling across his plate. Neither option was particularly appealing, but his stomach was winning the battle over his hesitations. He could either sit in his car and get stoned like some washed-up junkie, or take the risk of food poisoning.

His empty stomach won out. Even if the food was terrible, maybe the coffee would be decent. If not, he could at least doze off for a while and hope his car wouldn't be stolen by the time he woke up. Tom parked on the curb and switched off the engine, stepping out of the car with a sigh of relief as he stretched his legs. He almost forgot to lock the doors, cursing himself for being so paranoid. His parents would have been scandalized by his knee-jerk judgments. *"Being poor doesn't mean you're a criminal,"* he could hear his mother say.

As he pushed open the door to Elaine's Cafe, an old bell jingled, announcing his presence. The place was empty. A large Scandinavian-style counter dominated the room, with glasses and liquor bottles lined up neatly behind it. Everything seemed to be in its proper place, with the chrome of the old coffee machine gleaming like a prized possession. The owner had clearly taken great care of it.

The cafe had a strange layout—on the right, leather benches lined the walls, separated by small tables. On the left, a small stage sat alongside an ancient jukebox, its once-vibrant colors now faded. The walls were covered with old, worn photos of disco dancers, and posters of legends like Stevie Wonder, James Brown, Diana Ross, and Billy Ocean. Hanging from the ceiling was a sad disco ball, its glory days long past. It dangled from a patched cable, barely clinging to life. Round tables cluttered the middle of the room, leaving little space for service. The whole place felt like a time capsule, frozen in the memories of a happier era. But Tom couldn't imagine this part of town ever being happy.

The thought crossed his mind that there might be a secret room somewhere in the back, where shady poker games took place. The clientele was probably made up of old drunks, the kind who spun tales of their failed dreams over endless glasses of whiskey. Tom could almost picture them—people at the bottom of the barrel, clinging to alcohol as their only lifeline.

But none of that mattered now. Tom was hungry enough to ignore his surroundings. He slid into one of the leather benches and picked up a menu. The laminated paper had seen better days, handled too many times by indecisive customers. The ink had faded in places, and children's scribbles obscured the descriptions of most of the dishes. Holding the menu under a nearby lamp, Tom managed to make out "Full Breakfast." That was enough for him. He was already imagining crispy bacon and fries drowned in cheese sauce.

"You're not going to eat like poor Collins! An Invictus never gets belly fat, so forget the junk that makes you obese, bro!"

Wayne Beckett's voice echoed in Tom's mind. Wayne had always been obsessed with physique, convinced that a good body was the key to a successful social life. Wayne's personal trainer had shown up at the fraternity house every day to put the boys through grueling two-hour workouts, and a "dietician" delivered carefully portioned meals to help them "maintain their figure."

Growing up, Tom had never worried about his appearance. He was always thin, and his metabolism made it hard for him to gain weight. But the day he dared bring a hamburger back to the Invictus Residence, Wayne had nearly lost his mind. He grabbed the bag out of Tom's hands and tossed it in the trash, berating him all day about how eating like "poor people" would turn him into a fat slob.

"We're closed!"

Tom was snapped out of his thoughts by a booming voice. Startled, he looked up to see the owner of the voice—a man who looked nothing like the kindly grandmother Tom had imagined. Quite the opposite.

The man standing before him looked like a bad-tempered gorilla. His face was gaunt, his eyes as grey as his close-cropped hair. A toothpick hung from his thin lips, and though he was of medium height, his posture exuded authority. He looked like the type of barkeep who had thrown out his fair share of troublemakers over the years.

"We're closed!" the old man barked again, his voice full of annoyance. "Didn't you see the sign?"

Tom pointed toward the door. "What sign?"

The old man's face twitched in irritation. There was no sign. He muttered something under his breath, but Tom remained calm.

"I'd like a full breakfast and a coffee, please."

The old man scoffed. "Oh, I'd be delighted to serve you, sir, except we're CLOSED. Come back in thirty minutes."

He was clearly agitated, his voice dripping with sarcasm. Sure, the sign wasn't up, but that didn't mean some posh kid could waltz in and act like he owned the place. Tom, undeterred, dared to ask if an exception could be made.

The old man's fury boiled over. "Where the hell do you think you are, kid? You could be the Pope and it wouldn't matter. We're closed. Now get the hell out of my cafe!"

Without warning, the old man grabbed Tom's arm, ready to escort him out. He'd dealt with enough entitled customers over the years, and he wasn't about to let some smart-ass brat set the tone for his day. Exceptions ? Out of the question.

The old man caught sight of Tom's sleek convertible parked just outside as he rudely pushed him towards the exit. Cars like that didn't belong in Forrest Hill. It had to be worth at least 150,000, maybe more. The old man raised an eyebrow, nodding towards the car.

"Is that yours?"

Tom seized the opportunity to bluff, knowing that if it worked, breakfast might just be free—or at the very least, worth the hassle. He kept his tone calm and casual, hoping to throw the old man off balance.

"Yes, it's mine. And I've got a question for you—how is it that you're allowed to serve alcohol when you're listed as a cafe? Isn't that illegal? I imagine the fines for that could be hefty."

Bullseye. The color drained from the old man's face. His mouth tightened, and for a moment, he seemed at a loss for words. His eyes dropped, unable to meet Tom's. Of course it was illegal. His requests for the proper licenses had gone unanswered for years, so he'd taken matters into his own hands, improvising. But how had this punk figured that out? Between the way Tom was dressed, the car he drove, and now this... was it possible that Tom was working for the mayor? A mole?

MYTHOMANIA

Rumors had been swirling around town for a while. The old man knew how the game worked—developers and politicians had their eye on the neighborhood, trying to buy up properties for next to nothing. First, they'd send someone anonymous to snoop around, then they'd offer to buy his cafe and the surrounding buildings for a pittance. And what would come next? He didn't want to think about it. Everything would be torn down, erasing Forrest Hill from the map. The families here, people who had nowhere else to go, would be left with nothing. He couldn't let that happen.

The old man saw himself as the last line of defense, a guardian of the forgotten. If the council wanted Forrest Hill, they'd have to get through him first. The old man glanced back at Tom, who was watching him closely, waiting for a reaction. Grumbling under his breath, the old man relented, motioning for Tom to sit back down on the bench. Fine, he thought. Time for breakfast. He'd show this arrogant prick that people in the Forgotten District weren't savages. He called towards the kitchen, "Babou! Fire up the stove, we've got a customer!"

A huge man with dark ebony skin appeared from the back, wearing a crisp white apron over his chef's uniform. His face, in stark contrast to the old man's gruff demeanor, was warm and full of life. He looked like someone who laughed easily and took life as it came.

"Is this a VIP guest, Boss?" Babou asked with a playful grin.

"No questions, just make it good," the old man grumbled.

"Don't forget to pay my overtime, Boss!" Babou winked as he disappeared back into the kitchen, his laughter echoing through the room.

Tom watched the exchange with a smirk. The old man turned back to him, begrudgingly explaining,

"That was Babou, my cook. Breakfast will be ready shortly, so I'll make you some coffee in the meantime. But don't expect any soy milk or that fancy crap they serve downtown. We're traditional here, and I guarantee you've never had a coffee like mine."

Before Tom could respond, the old man turned his back on him, busying himself with the coffee machine. Tom leaned back against the bench, wondering if he'd made a mistake by insisting on being served. Normally, he never had to. The places he frequented were always more than happy to cater to his every need.

He thought about leaving, but something stopped him. Despite the worn leatherette bench and the strange, deserted cafe, he felt... oddly at ease. There was a strange calm in the air, a break from the relentless cycle of his days. Something about this place made him stay. Another sign, Tom thought, but he wasn't sure of what. He had never believed in God—not because he outright denied His existence, but because he'd never experienced any miracles firsthand. If Elaine's was a part of some divine plan, then God had a strange sense of humor. The idea that salvation could be found in this run-down cafe, in the grumpy old man who ran it, seemed absurd. But then again, nothing about Tom's life made sense anymore.

Tom's taste buds awakened as the smell of fresh, steaming coffee reached his nose. His stomach growled in anticipation—he was so hungry, he could hardly wait to start eating. The old man, sensing that Tom might be settling in for a while, had not only placed a mug of coffee on the table, but also a thermos. There was cream, sugar, and even two biscuits to accompany the drink.

Tom wondered briefly if this was the usual treatment for all customers, or if the old man was doing it out of fear after their earlier exchange. Either way, Tom wasn't about to complain. He added a spoonful of sugar to the coffee before taking a generous sip. The old man had been right—he'd never tasted coffee like this. It was rich, perfectly balanced with hints of caramel and cinnamon. The flavor was miles beyond the overpriced, artificial drinks sold in the city.

By the time Tom had finished his second cup, Babou appeared from the kitchen, carrying a plate of breakfast so large that Tom couldn't help but wonder how he'd manage to finish it all. The chef placed the dish in front of him with a nod, his expression calm and satisfied. The portion was enormous—scrambled eggs, caramelized bacon, sausages, toast, roasted potatoes smothered in creamy cheese sauce, and an impressive stack of pancakes.

Just as Tom was about to dig in, the old man returned, placing a plate of pastries on the table—peanut butter cookies, a slice of praline-covered brownie, and a chocolate muffin. Tom had already grabbed his fork and knife when the old man spoke.

"The pastries are on the house. To give you a taste of our local talent. My waitress bakes them, and I'll tell you, they're the best in town."

For the first time, the old man smiled, and there was something almost touching in his pride. Tom couldn't help but feel a little more at ease. For once, he felt free to be himself. No Wayne hovering over him, scrutinizing everything he put into his mouth. No lectures about diet and health. It was ironic, Tom thought, how people like Wayne were obsessed with avoiding food that made you fat or sick, yet worshiped drugs and alcohol without a second thought.

With every bite, that nonsense felt farther and farther away. Tom had eaten in many restaurants, some of the finest in city, but he had never enjoyed a meal as much as he did now. This breakfast was simple, yet filled with care. Every ingredient felt generous, made with love. In less than ten minutes, Tom had devoured the entire plate, and for the first time in a long while, he felt genuinely satisfied. He even considered ordering more, making up for all the tasteless, unhealthy food he had forced himself to eat over the years.

But first, the pastries. Tom had always been a chocolate lover, so he decided to start with the praline-covered brownie. The moment he took his first bite, he was transported back to his childhood. It was like stepping into a time machine, back to those carefree afternoons of after-school snacks. The taste of the brownie filled him with warmth, bringing back memories of his mother's comforting arms, the sense of love and protection after a tough day at school.

The doorbell rang, cutting through the moment of quiet nostalgia that had enveloped Tom. Curious, he turned towards the sound, wondering if what he saw was real. A young woman, about his age, had just entered. She was tall and slim, her blonde, wavy hair falling just to her shoulders. She moved with effortless grace, her long legs accentuated by the tight black lycra pants she wore. A light V-neck sweater revealed just enough of her figure, and an oversized haute couture gold leather blazer, cinched at the waist by a wide belt, emphasized her slim frame.

She walked with confidence, platform shoes adding to her height, but there was no vulgarity in her appearance despite the extravagance of her outfit. Instead, she seemed to own her look, as though it was an extension of her very being. Her face was striking, a subtle defiance of current beauty standards. A touch of black kohl framed her intense blue eyes, while her red lips stood out against her pale skin. She resembled a vintage model, one of those timeless figures from another era who expressed their femininity with a quiet, self-assured grace.

As she strode across the room, her arms laden with plastic boxes, the subtle scent of her perfume—roses with a hint of almond—drifted through the air, filling the space around her. Tom was captivated. His heart raced, his mind buzzing with questions. Who was she? Did she live here? He wanted to know everything. He had an overwhelming urge to approach her, to speak to her, to find out more.

"Madee, you're three minutes late!"

The spell was broken by the old man's gruff voice. Of course, he knew her. Tom's curiosity only deepened. What was her connection to this place?

With a smile, she removed her headphones and turned towards the old man.

"I'd say five minutes, but I'm glad you don't have a clock in your head. I was taking breakfast to Betty and helping her with her TV—she couldn't figure out how to change the channel."

"Tell the old bat she just needs to change the batteries in her remote!" the old man grumbled.

"Don't be mean, Earl. She's old."

"So what? I don't bother my neighbors, and I'm old too."

Madee's eyes sparkled with amusement. "What's with the grumpy old man routine? Everyone knows you're sweet on Betty."

Earl huffed. "I've got a reputation to uphold around here, girl. Don't go shouting it from the rooftops."

"Nobody's fooled, Earl. The whole neighborhood knows you're just a lonely old wolf taking care of his pack like a mother hen."

With that, she slipped gracefully into the kitchen to greet Babou, and the room filled with laughter and small talk between coworkers. Tom couldn't take his eyes off her. He watched her every move, waiting for another glimpse as she reemerged from the kitchen carrying a tray of pastries.

There was something mesmerizing about the way she worked. She carefully arranged the pastries, making several attempts until everything was just right. From his seat, Tom noted how the entire scene felt almost like a dollhouse teatime—an enchanting, delicate moment in the midst of this otherwise rugged, no-nonsense place.

The cafe doors opened again, and the first customers of the morning began to trickle in. They were clearly regulars, locals who greeted each other and the staff by name. Their faces were lined with weariness, the weight of daily struggles etched into their features. Wayne Beckett would have dismissed them with disdain, calling them "the sad-faced masses." But these were people in need of comfort, not judgment. They moved with a quiet urgency, but this place—Elaine's —was sacred to them. It was a warm, welcoming haven where they could sit for a few moments, have a cup of coffee, and share a few words with familiar faces. Madee greeted each one with a radiant smile, listening to their stories, comforting them with kind words, as if she knew all of their habits and burdens. Her presence lit up the room, making the café feel more like a community than just a place to grab breakfast.

Tom's fascination only grew. Madee seemed to belong here in a way that made him feel like an outsider, yet he was drawn to her light. She was the embodiment of something he couldn't quite name—something he hadn't realized he'd been searching for.

Madee had been running back and forth with customers all morning, and the first people to grab their coffee had already noticed Tom. Naturally, news of a stranger sitting in Earl's Cafe spread through the neighborhood like wildfire. Within half an hour, everyone knew. People started flocking to Elaine's just to catch a glimpse. Kids posed for selfies in front of the convertible, their eyes gleaming with excitement. For a brief moment, they forgot their poverty, daring to believe that maybe, just maybe, all dreams were within reach.

For the adults, Tom's presence was a rare distraction from the harsh reality of their lives. Some even smiled or waved at him from a distance, though no one dared approach. It was clear that by evening, Tom would be the talk of the neighborhood.

Madee, caught between serving customers and fielding nosy questions, had to navigate the rising curiosity with care. She arrived late that morning, so she smiled and gave polite explanations, telling the locals she didn't know much about the stranger. Disappointed, they went home with no new information.

Earl, meanwhile, had taken refuge in his office, satisfied that the morning rush had filled his cash drawer. But despite the influx of customers, Earl was furious. If this mystery man was really from the council, he should be fighting to delay the demolition of the area. Forrest Hill consisted of five main streets, and Earl owned buildings on four of them.

Babou, Madee, and fifty other families lived here. The area was unstable, cut off from the downtown area, with the train no longer stopping at their station. Now, residents had to walk twenty minutes to the new terminus just to get to work. Some with cars gave rides to their neighbors, but that was only a temporary fix. While the council let them rot away in their forgotten corner, the people of Forrest Hill continued to struggle.

Earl had once had hope. Two young, ambitious planners had stirred up excitement about a regeneration program. But like any new trend, it had attracted a wave of outsiders—hipsters with too much money and too little understanding of the neighborhood. They had made headlines, showing up with their fancy ideas and turning Earl's stomach with their pretentiousness.

Earl had cleaned up the place, refusing to let a bunch of hipsters suck the soul out of Forrest Hill. But the result had been a clash with the city planners, and the project was abandoned. The trendy crowd moved on, leaving the neighborhood to fend for itself, and Earl felt too old to get involved in any more fights.

The thought of legal battles gave him anxiety. For now, he swallowed his pride, hoping that by catering to the stranger on the bench, he might buy some leniency. If not, Forrest Hill would be lost. Earl would have no choice but to walk to the new train station, waiting for his own departure.

Earl sighed, glancing at the clock. The morning rush was finally over. Time to head back to the dining room and face the stranger once more. He blamed himself for leaving Madee to handle everything, but until he knew for sure who this man was, he wasn't going to sound any alarms.

But the bench was still occupied. Is this guy planning to take root here? Earl thought bitterly. Doesn't he have other places to investigate? His mood soured again. Grumbling, he grabbed the empty thermos, refilled it, and carried it back to the bar. He was too absorbed in scrubbing the counter to hear Madee approach. The scent of white chocolate and raspberry muffins should have tipped him off.

"Are you okay, Earl?" she asked gently.

"Well, why wouldn't I be?" he grunted.

"You haven't even tried to steal a muffin yet. C'mon, what's on your mind?"

Earl grumbled under his breath. "See that guy?"

"You mean the attraction of the day?" Madee chuckled. "With all the questions I've been asked this morning, it was hard not to notice him."

"I think he's one of those busybodies from the town hall. I'm worried about what will happen to the neighborhood if the politicians start poking around."

Madee tilted her head thoughtfully. "He doesn't look like a council worker to me. Jean Lamart suit, sports car..."

"Then what's he doing here if he's not from the council? Our charming little district is hardly a tourist hotspot," Earl muttered sarcastically.

"Calm down, Earl. We don't know anything about this guy yet. It's a bit early to get worked up, isn't it? Right now, he's just a customer. Let's treat him like one, okay?"

MYTHOMANIA

Earl grunted again, clearly unconvinced. Madee, ever the peacemaker, kissed him on the cheek like a granddaughter would kiss her grandfather and headed back to the kitchen to help Babou.

Madee... Earl thought to himself. She was the bright spot in the community, the one who could make light of any tense situation. Earl would never forget the first time she walked into Elaine's. It was the year before, not long after their former waitress Joanne had left for a better-paying job downtown. Earl had been ready to close the cafe for good. Forty years behind the bar had wrecked his back and knees, and even though his mind was still sharp, his body had begun to betray him. With no one to help him, it seemed like the end of the line.

The community had rallied around him, begging him not to give up. But who would come work in this forgotten corner of the city? Days passed, and Babou tried his best to cover both the kitchen and the dining room, but it wasn't sustainable. Earl had resigned himself to closing shop. Then, without his permission, Ginny from the grocery store had posted a job ad online. Earl was livid. He hated the internet—he thought it was the new cesspit of the world.

But Ginny had insisted, and despite Earl's grumblings, she was right. One cold day, the doorbell rang, and in walked a shivering young woman, her cheeks pink from the cold. She asked to speak to the owner, having seen the job ad online. Earl had almost laughed in her face, ready to send her packing. But when she mentioned she had walked all the way from downtown, he paused. He looked at her carefully. She clearly wasn't from their world. But something made him stop and reconsider. She wasn't going to find it easy here—Forrest Hill was a far cry from the lights of the city. Could she survive in this place?

Her name was Madee, and her resume was flawless. She had experience, was ready to start immediately, and came across as motivated and polite—almost too good to be true. Even more surprising, she had asked Earl if he knew of any places for rent in the area. A small room would be enough, she'd said. Earl could tell from the desperation in her eyes, from the soft, cautious way she spoke, that this girl was running from something. What was it? A bad boyfriend? Abuse?

Madee was shy, and her polished, sophisticated style didn't fit the profile of someone who might bring trouble. Whatever she was hiding from, Earl didn't think it would put the community in danger. It took courage to walk all the way to Forrest Hill, and Earl could sense the weight of personal tragedy hanging over her. You can't fake that kind of need, and that was why he hired her.

Earl had plenty of empty properties under his name—land that had once been worth something, but now was nearly worthless. His family had lived in Forrest Hill for generations, working tirelessly to build something lasting. Earl was proud of his roots, proud of the legacy left by those who came before him. What he owned was a reminder that hard work paid off in the end. Without a second thought, he had pulled a key from his desk and handed it to Madee.

"You start tomorrow," he told her. "I'll deduct the rent from your salary."

Madee had almost cried. The flat was small—just one bedroom, a cramped living room, a kitchen, and a bathroom. The furniture was basic—a bed, a table, four chairs, and a fridge—but to her, it was everything. She thanked Earl over and over, her voice thick with gratitude.

And that was how she had arrived, with nothing but a handbag and the clothes on her back. Since then, she had become part of the family—Earl's family—protected and loved by the community. Madee, his Madee.

She wasn't upset that Earl had come out of hiding. His gruffness had always been part of his charm. Working downtown had taught her how to handle pressure. She no longer counted the number of strangers who brushed past her each day, most of them treating her like she didn't exist. Downtown customers despised the "worker ants," looking down on those who spent their days in shops or restaurants as if their lives had been wasted. She had endured insults, been called stupid, and on more than one occasion, had hidden in the restroom during her breaks, crying quietly. By comparison, Earl's grumpy moods were like a sunny vacation.

Now, she took the chance to slip back into the kitchen with Babou as Earl returned to the cafe to watch the stranger on the bench. She busied herself grating potatoes, her mind barely registering the cook's cheery mood. Instead, she thought of Earl's words. If the council started to take an interest in Forrest Hill, she would have to leave. The very thought of running again, of leaving behind the life she had managed to build here, made her stomach churn. She didn't want to say goodbye to her friends, to the family she had found.

"He's a handsome boy, don't you think?" Babou's voice jolted her out of her thoughts.

"What?"

"The guy at table four. Handsome, no?"

"If you say so..."

Babou's grin widened. "Come on, Madee. Aren't you attracted to him?"

"What are you insinuating, Babou?" she said, flushing slightly.

"You're a beautiful, single girl. You need a man who'll love you and take care of you."

Madee rolled her eyes. "And you think this customer is some knight in shining armor, here to sweep me off my feet?"

Babou laughed. "When he's around, I can smell love in the air. He's been staring at you since he sat down!"

"Nonsense," Madee muttered, turning away. "Pass me the bacon and cheese. These potato pancakes won't make themselves."

Her heart beat a little faster, but she tried to push the feeling down. Babou was just being playful. He saw her through the lens of friendship, not reality. Madee wasn't beautiful, and she knew it. Babou was only saying that because he cared about her, but his judgment was clouded.

Men rarely showed interest in her, and Forrest Hill wasn't exactly brimming with single guys. Madee knew everyone here, and she wasn't naïve enough to believe that meeting someone was likely. Sure, the guy at table four was attractive—anyone could see that—but he was probably already taken. He had the look of someone who came from a different world, one where girls were born under lucky stars, beautiful and rich.

Handsome boys don't fall in love with girls like Madee. They fall in love with perfect women. That's just how the world worked, and Madee had been reminded of that fact from the time she was a child. He's only looking at me to judge my faults, Madee thought bitterly. Back in town, he'd probably meet his friends, and between martinis, he'd tell them about his trip to the poor part of the city. He'd give them a detailed account of the ugliest waitress he'd ever seen, and they'd all laugh until their sides ached. Then life would return to normal.

Madee had long accepted that she would always be a last choice. She needed to stop dreaming of a man she loved, because it wasn't going to happen. Since she was a child, she had been conditioned to believe that she should be content with the man who wanted her—whether she liked him or not. Ugly people take what they can get, she thought. With time and routine, maybe love would grow. But her throat tightened, and tears threatened to spill from her eyes.

Determined not to cry in front of Babou, she walked briskly out of the kitchen. She needed to escape, to forget these sad thoughts, and a cigarette would help. She dug through her disorganized handbag, cursing under her breath. How did Mary Poppins keep everything so neat?

Her eyes flicked to table 4, where the man from the convertible was rummaging through the pockets of his blazer, muttering to himself, "Where the hell can it be?"

She knew that look—the panic of a smoker who couldn't find his cigarettes. She glanced at the table and spotted a lighter.

Before she could second-guess herself, Madee walked over to him, holding her pack of Calvin Silver.

"Looking for these?" she asked softly, setting the pack down on the table. "Use mine if you need them. I've got more stashed under the register."

Without waiting for a response, she turned on her heel and walked quickly out of the cafe, her heart pounding. She didn't want to stick around long enough for him to think she was crazy. She rushed into the alley behind the cafe, crouching behind the rubbish bins, her hands shaking as she lit her cigarette. Just as she took the first drag, the back door to the kitchen swung open.

"Babou! You nearly scared me to death!" she hissed. "Good thing I've got a strong heart!"

Babou's laughter echoed off the alley walls. "Madee, you should've seen it! That was epic."

"Shut up, he'll hear you!" she whispered urgently.

MYTHOMANIA

"What were you thinking? Running off like that? He looked so disappointed! You could see he wanted to talk to you..."

Madee groaned. "What was I supposed to do, Babou? Ask him about the weather? Get real. It's impossible..."

Babou shook his head, a grin still on his face. "Madee, I'm telling you, he likes you. Go back in there and believe you're the beautiful woman you are!"

"Stop it. You're just being nice." Her voice wavered slightly, and she turned away. "Just do me a favor—keep an eye on the entrance and let me know when the coast is clear."

Babou's smile faded a little, but he nodded. "Alright... I won't push it. But think about what I said. Give yourself a chance to live."

Meanwhile, inside the cafe, Tom was cursing himself for how cold he had been. Normally, he didn't have to put in any effort with women. The ones he met knew exactly what they wanted, and he let them take the lead without a second thought. But today, he had waited all morning for Madee to approach his table. He had even rehearsed what he would say, prepared a few lines to break the ice. And yet, when she finally came over, he froze. He let the moment slip away.

Now, the craving for a cigarette gnawed at him, amplifying his frustration. Just as he was about to give up hope of finding his pack, she appeared. Her simple gesture, offering her cigarettes, touched him more than he expected. No one had ever done something so spontaneous for him, except maybe his parents. And instead of seizing the moment, he had let her slip away again.

Tom sat there, berating himself. In Madee's eyes, he must seem like a pretentious jerk, too full of himself to even say thank you. The only impression he'd left was that of an ungrateful fool. It was a disaster. His first attempt at connecting with "normal" people, and he had failed miserably.

Feeling defeated, Tom asked Earl for the bill. He needed to leave. Even the idea of returning to his loft felt like a punishment, but he didn't see any other option.

Earl, barely hiding his relief, approached. "You're leaving already?"

"Yeah. I've got meetings downtown." Tom hesitated. "Can I get some cakes to go?"

Earl eyed him for a moment before grumbling, "I'll seal 'em up in a package, but you gotta bring it back."

"Deal. Two brownies and three muffins, please."

"Gladly, Prince!" Earl replied, his mood lifted at the thought of seeing Tom leave.

Without waiting for the total, Tom placed a note on the counter and told Earl to keep the change. It had been the best breakfast of his life, and the muffins were worth whatever he'd just paid. Earl, in an unusually good mood, shouted, "Royal tip!" and threw in an extra muffin for good measure.

As Tom left the cafe, he stored Elaine's address in his GPS favorites and set an alarm on his phone for 6 a.m. He knew he'd be back. Not just for the returnable box, but because he wanted to see Madee again. He settled into his convertible, already planning his next visit, and as he drove home, all he could think about was the beautiful waitress from the Forgotten District.

CHAP 5

THEN, HERE, AND NOW...

Eternal rest... Tom wondered: What is death like? Do the dead truly find peace? Are they really reunited with their loved ones in some eternal afterlife? Or do they simply fade into nothingness, watching over the living in silence?

People love to comfort themselves with theories of heaven and hell, but in reality, no one has ever come back to tell the truth. Death is like a secret society, one where only the initiated gain entry. Once you cross through the armored gates of the afterlife, you become part of an eternal holiday camp, where the virtuous and the damned rub shoulders, trapped between light and flame. The good and the bad mingle, and watch as the weak humans below repeat the same mistakes over and over again. Isn't that a ghost's role? To haunt, to sow suffering, to remind the living of their fragility? Perhaps they linger to push the strong toward enlightenment while pulling the weak into the abyss. Do the dead even know the difference between fear, love, and hate anymore? In the end, it's all about decisions, choices made and unmade, and keeping score until the final KO.

Upstairs, Laura was still throwing things against the walls. Tom could hear the dull thuds as more of their possessions met their end. What little was left to break had probably already surrendered. She was hoping—no, expecting—that he'd come upstairs, smooth things over, fuck her as she had asked, make her feel desired. She wanted him to feel guilty, to regret pushing her away, to give in just so things could go back to their miserable "normal" until the next time.

This little game disturbed Tom. Without drugs, it was difficult to perform, and he didn't care about pretending anymore. He only wanted the drudgery of forced sex to end as quickly as possible. The truth was, the only woman he had ever truly loved was gone. Madee. Laura meant nothing to him, and the idea of forced intimacy disgusted him. His body was not a tool at Laura's disposal. To avoid her wrath, he often handed over his credit card like a bribe, letting her buy whatever she wanted. Money was their referee, and it bought him temporary peace.

This time, though, Laura could have destroyed the entire floor, and Tom wouldn't have moved from his seat in the kitchen. He sat shrouded in smoke, drowning in his memories. I should have seen this coming, he thought, but I wasn't paying attention.

The house was big, too big for the two of them, and Tom often deluded himself into thinking he could have space, a sanctuary within its walls. But how naive he had been. Laura invaded every corner of his life, her obsessions creeping into every room.

After germs, bad odors were Laura's second greatest obsession. The faintest hint of tobacco smoke sent her into a blind rage, her nose attuned to even the slightest unpleasant smell. It was only a matter of time before she noticed. She stormed into the kitchen, eyes wild. The ashtray on the table was already half full, and Tom had been lighting one cigarette after another, his only solace from this nightmare.

With a swift, violent motion, Laura snatched the ashtray from the table and hurled it against the bay window, shattering glass in every direction. The sound echoed in the silence, and before Tom could even react, she was on him. Her small frame seemed to have multiplied in strength, her fury giving her the force of a hurricane. Gone were her demands for sex—now it was pure rage, pure venom. Insults poured from her like a torrential rain, punctuated by the stinging blows of her fists.

"You're nothing," she screamed, "you're worthless! A fucking coward! You don't deserve to live!"

Tom didn't understand what was happening. His reflexes were gone, dulled by shock. He let her hit him, made no move to defend himself, only managing to shield his face as best he could. He felt the sickening crunch of his nose breaking beneath her fists. He hadn't even done anything wrong. Such violence... over cigarettes. When the rage had burned itself out, Laura calmly fixed her hair, her breathing returning to normal. She slipped away, leaving Tom where he stood, dazed and bleeding. Let that be a lesson to him, she probably thought. Next time, he'll think twice before smoking in the house.

React! a voice screamed inside Tom's head. Don't be weak! But he couldn't. He was too stunned, too lost in the fog of disbelief. Slowly, he stood up, his only thought now to run away, to get out of the house he had grown to hate. The broken bay window seemed like a final symbol, a crack in their already shattered relationship. This breakup had been written long before tonight.

He grabbed his car keys, phone, and wallet. His credit cards were still in place, but the cash was gone—likely spent by Laura during another one of her drinking binges. He didn't care. All that mattered now was getting away, getting safe. Laura had crossed a line tonight, a line that had turned her cruelty into something far more dangerous. With the engine running, Tom's first instinct was to drive to the police station. He laughed bitterly at his own stupidity after barely a hundred meters. What kind of cop is going to take a six-foot-two man seriously when he files a complaint about domestic violence?

They'd give him a breathalyzer test, probably suspecting he was the aggressor. And then Laura would be called in. She'd arrive at the station with her crocodile tears, spinning some lie about self-defense. The fragile little woman with the sweet smile, adored by her followers and fans, couldn't possibly be guilty of such madness. In society, men were always cast as the villains—the predators, the bastards, the manipulators, the abusers. Women were the eternal victims. But violence doesn't care about gender. It's universal, indiscriminate. Men, women, children... anyone can be caught in its grip. The weak, the vulnerable, the unlucky.

Tom knew this now, but where could he go? His parents? That was out of the question. He hadn't spoken to them in years, not since he'd disappointed them for the last time. His selfishness had driven them away. Forrest Hill? He could go there, see Earl, Babou, and the others—his only real friends, the only ones who had ever given him moments of simple joy. But he had pushed them away, too, preferring to wallow in his own misery. The only person who could have truly understood him, the one person he would have confided in, was gone. He was alone now. Alone with his mistakes, his failures, and Laura.

* * *

Laura Wilkins was part of the "in" crowd. She had risen from anonymity through sheer manipulation of social media. She wasn't a model, actress, or singer—she was simply Laura, the girl-next-door type who had figured out how to market herself as the perfect friend. Her fans loved her because she wasn't too intimidating. She was pretty, sure, but not in a way that overshadowed anyone else. She made her followers feel like they could relate to her, like they could be her. Unlike unreachable celebrities, Laura had managed to build a community around herself, a persona that seemed down-to-earth and friendly. She replied to comments with girly emoticons, shared her life in cleverly edited posts, and pretended to keep it simple, all while subtly reminding her audience that she was, in fact, still above them.

As her following grew, so did her influence. The likes, the views, the contracts—they all came rolling in. Brands began to trust her to sell their products, and before long, her opinion was one that counted. She entered the elite world of celebrity influencers, where every hashtag was a calculated move, and every post had the potential to earn her thousands. Thanks to the media's obsession with online stars, even people who had never heard of Laura were starting to see her face everywhere. And with every new follower, her ego swelled. Her heartache, whatever real pain she may have once felt, had been replaced by a hollow, oversized sense of self-importance.

In the end, Laura was just another empty starlet, glimmering under the spotlight, nothing like the real person hiding behind the filters. Her fame was built on imitation gold, glittering on the surface, but rotten beneath.

A month after Madee's death, Laura appeared in Tom's life. At that time, Tom was a wreck of a man whose main activity was buying alcohol at the local grocery store. He wandered the aisles, lost in thought, when Laura bumped into him, the day of their fateful meeting. Seeing the small blonde briefly apologize reminded him of Madee. And then there was the perfume... she was wearing the same fragrance as Madee.

Tom quickly pulled himself together, annoyed at being disturbed in his solitude. But the girl insisted on offering him coffee to make up for her clumsiness. He accepted, despite his reservations. The faint resemblance to Madee in the girl's face gave him the illusion that he was rediscovering his lost love—classic transference for someone who hadn't fully grieved.

They sat down in a cafe across from the grocery store, and thankfully, Tom didn't have to carry the conversation. Laura spoke for both of them, effortlessly filling the silence. She tried hard to appear simple, kind, cultured, but her face betrayed her. When she realized Tom was barely listening, a sneer of irritation would twitch at the corner of her lips. Quickly, she would slip back into her mask—the smiling, positive, "friendly" Laura.

To Tom, she was just another shallow socialite like the ones he had known in his previous life. She was ambitious—too ambitious, really—and willing to do whatever it took to get what she wanted. But Tom ignored all the signs, choosing to focus on her resemblance to Madee. It was the only reason he kept seeing her. Without that, he would have disappeared long ago.

Every day, at the same time, she was at the store. Every day, Tom hoped to avoid her, but there was always something about her that drew him in. Her blouse, her long hair, her pink wallet, her nail polish, and that perfume... the powdery scent of rose and almond, subtle but persistent. There was always some detail that reminded him of Madee. So, he listened to her gossip about people he didn't know, went for coffee with her every day. And when his attention drifted, her friendly look would turn cold, and she'd bang the table to snap him back.

Soon, they stopped going for coffee. Laura was staying in a hotel just a block from Tom's house. She had lost her apartment after a pipe burst, causing major water damage. The fire department evacuated everyone, and her insurance had arranged for her to stay in the hotel until repairs were made—a real tragedy, as she liked to call it.

One morning, Tom agreed to have breakfast at her hotel, even though he didn't want to. That day, she was wearing a moon-shaped pendant, just like Madee's. Hypnotized by the necklace, Tom barely noticed as Laura scooted closer, unbuttoning her shirt to reveal more cleavage, her hand sliding up his thigh under the table. She wanted sex. And Tom couldn't bring himself to tell her he didn't want her. He wanted the memory of Madee. And that's how he got hard. They went into the bedroom, and Laura undressed slowly, showing off her perfect body, searching for adoration in his eyes. But her ass and pussy did nothing for him. It was just like the old days—like those endless orgies. She was no different from the others. Predictable.

Before she started sucking him off mechanically, she masturbated to get herself worked up. She was used to this routine, her mouth having seen it all before. To her,

MYTHOMANIA

Tom's cock was just another toy to play with—something to shove between her fake breasts or down her throat. Tom remained impassive, letting her do as she pleased. She fucked him eagerly, offering her holes and cumming loudly, probably thinking she was the best he'd ever had. She wasn't. She was just another beautiful, worn-out, vain, boring woman, believing she was delivering Nirvana to the man caught in her web.

Every day, they fucked. Laura had an insatiable thirst for sex. No more monologues at the cafe. Now she waited for Tom at her hotel, panties already wet. Sometimes, she'd wear a plug in her ass while waiting for her dose of cock. Sometimes, she kept it in during penetration, imagining she was being taken by two men at once.

She sold the idea of true love to her followers. She couldn't resist snapping a selfie with Tom and plastering it across her social media, despite his adamant refusal. That was Laura's first outburst—she hated it when people didn't follow her script. Once Tom's face was shared thousands of times by strangers, there was no going back. He had to accept it.

The public adored her radiance, and girls eagerly wrote to ask the secret behind her glowing complexion. Laura raved about another miracle cream, generously handed out discount codes, sales soared, and her pockets were lined with cash. Tom was just a trophy, something Laura could proudly display. The fatality of being a dehumanized man was catching up to him. He didn't find Madee in Laura—he had become a puppet once again, a man fumbling without direction, waiting for time to swallow him whole.

When Tom decided to move out of the city, Laura stepped in. To her, their relationship was serious enough to move in together—Tom disagreed. He warned her that she'd get bored living in the countryside, tried to dissuade her. But Laura, furious, took the matter to her networks. In a tearful video, like a guru rallying her cult, she painted Tom as a commitment-phobic bastard. The public sided with their beloved good friend Laura, and before long, #supportlaura was trending.

Tom couldn't handle strangers meddling in his private life. His parents had always avoided the media for this very reason—to protect the family. Celebrity was just a shiny veneer, a never-ending source of problems that cost far more than it was worth. Money and luxury were perks that made daily life easier, but they didn't spare anyone from disaster when it struck.

From the moment they moved into the house, Tom was reduced to a mere accessory. Laura monopolized everything, imposing her lifestyle on him. Tom became her number one target, as she began to reveal her malice and intolerance. A wrong word or gesture, and accusations would fly. Spoiled, jealous, the little princess had an excuse for everything.

Being with Tom gave her access to the upper class. Where once they wouldn't have given her a second glance, the snobbish elites now welcomed her with open arms.

From wardrobe upgrades to invitations to exclusive parties, Laura treated Tom like some pitiful man she had rescued from the gutter. One of her favorite weapons was making him feel inferior. Tom wasn't fashionable enough, didn't spend enough, was too discreet, and the Collins name paled in comparison to her exes... He managed to become invisible, yet Laura constantly reminded him that he wasn't good enough for her... Once, he had believed in his relationship with Madee with all his heart. But now, with Laura, he was back to being "Collins' bitch." The rules were simple: obey, look good, shut up, get fucked, and open your wallet wide. Tom resigned himself to this fate. Life had brought him full circle, back to a boring, inevitable future. Whether it was Laura or someone else didn't matter. He'd be tied down, trapped in a loveless union, with a wife who spent money to stay young and beautiful, flashing her wedding ring as a badge of success. It wasn't worth fighting for anymore.

Deep down, Tom knew he was betraying Madee. His relationship with Laura was a farce, a sign of his cowardice. He couldn't honor Madee in death. If she was looking down on him now, she'd be ashamed. How could she have loved such a pathetic man? Madee hadn't been able to save him, and Tom didn't deserve the love she had given him. There was no escape for him now—he had to pay for his mistakes, no matter how high the cost.

Tom hesitated, but eventually turned back, resigned to going home. Resigned to the idea that he would be forever miserable with Laura. She had won. The little dog was coming home, obedient as ever. When he stepped inside, everything was still. Silent. The downstairs was untouched, and on the upper floor, most of the rooms were locked. He entered the bedroom—empty. The dresser drawers had been hastily emptied, some clothes remained on hangers in the closet, but the rest was gone. Laura had packed up and left.

Relief or anger? Tom wasn't sure. He had been pitifully abandoned by his tormentor. Laura had the nerve to throw a tantrum and leave just because he refused to fuck her. And for what? For being too patient? For letting her push him around? It was so typical of Laura—selfish and domineering. If her followers could see the "good friend" off-camera, they'd be disappointed.

Tom noticed Laura had even made the bed before leaving. On his side, there was an envelope, some notebooks, and a cardboard box. Laura had never given him anything before, so what kind of trick was this?

He picked up the envelope and opened it. Inside was a short, hastily scrawled note:

"Read this first. Then the notebooks. Then the box. If you don't follow this order, I'll know... Be a man, Collins. And now suffer, you son of a bitch."

What else has she dreamed up to torture him? Does the box contain a bomb, ready to explode in his face? Even though he's alone, Tom can feel Laura's malevolent presence hovering around him. Cautiously, he picks up the first notebook and opens it. An old photograph is pasted on the very first page. In the photo, two teenage girls, around fifteen, are wagging their fingers at the camera.

MYTHOMANIA

The face of the girl on the right is completely obscured by black marker. She's wearing a backwards cap over her long chestnut hair and a big oversized skateboard sweatshirt. Her hands are gloved in woollen mittens, and her nails are painted black. The other girl has long straight black hair, parted down the middle, with heavy kohl ringing her eyes. She's wearing a spiked leather collar around her neck, her skin almost unnaturally pale, and her black clothes drape over her frail frame. She, too, is wearing mittens—mesh ones—and her nails are painted black. A caption, written in thick gothic ink, sits beneath the photo: *"Joy and Laura best friends for life."*

Tom stares at the image, blinking twice to make sure the girl in the photo is really Laura. He would never have recognized her if her name wasn't written right there. Intrigued, he flips the page, his eyes scanning the lines filled with the rounded handwriting of a teenage girl. It becomes clear to him that Laura has left him her old diary. But why?

Probably some pathetic teenage drama, he thinks, rolling his eyes. Yet, curiosity begins to gnaw at him. He's about to meet a version of Laura he never knew—a young Miss vampire lookalike who, alongside her best friend, seems to have once wanted to rebel against the world. Up until now, all Tom knew about the woman who had briefly shared his life was what she had allowed him to see. But who was she really? What's the story behind this moody rocker girl who grew up into the plastic, manufactured bimbo he knew?

He grabs a second pillow, tucking it under his neck, and lies back on the bed. Snug and settled, he turns back to page two and starts to read...

CHAPTER 6

LAURA'S DIARY - Y2K

I'm Laura, I'm almost 16, and it's 2006. I've always thought it was stupid to write about my life in a diary. In fact, I'll never start my pages with the classic "Dear Diary." That's so cliché, like something out of a marshmallow film for brain-dead teenage girls. My room doesn't have a canopy bed, my walls aren't pink, I don't have a dumb teddy bear, and I don't spend hours on the phone with my friends. I don't even have friends to talk to. I guess that's why I'm writing in this old notebook I found in my desk drawer. No, you won't be my dear diary. You're not my friend. You're not even alive. You'll cease to exist when I throw you in the fire or toss you in the trash, along with all my feelings. I write because I know you won't argue with me or disagree. You're the deaf-mute friend I can tell everything to without shame or judgment.

I go to Richmond High School in Birdtown, the rich suburb closest to downtown. The kids in my neighborhood are middle-class, not rich enough to live in Sun Valley but well-off enough to be shown a little respect. We're not like the riffraff from the outside. They reek of poverty from every pore, wearing the same clothes day after day, 365 days a year. Parasites on the system. Fucking losers who don't belong in our school.

Despite living in a good neighborhood, I was never popular. I've always had this skinny, awkward body and limp hair, which pretty much disqualified me from being one of the popular girls. My wardrobe was a mess, I didn't go to dances after school, and I wasn't passionate about anything. Personally, I'm what you'd call a copycat. I've always found it hard to have my own tastes or preferences. And the one time I tried, people said I was old-fashioned. It's easier just to wait for trends and copy them. You have no idea how much I hate people. I've always envied them for being cooler, for having more. I'm jealous of every little scrap of happiness that comes their way, because it should be me.

One of the perks of being unpopular is that I don't have many friends. In fact, I only have one: Joy. We've known each other since we were 4. Joy's lucky enough to be everything I'm not—pretty, an only child, rich parents. I love her as much as I hate her. She's always surrounded by friends and has this insane ability to make new ones like it's nothing. She's a bit of an artist, switching styles as easily as she breathes. It doesn't hurt that her parents have the money to keep up with her, and she doesn't have to share anything with a sibling.

She has no problem being the center of attention. Her parents buy her everything new as soon as it comes out, so of course everyone flocks to her. But none of her friendships last more than six months. I'm the only real friend Joy has. She's super picky and doesn't like most people, even though she pretends to be cool about it. She loves being noticed, but her friends are always interchangeable depending on her latest look or phase. To be honest, Joy is a little hypocrite who uses people.

I guess it's convenient to have a "transparent" friend like me to help her shine. Sometimes I feel like I'm just a prop in her life. She's ditched me plenty of times for her new friends when she wants to live life to the fullest. But when things go south and she ends up alone again, she comes back to me like nothing happened.

Our relationship is a roller-coaster—either we're inseparable or we're not speaking at all. It feels unfair that she has everything I don't. I try to copy her styles, but it never works for me. Nobody notices me. My life is a fucking mess.

That's teenagers' number one complaint, but my life is a thousand times worse—I'm not exaggerating! The only good thing about school is that I get good grades. I'm a natural learner, even though I can't stand my teachers or my bastard classmates. Unlike Joy, who's an average student, I have to work really hard to maintain my good marks.

Teenagers usually glorify stupidity, so at least I have an intellectual advantage over her. Intelligence is considered incurable…

When I was in nursery school, one dumb teacher called my parents in to rave about me. According to her, my intellectual abilities were way above average, and she saw me as some sort of genius… top of the class in stickers! My parents, of course, ate it up. At home, I became the family's "little gifted girl." When I throw tantrums or have fits of rage, they pass them off as poorly channeled bursts of genius. That label comes in handy… I haven't mentioned my parents yet, have I? Other teenagers complain about their parents, but they don't live with mine!

My dad, Jeff, is a first-class asshole. He's resigned, absent, short-tempered, rigid, authoritarian—he has no redeeming qualities whatsoever! When he's home, he's terrifying, and you wonder why the poor bastard even bothers. He's an expert at humiliation, always saying, "Words hurt more than fists." He yells all day, lashing out at any excuse: the dishes aren't put away, his favorite show is late, dinner isn't ready on time, we're playing too loudly… When he gets really mad, he hits. Anyone who dares to defy him gets hit, hit, hit until they shut up.

He hates the simple pleasures of life. No restaurants, no vacations, and any outing has to be planned meticulously at least 15 days in advance. It's like he enjoys seeing our happy faces turn to disappointment when he cancels last minute. The bastard always has an excuse: no gas in the car, bad weather, too much traffic, no money… The only option is to bow our heads in submission to his will. Be reasonable... I couldn't care less about being reasonable!

I know he hates me, and I hate him right back, but I never confront him because I'm terrified of what he'd do. I always fake it, and to keep the peace, I shift the blame onto someone else. He's a bastard, but I swear one day, I'll get him.

Luckily, there's Mom to stop him... Mom... She's my protector. In a way, I'm her little queen. Annie was a beauty once, but she's always been hung up on her lost youth and the body that pregnancy ruined. As far back as I can remember, I've only seen her depressed and miserable. She and my dad don't get along. They're married out of habit, but they've got nothing in common.

Mom loves to talk about her glory days—the wealthy childhood, the happy teenage years, when she was a rising star on TV. Casting directors spotted her young, and soon she was landing roles in hit shows. Then, for reasons she's never shared, her career came to a sudden stop, just when the film industry was starting to take notice of her. Apparently, a heartbreak cut her wings in mid-flight.

You can hear it in her voice when she talks about meeting my father. I don't think she ever really got over that failed romance. One day, Jeff came into her life, and she swallowed her pride and expectations, marrying him out of necessity. Time passed, her friends got married, and Jeff was there... You had to do what your friends did so you wouldn't get left behind.

Now she's bitter, stuck in an unhappy marriage. Who could ever be happy with a man like Jeff? She spends her days crying, brooding over her lost opportunities. Jeff avoids the house, searching for a life elsewhere. She often confides in me about her suspicions that Dad's having affairs, and she's developed this hatred for all women, seeing them as sluts who just want to steal husbands. Since my father deserted her emotionally, Mom's poured all her love into her kids... well, into me, that is.

Demanding and high-strung, she's kept her showbiz attitude. Having people work for her for years only reinforced her controlling side. Mom loves beauty, luxury, and intelligence, and she has zero tolerance for flaws or weaknesses. Her old world of glamour and showbiz was everything to her—the ultimate success in life, the holy grail she never quite reached. Now, her kids are her property, the next best thing to fill that void.

She's a master of emotional blackmail. While my dad vents his frustrations through violence, Mom uses manipulation to get what she wants. She calls us "brats" but doesn't give us a moment's peace. She can't tolerate any rebellion. If she can't get her way, she complains to Dad, and then he steps in to put the "scum" in their place.

Despite her flaws and weakness, my "gifted child" status gives me an edge. I tick all the boxes for her perfect child: I'm slim, I'm smart, I'm almost perfect in her eyes. If I need something, or if I'm jealous of Joy, I just have to make Mom believe it's for her own good. She'll make sure I get priority in household spending.

Speaking of money, things are rough. Dad makes good money, but since Mom doesn't work, the end of the month is always tight. We get by thanks to the occasional check from my grandparents. Living in a middle-class neighborhood, owning a nice house—that's all Mom has. Her specialty is hiding what's wrong and putting a spotlight on the good family image. You have to make people believe... make them jealous of you, make them adore you. That doesn't come cheap. Mom loves looking down on shop workers and anyone who serves her. She's taught me that money opens doors, and people crumble like shit when power's in play. According to her, I'm above the rest of the world, and I'm not made for work. Killing yourself at work is for the proletariat. Her little princess—me—isn't meant to crawl in the mud.

My dream is my parents' divorce! They don't belong together, and I'd be relieved to get rid of Dad. The only downside is that he brings in the money, and since we need it, I suffer silently. But whenever I look at him, I imagine him dead and buried. Ever since I was five, I've prayed for their separation, so I could have Mom all to myself and finally get everything I want. What's the point of living in a middle-class house if you're always left wanting?

On the outside, Mom won. Our family seemed happy, settled into its comfortable routine. But inside, it was always the same: No, we can't afford it, No, because we don't have the money. The rich get everything; they're allowed to show off, to buy whatever they want, and everyone respects them. Why can't I be like Joy and have the latest MP3 player, trendy shoes, a RedStar computer, a luxury bag? Why can't I go out whenever I want? Why do I never get any pocket money? I'm so tired of feeling ashamed.

My father is enemy number one, but there's another culprit: Madeleine, my fucking sister. Next to Joy, Madeleine is the person I'm most jealous of. She bleaches her hair like Kelly or Bellinda, those famous blonde girls on TV, always thinking they're better than everyone else , so I've nicknamed her the blonde. I hate all those blondes who turn heads with their fake, bitchy smiles. Everyone knows their hair's fake—you just have to look at their pussy hair to see the truth.

The blonde has a real personality, unlike Joy, who just buys style with her parents' money. She reads boring books no one cares about, listens to shitty music like disco and EDM, and she's passionate about all kinds of things… She goes against the trends, adopting them long before they're cool again. It's her resilience and kindness that really piss me off. The blonde isn't obsessed with money; she appreciates people for who they are, without trying to take advantage of them.

The worst part is, the blonde is Mom's biggest disappointment. She doesn't fit Mom's idea of perfection. Madeleine was two years old when I was born, and my parents love to tell the story of how she ran to the bathroom to throw up when she saw me at the maternity ward. It's one of Jeff's favorite humiliations. He grabs her by the hair and calls her a degenerate, a piece of trash, an animal.

MYTHOMANIA

My parents decided early on that Madeleine was jealous of me, a danger to the family. If I cried, it was automatically her fault because she'd obviously hurt me. I'm not ashamed to admit I used that to my advantage. Whenever I wanted something, I blamed the blonde, and my parents would take it out on her.

The blonde used to be overweight, which only made things worse. My memories of her are of a fat kid with rolls of dripping fat. My favorite game was "horseplay"—I'd make her get on all fours, climb onto her back, and slap her hips to make her go faster. If she didn't, I'd cry. Mom would rush in, scoop me up, and slap the blonde across the face to teach her a lesson.

The blonde was really creative, and I loved stealing her markers or breaking her favorite Jenn doll's head off. No matter what I did, she was always in the wrong. She was fat, and in our house, that was unforgivable. Mom never let her forget it.

When it was time for my bath, I'd go first and soak in the water until my fingers wrinkled. Once I was done, the blonde was allowed to bathe in my water. Never the other way around! If she went first, Mom would've considered it an insult. Fat equals dirty, and I wasn't about to be infected by her obesity!

Mom put the blonde on a strict diet when she hit her teenage years. My years of spying paid off—I loved snooping through her things, sometimes stealing stuff to stash away. I'd find candy wrappers hidden in her drawers. It didn't take a genius to figure out she was sneaking food. Of course, I went straight to Dad to tell him, and he lost it. I still laugh when I think about how many times that idiot rushed headlong into a beating.

I remember those tiny portions of green beans she had to choke down while the rest of us ate real food. "You need to be thin, like your sister," they'd say. The worst part? Despite all the shit she went through, she actually managed to lose weight. She's not model-thin, but she looks good enough.

I can't stand that she became pretty. That wasn't supposed to happen. I'm sure she only lost the weight to get our parents' attention. And with that successful diet came a new wardrobe, a reward she didn't deserve. And guess where the money for that came from? The trip my class was taking to an amusement park! The parents had promised, but my amusement money went straight into the blonde's new clothes.

I made her pay for that betrayal. I stole her favorite top, wore it around, then gave it back to her after I'd had my fun. Except I'd cut little holes into it with my scissors. Weirdly enough, she never wanted revenge. She stayed kind, helpful, always in her own world, ignoring me most of the time. I guess I'm not good enough for the fat bitch... and maybe she's just jealous that I'm so close to Mom.

But if she's not the favorite, why do I hate her so much? Because of what she costs our parents! Our family is all about appearances. I should be the priority, but I have to share. If it weren't for the blonde, the kids' budget would be mine. She's got simple tastes, but I miss every penny spent on her. In my perfect world, Madeleine is nothing more than an annoying obstacle. Bullying her is my favorite pastime, but she's a dangerous enemy who needs to be destroyed if I'm going to be happy.

I can't stand her shadow, hanging over me, full of untapped potential. I'm already living in Joy's shadow at school. I don't know what I want to do with my life yet—the future feels so far away. I just want to be admired by everyone. I want them to shut up when I'm in front of them. I want power. I want to exist. I want to live, and I'll do anything to get it. Now, I just need something to boost my popularity. I need something Joy doesn't have. I need to pull the rug out from under her.

CHAP 7

LAURA'S DIARY: BRANDON AND ME

I haven't written to you in three months... I had some stupid homework to deal with, don't worry. I'm not here for you, so don't complain! Don't switch the roles! You're here for me, on my terms, because I make the rules. If you protest too much, I'll get a lighter and that'll be the end of you, got it?

I'll continue my story if you don't mind. Be quiet and keep your stupid opinions to yourself! So, where was I? Right, I've shared my crappy life with you. The people around me aren't exactly glamorous, as you can see. Everything happens in its own time; I'll deal with them later...

I have good reasons for my silence. I've finally found a passion, a sense of purpose in my life. And guess what? Joy is connected to this new interest... Two months ago, I was supposed to meet her when she came back from her winter vacation. I knew she'd return with lots of exciting stories to tell me. But, as usual, I hadn't done anything special except stay home and be bored.

My dad did us the great honor of taking us for a walk in the woods to go mushrooming. For going out and doing crap, Jeff deserves top marks! Mom dressed like she was going to a gala, she told me you must look smart in the woods too. The blonde was thrilled to go out into the fresh air... She really pisses me off, being so happy about everything. Just to shut her up, I wanted to shove mushrooms in her mouth! For me, outings are only worthwhile if I come back with presents. If you don't spend any money, what's the point of going for a walk?

I grumbled about mushrooming, but Jeff had his way. I did what Mom did and dressed in a pair of stiletto boots, completely unsuitable for a walk in the woods... To shorten the ordeal, I pretended to twist my ankle... I was glad to have the last word with my father. He insisted on forcing us, and paid the consequences... You can't go against me; I screwed him over!

Aside from this not-so-interesting episode, I was dreading Joy's return. We chatted briefly online, but thankfully not long enough for her incredible adventures to ruin my mood... It's always been like this from the start, she's used to me not having much to say... I'm the loser she likes hanging around with, raving about everything she does...

She arrived around 6 p.m. on the Saturday of her return. Joy is the only friend allowed to visit because the parents don't like outsiders in their home. As Mum says, "The house isn't a hostel or a restaurant." I barely recognized her when I opened the door. Where was the dreadlocked, tie-dyed Joy?

The girl standing before me wore fishnet stockings, platform boots, a faux leather miniskirt, a gothic bustier, and a black leather choker. Her left ear, still reddened, proudly displayed an industrial piercing. Even her makeup had changed—from subtle black eyeliner to a dramatic splash of kajal. Only her long, wavy chestnut hair remained the same. Her new style dazzled me, and if I were into girls, I'd have kissed this dark beauty passionately. I was enchanted by her outfit, but instead of feeling happy, I started to feel a pang of jealousy. Joy had outshone me once again... She would undoubtedly be the center of attention at school!

Joy looked at me with a smirk, clearly pleased with the effect she was having before she hugged me. Mum, passing by, was taken aback by my best friend's new look. They exchanged a few brief words before we went up to my room. I had never seen her like this—laughing and jumping on my bed like a child. I was accustomed to her eccentricities, but this was something new. My curiosity overcame my growing jealousy, and out of politeness, I asked her what had put her in such high spirits. She seized the opportunity to tell her story.

She had met a guy named Troy at the ski resort where she'd spent her holiday. Unlike the popular teens at school, he was already 21 and had a car—he was a man, not a boy. After a series of trips with his father, he had come to the ski resort for a break. Joy couldn't wait to see my reaction. Troy's father is the head of security for the rock band Paradoxical Heights!

I had no idea who they were, but Joy insisted she'd mentioned them a million times and that she'd always been a fan. I might be invisible, but I remembered her never mentioning the band. Joy was playing her social role perfectly, pretending to be an early fan to impress Troy... Anyway, they were inseparable. Troy, who resembled my best friend but as a male version, had told Joy that it was Brandon Stevens himself who had helped him develop his style. Who on earth was Brandon Stevens?

Annoyed, Joy accused me of never listening, of being inattentive... The familiar refrain. Brandon Stevens was the leader of Paradoxical Heights, and Joy was talking so fast I thought she might suffocate. I sat down at my desk, opened a new tab, and typed "Brandon Stevens" into the search bar... Wow, he's stunning!

I must be living under a rock not to have heard of him. He could easily pass for fifteen years younger, despite being in his thirties. Small and slender, he looks like a perpetual teenager. His long, glossy black hair and heavily made-up face—eye shadow, foundation, and lip gloss—give him a strikingly androgynous appearance. I was taken with his look, but it was his eyes that captivated me: deep blue with a cold, unfeeling expression. I'd never seen eyes like that before!

To remind me of her presence, Joy shook my arm. I was smitten with Brandon Stevens! I closed the tab, promising myself to do more research later when I was alone. It turns out that it was Troy who inspired Joy's style transformation. Apparently, they had gone shopping together, and she bought some black clothes to start with. On her way home this morning, she had stopped downtown to get her ear pierced and buy new clothes.

She and Troy decided to stay in touch, having exchanged contact details on instant messaging to keep their romance alive despite the distance. The next time the band comes to town, he promised to introduce her to Brandon. I thought my heart would burst with anger... If she wants to date the security guard's son, that's her problem, but she should stay away from Brandon. As if he were already mine, I called him by his first name.

She saved the worst for last, revealing that she wasn't a virgin. No, Troy wasn't pressuring her; he was simply captivated by her beauty and asked if she would be willing to give him oral sex. According to Joy, it wasn't unpleasant; she compared the feeling to swallowing an earthworm. It made her laugh... It was a long experience with a sticky finish. She laughed so hard she couldn't stop...

Then Troy played with her nipples, and when she consented, he moved to her panties, touched her intimately, and did his thing... It was quick due to their exhaustion, but they made up for it with three more rounds. I was fed up with listening to Joy, who seemed to feel like a woman now. I wanted to be alone. I also longed for a boy to take my panties off...

It was difficult to get rid of Joy; she wanted to stay for a sleepover with popcorn and movies, but I couldn't stand her anymore. I had to be crafty to get her to leave. I pretended to be happy for her and Troy, who was probably waiting impatiently at his computer for her to log on. She bought my act and left, thrilled to be wanted by "the man."

I was anxious all evening, and at the dinner table, Mum gave me a murderous look when she asked if I was all right. Her eyes seemed to say, "What have you done to your sister now?"

I was too upset to confront Madeleine, so a little rest wouldn't hurt her until my next attack... I lied and invented imaginary homework to get away. Finally, I managed to lock myself in my room after Mum brought me a plate of cake. I was not to be disturbed in any way!

I spent the entire night searching for information about Brandon Stevens on the internet. I needed to know everything about him now that I was infatuated! Back in the 90's, when the entertainment industry still gave young people a chance, he started as a musician. He was discovered by a producer at a village festival where he was arrested for indecent exposure. Alone on stage with his guitar and his melancholy, he sang his hatred for the world and pulled down his pants in front of a bunch of rednecks to reveal a spider's web tattooed around his anus...

MYTHOMANIA

The producer had an eye for talent. With his soft voice (a rarity in rock), poignant lyrics, and provocative attitude, he took Brandon's musical future into his own hands and made him a rock star. To shine even brighter in front of his fans, Brandon needed a band. The producer recruited gothic bassist Amy, eccentric backing vocalist Olaf, relentless drummer Sonja, and pianist Vince. There's no real individuality among them; it seems that over the years, the band members adapt to Brandon's style but never express their own.

During my research, I took the opportunity to listen to Paradoxical Heights' greatest hits. Brandon's voice captivated me; when I heard it, I didn't feel alone. I wasn't abnormal; envy and hatred are human emotions, and it's natural to express them to be a true rebel. Brandon resonated with my feelings. His biggest hit, *"Dancing with Death,"* and the aggressive riffs of *"Alternative Drugs"* swept me away. The lyrics of *"Heavy Life"* drove me mad...

I re-listened to all five studio albums and read every available interview. I'm convinced that I'm on the right path and have the right attitude. Brandon often says that you must take what you want and never be happy for others. Wishing ill shows a genuine spirit in this hypocritical world!

Mum has always instilled this way of thinking in me, and I completely agree. She always said, "Honey, if you're not happy, don't let anyone else be happy. You must be served first because you're above everyone else." Hearing this from someone as influential as Brandon reassured me.

I can be as mean as I want; I can be myself, free to live out my jealousy and lack of empathy...

I investigated Brandon's private life, and it seems his chaotic love affairs are widely discussed. Between casual flings and rehab stints, he frequently changes girlfriends. All the girls in his bed look like Joy, and rumors suggest he enjoys having fun with his fans too... Everything will end quickly; he doesn't have me yet, which is why he's so unstable. With me, the nonsense will stop; he'll have to obey!

Am I sure I've got him? I have no doubt. He's already my lover; it's written in fate. To become part of the community, I registered on all the fan forums. In a few days, I knew everything about Brandon Stevens. As Loliblue (my username on the forums), I already had about thirty virtual friends, select fans who had met Brandon at least once and who had connections within his team. I swallowed my jealousy and cursed them in silence; soon, these vultures would be banned from the backstage area...

I worked diligently to get in touch with Brandon. Of course, there was Troy, Joy's boyfriend, but I was already so dependent on her... To hell with them both! Troy would get bored, as expected, and Joy would be heartbroken at being deceived by the first guy she ever performed oral sex on. She'll get over it; she'll find other guys! I'm not the friend who worries; it's not my job to prevent or protect... I don't exist, so Joy's future heartbreak is not my problem, even if I cared.

Convincing Mum to go shopping with me was the hardest part. To make her agree, I set a trap she couldn't resist.

I exaggerated how Joy and Troy met, and as soon as I mentioned a showbiz event, she was hooked! From that point on, she said yes to everything, even if it meant stretching the household budget to get me the attention of a world-famous singer.

For my hair, we entrusted the task to the blonde. I was so particular about my hair that no salon would take me. With the blonde, I knew I could annoy her and nitpick at every little flaw. All I had to do was claim she ruined my look out of spite, and she'd get a proper dressing down!

Luckily, the result was stunning, and I didn't have to criticize her. Even Mum was impressed and congratulated herself on saving so much money... She's a talented blonde, but I don't like her much... Although she did a good job, I stole her makeup as punishment. Physically, I'm ready for Brandon; my wardrobe is now full of dark clothes, and I've got the perfect doll-like hair. You can see why I haven't written to you since, and I'll leave my IM icon blinking; it's important... See you later when I decide!

CHAPTER 8

LAURA'S DIARY: LOVE, GLORY, LIES AND BETRAYAL...

Luck... For simple minds, it's a shitty concept. Every time I hear "I'm lucky," "it's my lucky day," or "my luck has changed," I want to spit in the faces of these idiots! Luck isn't a cosmic force or chance; it's just a fancy word to mask the baser instincts—the politically correct term for the law of the jungle. In the game of life, luck is just one card you play. You need to crush, seize, and show no mercy to make the most of it. It's kill or be killed, becoming the best strategist on the battlefield...

I used to see myself as an unlucky girl, a victim of life, before I fell for Brandon. I didn't realize there's no such thing as luck in any "trial." It's about bouncing back when things go wrong, not the sum of favorable probabilities. I was naive, but I went through the crucial "luck turning" phase. My starting hand was shit, but I turned it into four aces...

Out of all the asshole fans I chatted with online, one really caught my attention. Understand that Brandon Stevens's fan base is a tight-knit circle, with status depending on how cool you are. You just need to invent a life for yourself online, and it's easy to be cool. In my case, I was only half-lying, using Joy's crush on the security guard's son to infiltrate the inner sanctum! Don't kid yourself: die-hard fans lead shitty lives!

They take their shortcomings out on their favorite artist! Anyone who's ever met Brandon thinks they're his best friend, but in reality, they're just pathetic suck-ups. As long as they pay... they'll be the guarantors of my future survival... I told you there was one girl who didn't annoy me in this ravenous bunch of freaks. Not yet... Her name was Lou, and we were the same age. She was the villain in the discussions, always putting the others in their place and dashing their hopes of becoming Brandon's close friends.

I liked Lou! I enjoyed her pithy remarks. Some evenings, I didn't even take part in the exchanges; I just waited for her punchlines to appear on my screen. My bedroom became a shrine to Brandon. I devoured his albums, lined the walls with posters, and felt him close... Lou, without knowing me, was doing me justice by humiliating this gang of arseholes who were sticking a knife in my heart with each of their messages.

That famous night when my luck changed, I thought I'd become the happiest girl in the world. While waiting for Lou to log on, I read the day's fan crap on the forum. Brandon's spiritual retreat after his umpteenth overdose was the big topic. Where Brandon had gone, the idiots theorized. Alone in an isolated place, it would be easier to approach him... I hadn't seen Lou join in; it wasn't like her to be discreet. Imagine my surprise when she invited me to chat... I couldn't believe my eyes!

She asked me why I never participated in the debates with the others. I told her I didn't get the fuss about Brandon. She must have liked what I said because she sent me her instant messaging address, which she said was a better way to chat... Did I want to? Of course, I did! I was thrilled!

The others crumbled in front of Lou, even though she didn't treat them kindly, but she had a power over them that I didn't understand. If she felt secure, maybe she'd share her secret... To appear detached, to wear the mask of a fan who loves Brandon's music without being too interested in the character. To give the impression of being a purist in a way!

My initial private conversations with Lou felt like stepping back into the Inquisition. She would grill me with a million intrusive questions, sometimes phrasing the same one differently to see if my answers stayed consistent. I think she wanted to uncover what I was hiding. Too bad for

Lou – when it comes to lying and hiding, I'm pretty much an expert. Thanks to my family for being my guinea pigs!

I passed the test with flying colors, and after a week, Lou was more relaxed. We chatted every night as if we were two old friends who had known each other forever. She never talked about Brandon, so I made sure not to bring him up, fearing it might upset her. It was a positive sign that she hardly ever logged onto the forum. It meant I was interesting enough for her to leave behind the crowd of nobodies. I had Lou all to myself without needing to share her, and this total possession was exhilarating for my battered ego.

Another two weeks went by before our virtual friendship changed. I was getting a bit tired of Lou's idle chatter – I'm not a patient person; when I want something, I need it immediately! You need to challenge their words and push them to the limits of their sincerity to get them to confide in you. The idea is to weaken your prey without raising suspicion. I told Lou that our friendship could no longer continue because I felt she was hiding things from me.

I played the devoted friend, hurt that I wasn't being trusted. Despite her big mouth, Lou was very lonely; otherwise, she wouldn't be spending her nights chatting with a stranger online. She confessed that she was bored with her life because her family was often away. I pretended to be gentle to get her to tell me more, and that's when my life changed. Lou enjoyed visiting fan forums because she is Brandon Stevens's niece!

Lou's mother works for Brandon's team. She operates in her brother's shadow, helping him stay grounded when he strays a bit too far off course... Often left to her own devices, Lou explained that infiltrating the fan forums and reading the nonsense written about her uncle is her way of giving her family the finger. She had found a friend in me; I was different and discreet...

I knew she wasn't lying, but I wanted to play a little game with this unsuspecting rich girl. I needed more than her tearful story to believe her. On the internet, especially among Brandon's fans, mythomaniacs are a dime a dozen! I opted for a passive-aggressive approach, taking advantage of her sensitive mood to turn the tables. If Lou was serious about our friendship, she had to reassure me and provide something concrete to avoid being blocked. I wasn't going online to get scammed!

She saved herself with dozens of photos of her and her mother with Brandon. Moments of family intimacy away from the spotlight and public life – there was no doubt about their authenticity. I disconnected, making sure to save the photos beforehand; making Lou think she had scared me off was the best way to get her...

My new look didn't go unnoticed at school. Proud to stand out, Joy and I strutted through the corridors like conquerors. Suddenly, students who had never acknowledged my existence began to notice me. They called me by my first name, greeted me, and invited me to join their tables in the cafeteria or to their parties.

Although I relished this newfound attention, I maintained an air of indifference. I claimed I had a busy social life outside of school with friends who were already of age, and I turned down their invitations. I'd never admit that my parents had banned me from going out!

Joy, with her naive enthusiasm, adored my new attitude of snubbing others. She agreed with me; I should make them pay for their ignorance. Lou had transformed me; I began to trust myself and feel empowered. If I could set the rules at home, I could bring the whole school under my control.

I started to distance myself from Joy. Her constant lamenting about Troy grated on me. Despite their steamy text conversations, her Prince Charming had deserted her. Troy had moved on to other horizons, or rather, other girls. He was tired of the little virgin who offered herself without discernment. Joy got a monumental slap in the face—she who had let others down was now abandoned herself. Bad karma, well deserved!

We remained friends, and I enjoyed our rebellious duo, but I was determined to teach her a lesson. I felt no guilt about doing the same to her, considering the number of times Joy had used me. But... I was furious with her for losing her virginity. We had promised each other that we would lose it together with a guy we both chose because we were both a bit apprehensive about sex... and she had just betrayed me!

Lou was my secret weapon, to be deployed when the time was right. The advantage of virtual relationships, which require no commitment, was that no one knew she existed. I was clear that I wouldn't let Lou gain any power over me, having suffered too much from being the enforcer in real life. She would never know that she was helping me become the biggest fish in my pond. I had a plan in mind—a rough draft at least. I needed a few elements to perfect it, and then the good life would be mine!

For gratification, I left Lou hanging with no response for a week. Even offline, she sent me apology messages, expressing her regrets about her relationship with Brandon, realizing thanks to me that not everyone is opportunistic, and so on. If only that poor girl knew that I was manipulating her like a puppet...

I love to make people beg for forgiveness. Their stupidity is overwhelming, their emotions robbing them of their intelligence. They are convinced they've wronged me, and they would do anything to hear me say the magic words *"I forgive you."*

During this period of silence, I positioned my pieces on the chessboard. To succeed, I needed a sum of money that would be a fortune for a teenage girl. I knew my father would be adamantly opposed, and convincing my mother would be challenging.

So, I turned to the only fool I could find: the blonde! She had a job in a restaurant at the weekends for a bit of extra cash. Madeleine was rich compared to me, who had to beg my parents for my pleasures. I knocked on her bedroom door, having prepared a convincing speech. I went in when she didn't answer. No one!

Even better, I didn't have to ask. I'd done enough of a search of the blonde's room to know where she kept her valuables. I made a one-way trip to her dresser, opened the second drawer, and found her savings envelope under her panties. It was a treasure, at least 2,000... I took half, that bitch won't notice, worst case scenario I'll tell her parents and they'll take her money. She's too afraid of my reprisals to risk opening her mouth! I have also stolen two pairs of sexy black knickers. The blonde is an M and I'm an XS, but they'll do for my project...

I invented a story about Joy so that Mum would take me shopping. She needed some software for her art class, but she didn't have time to go because of Troy. She gave me the money, I'd promised to do it for her... Mum believed me, she said that a child who puts a lot of effort into his studies wouldn't think of doing anything stupid. I played the good teenager, full of gratitude, and had to stop myself from laughing at such naivety. Mum is so predictable...

I spent the rest of the day and night learning how to use the photo editing software. The collage aspect was too obvious, and my first attempts were inconclusive. I watched tutorials until my eyes popped out of my head, but I managed to get results that were truer to life. The first part of my plan went flawlessly.

I texted Lou to say that I wasn't angry with her. I added that, as a normal teenager, I'd been worried about having the niece of a famous singer as a friend, but on reflection it didn't change anything about our friendship. Lou was trapped, flattery always works with people.

I then undressed and put on one of the blonde's sexy knickers and my favorite pair of boots. The knickers were way too big for me, so I had to tighten them up. If she couldn't get down to a size XS, what was the point of her diet? How did she live in a body so imposing? I felt like I was wearing a parachute. Fortunately, I solved the problem with a safety pin. I did my make-up, added volume to my hair and turned on my webcam. Pictures needed to be perfect. I dimmed the lights, and the shoot was on!

I posed provocatively, Brandon on the walls watching me caress my boobs and pussy. I had visions of him melting my body with pleasure during endless foreplay... I was excited, thinking of Joy and how she'd betrayed me... Wrongs would soon be righted... I grabbed the black candle I kept on my bedside table, took off my panties, the webcam was still taking pictures at regular intervals, I set it to video to continue...

Lying down, my thighs spread, rubbing the candle against my clit, it felt good but did not make me moan. I wanted to go further, I wanted to push it deep into my pussy, but I was afraid... Joy told me it hurt for a few minutes... Afraid to go any further, I hesitated, barely inserting the tip. What would happen if the pain became unbearable?

I could feel a liquid dripping from my crotch, the mixture of fear and excitement making me wet like crazy. I was so wet that I wouldn't feel anything and then I had to do it now, while I was alone, rather than be ashamed when the time came... As far as I could, I pushed the candle inside me. It hurt a little, but nothing I couldn't handle - what a wuss that Joy was! I moved quickly back and forth with one hand while stroking myself with the other, harder and harder, faster and faster... I fucking liked that. Not moaning, not screaming my desire for a real cock... My plan had to work...

My cum flowed freely as my vagina contracted, I thought for a moment I was going to pass out from the pleasure... Mum was right when she said a woman's pussy is her greatest weapon if she knows how. I was ready to welcome a man inside me when I'd managed to feel like this on my own.

Since I wasn't exactly a virgin, I felt ready to take the next step. I decided to add Troy to my instant messaging list after blowing a kiss to my Brandon posters. Joy had insisted on giving me his contact info, hoping I would talk to him and sing my best friend's praises. It was two o'clock in the morning, so I wasn't expecting a response, but he accepted my invitation almost immediately. I contemplated deleting the request right away, pretending I'd added the wrong address. But Troy asked me to stay for a while...

We exchanged our first names, ages, and engaged in some light conversation. Just as I had hoped, he asked me for a photo. I began with a seductive shot of me caressing my breasts. To my delight, he seemed pleased with the photo, believing it was his lucky day because of the supposed mistake with the address. It was clear he was thinking with his dick. Thanks, Mum!

MYTHOMANIA

I never told him about Joy; that bitch could have handled her own business. Troy suggested we video chat, and as soon as the webcam was on, things heated up. Still naked and dizzy from my solitary pleasure, seeing his erect cock turned me on. I pushed my chair back, spread my legs with my feet on the edges of the desk. I slid my middle finger into my wet pussy, then put my slick finger in my mouth. It felt strange to taste my own juices, but I could tell Troy was enjoying it. The harder he jerked, the harder his cock seemed. Frustrated by my desire, I grabbed my candle and got down on my knees in the chair, my back to the webcam. The angle was perfect; I pushed the candle into my pussy where I could see it. Sex and pleasure were all I could think about. Pussy is the most powerful weapon I have...

Troy promised to come before I logged off. He kept his word because he was there on Tuesday, and we had an appointment at his hotel. Mum dropped me off at school as usual, and when the car was far enough away, I waited for the bus to take me into town. I'd never skipped school before, but this time it was for a good reason. Once in town, I stopped by a shop to buy condoms. Troy and I didn't want to waste any time talking, so it was safer to arrive prepared...

Troy was waiting for me when I arrived at the hotel. As soon as I walked into the room, I became uncontrollable; I wanted sex so badly. I rushed to get undressed, wearing nothing underneath to make it quicker. Troy had already taken off his pants, so I threw them on the bed and got on all fours on top of him. I offered my pussy to his mouth, imagining his cock like one of those candies you suck on slowly before swallowing.

For the first time, I think I did it right. He wasn't bad either, running his tongue over my clit while sticking one finger in my vagina and another in my ass. I thought I was going to faint, the pleasure was so overwhelming, and in response, I swallowed his cock as deeply as I could. Not cumming, not cumming...

I pulled myself up before I lost control and straddled him, rubbing my pussy against his cock as I mentally prepared myself to be penetrated. I'd done the hardest part myself; I was too close to back out now. With my hands on his thighs, I eased Troy's cock a little inside me. It was bigger than my candle, so I took it slow, but Troy, at the height of his excitement, shoved it all in at once. The brief pain faded quickly, and I let out a scream. That was it; I was no longer a virgin!

The sensation of being filled by my best friend's boyfriend's cock was overwhelming. My hips moved fast and erratically; I was ravenous... I screamed with pleasure, victorious over Joy. More, more, more... Troy pulled out, had me get on all fours, and then drove back into me. I loved his roughness; I arched my ass to let him go deeper. I begged him to put his finger in my asshole again, oh yes, so I could come... We fucked into the afternoon until I had to head back to school and resume my role as the good girl at home... Troy wanted me back soon... I had my revenge; justice was served!

When I got back, there was an email from Lou waiting in my inbox. It wasn't her usual way of communicating, so I was a bit apprehensive when I opened it. Maybe I'd been playing with fire? No way, I'd just fucked my best friend's boyfriend; I was invincible... I wasn't intimidated by anyone now, I'd entered the big leagues, and my formidable weapon was activated. I'd never be transparent again! With men, you had to be beautiful and spread your thighs, but with women, those vipers deserved nothing but suffering!

After all, I didn't care about Lou, and whatever she said didn't affect me. Her words were flattering; she was glad nothing had changed between us and hoped our friendship would last a long time. She had a little gift for me, and I had to check the attachment at the bottom of the email... I looked at Lou's gift at least a hundred times, my heart pounding as I listened to Brandon's message.

For Laura, a good girl, a friend dear to her heart, she'd asked her uncle to make a video... She'd even shown him a picture of me. Here's the message my love sent:

"Hi Laura, I'm making a video to thank you personally for being one of the people who loves me. Your support means the world to me as an artist. I'm going into the studio soon to record my next album, and I'll be thinking of you. See you soon!"

He finished with a wink! He likes me! It was the happiest day of my life; I'd paid Joy back in spades, and Brandon was interested in me. The heavens were with me!

I called Mum and she rushed into my room, worried. She thought Madeleine had bullied me again, so I told her to leave that loser alone and come and see. She cried as she listened to Brandon's message, her darling daughter had made it. Of their two children, it was fortunate that Laura had set the standard, this little girl was as delicate and precious as her mother... Not like the other... Fat, ungrateful and disobedient, a true daughter of the people, a slob who took everything from her father... She looked lovingly at Brandon, as if the message was for her. She told me that he reminded her of the great love of her youth, also a rocker. Except that the bastard had left her for someone else... All whores!

She promised to help this relationship blossom. She advised me to be wary of Brandon professional entourage as all the scum of the earth gravitated towards the stars. She would do everything in her power to have Brandon marry me, it would be a challenge, but together we would be the champions!

Yes, I've had the good life, I've been lucky. For 6 months I touched the stars... At school I showed Brandon's video and my retouched photos to some very chatty pupils. Laura was Brandon Stevens' new girlfriend and the news spread like wildfire!

Joy gave me the cold shoulder; I think she couldn't stand the fact that I was in first place. I became the most popular girl in school, and she wasn't the star anymore. I was still having sex with Troy and he was teaching me about dirty sex, how to fuck rock, with no limits or taboos. Sometimes he'd film me giving him a blowjob or putting a plug in my butthole. He liked to get a close-up of his dick in my pussy. He also immortalized my first sodomy, when his cock entered my dilated arse, glistening with lubricant and sperm...

I told Mum I wasn't a virgin anymore, but I forgot to mention that I was screwing Joy's boyfriend. That was my secret! She would take away all my rights if she found out that her precious daughter was screwing a common man. But Brandon... My Brandon... In my mind I was already in love, I believed in it, and I still do. I got into God's right hand by making everyone think I fucked a star. Money, sex, and power obsess people. And so, blinded by the illusion of a better future, the weak man advances unsuspectingly.

According to the official version, Brandon moved to the city under a false name. To live our love story away from the media, these precautions were necessary. Because I was a respectable little girl, I thought long and hard before I had sex with him. Mum covered up my absences from school because she was proud of what I'd achieved.

She always said I was ill when the school called. Pupils imagined a thousand things about me, some of them wanted to screw the captain of the football team, while Laura was going to live like a rock star... In short, in my suburb, in my family, in my school, I was a superstar. I was untouchable, the underage girlfriend of the great Brandon Stevens, the pretty kid with the dark eyes who was about to step into the spotlight...

How did my lie hold up? I'll tell you; I became an expert at retouching photos. Lou trusted me, she told me everything about her uncle and sent me the photos she'd taken of him. I just changed his face for mine, no?

If a jealous person questioned my word, I'd show them the photos to stop them in their tracks. Who could argue with such proof? Personal moments that don't exist online. At home, Mum took her role as guardian to heart. Jeff and she argued more and more about my relationship. Dad wanted Brandon to come home, but Mum forbade it. She said that an artist didn't have the same sensitivity to people and things, so we had to adapt to his rhythm... I suspected that Mum was falling in love with Brandon, and I often found her in my bedroom, sitting on my bed, staring tenderly at my posters... Pathetic!

Until the day when everything changed... Whether it was karma or overconfidence, I don't know. Everything was under control; my dogs were firmly on the leash. Except for one detail I hadn't reckoned with: Troy falling in love with me! The little shit turned up at school without telling me, instead of waiting for me at the hotel as usual. Joy was crying a lot, her handsome prince wasn't answering her messages at all, so her eyes lit up when she saw him arrive.

She thought he came out of love... She'd gotten used to better than childish and disappointing. The first cold shower! He walked past her without looking at her. Then he stopped before me, took my face in his hands, and kissed me before everyone. His words were incoherent, he was tired of us hiding, he wanted us to be a real couple, he'd loved me since the first time on the webcam...

How could I salvage this disaster? I made him look like a maniac—someone I'd never seen before—so he had to stay away from me. He pleaded, crying out his love and confusion over being rejected. I thanked the heavens when the school security finally escorted him out... Rescued!

Joy fled without a glance at me, and I couldn't endure another scandal! I told everyone he was a crazy fan who'd followed Brandon everywhere and had stumbled upon us once, becoming obsessed. The only thing that really upset me was not getting my sex fix. I desperately needed a backup dick to keep me going... I'd handle that later, but for now, I pretended to be in shock. I asked to see the school nurse and managed to stay in the infirmary for the rest of the day.

I was anxious about the confrontation with Joy; I knew she'd come at me hard. I've never understood why people whine about being set up when they've been the ones to betray first. Joy provoked me by meeting Troy; she broke our "virgin promise." I only got back what was mine. What's the big deal about a dick? It was just a fling! I refused to feel guilty for taking what I deserved. I had my experiences, and Troy didn't belong to her. In fact, he belonged to both of us, but more to me than her...

Silence! My worries were unfounded. Joy didn't show up. The fight I feared didn't materialize. She hadn't been to school all week, but no one noticed her absence. Everyone was focused on me. With fake tears and a trembling voice, I told anyone who'd listen that Brandon was concerned about me since the incident. My life as the little queen was returning to normal. I was entitled to respect and privileges, and if those idiots could've wiped my ass, they would have. Brandon Stevens' girlfriend deserved it... But everything unraveled in an instant... Damn bitch...

The atmosphere was off when I arrived at school on Monday morning. Pupils whispered in the corridors as soon as I walked by. They weren't friendly. If this gang of idiots kept it up, I'd have to complain to the headmaster to sort it out! A crowd had gathered around my locker, and if those bastards didn't move, I'd be late for class. What was security doing?

As I approached, they parted to let me through, and that's when the floor seemed to collapse beneath me. Everyone was wearing a *"Where is Brandon?"* T-shirt, and all I could see were big red letters. My locker door was plastered with photos of Lou with her uncle and, even worse, images of me screwing Troy. A sign hung over the mess, reading *"Mythomaniac."*

Joy was wearing the T-shirt too, so I didn't see her coming. The first slap she gave me was for Troy, the second for the lies I spread to make her look bad. The crowd chanted *"Mythomaniac,"* their cheers echoing like those at a sports match. My head spun, I felt nauseous. I never thought Joy would do this to me... Why did someone hurt me?

A Day of Disgrace! I fled, a barrage of boos echoing behind me. I ran as fast as my platform boots would carry me, heading straight home. In the red stone building, now the cursed site of my shattered popularity, I could still hear the mocking laughter. I hoped my parents hadn't heard about the fiasco... The show must go on. Whether they liked it or not, I was in a relationship with Brandon. The relationship might only exist in my head, but it was there, and that's all that mattered! Damn karma and its pathetic justice; the only judge here was ME, and my sentence would be ruthless!

I stopped at a cyber cafe on the way. I knew I'd never return to school, but to convince my parents to pull me out, I needed a clever plan. I scoured the internet for anything on Brandon's writing, looking for material for my makeshift plan. Writing a fake letter shouldn't be too hard—I was adept at forging signatures.

I tore a blank sheet from my sketchbook and meticulously copied Brandon's handwriting—both solid and broken lines, as tortured as our souls were. Yes, I said our souls; he and I were forever connected. I was pleased with the result. Using a formal tone, as if the future son-in-law were addressing his prospective in-laws, I wrote:

"Dear Mr. and Mrs. Mitchell,

This morning, I was deeply distressed to hear that some envious classmates had humiliated your daughter, Laura, out of sheer jealousy. Laura, my beloved girlfriend, called me in a panic, and this disgraceful act by troubled teenagers was met with severe displeasure by my management. To address the negligence of the school administration and to ensure a secure environment befitting my status, I have instructed my lawyer to take immediate legal action. The incident today has compromised the discretion and security expected of my entourage. Therefore, my request is for Laura to be removed from school immediately. Although I understand this is a significant sacrifice for you, I hope you will support our relationship. I am committed to making it work, and I wish to provide Laura with a life free from the cruelty of the common world.

Sincerely, Brandon Stevens"

When I got home, I threw myself into Mum's arms, weeping. Between sobs, I recounted Joy's diabolical scheme and Brandon's heroic rescue. I handed her the letter. When Mum said she'd agreed with Brandon's request for me to leave school, I nearly leapt with joy. My life was about to change dramatically. Becoming the official companion of a star would leave me no time for studying. Being his muse meant being with him constantly... Victory was in sight!

I blocked Joy, Troy, Lou, and everyone else... I also erased Loliblue from the web radar. I never figured out how she discovered me—probably through that bastard Troy! My hatred for her grew with each passing hour. I'd have torn her eyes out if I could. Betrayed for a cock... That bitch deserved something worse... No, death was too kind. Joy needed to suffer both physically and psychologically, but I didn't have the means to hire a hitman. I wouldn't risk prison for a little whore! How could I channel all this hatred? I needed a frightened, unpopular, easy target—someone I could destroy without raising suspicion. My first victim... I smiled as I thought about that fat lump. She would pay dearly—she would pay for Joy... Blonde, prepare for martyrdom!

CHAPTER 9

THE NIGHT OF TRAGEDY, SIX FEET UNDER...

The black pickup pulls into the lit driveway. Up close, the house is even more impressive than the photos suggested. The king's residence looms over the heights, like Zeus' palace on Mount Olympus. Only the chosen few are allowed into this den of excess. For a moment, the man forgets why he's here, dazzled by the sheer wealth surrounding him. Focus... Stick to the plan... and then he'll be free.

He quietly steps out of the truck, careful not to slam the door. Not a soul for miles, so there's no risk of being heard. The CCTV is off, and the estate is surrounded by acres of sloping land dotted with hundreds of palm trees. One wrong step, and you're dead. But peace is a luxury the man doesn't have. He's seen more than a few deals go wrong, and this one is worth its weight in gold. Failure is not an option.

He pops the trunk and pulls out a heavy-duty blue bag, the kind used on construction sites. He'd been told he'd need at least this much. To his surprise, it weighs less than he expected. He tosses the sack onto the ground, dragging it down the driveway—it'll be quicker and less exhausting. He'll need all his strength for what's coming.

Men like him don't use the front door; they're condemned to the back entrance. Turning his back on the lights, he follows the gravel path to the staff quarters. The bag swings behind him, scraping along the ground until he reaches the gardener's quarters. According to the instructions, the trapdoor should be nearby. He finds it, swings the load into the dark pit, and climbs down after it.

The stench of damp and rotting flesh doesn't faze him. His job isn't to admire the place; it's to clean up. He's seen enough horrors. A legend before he became a fallen angel, they didn't call him Death Face for nothing. But there's no time to dwell on the past. If he wants to get paid, he needs to move. He pulls a flashlight from his leather jacket, the beam sweeping quickly over the room. Hundreds of photos cover the walls, some of very young faces, others older. Famous faces, nobodies—all immortalized in moments of intense sex. Alone, in groups, there's something for everyone.

Where's the damn light switch? In this glossy den of filth, he can't seem to find it. Time is slipping away, and he still has a little bonus to claim. He spots a table at the back, a chair, and the camera waiting on its tripod. Finally, he sees the switch. Now, the real game begins...

The man presses the button, and in an instant, the magic happens. The vestibule of vice is bathed in a blue glow. Like a shower of stars on a clear night, the women's faces are dotted with fluorescent specks. His attention drifts back to the bag, noticing a slight movement inside. Not yet... Irritated, he steps forward and delivers a violent kick to the still form. Quickly, he sets up the camera, the red light blinking on. Everything's working. The boss will be pleased.

He begins undressing, folding each garment with meticulous care. Even in the horror of his work, he likes things in order. From his pocket, he pulls out two brass knuckles, made of the same titanium as his teeth, before placing his leather jacket on the back of the chair. His only adornments, the tools of a jailer...

The tattoos on his naked body come to life under the blue light. Bone-like patterns, inked with eerie precision, trace the structure of a human skeleton. His face is masked in black, with hollowed cheeks and ears cut off to complete his reaper-like appearance. Death Face is ready.

Finally, he takes a moment to look at her. With a feline grace, he moves toward the bag of rubble. Earlier, in the heat of the moment, he'd simply come up behind her, knocked her unconscious, and loaded her into the car's trunk before injecting her with a powerful sedative.

Now, he lays her on her back, her wavy blonde hair framing her face, glowing pale under the blue light. He undresses her with the same methodical precision as he did himself. She won't need the clothes again, but that doesn't concern the skeleton man. His job is to keep them alive until the client decides otherwise.

Folding her clothes, he leaves them neatly by her side. It's his way of giving them one last illusion—an illusion of dignity. In his twisted logic, it's how he keeps them holding on to a sliver of humanity, a flicker of hope, even when there's none left.

* * *

In his prime, Death Face was the best—a key member of The Guardians. His work thrived on corruption, vice, and cruelty. His job? To give kidnap victims a five-star welcome and ensure their captivity was a nightmare. His role was simple: prolong the client's pleasure and dispose of the victims when they were no longer useful. His reputation for brutality was well-earned. Hiring him meant the job would be done—no questions, no hesitation. But his downfall came when a boy died before the client could... make use of him. That failure led a powerful politician to lock him away for years.

Recently released from prison, a slick man in his thirties approached him with a job offer. Death Face hesitated at the terms. He never dealt with women—his twisted code forbade it. Flattery didn't sway him. He knew too many men who would do anything for the right price. But when the client produced a bag full of cash, things changed. For someone with no future, this was his chance to vanish and start again. The deal was sealed, and a few bundles of money exchanged hands. The rest would come when the job was done.

Now here he is. With her. Both naked. The skeleton man admires the girl's body. He doesn't usually like them too thin, but this one... she has just the right allure. She reminds him of Sandra.

He loved playing with dolls as a child. His grandmother had let him have his dolls, and he would spend hours styling their hair, making them look pretty for their imaginary walks in the park. The happiest day of his life was his 6th birthday, when Grandma gave him his very own doll. She had wavy blonde hair, blue eyes, rosy cheeks, and a long flowery dress. Like his mother, who had gone to heaven, he named her Sandra.

Sandra became his best friend. With Grandma's help, they made clothes for her, knitting little sweaters and dresses. Sandra drank tea with them, sat with him during homework, even had her own pram for walks. That doll gave him joy, bringing light back into his world. Life without Sandra was unimaginable.

But the boys at school didn't see it that way. They mocked him, calling him names he didn't understand. During breaks, they'd corner him in the bathrooms, their cruel laughter echoing. It was their punishment for a boy who played with dolls.

The day Sandra disappeared, his world collapsed. He and Grandma searched the entire house, but Sandra was gone. Desperate, he made flyers and posted them on every electricity pole in the neighborhood, offering a reward of chocolate cake to anyone who returned Sandra safely.

One afternoon, the doorbell rang. He rushed to answer, but no one was there. He searched frantically until, at last, he saw her—Sandra—propped up on a chair on the veranda. Her face was mutilated, arms twisted and broken, her beautiful blonde hair hacked off. His heart shattered as he held what remained of his beloved doll. Not even Grandma could console him. He buried Sandra beneath the weeping willow, the place where his mother had also died in his heart...

* * *

Death Face thought this mission would be easy—routine, like the others. But she... something about her was different. Sandra had grown up, and the school bullies had returned to break her all over again. He needed to fix Sandra.

At the sight of her lifeless body, his pulse quickened. Her round hips, her pale skin—it stirred something inside him, something dark. He moved around her, his breath growing heavier, hands shaking. He stroked her body, imagining the softness of her skin beneath his rough touch. His fingers trembled as he began to pleasure himself, circling her like a predator in a ritualistic trance.

MYTHOMANIA

Women are like flowers, he thought. They need to be nurtured, watered with the seed of life, so they can blossom and pass it on. His movements grew faster, more frenzied, until he could barely contain the wave crashing over him. His body shuddered as he came, spilling his seed like an offering into her navel, his twisted homage to creation.

Death Face had never felt guilt for the atrocities he committed. Breaking bones, feeling the snap of limbs beneath his fists—it made him feel alive, useful. Each tattoo on his skin was a tribute to those he'd beaten, a way to exact revenge for Sandra. He took a bone from each of them, a token of his satisfaction.

He had never been gay, no matter what the mafia said. He didn't need to fuck women to feel power over them. He loved them—mothers, aunts, sisters. To violate them would be to rob them of their purity, their sacredness.

He brushed a hand across the girl's face, inhaling her scent, which reminded him of roses and something familiar, like homemade cake. His anger flared briefly—he hated himself for hurting her. Grandma would never forgive him for that.

He didn't want to break her, not like the others. He wanted to care for her, to make her beautiful, like Sandra, so they could go to the park together. He cradled her face in his hands, her hair so soft, like Sandra's.

Then, her eyes fluttered open. Fear filled them, but she didn't scream. She barely moved, only looking at him with wide, terrified eyes before slipping back into unconsciousness.

CHAPTER 10

FORREST HILL, 8 MONTHS BEFORE THE TRAGEDY...

"Morning. Breakfast as usual?"

Tom wouldn't miss those words for anything. Every morning, sitting at his usual spot in Elaine's, he waited eagerly for Madee to take his order. Their exchange was simple, limited to the polite interaction between waitress and customer. She remained professional, never too familiar. Yet, her smile—awkward as it sometimes was—brought a ray of sunshine to Tom's otherwise gray mornings.

An encounter can change everything... Tom used to scoff at that idea. His past experiences had proven the opposite. But... for the last two months, his life had felt different, all thanks to a chance moment on a forgotten road in the middle of nowhere. On the outside, the change wasn't obvious. People expect grand, heroic stories when they talk about personal growth—tales of miracles and inspiration. For Tom, it was simpler: a forgotten pack of cigarettes and a daily smile.

Hardly the stuff of bestsellers or talk show interviews. But it was enough to get him out of bed at 6:45 every morning. He'd shower, get dressed, slip into his convertible, and drive to Forrest Hill just to be at Elaine's by the time Madeestarted her shift. She usually arrived by 7:30, so if he came a little late, it meant he could avoid Earl. The old man never made an effort to be pleasant, and Tom always felt unwelcome despite his generous tips. But as long as he got to see Madee, he didn't care what the grumpy old man thought.

Tom thinks about her constantly. Feet on the ground, head in the clouds, he lives in a sort of daydream. Their relationship may be purely platonic, but he only ever feels truly at ease when she's near. A thousand times, he's imagined asking her out for a drink, spending an hour getting to know her. But instead, he just sits, watching her work, drinking coffee after coffee.

In the early evening, when he drives home, the anxiety creeps back in. Before eating the takeout he picked up from Elaine's, he goes for a run, trying to clear his head. It's his way of taking a piece of Madee with him... the last blessed moment before the darkness of night swallows him again.

MYTHOMANIA

Tom doesn't go out anymore, and oddly, he's okay with that. The meaningless flings of his past have brought him nothing. The only shadow hanging over his perfect little world is the drugs.

He's tried to quit twice. Locked in his flat, pacing like a caged lion, Tom thought he was going mad. But he needed the fix, and convinced himself it would be fine. The coke called to him like a seductive whisper, and he couldn't resist. He was weak, a loser with no willpower. The guilt set in immediately—using alone, crossing that forbidden line. Convinced he had it under control, he'd snort tiny lines, spaced out over hours. Small quantities, nothing major. An addict's denial, just enough to clear his conscience.

He knows he'll never beat this. Drugs are in his DNA, etched into him like a genetic curse. Rehab? He's not even sure it works. The rich kids who go to those overpriced clinics usually relapse as soon as they're out. Talk to a psychiatrist? And say what? He didn't want to talk about his misery. He was Tom Collins—the golden boy, the one life always smiled on. No one would understand the emptiness that comes with a life of ease. Not even Madee should know.

It bothers him that she doesn't seem interested in him. Tom thought he knew women, that his money and status would attract them. But Madee isn't like the others. She must think he's a shallow, vapid loser. Better not add *"cocaine addict"* to the list of reasons why she'll never see him the way he sees her.

It was the 61st morning Tom had walked through Elaine's door, and the familiar chime of the bells lifted his mood. As usual, Earl barely acknowledged him, giving only a brief, disapproving glance. The old bastard had it out for him, that much was clear. The first customers didn't notice him anymore. At first, he was just a curiosity—a new face. But now, he had become part of the scenery, known as the guy who left the best tips. An outsider, now part of the landscape.

But today, his usual seat was taken. A man well-known around here was sitting in his spot. The doctor's bag beside him gave him away—Tom had heard the others call him "Doc." He had that rare aura, the kind that commands silence the moment he enters a room. Physically unremarkable, like a man carved from the trunk of an old tree, he exuded mystery and wisdom. He was the only one who ever greeted Tom with a handshake, treating him like an equal. It didn't bother Tom. It was just a bench. He didn't want to disturb Doc while he enjoyed his breakfast. Besides, they'd never spoken—it would be inappropriate.

Tom took a seat at another table, scanning the room for Madee. She wasn't in the dining room, probably busy in the kitchen. He wondered what she'd be wearing today. Madee was different—she didn't stick to one style like most people. She wore a kaleidoscope of colors, prints, and daring cuts, blending vintage with modern. Her clothes seemed to have lived through the ages, never going out of style.

MYTHOMANIA

Critics might say she raided her grandmother's wardrobe or recycled her teenage jeans, but it worked for her. Only someone truly confident in who they are could pull off a style like that, and Tom admired her for it. He had needed a Wayne Beckett makeover to find his own look, but Madee seemed to be effortlessly herself. She didn't care what people thought—she wore what she loved, unaffected by trends. In a world of conformity, she was a breath of fresh air.

The clock ticks, and still no sign of Madee. As usual, Earl has slipped off to his office. The old man is like clockwork—every morning it's the same routine. He claps his hands, announcing to his staff that he's off to do the accounts. Tom imagines him, like a proper landlord, sitting at a table overflowing with dusty books. Surrounded by boxes and cobwebs, he counts the banknotes with hands as wrinkled as the paper.

Madee finally appears, snapping Tom out of his thoughts. She storms out of the kitchen, her annoyance obvious. The door slams behind her. She takes it out on the coffee machine, banging it like she's willing it to work faster, not bothering to look at the few customers scattered around. Old Earl would have a fit if he saw her mistreating his precious coffee machine like this.

From his table, Doc asks, "Is everything all right?"

No answer. That's not like Madee.

With her usual light step, she walks over to Tom's table, a coffee in each hand. For the first time, she speaks to him in a different tone, catching him off guard.

"Come with me."

Tom stands up, heart racing. She's never been so familiar with him before. He's imagined this moment so many times, rehearsing what he might say when they're finally alone. He follows her, trying to calm his nerves.

They enter the kitchen, and Babou clasps her flour-covered hands together in mock prayer.

"Thank you, Lord! I thought she'd never talk to you!"

Madee pretends not to hear her friend's comment. She pulls a clean apron from the cupboard and hands it to Tom.

"Virgin wool blazer, Egyptian cotton shirt... You'll need this if you want to avoid the dry cleaners."

"May I ask what's going on?"

"Babou and I are making cookies for the kids' snack. You're here all day anyway, might as well help out. We've got fifty little stomachs to feed by playtime!"

For Tom, this is new—feeling useful. He's never had to look after anyone but himself. The idea of doing something selfless, especially with Madee, gives him a strange sense of relief, like it might balance out some of his past indulgences.

Unsure how to explain that he's never cooked a day in his life, Tom slips on the apron. He glances at the worktop, full of utensils. Do cookies really need all this? He hesitates to ask; afraid Madee might think he's clueless.

"Have you ever made cookies?"

Tom flushed. He felt the tension rising. Should he lie and risk getting caught, or be honest and look like an idiot?

His eyes dropped, expecting some comment like, Typical rich guy...

"I don't know how to cook."

It slipped out, unplanned. Tom braced himself for laughter, expecting them to roll their eyes and send him away.

"Never mind, I'll show you!" Madee said. "Babou and I already made the dough. Here, take this spoon, make little balls, and put them on the tray. Leave some space between them. Perfect! When the tray's full, stick them in the oven."

"It looks easy..."

"Child's play! You seem like a smart guy; you can't mess this up."

"I'm not sure I deserve that compliment..."

"You don't have to. But it's nice to be recognized, right? Anyway, you'll do great."

Madee was just being nice, he thought. She didn't really know him, couldn't possibly believe he was smart. If she knew how many mistakes he'd made... Determined not to disappoint her, Tom carefully shaped the dough, making sure each ball was identical. The kitchen buzzed with quiet joy, Babou humming an old Etta James tune. Suddenly, Earl appeared in the doorway, eyes narrowed.

"What the hell is he doing in my kitchen? No clients allowed!"

Earl's grumpy, vindictive tone always spoiled the mood.

"It's fine, Earl," Madee said calmly. "Tom's helping us out, Babou and I have our hands full."

"Are you sure about that?"

"Yes, Earl."

"All right. I'll trust you this time. As for you"—he jabbed a finger at Tom—"when you're done, fold that apron and get out."

The old man shrugged and left, unable to refuse Madee's requests. Babou let out a sigh of relief.

"Thanks for saving us from one of his legendary tantrums," Babou said, laughing. Madee giggled.

"He's not that bad," she assured Tom. "He has a temper, but he's not mean. You'll get to know him."

"What did I do to him?" Tom asked.

Madee and Babou exchanged glances, debating who should explain. Finally, Madee spoke up.

"No offense, Tom, but Earl thinks the Council sent you."

"What? That's nonsense! Why would they send me? I've never worked for the Council."

"You've seen our neighborhood, right? To them, we're cockroaches, something to get rid of."

"Madee, Babou, I swear, I'm not some city-assigned spy. I got lost after a party. My GPS messed up and brought me here. I found Elaine's, and... I stayed. I love it here. I feel better here than I do at home."

His answer caught them off guard. No one stayed in the Forgotten District because they wanted to. Not someone from his background. Madee studied him closely, the silence hanging heavy. Tom felt like he'd played his last card—everything hinged on her next move.

"I want to be sure of one thing, Tom," Madee said slowly. "You come here to feel normal, right?"

"And for breakfast, too. I've never eaten anything so good!"

Tom wanted to add and to see you every day, but the timing wasn't right. Madee held his gaze a little longer, then took off her apron, gesturing for him to do the same.

"All right! If you love it here so much, you can come to school with me and bring the cookies to the kids. We're all family here. Just so you know, everyone helps out, and everyone knows everyone else. If that doesn't bother you, welcome to Forrest Hill, Tom!"

CHAPTER 11

LAURA'S DIARY: BATTLE PLAN

It's a delicate operation to destroy someone you hate. Success requires skill and patience. Like a spider, you have to meticulously weave your web before trapping your prey in its silken cocoon. First, you have to neutralize your enemy's suspicion. I've told you before what that bitch Joy did to me. How she humiliated me at school. My first instinct was revenge, but I realized it was risky. So what made me change my mind?

That's where the fun begins. All those sheep at school, blindly following Joy, got to know my little secrets thanks to that slut. I managed to manipulate those idiots for a while, but the truth caught up with me. They're still strangers to me, and my control over them is limited, despite their stupidity. I made a miscalculation, and I paid for it. If I attack them directly, they'll fight back. And if they feel threatened, they'll complain. Cops, judges, prison—or worse, a psychiatric hospital—terrify me. Manipulating teenagers is one thing, but dealing with official institutions is a whole different game. Honestly, how could I call the cops liars? How do I deny facts, dates, accuracy?

I'm not ready to take on the authorities, though I can destroy a nobody's reputation in my sleep. But imagine if they traced it back to Brandon. The investigation would be over in a flash, and his management—probably alerted by Lou by now—would have me under house arrest and in therapy. That would ruin any chance I have of marrying Brandon. So for now, the less he knows about this, the better. I don't think Lou had the guts to spill everything anyway. She'd be scolded for trusting some internet kid and her uncle's fan. I can relax... for now.

I saw she sent me several emails. Straight to the trash. I've got better things to do than read her whining. A rich kid, desperate for friends, doesn't get to lecture me. She knows the world is cruel. Friendships don't last. People use each other, it's how it works. There are rulers and the ruled. If she's upset, that's her problem. I'm not letting her drag me down with her toxic drama. I've cut myself off from the internet. As far as she's concerned, I'm dead. Case closed.

Joy? That bitch will pay later. I've already found the perfect way to take her down—undetectable, of course—but

MYTHOMANIA

first, I need to focus on something bigger. My brilliant plan starts with my family. My parents are practically divided, and I've always ruled the house. Brandon's fake letter worked like a charm. Now, they think they're part of his inner circle (which, soon enough, they will be) and they're worried about my safety. They're waiting for Brandon's lawyer to swoop in and fix everything. They'll be waiting a long time.

Blinded by this illusion, they've got my back. They tell anyone who'll listen that Brandon took me with him to record his new album. They look so smug when people say anything negative about me—jealousy, of course. I mean, who are people going to believe? Teenagers with a grudge, or my parents? Obviously, my parents.

At home, I'm the victim of everyone else's nastiness, and that's where it ends. This is where my genius comes in. Out there, they call me crazy, but at home, I'm God. The game is just beginning, and it's going to be fun, because I'm pulling all the strings of my little puppets. What's that? You don't understand family? Let me explain.

Family is a sacred institution, a place of protection and love. Based on that, even when there's disagreement or abuse, what's the number one rule? Silence. A family falling apart in public, or one member denouncing another—it looks bad. Very bad. In the family, everything is forgiven, even the worst crimes. Just look at the news: how many mothers report their children's abuse? How many battered wives denounce their violent husbands? Zero. Because speaking out is "wrong." No one wants to betray the family. Everyone turns a blind eye.

Family is the perfect shield against repercussions. A space full of unspoken truths, taboos, and appearances. And this is where I've chosen to play. I can make them believe whatever I want. I can put them through hell, and they'll never say a word. They're too scared of what people will think, too afraid of social exclusion.

In my case, if I throw them a bone now and then, they'll never insult me by questioning what's real or fake. They hope their brilliant daughter will marry a star, and I've got plenty of time before their patience runs out. I keep their suspicions at bay with a steady stream of lies, manipulation, and just enough "evidence" to maintain my good faith as a teenager navigating a "complicated" relationship. Showbiz is full of sharks, and they just want to protect their baby from powerful, jealous people... Second, you need a scapegoat.

The blonde will be first. I can't stand when my sister doesn't kiss my ass. I've chosen her as my stand-in for Joy, and she has no idea what's coming. Fatty thought she'd seen it all... Well, she's about to go through hell.

I've loved ratting her out since we were kids, even making up things just to see her get punished. It's the greatest satisfaction. Even though I'm the youngest, I've always hated sharing. In my mind, she's an intruder—someone who never should've been part of this family. I should've been the only one. I had to fight for space. Why do I hate her so much? She's mediocre, but in that mediocrity, she has something I'll never have. She's dangerous, radiant, free. And me? I'm the prodigal daughter.

She doesn't believe in my relationship with Brandon. Mom is so proud when she talks about it, but the blonde shows no jealousy, no resentment. She says nothing. When the family raves about it, I smile and watch her. I secretly hope she'll explode with rage, but she just sits there, indifferent. She doesn't admire me. That's her crime, and she'll pay for it. She thinks she's strong? We'll see who's stronger. She'll be the perfect scapegoat. The parents already hate her—they're so disappointed.

I'll use the classic dictator method to make it worse. All these infamous figures mastered the art of manipulating their followers. It's foolproof. To gain power, dictators believed in what they preached and fed on the desperation of their people. They presented themselves as martyrs, as the ones who understood the world's suffering and could fix it if given the means. But to climb the ladder of power, they needed a scapegoat—a public enemy to distract from the real problems. They hid the truth and invented a target for everyone's anger.

You've probably guessed my next move. I'll stir up my parents' hatred. I'll tell them she's jealous of my relationship with Brandon, that she's spreading rumors about me online, and trying to have me committed to a psychiatric hospital. Her goal is to destroy our family just as we're on the verge of success. Would they doubt her jealousy? No way.

She's the ugly duckling, always second best to me. Socially, she's fat, plain, invisible—the kind of person who'll go through life without leaving a trace. And when I'm Brandon's wife, I'll have the money and the connections to crush anyone who gets in my way. She's the perfect scapegoat.

I'll play the good daughter, preaching that family is everything. I'll flatter their egos, put them on a pedestal, even though in my head, I'm laughing. I'll make them believe that my relationship with Brandon is their success too. If I have access to the top, so do they. I'll share my husband with them, in a manner of speaking...

From this perspective, the blonde has nothing to offer them. Add her selfishness and indifference, and all I have to do is watch her fall. Isolation is the final stage of destruction. A scapegoat can escape if they manage to build a normal life—friends, a job, some money. But I'm not worried. The blonde has no friends. She's a loner, and no one wants to be seen with her. Her love life? A string of disappointments. Guys will have sex with her, but commitment? No way. I get it. In private, sure, they'll sleep with her. But to show off a fat girl in public? Unthinkable. She's a romantic, dreaming of true love... That only makes her weaker. More reason for her to be jealous of me. It must kill her to see how happy her pretty little sister is with the perfect boyfriend.

For the blonde, work and money are everything. That's where Brandon comes in. She buys whatever she wants with her salary, since the parents don't buy her much. I can't stand it when she comes home with shopping bags full of new things. She can work, but she can't show off. No job means no money, which means she'll spiral back into her eating disorder. She'll gain weight again, her clothes won't fit, and I'll take it all back.

All I have to do is write Brandon, ask him to tell the parents not to let her go to work. She's a danger to me, I'll say. I'll add a list of strict instructions: limit her outings, only use the internet for emergencies, no music channels or variety shows, confiscate her phone, stop buying magazines. Most importantly, they must trust Brandon's love for me.

I'll play the guilt card, apologize for these restrictions, and swear it's only temporary—until I'm no longer Brandon's secret love. They'll believe it, and the blonde will have no choice but to submit. If she resists, I'll beat her into submission, and the parents will back me up. She's nothing now, and soon, she'll be less than nothing. I can't wait to start. I'm so excited!

CHAPTER 12

SIX FEET UNDER, THE NIGHT OF TRAGEDY...

"You'll wake up. It's just a nightmare. You'll wake up..."
Madee repeated the sentence over and over in her head. No, this couldn't be real. None of this was true. Any second now, she'd open her eyes. She'd be safe, in her apartment, curled up in Tom's arms.

But her head was heavy. Her body ached—first her legs, then her back, her stomach, her arms. Slowly, the pain crept over her, like she'd been crushed under a steamroller. A migraine pounded in her temples, gongs echoing inside her skull. She wanted to move, but her body refused. She couldn't even twitch. Just before, she'd managed to wake briefly, catching a glimpse of a terrible face staring at her before the darkness pulled her back down. She wasn't alone.

But she refused to look, to acknowledge what was happening around her. It had to be a hallucination, a panic attack—her mind playing tricks. After everything she'd been through, this had to be her subconscious, trying to sabotage the happiness she'd fought so hard for. This wasn't real. Don't panic. Just breathe. Deep breath in, slow exhale. Madee's first goal was to move again. But she needed to relax. If she didn't, the tetany would last for hours. The weight on her chest made breathing difficult, and the harder she tried to calm herself, the more her anxiety spiked. OK, try something else. Distract yourself. Go over the day. What could have triggered this?

Madee forced herself to rewind, though the migraine made thinking a struggle. Flashes of the day came in fragments. She'd left work early. The model spaceship she'd ordered for Tom had arrived. She had to go downtown to pick it up—the delivery man wouldn't come to the Forgotten District.

Downtown made her nervous. What if she ran into someone from her old life? Or worse, what if she ran into them? Unlikely, she told herself. Tom's smile was worth the risk. People change, even if only a little. Hate can't last forever.

She had walked calmly toward the old railway line. She remembered crossing it. She'd reached North Station and stopped at Hassan's Food Truck to grab dinner. Then, she'd hurried to public housing and put on her headphones. She had always been wary around North Station. She knew the homeless community well, but the new faces—small-time dealers staking their claim on the area—made her uneasy. The violence in North Station was constant. Better to keep her head down, stay alert, and move quickly.

She was just 800 meters from the station when she let her guard down. Joyful, confident, she turned up the volume on her headphones, losing herself in the chorus of her favorite song. No more tears. She imagined a bright future, one where she would never be alone again. Everything had changed. She had changed. But happiness can blind you to the danger lurking in the shadows. She didn't see it coming. The blow landed sharply on the back of her head, clean and precise. Her song ended.

Ignore the pain. Face the situation. Whatever it is... She's strong. She'll get through this. One eye, then the other. It takes Madee a few minutes to adjust to the darkness, bathed in an eerie blue light. The space is small, windowless, and covered in pictures... Her thoughts are interrupted by the overwhelming stench of rot filling her nostrils. The smell sharpens her senses, and her aching body slowly comes back to life. She can move—barely. Her arms, her legs—they tremble uncontrollably, but it's her first victory.

But then she freezes. Desperately, she searches for her sweatshirt, only to realize she's completely naked, her skin slick with a slimy, whitish liquid. Horror sinks in. Is she in one of those caves where the gangs take girls to rape? Madeeswallows hard. Babou had warned her about the dangers near North Station... How many guys had raped her? One? Two? Ten? She'd rather not know.

Stay calm. Think. If she's still near North Station, they might let her go when they're done playing with her. These bastards know their victims won't press charges. She knows how this works—keep your head down and pray there's no next time. Anger begins to replace fear, fueling her strength. She tries to stand. Earl won't appreciate this insult... The riffraff who took her don't know the rules between the neighborhoods...

That smell... It must be a dead dog, tortured and left to rot. Rats will finish the job. Madee feels sick imagining the poor animal's suffering. She looks again at the photos on the wall. The entire room is covered in a grotesque pornographic fresco. Women, immortalized as nothing more than sexual objects—disposable, replaceable. Fresh meat for the slaughterhouse, discarded when no longer useful.

"Are you awake, Sandra?"

The voice startles her. A figure emerges from the darkness at the back of the room. Morbid. Terrifying.

"The kids broke you, Sandra. They broke you."

Madee's heart pounds. This man isn't from North Station. He's something worse. Covered in tattoos—bones, tendons, a disembodied face—he looks like a human skeleton. He moves closer, his smile revealing steel teeth that match his fists. A predator. Madee won't be his first victim, and she certainly won't be his last. She has no chance of escaping him.

She's read enough thrillers to know how this ends. Girls like her don't survive psychopaths like him. They're found in dumpsters—raped, beaten, and broken. He keeps calling her Sandra.

Madee has two choices: stay silent and try to disappear into herself, or play along with his delusion. Pretending to be Sandra might speed up her punishment. Staying quiet... maybe that will buy her time. For now, it's safer to let him live in his madness. There's no point angering him with contradictions.

Suddenly, the skeleton man stops. There's a noise above their heads. Madee, trying to retain some semblance of dignity, pulls her legs up against her body. A hatch opens in the ceiling, cool night air rushing in as a second man descends, grumbling about getting dirt on his suit. He doesn't look like a lunatic—more like some pompous daddy's boy addicted to excess. She doesn't trust him.

"Oh, there she is! Madee, Madee, Madee... May I call you Madee?"

He stretches out his arms, as if they've known each other all their lives. Madee grits her teeth and stays silent.

"Welcome to my museum, Madee! Have you seen my photos? Come, take a look. I'm sure you'll spot your boyfriend in one of them! They're all over his dick, you know... Good ol' Collins, what a serial fucker!"

His words hit her like a slap. Madee's mind reels, but she tries to stay calm. Does he know Tom? No, it has to be a bluff. But doubt creeps in. OK, Tom's no saint—he's had his issues with drugs—but this? He would've told her... right?

Maybe he didn't trust her, didn't think she could handle it. Or worse, maybe Tom had been playing her all along...

"My name's Wayne! You must've heard of me—Collins' bitch probably mentioned me! I don't know how things work in your world, but here, we're civilized. Let's introduce ourselves properly!"

In your world. Madee's heard that sneer before, too many times. She wants to spit in his face, tell him that when he dies, the maggots won't care about his status. Death doesn't discriminate. Wayne steps closer, pretending to take her picture.

"You know, you could be hot if you weren't so fat. You don't fit in here, so I'll put you on a diet!"

He laughs, delighted to humiliate her in front of the skeleton man and the grotesque display of photos on the wall.

"Collins has shit taste. I'm used to better! He's fucked the most beautiful women, and what does he end up with? A fat one!"

Madee feels tears burning behind her eyes, but she refuses to give him the satisfaction. The confidence she had this morning is gone. Was Tom playing with her all along? Was it all just to see what it's like to sleep with someone ugly? Maybe Tom had orchestrated this whole thing, luring her in with fake affection... Maybe he always meant to hurt her. Wayne pulls out a packet of powder, spreads some on his hand, and snorts it hard.

"You want some? You must be on something, because I really don't see what Collins sees in you!"

Madee feels the walls closing in. Shame and anger rise in her chest—ashamed of herself despite all her efforts, and furious that her poverty, her insignificance, has caught up with her again. How naive she'd been, believing in a happiness that has now gone up in smoke.

"Let's get down to business. I'm going to teach you some manners. And if you behave, you'll get a surprise!"

Wayne winks at her, clapping his hands as he shrugs off his jacket. The skeleton man moves toward the trapdoor, ready to leave. But Wayne, his face flushing red with anger, stops him. For a moment, Wayne forgets about Madee entirely as his temper flares.

"What the hell are you doing?"

"Contract conditions were clear. You do your business, and I'll come back later"

"You stay here!"

"That's not the deal..."

"You want cash? Then you do as I say, or I'll make sure you rot in prison for the rest of your fucking life. Got it?"

"This isn't what I signed up for. The Honor Code—"

"Fuck your code! Sit down, film, and shut the hell up. That's all we ask!"

The skeleton man hesitates but finally shrugs and sits. Wayne, like a magician pulling a trick, pulls out a wad of cash and tosses it to him.

"A gift. Use it to wipe your ass... or shove it up the bitch's ass!"

Wayne spits on the floor, ranting about the lack of professional integrity these days. Madee watches, disgusted.

People like Wayne think their money makes them untouchable, respectable. It's a twisted world. He's just like Laura, his mirror image—a spoiled child, convinced they have the right to decide who lives or dies.

"On your knees. Let's see how well you suck."

He unzips his pants, but Madee doesn't move. Wayne leans down, smirking.

"Are you deaf? This could go so smoothly if you just play nice..."

When she doesn't react, he punches her hard in the face. Madee staggers, falling to the ground as Wayne pounces, hands around her throat.

"Won't suck, huh? You weren't shy with Collins when you had his dick down your throat. You even seemed to enjoy it... Well, guess what? I'm skipping the foreplay. I'm going to fuck you so deep you'll feel me ripping you apart."

Madee gasps for air, her vision fading as the pressure on her throat tightens. She prays to pass out, to escape into unconsciousness before the horror begins. She feels his erect body pressing against her, and just as she thinks she might black out, he releases her neck and flips her over.

"Let's see if I can find your hole under all that fat," he sneers. "I bet you'll make a fine bitch."

Madee squeezes her eyes shut, fists clenched so tightly her nails cut into her palms. Wayne spreads her apart. She hears him mutter, *"Splendid,"* as he orders the skeleton man to come closer with the camera. Wayne mocks her, telling his invisible audience that Collins never had the guts to take her this way.

He spits to make it "easier," takes a deep breath, and thrusts into her. Madee's screams echo in the small room, but Wayne doesn't care. He pulls her hair violently, quickening his pace. Between gasps of pleasure, he murmurs to himself:

"That's it, bitch. Keep screaming. No one can hear you. You're mine now, my toy."

CHAPTER 13

LAURA'S DIARY - MY LIFE IS A LONG QUIET RIVER...

You're just dumb paperwork. But I have to write to you—I'm so proud of myself that I need to leave my mark in history. I could have thrown you away, but I can't. You're my link to the world. I'll make sure no one ever finds you, not even that blonde bitch.

I'm almost 18 now. I stopped confiding in you after the school scandal, but so much has happened since. I've been fighting on every front, and I never imagined my plan would work out this perfectly. The world is mine! Well, not yet—the billions of shitty lives on this planet can wait—but I already have supreme power over the three idiots I live with: my mother, Jeff, and the blonde. They're at my mercy.

I control them completely, and it's not going to end anytime soon. My moods, my stories, my twists—I'm the one who sets the pace in this house. An exciting life is full of surprises, after all.

First off, I quit school. My parents didn't force me to take any courses, not even correspondence. At least I'm safe from that! After what happened at school, I have no reason to see people. When I reemerge into the world, it'll be on Brandon's arm, untouchable. No one will dare question me. But until I have that absolute social backing, I can't crush anyone beneath my heel. Not yet. So for now, I practice with what I have—training for the day when I'll destroy anyone who dares stand in my way. Studying? What a joke. Why waste time on school? Learning... pfft. Bullshit.

All I need is to stay beautiful and sexually irresistible. That's all it'll take to become Brandon Stevens' wife. The public will only see perfection. As for Brandon, as long as I have him between my thighs, I know he'll worship me. Men are weak that way—get near their dick, and they forget every principle they ever had. The rest comes second. With Brandon's name and money, who cares about diplomas?

Where was I? Oh, yes—my little puppets at home. It's amazing what families are willing to accept, to forgive. That's the beauty of family—I can put them through the worst horrors, throw tantrums, and be an absolute nightmare, and it stays inside these walls. And even if people found out about my little games, no one would care. *"Every family has its problems,"* right?

MYTHOMANIA

Two years ago, ours had a tragedy. My grandparents, those two assholes who raised Jeff, died. I wasn't sad. I hated those old bastards. Just like their son. Good riddance. But, of course, I cried. Made a whole show of it. Jeff and Annie thought I was devastated. Another win for me.

I even wrote a fake condolence letter from "Brandon." The day my mom got it, you should've seen her face light up. She wouldn't let anyone touch it—took it to her room and hid it in her jewelry box like it was sacred. And the bouquet! I used Jeff's credit card to order the biggest arrangement I could find online. The delivery guy had strict instructions to ask for Mrs. Stevens and offer his condolences. When the doorbell rang, holding that huge bouquet, it was priceless. Even without Brandon there, he was "supporting" the family through their grief. You should've seen them.

My mom placed those flowers on the sideboard in the living room, stroking each petal, raving about the scent. I waited for the perfect moment before telling her that Jeff had a mistress. When she saw the florist's charge on the bank statement, she never suspected I'd bought those flowers with house money. Nope. Her resentment toward Jeff turned to pure hatred. The bastard was cheating on her and using household money to buy his mistress gifts. It was child's play to make her believe Jeff was unfaithful. All I had to do was turn her own misery against her.

The only good thing about my grandparents' death was the massive sum of money they left Jeff. I needed it desperately for the next phase of my plan. It was an unexpected miracle. Now, Jeff's more tolerable—his bank account makes him interesting. He's still a jerk, but he provides the household's financial security. I'll deal with him when the money runs out. Until then, I'll keep the peace.

I've been working quietly to drive a wedge between him and Mum, but it takes daily effort. Money is the perfect salve for any wound, and it helps keep things under control.

Every day, I check the internet for news about Brandon. To keep the blonde from snooping and getting back at me for everything I've done to her, I put a parental lock on the phone line that only I know. My safety comes first.

But my heart shattered when I found out Brandon was in a serious relationship with some trendy starlet. She had the look—sophisticated, chic. Perfect for Brandon's new style. Gone were the wild days of Paradoxical Heights. He'd swapped his musicians and transformed into a rock dandy. The only thing he kept was the makeup and black-painted nails. Needless to say, my gothic Lolita look doesn't fit his new ideal.

I spent hours in front of the mirror, staring at my face, seeing every flaw. My mouth was slightly asymmetrical—tragic. My breasts, nonexistent. My butt, flat. I envied the blonde's curves, her full breasts, her hips. I didn't want to be her. I didn't want to be fat, but I wanted a proper woman's body. I had to act. My mouth, my breasts, my butt, my stomach—everything had to change. I had to wage war on fat and sculpt a body worthy of a magazine cover.

Using Brandon's girlfriend as leverage, I convinced Mum to take me to a plastic surgeon. One morning, I went to the kitchen, crying. Annie, of course, panicked and asked what was wrong. I told her Brandon had cheated on me, and I knew that would work. Infidelity always set her off. Watching her crumble was my key to getting what I wanted.

I showed her a picture of the girl, and as expected, she hated her. She called her ugly, vulgar. Mum became obsessed, convinced Brandon had destroyed his "perfect" daughter's happiness by cheating with the first slut he found. Her reaction, predictable as ever, told me I'd won. Behind Jeff's back, she made an appointment with the best surgeon in town, and in one consultation, my surgery was scheduled. It cost a fortune, but who cared? Jeff had the money!

Mum was obsessed with my happiness, with ensuring I beat this "whore" in the battle for Brandon's affection. It became personal for her. Jeff didn't understand. He kept saying that if Brandon truly loved me, he'd accept me as I was. The back-and-forth dragged on for two weeks, but in the end, Annie won. The day I went back to the clinic, the operation was paid for.

The recovery was agony. My stomach hurt the most. I yelled at the surgeon for not letting me see the results immediately. The bandages hid everything, and I accused him of scamming my parents. I made the nurses' lives hell until I got what I wanted. When I finally saw the bruises and scars, I almost cried. On top of the pain, I was far from the perfect body I'd seen in magazines. The surgeon assured me it was temporary—just postoperative shock. I didn't want to hear it, and neither did Mum. We wanted results, and fast.

Finally, after two months, I started seeing the changes. My mouth was perfectly symmetrical. My breasts were like those of a bimbo. My butt was firm, and my stomach was flat, with visible abs. I was perfect. At last.

I went shopping with Mum and bought nothing but smart, expensive clothes. The only trace of my gothic past was my black hair—blondes disgust me. I'd rather die than look like one of those peroxide whores. I was living the high life, always finding new expenses, new desires, and Jeff paid for it all. You're probably wondering how I managed to keep up the pretense with Brandon. Let me tell you.

God, it's been easy so far. I kept things going with the same basic lie: Brandon loved my family, considered them his, but he was too afraid to introduce himself. Mum was a huge help, of course. But that one lie wasn't enough—I had to keep feeding it. So I created rituals. I made my parents believe that Brandon visited me in the afternoons, but only on one condition: I had to be alone. They gave in, despite Jeff's frustration, convinced that our relationship would end in a glamorous media wedding.

Every day at 2 p.m., no matter the season, no matter the weather, they had to leave. They'd only come back when I called to say our "visit" was over. During that time, I'd go through the blonde's clothes, rummage through her things. I missed sex, so I'd put on porn, blast the volume loud enough for the neighbors to hear. Let them think little Laura was having a wild affair with her famous fiancé.

I had to live like a rock star, every day an emotional roller coaster. I kept up with Brandon's media presence so I could embellish and twist things when the idiots came home. Between me, Mum, and Brandon, I created a love triangle. I needed to give Mum something in return for her support, so every afternoon, I'd forge letters in Brandon's handwriting, addressed to my dear mother.

Mum would write back quickly, pouring out her heart to her "favorite son-in-law," confiding in him. If only she knew it was her own daughter reading and responding. I pretended to be the man she'd always dreamed of. In my replies, I'd paint a picture of Brandon far removed from his wild, media image. I made him into a simple guy, scared of fame, someone who only wanted peace and love.

Mum was hooked. I could see it—she was in love with the imaginary lover I'd created. And I fed it. The letters became more intimate. I even went as far as telling her that Brandon didn't know who to choose between mother and daughter. Mum was living a second youth, dreaming about her fantasy man—the one who would join her in bed after he was done screwing her daughter.

On those afternoons, after I'd finished masturbating—sometimes thinking about Troy's cock—I'd turn to my new passion: witchcraft.

I first stumbled on it while scouring the internet, looking for ways to destroy Joy and push the blonde to suicide. I found incredible rituals, ones that could hurt someone without them ever knowing it was me. The blonde was my first guinea pig. I performed a ritual to plunge her into deep depression, make her gain weight, and completely ruin her life. The results were instant. After that, I moved on to Joy, ensuring that none of her relationships would ever work, making her feel the same heartbreak I did. I even performed a ritual to break up Brandon and his girlfriend, another to bind Brandon to me for life, and a final one to kill any woman who dared come near him. All I had to do was rub the lamp and make a wish.

I'd sit in my bedroom in the dark, lit only by candlelight and the glow of the computer screen, which was playing my favorite porn movie on loop. It showed a girl being taken by four guys at once, and while I watched, I worked my magic. Those lonely afternoons were always busy—I barely had enough time. I'd deliberately delay calling my family. I loved knowing they were waiting outside, aimless, wondering when I'd finally bring them back home. When they arrived, I'd greet them half-naked or dressed in the blonde's favorite clothes, the ones she could no longer fit into.

Mum would run to my desk, desperate to get her hands on Brandon's latest letter. I'd tell her about my imaginary sexual exploits, the wild orgasms I'd had. Depending on my mood, I'd force myself to cry, spinning some drama about how things were going wrong between Brandon and me—how we'd fought, how he wanted to leave me because everything had become too hard. I'd show them pictures of luxurious properties, telling them Brandon was buying houses to protect us all.

Jeff, though... I had a feeling he wasn't as fooled as Mum. He never understood why Brandon never showed up, and once, he even suggested they stay one afternoon to catch Brandon when he came home. I was afraid he'd follow through, but he was stubborn. So I used Mum to rein him in.

I pretended to call Brandon and faked a conversation, making it sound like he was furious about Jeff's decision. I told them Brandon was done protecting the family and wouldn't see me again until it was on his terms. Jeff eventually gave in, terrified of losing the money as it melted away, hoping for some kind of return on his investment. I have them all in the palm of my hand. If they disobey me, I'll make sure they know their place.

I haven't mentioned the blonde yet... She's another story. As for my parents' hatred of her, I'm not worried. I've used the dictator technique—made her the scapegoat for all our problems. Everything is her fault. I've told my parents that Brandon doesn't come because of her, that she's leaking everything that happens at home, and that he's waiting for proof she's a mole before he retaliates.

It worked perfectly. Now, she's completely excluded from family conversations. I've condemned her to perpetual silence. The moment she walks into a room, we all stop talking, and if she dares ask what's going on, we tell her to shut up—it's none of her business.

I'm always on her back. I love treating her badly. I mock her music, her attitude, her taste, her very existence. I blame her for everything I do wrong, accuse her of being shallow, of being the reason our family's life is ruined. The harassment is daily. If I could, I'd torture her in her sleep. Every day, I erase a little more of her. She's nothing but a freak to my parents now.

Jeff and Annie are furious with her. They keep telling her she ruins everything, that she's sabotaging my marriage and their social climb. To make it worse, I pretend to be her confidante. I dress in her clothes, imitate her, mocking her behind her back. Mum and I have this little habit of speaking over her, and when she says something smart—which, unfortunately, happens too often—we twist it so it sounds like the idea came from us. She's nothing but a burden now, an extra mouth to feed. We keep her locked inside, only allowing her out in the afternoon with my parents. Her life is hell.

Beyond my expectations, the ritual I performed on her worked. Her eating disorder came back with a vengeance. She's gained 34 pounds. She hides when she eats, stuffing herself in secret. I take advantage, reporting her binges to my parents, just like I did when we were kids. Money is everything in this family, so I tell them Madeleine's eating is costing us a fortune. When she tries to diet, I shout that her mental problems are making us all suffer.

My parents are desperate. They don't know how to get rid of her. I play the role of the concerned sister, pretending to care. I tell them she's lost, that she has nowhere to go, no future. Families stick together, I say, even when there's a black sheep.

She's fat now, and it gives me so much pleasure to show off my perfect body. Mum often tells her to follow my example if she ever wants a man to want her. The blonde punishes herself, cutting, sinking deeper into depression. This fat, pathetic bitch... Three times she tried swallowing sleeping pills and Mum's antidepressants. Mum and I found the drugs, but we just let her sleep it off. We said it wasn't serious, that she was just a junkie, a problem with no solution. We calculated how much she'd taken compared to her weight. It wouldn't kill her. And if it did, what did it matter? She's nothing. Just trash. An obstacle to my happiness.

I used to love seeing the tears in her eyes when Mum and I came back from shopping. We'd tell her, with innocent smiles, that there was nothing in the shops for someone her size. That you had to be an XXS or XS to find anything decent. Mum would brag about all the compliments I'd gotten from the salesgirls and glance at the blonde with disdain, as if to say: You're ugly and fat. You'll never have this.

Of all the nasty things I did to her, my favorite was that afternoon in the city center. I'd told my parents I needed new clothes for my next visit to Brandon. The blonde, dreaming of clothes she'd never get to wear, stared longingly at the shop windows. A pair of cowboy boots caught her eye. I laughed in her face and told her they were old-fashioned. Then, with fake enthusiasm, I said I loved the boots and that Brandon wanted me to have them. When Jeff and Mum met us outside, fifteen minutes later, I had the boots in my hands. The blonde looked devastated. She tried to ask for a pair too, but Mum and Jeff shut her down, telling her she didn't need them.

One day, she asked to borrow my boots. I said yes, knowing exactly how Mum would react. When Annie saw the blonde wearing them, she slapped her twice. I laughed with satisfaction. Her weight had crushed the heel, and Mum ordered her to take them off immediately. Watching her obey and cry was priceless. It's simple. Because she's fat, her parents will never buy her anything. It's my little revenge for all those months she spent buying herself clothes with her miserable waitressing wages. I forgot to mention that she had to lend me her clothes—too small for her now—and if she dared say no, I'd beat her. So would Mum and Jeff.

I loved hitting her. I'd hit her as hard as I could, the way you beat an animal in a cage, to keep her under control and remind her of her place. When she had bruises, her parents said she had serious psychological problems and was doing it to herself. People could hardly believe we were sisters when they saw us together. I am beautiful. She is a beast. Sisters? Impossible. I'm grace. She's shit.

I even told everyone she was adopted. Word spread quickly in the neighborhood, and soon everyone thought that explained why we didn't look alike. The Mitchells had rescued an orphan, done a good deed. Madeleine was the daughter of some crook and a prostitute, one of the many unwanted children from North Station. She has no identity.

MYTHOMANIA

She waits for death to free her, and no one will mourn her when it comes. Yes, my life is a calm, easy river. I love playing with my three dolls, and I hope it lasts until I become Mrs. Stevens.

CHAPTER 14

SIX FEET UNDER: IN THE DEN OF VICE...

Lifting her body is excruciating. Madee refuses to stay on the dirt floor of this sad, filthy cell. She's still reeling from the rape, trying to reclaim herself after those endless moments when she was reduced to nothing more than a sexual object. Until now, she thought she'd seen the worst, thought she had escaped the darkness. Life is punishing her for daring to be happy, for allowing herself even a sliver of joy.

Wayne had taken her over and over, violently, until she was nothing more than a rag doll, ready to collapse. When he finally decided the game was over, he left her there, under the cold, watchful gaze of the skeleton man. As a parting gift, Wayne beat her senseless, telling her to be more cooperative next time. But whatever the cost, Madee is determined to stand. Wayne will never win. He will never defeat her.

She doesn't know how long it's been since she last saw daylight. It doesn't matter anyway. Wayne had made it clear: no one was coming for her. Her captivity would last until her body gave out—until she reached the absolute limits of endurance. The taste of blood in her mouth gives her a bitter preview of what's to come. A painful, indifferent death. In her fear and agony, she barely notices her bladder and bowels had emptied themselves. The smell of urine and faecesmingles with the stench of decay. Shame claws at her. Her dignity, her humanity, stripped away.

She wonders if it would be easier to embrace death rather than drag herself through more torment. But she has to get up. She wants to see those perfect women, the ones on the walls. She has to rise. The searing pain in her head, her ribs, and her gut scream at her to stay down, but she knows—either she stands or she dies here.

She knows the skeleton man is watching her. He hasn't moved, but she can feel his eyes on her, cold and detached. His orders are clear. Even if she wanted to, she could never make him her ally. She remembers how he reacted when Wayne threw money at him. Money makes people do anything. Madee knows that all too well.

Before they take away what little sanity she has left, Madee tries to stay strong. Hope is gone, but she won't let them take what's left of her soul. After several failed attempts, she's finally on her feet. The tiny room Wayne locked her in feels impossibly low, the walls pressing in on her. There's nothing to indicate where she is. She can't hear anything from outside—not even the faintest vibration. This place could be hundreds of meters underground. It's just her, the monster, and those women. The ones Tom fucked. If Wayne is telling the truth...

Madee has never had much self-confidence. In fact, she's never really loved herself. If she were so special, why would life keep hurting her? She starts to wonder how much she really knows about Tom. He never talked about his childhood, his family, his past. She'd been so focused on helping him with his addiction that she never pushed. She thought they'd have all the time in the world to learn about each other...

With difficulty, she takes a few steps toward the photos. The women are stunning, their bodies perfect, but their faces... their faces reveal their enslavement. Madee can't believe it—her Tom, kind and caring, enjoying this? No men in the photos, just dicks that could belong to anyone. She tries to convince herself that Tom isn't part of this debauchery unfolding before her eyes.

She remembers their night together. Impossible. He would never degrade a woman like this. He was gentle, respectful—almost clumsy. Madee gave herself to him with full trust, despite her insecurities and her flabby body...

"Do you like them?"

She didn't hear Wayne come back. She's too focused on the photos. The bastard can wait. She won't give him the satisfaction. Silence is her only weapon. Feign indifference, even as her body screams. Don't let him destroy what's left of her... again.

"You're not much of a talker, are you? Just like Collins. Always brooding, acting like he's better than his brothers."

Wayne lights a cigarette, taking a deep drag before blowing the smoke in her face. Her indifference frustrates him, and that makes her feel just a little more in control.

"Wait a minute. I've got something that'll get that bitch mouth of yours moving."

Without looking at her, Wayne walks over to the wall and pins up a new photo. The neon light strips it of any sentiment. Madee's heart stops as she recognizes the couple in the image—caught in the act of love. It's her. And Tom.

The photo was taken in her apartment. How had Wayne gotten it? Only one other person had a set of keys... Coldness invades Madee's heart. Everything she thought she knew crumbles. All those months with Tom mean nothing. Among all the other images, her precious night of love is reduced to something vulgar, something dirty. The warmth of Tom's arms disappears. He's a good actor.

Despite everything he made her believe, she was just another challenge. Another girl to fuck. Enjoying her confusion, Wayne grins, taking pleasure in every second of her torment.

"C'mon, that's enough bullshit—the emotional sequence is over!"

Before she can react, Wayne's hand comes down hard on Madee's back, the sudden pain sending her sprawling to the ground. She barely registers the sting before another blow lands.

"If my coach saw an ass that big, he'd have a heart attack! That's what happens when you don't work out. Look at you—you're disgusting. You've even shit yourself!"

Wayne unzips his trousers and starts to urinate on her. He takes his time, spraying her thoroughly as if marking his territory. Madee doesn't move. Can't move. Her body has betrayed her, and now she's nothing more than prey.

"You're getting the hang of it, bitch! Let's see if you can stand up now, covered in piss," Wayne taunts, his voice dripping with cruelty. "I hope the other idiot's been filming this."

He crouches over her, dropping his full weight onto her limp, soaked body. Holding her head still with one hand, he pulls something out of his blazer with the other—a small black box.

"I'm finally going to hear your bitchy voice... And that's just the beginning. Soon you'll be begging me to stop."

With a sadistic grin, Wayne presses the button. The electric shock is instant and violent, ripping through Madee's body, making her convulse like a puppet with its strings cut. He pauses, only to press the button again, over and over, commanding her to scream. But no sound escapes Madee's lips. She's too stunned, too far gone to react. Wayne grows frustrated, rising to his feet, pulling up his pants, and grabbing her wrist to check her pulse. She's still alive, for now.

"Damn it. Still breathing," he mutters, then turns his attention to the Skeleton Man.

"You, stop standing there like an idiot with that camera. Clean her up. Make sure she's more lively when I come back to fuck her tonight. I'm tired—I need to sleep."

Without a trace of guilt, Wayne walks away, leaving Madee to her torment, as if what he'd just done was nothing more than an afterthought.

CHAPTER 15

FORREST HILL, 8 MONTHS BEFORE THE TRAGEDY...

Tom and Madee walked through the Forgotten District on their way to school, their arms full of boxes of cakes. A fresh breeze ruffled their hair, an early sign that autumn was on its way. The streets, empty in the early morning light, seemed just as deserted as they had at dawn. The neighborhood was crumbling, a vast dormitory for the poor, despite the few open shops offering a semblance of life. From a distance, Tom had already noticed the poverty, but up close, the decay was undeniable. Cracked walls, poor insulation—one jolt too many, and the whole house of cards would collapse. Elaine's Cafe was the best-preserved building in the area.

Tom understood Earl's suspicion of outsiders. If the council started taking an interest in Forrest Hill, the politicians wouldn't hesitate to order its demolition. Sentiment wouldn't factor into their decision.

"Seen from here, the reality isn't very pretty, is it?" Madee's voice cut through the silence.

Tom didn't respond right away. He could feel her steady gaze on him, but was this a test, or just a simple question? Sure, the Forgotten District looked like a shithole, but there was no point in telling Madee that. It would take more than judgments to fix a place like this. He could see the efforts of the community to make things better, but the chaos was too overwhelming.

To bring dignity back to this neighborhood would require more money than these people could ever hope to earn. The mayor would never approve funds for such a risky project. Tom could already imagine the backlash from taxpayers. No politician would jeopardize re-election for a place like this.

Madee was still watching him, waiting, but not pushing. She must have taken his silence for contempt. Tom felt a pang of guilt. He didn't want to talk about the state of the district; he wanted to talk about her, to know more about her. Madeeintrigued him. He wanted to ask about her past, her life... but he didn't dare. What if he said something stupid? He wasn't sure how to start a conversation like that. For now, he was content just walking beside her, each step feeling like the beginning of something deeper, a prelude to a long journey together.

"Tom... You have the right to change your mind, you know," Madee said softly. There was a note of hesitation, even sadness in her voice. She stared straight ahead, as if afraid of hearing him say he regretted coming here. "It's never easy when poverty hits you in the face."

"Why would I change my mind?" Tom asked, frowning.

"I don't know..." She sighed. "You come from a different social world, obviously. People here aren't exactly rolling in money, as you can see for yourself. We don't have much to offer..."

"What makes you think that, Madee?" Tom's voice was gentle, but she continued as if she hadn't heard him.

"You're the pride of the community. Everyone's gotten used to seeing you. A well-dressed man with a nice car, coming all the way from downtown every day... You make people here feel important. A stranger who cares enough to spend time in their world. They really like you, Tom. It wouldn't do to disappoint them."

Madee's voice grew quieter. "I don't want you to be here out of pity, or boredom, or distraction..."

Tom felt a flicker of disappointment. Madee was talking about the community, but she wasn't saying what he really wanted to hear. He longed for her to say, I want you to stay. Her argument didn't make sense to him. How could these people like him? They barely spoke to him. He could try to push her, to force her to say what she was truly thinking, but that would be a mistake. She'd taken so long to open up to him—he didn't want to ruin that.

"Madee, I don't understand what you're getting at."

She took a deep breath. "What I'm trying to say, in a very clumsy and confused way, is this: By coming to breakfast every morning, you've become part of our community. You don't show up like some conqueror, full of contempt for the lower classes... No. You come to spend time with us. We're invisible. Nobody cares about us, except to treat us like shit. But you—Tom—you're not ordinary. Thanks to you, everyone's realizing they have the right to exist. We're not just stupid handmaidens made to serve. Despite the misery of our little hiding place, we're no longer rats."

"Madee, they can come and talk to me. You could've come to me sooner."

"I think... I think you impress me," she admitted, her voice softer. "You impress us all."

Madee's cheeks flushed, and Tom noticed how vulnerable she looked. Beneath her shimmering clothes and her strong-woman persona, there was a sensitive, fragile side to her. Tom was captivated. There was something so pure and complex about Madee, a naturalness that drew him in. He longed for her to open up fully, to trust him.

"Madee, to be honest, I've never been faced with poverty like this. It's all new to me. But you can be sure of one thing: I'm not leaving. I'm happy here. With you. So, no—I won't change my mind."

Their eyes met, and both of them smiled, the tension between them dissolving in that moment. Tom felt a sense of relief. He believed, for the first time, that they could talk freely now—that the social barrier between them had finally fallen. As they continued walking, they passed a park that Tom saw every day on his way into Forrest Hill. He asked Madee if it had always been there.

"No," she explained. "The project started just after I arrived in Forrest Hill. It's the pride of the community now, because everyone was involved in creating and maintaining it. We call it the *Oasis*. The kids spend their breaks here because the school's right behind it."

Madee spoke with such joy and love about the neighborhood, about how they had to create makeshift classrooms in the chapel and Doc's medical practice because there was no school bus to downtown. Tom admired the strength and resilience of the people here. They had built something beautiful out of nothing. But one question still burned in his mind, one he couldn't push away...

"You've been living here long?" Tom asked, trying to dig deeper.

"I arrived a little over a year ago."

"And?"

"I lived and worked in the downtown... Now I'm here."

"Don't you miss city life?"

"Oh no, I don't! I'm happy in Forrest Hill. I have friends and family... I wouldn't change a thing!"

Her response was polite, but Tom could feel the evasion in her words. It was clear that Madee liked her life now, but why had she come here in the first place? His curiosity wouldn't be satisfied today.

They approached the school building, a three-storey structure that looked like an abandoned sanatorium. Tom half expected to see a poltergeist emerge from the crumbling grey walls. With some renovation, the place could be decent, but right now it was a depressing sight. Tom felt a pang of sympathy for the children and elderly who spent their days in this gloomy place.

As they neared the entrance, memories of his own disastrous school years resurfaced. Tom's pace slowed. Over the years, he'd developed a phobia of teachers, seeing them as tormentors. For him, school was a place where rich kids like him were treated as the bad seeds, no matter what they did.

"Tom? Is something wrong?" Madee's voice pulled him out of his thoughts.

"I can wait for you here if you want..."

"Are you afraid of the building?"

"No... I just don't really like schools."

Madee studied his face for a moment, then nodded with understanding.

"I get it. If it helps, I didn't like school either. The kids made fun of me, my grades were awful, and I hated the teachers. The second I was old enough to skip class, I did!"

She laughed as she said it, and Tom was struck by how unexpected it sounded. Sweet, orderly Madee, skipping school? She didn't seem like the rebellious type, yet here she was, admitting she hated school too. For the first time, Tom realized that he wasn't alone in his suffering. Bullying didn't discriminate—it could touch anyone. But unlike him, Madee seemed to have moved past it, carrying no bitterness from her school years. He wished he could learn her secret, to let go of the resentment that still gnawed at him.

"If it's too much, try my method," she said, her voice softening. "You're not that kid anymore. You come here as an adult, a savior to these children who only eat once a day. Leave your fears behind, Tom. It's going to be fine. We won't be here long, and the kids are sweet. I'll protect you. Just breathe, okay? Stay close to me."

She winked at him before climbing the steps to the entrance. Tom hesitated. He didn't want to be left alone, but stepping inside that building terrified him. The old fear resurfaced—of being the rich boy who needed discipline, the prince with the perfect life who didn't belong. He glanced down at the boxes of biscuits he was still holding. He'd come this far. There was no turning back now. Whether he liked it or not, his past was catching up with him.

Tom couldn't shake the irrational fear that the biscuits were part of some elaborate trap. Maybe Madee was a temptress with an angel's face, luring him into the school where Mrs. Atkins would be waiting at the end of the corridor to punish him for being Tom Collins, born into privilege. The idea was absurd, but as Madee walked ahead, smiling like a beacon at the end of the tunnel, he was already thinking about putting down his boxes and turning around, desperate to escape the sinister building.

Madee noticed his absence and came back to look for him. No one had ever come back for him before. She scooped up his boxes and added them to her own pile, balancing them with her right arm while using her chin to steady the top. Tom's heart warmed as she took his hand, intertwining her fingers with his. He clung to the softness of her touch, hoping to prolong this unexpected contact. In that moment, all his fears melted away. Madee was right. He was safe.

Inside, the building was far from the gloomy prison he'd imagined. Abstract drawings, born from a child's wildest dreams, covered the walls. On one side, a bright day with an eternal sun, trees, birds, hot-air balloons, and animals danced across a sky-blue background. On the other side, the night scene unfolded: a giant moon surrounded by stars, a lake full of water lilies, swans, and owls. Superman, an astronaut, Thor's hammer, flying shoes, and skateboards were scattered throughout. Each child had clearly created their own world, a place where fantasies took flight.

Madee explained that the children called this part of the school the *"Dream Corridor."* Tom was mesmerized. He wished he'd had the freedom to express his creativity like this when he was young. He realized now how much of his childhood he had missed, even though Margaretha would never have forbidden him from painting his own walls.

The classroom was the real surprise: the desks were arranged in a circle, with no blackboard in sight. Strings of lights hung from rainbow-colored walls, casting a warm glow. On the shelves, an old hi-fi system was almost buried under stacks of records, while books were guarded by a miniature skeleton and an ancient lava lamp. A group of kids took turns playing Space Invaders on a computer. Tom's mind played tricks on him—Mrs. Atkins would never have taught in a room like this. As the seconds ticked by, he began to relax. The children let out a collective *"Ohhh"* of surprise when he and Madee entered the room. They were in awe, fascinated that their friend Madee had brought along the man with the fancy car. Two boys mimed a kiss and teased that Madee had brought her boyfriend. Tom chuckled at their antics. Seeing these kids try to play the provocateurs made the bullies of his past seem almost laughable. Maybe some clever children from every generation had the urge to make themselves interesting.

The teacher kindly asked for a little silence. Madee introduced Tom to everyone, and one by one, each child solemnly shook his hand. A few of the lucky ones with mobile phones even dared to ask for a selfie with him. It was surreal. Not long ago, Tom had been a cocaine-addicted loser, yet here he was, treated like a world star. He wasn't exactly an example to follow, but for the first time in a long while, he felt important.

Without thinking, he took over distributing the cookies, energized by how good he felt. Madee had stepped back, letting him take the lead. She was surrounded by three little girls, helping them choose a record to play later. She smiled as she watched Tom, so patient with the children. He had no idea how much he was learning about himself, how Forrest Hill was slowly changing him. She could see it already.

All good things must come to an end. The kids begged Tom and Madee to stay, but they were back in class, and it was time to go. Madee promised to return the next day with Tom, and if they behaved, she'd bake her famous chocolate praline brownies.

As they stepped outside, the wind picked up. They walked side by side, each lost in their own thoughts. Leaves fell from the few trees lining the street, swirling around them gracefully before settling on the tarmac. Tom's mind buzzed. The kids had pulled him out of his comfort zone, and he was amazed at how easy it had been to devote himself to them. He'd always thought he was a failure, a man without direction, but these small moments—handing out cookies, making the kids laugh—had made him feel... whole.

He never thought he could be cool or interesting without showing off, without being a chameleon who changed his personality to fit in. Looks had always come first. That was what Wayne Beckett had drilled into him. Kids, Wayne had said, were a man's worst curse—nothing but fashion accessories or pawns in the game of social advancement. Starting a family? That was for losers, the desperate.

"Enjoying yourself with the rednecks, Collins?" Wayne's snide voice echoed in Tom's head, his words sharp and cutting. "You're breaking the Invictus code of honor... Giving cookies to kids... What the hell, man? Be a man, Collins.

Fuck her. Take your car and get out of this shithole before these losers eat your soul."

Tom could almost see Wayne's tanned face, the smug, ironic smile. The bastard was trying to pull him back, back into the life of vice.

"Why are you wasting your time, Collins? Act, don't dream. Fuck her and disappear, just like you did with the others. Stop letting her fill your head with this sentimental bullshit. Stick your dick in her and get out. You're a piece of shit, Collins. You'll always be a piece of shit."

The voice grated in Tom's mind, dragging him back into a world he was desperately trying to escape. The toxic, selfish mantra of Wayne's world clashed violently with the warmth of the day he'd just had. For a moment, Tom wavered, caught between two versions of himself—one who wanted to embrace this new path, and one who still believed he was beyond saving.

Tom's mood plummeted, the joy from earlier evaporating in an instant. Wayne's voice hissed like a rattlesnake, slithering through his thoughts, squeezing out any sense of peace. You're nothing, it said. Nothing to show Madee... Nothing but a failure. The words were unbearable, they coiled tighter, suffocating him. Wayne's speech became unintelligible, a poisonous blur of contempt. His low opinion of himself, of Madee, of the children, of the poverty—all overlapped until he could no longer breathe. He felt dirty. Worthless. In short, he desperately needed a line. Just one. To feel his brain frying, his body splitting apart for the thousandth time, then he'd stop. He promised.

Wayne laughed, called him weak, and congratulated him all at once. The bastard was enjoying this.

"Shut the fuck up!" Tom snapped.

The words echoed, loud and real. He hadn't just thought them—he'd spoken out loud. Wayne was gone. Only Madeestood there, a few feet away, her face clouded with worry. They'd reached Elaine's. Her car was just a few steps away.

"Tom, are you okay?" Her voice was soft, gentle, but it cut right through him.

"Yes... Madee, I've got to go... Thanks for this morning."

She tilted her head, her eyes searching his face for something.

"Do you want to come in for a coffee, Tom? You don't look well."

He couldn't bear it. "Madee... See you tomorrow. I'll be back soon, I promise, but I need to do something urgent right now!"

Without waiting for a response, Tom bolted to his car, his hands trembling as he fumbled with the keys. He didn't dare look back. In the rearview mirror, he saw her, standing alone on the pavement, watching him speed away. She stayed there until she was nothing but a speck in the distance. Tom pulled into an empty lot just before the main road. At least here, he thought, I'll have some peace. No one would see him. No one would care. He reached for the glovebox, pulling out the small, crumpled bag of powder. His hands moved fast, almost on autopilot, as he made two neat lines on the leather of the passenger seat—one for each nostril. He bent down and sniffed greedily, the familiar burn spreading through his nose, lighting up his brain. He straightened up, his heart racing, the world spinning in sharp relief. Shame hit him like a freight train. He slapped the steering wheel, furious at himself. Weak, he thought. Pathetic. You'll never lead a normal life... Madee was right to stay away. He might as well forget her.

"Another failure, Collins!" Wayne's voice slithered back, venomous and mocking. Tom glanced at the passenger seat. Wayne was there, sitting casually, grinning like a devil.

"Next time you'll listen to my wise advice."

The hallucination scooped a handful of powder from the bag and, like some twisted version of the Sandman, blew the white dust into Tom's face. The powder danced in the air, swirling around him as Wayne disappeared, leaving behind nothing but the guilt and the smell of cocaine.

CHAPTER 16

SIX FEET UNDER, IN THE DEN OF VICE...

Despite the cold November afternoon, Madee slipped out into the garden, humming the song she kept playing over and over in her head. Now that she was alone, she allowed herself to sing. The little girl adjusted the bonnet over her baby blonde hair. It covered her head completely—a hand-me-down from Laura, the little princess who refused to wear it because it wasn't like those of her school friends. Madee had inherited it. It was good enough for her. The bonnet was ugly, but it hid the choppy bob Annie insisted on giving her.

A week earlier, Madee had turned eight—the age of reason, according to Annie. It meant she had to work harder at school, be good, and behave like a "big girl." But Madee already knew that to be "good" in her mother's eyes meant to be invisible. Madee tried to disappear, but no matter what she did, she always took up too much space. Just this morning, she had been scolded for eating one waffle too many. Food was her comfort.

What did they care? They always told her she was fat, that being overweight was her destiny. Leave me alone, she thought. It's already been decided for me. Madee's dream was to be pretty—to be like the other skinny little girls who smelled of perfume and got to be the queens of their own songs. The ones who were watched and admired.

There wasn't much to do outside. Jeff always took the swing down in the cold season, and the basketball hoop over the garage door hung unused. Madee would have made a few baskets, but the ball had a hole in it, and her parents never bothered to buy another one. It didn't matter. She often made up stories about magical lands, befriending animals and fairies who would come to save her from the ogre's clutches. But today, the inspiration didn't come. She felt too sad. Would she ever leave this hell?

Several times, she had written letters to her parents, saying she was leaving for a better world—one where people didn't care that she was fat because they loved her. She would slip the letter under the front door and go out into the garden, schoolbag in hand, waiting for Annie to come and hug her, to tell her, "I love you." But it never happened. When she returned to the house, the letter was always there—sometimes trampled on, unread. Once, Annie had opened it, glanced at the words, and said, "Nonsense! This child is completely mad."

Ashamed, Madee had run to her room to cry. She tried to be normal—but in her child's mind, she already knew she wasn't well. At school, they made fun of her. Teachers called her stupid. At home, she was "the fat girl," her parents' and Laura's whipping boy. She didn't fit in anywhere. So she spent her time alone, reading and listening to music, hoping for a future far away from all of this. A future where no one could hurt her.

Madee didn't realize that she was humming louder and louder, her small body beginning to sway to the rhythm of the song inside her head. It was feeding her, lighting her up from the inside. She imagined herself transported, like the singers on TV whose lives always seemed to have a happy ending. She admired the fancy outfits, the way they moved with the music, swaying in perfect rhythm. The little girl didn't understand the lyrics, but she felt that they were meant for her—that these singers were angels speaking directly to her.

The beat quickened. Madee could almost hear the whistle in the song as the sexy girl appeared, and the man saw her, knew she was the one. The dark, cold garden around her vanished, replaced by a smoky disco room full of people in platform shoes and sequined shirts. The volume swelled, the party was in full swing, and the disco ball on the ceiling reflected millions of stars onto the walls. The king of the crowd came down from the stage, his leopard suit drawing every eye as he made his way toward Madee, singing into the microphone. The crowd erupted in applause as Madee twirled in the middle of the floor, her laughter echoing like the sweetest melody. A shimmering gold jumpsuit appeared on her body as the singer touched her shoulder, welcoming her into the spotlight. For the first time, Madee was like everybody else. The rhythm pulsed through her, and she was free. Bernie, her little dog, came bouncing into the scene, barking in excitement. He stood on his hind legs, and Madee, giggling, grabbed his paws. Together, they spun around the room, her small arms holding on as her legs tried to keep up with the infectious beat. She laughed so hard her cheeks hurt.

But then, suddenly, the lights went out... The joy disappeared in an instant, leaving only the cold, harsh reality. Pain snapped her back to the present. Jeff's rough hand gripped her arm like a vice, pulling her out of the dream and into the nightmare. Madee's heart pounded, her body frozen in fear. She knew what was coming. Jeff dragged her toward the house, his face twisted with rage. The applause of the imaginary crowd turned into the silent, judgmental gaze of a jury. Annie watched, indifferent, as her daughter was yanked past her. It wasn't worth intervening. Madeleine was a lost cause, a child who would never be good enough. Laura peered from behind her dolls, her eyes gleaming as she witnessed her sister's punishment unfold.

Jeff tore off the bonnet, grabbing Madee's hair with one hand and yanking her head back. Her scream echoed in the narrow hallway. The blows came fast and hard—first his open palm, then his fists. Madee's body curled in on itself, but there was no escape. Her small arms were useless shields against his fury. Her head slammed against the sink, the sharp edge biting into her skull. Everything blurred. The taste of blood filled her mouth as her teeth cut into her tongue. She was too weak to scream anymore, her body convulsing from the shock.

"What did you do with the dog, fat girl? You looked like a damned elephant, flailing around like that!"

Madee's mind reeled. What had she done wrong? All she wanted was to dance. To feel free. The tears that she had tried to hold back came pouring down as Laura's fake sobs echoed through the door.

"Are you happy now? You've made your sister cry again. You're nothing but carrion, nothing but trouble, you fat girl. If anyone had told me I'd have a child like you, I'd have had my balls cut off!"

The final words cut deeper than the blows. They were sharper, more permanent.

"Now stop crying and go to your room. I don't want to see your face until dinnertime."

The sentence was passed. Broken and humiliated, Madee crawled to her room, each step heavier than the last. When she finally reached her wardrobe, she buried herself inside, hiding beneath a mountain of clothes, as if they could somehow protect her. The plaid ball was her only comfort, and she pulled it over herself, pressing her hands tight against her ears, desperate to block out the world. She retreated into her mind, clinging to the music.

To the songs that made her feel alive. Back to her dreams, back to a place where no one could hurt her.

*　*　*

"Suck my dick, you need to taste your shit, bitch!"

Madee's childhood refuge felt like a distant dream, slipping further away with every day of her captivity. Wayne's visits grew more violent, more degrading. His methods of inflicting pain were disturbingly creative, pushing her to the edge, further than she had ever imagined possible. The torment she'd once endured at the hands of Jeff, Annie, and Laura now seemed like a reprieve compared to the horrors unfolding in this underground hell. Wayne was killing her, slowly, methodically, breaking her piece by piece. Even the music that had once been her escape offered no solace here.

The ritual was always the same. Wayne would strip, screaming at both her and the skeleton man, snorting lines of coke before violating her. Once, twice, three times, depending on his mood. Brutal sodomies, each one longer and more violent than the last, leaving her a hollow shell. He craved her moans, demanding to hear her enjoy it, but she never did. And for that, he punished her.

He threw buckets of icy water over her trembling body, choking her with a rope or pulling a bag over her head until she was on the brink of death. The electric shocks were reserved for moments when he wanted to push her to the edge, but not too far—he needed her alive to satisfy his sick urges.

"Open your mouth, bitch!"

She was numb, her body drained of the will to resist. The cold seeped into her bones, her strength ebbing away with each assault. The skeleton man held her on her knees while Wayne loomed over her, ready to force himself into her mouth again.

"Open her mouth! This bitch isn't even trying!"

He reveled in his power, slapping her face with his cock before jamming it deep into her throat. Madee gagged, her body convulsing as her airway closed. She knew she was going to die this time. Tears welled up in her eyes as her body betrayed her, choking on her own breath.

"You like your shit... hmm... wait, I'll stick it in you some more..."

Wayne's grip tightened around her head, forcing her face into his pelvis, cutting off her air completely. She felt the darkness closing in, her body going limp, the will to fight slipping away with each second. Her eyes filled with tears, a pitiful reminder of her fading humanity.

"Boss, she's not well..."

"Is it because you're a fucking doctor that you know that? Shut up, shut up, shut up! Seconds to go... Oh yeah..."

Wayne pulled out just as she vomited a mixture of saliva and semen, her body convulsing as she coughed. He didn't care. He laughed, finishing himself off on her chest, declaring it an honor to have his cum on her. Madee could barely register what was happening, her senses dulled by exhaustion and despair. Still not satisfied, Wayne tossed her to the floor like a rag doll. He barked orders at the skeleton man to clean her up, but not before reminding her to keep her eyes open—he had something special planned for her next.

"You see me as a torturer, but you're wrong... I'm your savior, and to prove it, I've brought you a present..."

Madee kept her eyes squeezed shut, her mind reeling from the lack of oxygen, barely comprehending Wayne's words.

"Don't you like gifts? You're not a real woman if you don't. Wait until you see what I've got for you... Then you'll be grabbing Wayne's dick and sucking it with gratitude!"

Wayne moved across the room to a large bag in the corner, the Skeleton Man assisting him in dragging it over. Wayne sniffed loudly, twitching—he was close to needing another hit, but first, he wanted to show Madee just how generous he could be.

"Madee, say hello to Mummy..."

With a sickening theatrical flourish, Wayne unzipped the bag, revealing its grisly contents—a decomposing head, writhing with worms.

"Aren't you happy to see her again, Madee?"

The sight hit Madee like a blow. Her mother's necklace, the tiny diamond pendant with the initial, was unmistakable. The face was bloated, blue, barely recognizable except for the undeniable features of her mother, Annie, now rotting in front of her. Madee's heart sank. She had never imagined she would see her mother like this. Somewhere deep down, she had clung to the hope that Annie might one day come to find her, that there would be a chance to rebuild, to form the relationship they never had. That hope was now dead, along with her mother. How did Annie end up here?

A flood of doubt about Tom surged back into her mind. Could he have played her? Was he as twisted as Wayne? Did he choose her, knowing exactly how vulnerable she was? The dam broke, and her sobs came hard and fast, her restraint shattered. Wayne, thrilled by her reaction, sneered at her tears.

"Oh no, Madee's crying over her evil mummy's corpse... I didn't know you had Stockholm Syndrome... That's good news for me. It means you'll love me eventually... Oh yes, Madee, you'll love Wayne with all your heart... because I'm all you have left!"

Wayne's words echoed like a death sentence. It was true—Wayne was now her entire world. And the realization hit her like a punch to the gut, a reason for her tears that went far beyond her mother's death.

CHAPTER 17

FORREST HILL, 7 MONTHS BEFORE THE TRAGEDY...

Forrest Hill wasn't the only deprived area in the city. In terms of social decay, Earl's community was relatively fortunate, ranking only third. The media, uninterested in stories without shock value, ignored the working poor packed into crumbling homes. The real hotspot, the epicenter of crime, was North Station—the undisputed capital of the city's worst stigmas.

During the day, drug dealers occupied every corner, promoting their promise: *"A solution for every problem."* Their market thrived on easy access, with the train station serving as a prime spot for young recruits eager to make quick money. These street dealers, most of them school dropouts, occupied the lowest rung of the drug trade.

Occasionally, the police would stage raids at North Station, just to satisfy the media's hunger for a crime story. But the real addicts, confined to their estates, stayed hidden away, their lives dictated by shame and addiction. Meanwhile, the wealthier residents of the city discreetly picked up their fixes, pretending the problem didn't affect them.

Between Forrest Hill and North Station, a fragile truce existed. Despite the council's rhetoric of tolerance and coexistence, these neighborhoods were filled with families society wanted to forget. North Station, in particular, was any part of Forrest Hill not controlled by Earl. The destruction of the old swimming pool, hospital, fire station, and the two blocks of dilapidated bungalows were out of his hands. He lacked the financial resources to fight against the powerful council's housing project.

Thus, Eldorado was built despite Earl's protests—a decaying high-rise meant for those unable to afford rent anywhere else. These residents, promised temporary housing, soon found themselves trapped in a permanent ghetto. Young people dreamed of escaping, of rebelling against the systemic oppression, but over time, crime became the neighborhood's defining trait. For them, selling drugs to wealthy clients became their way of flipping off the system. Graffiti-covered walls bore slogans like *"Fuck the system"* or *"The cockroaches profit from your misery—North*

Station wins." It was a clear message to anyone who dared cross into their territory.

Earl quickly put an end to the invasion with guns and threats when the kids tried expanding their business to Forrest Hill. The most daring among them got a brutal beating from the boss of Elaine's, halting their plans to merge the two neighborhoods into one massive drug market. Urban legends about Earl's violent outbursts spread like wildfire. The young ones whispered that the cafe owner had a mafia past, claiming he'd been the ruthless right-hand man of the city's most notorious crime bosses. This myth drew an invisible border between Forrest Hill and North Station, securing peace for the community under the watchful eye of its old protector.

In the middle of it all lay an abandoned rapefield, now a strange haven of calm. On one side, a group of homeless clustered together, and on the other, Hassan's humble food truck stood. Hassan, one of the earliest residents of North Station, had been cast out of the city center when the council offered him a tiny studio in the social housing block. He didn't complain—his former life as an immigrant fleeing oppression had prepared him for the trials. Instead of giving in to resentment, Hassan rolled up his sleeves and started serving his famous spicy chicken, a small symbol of resilience in the free zone.

His cart became the only neutral ground where rival clans, dealers, and outcasts crossed paths without open hostility. Even the street dealers, hardened by the violence of North Station, stopped judging the poor folks who worked themselves to the bone for little gain. In this fragile balance, Hassan's warm smile and perfectly seasoned chicken brought everyone together in silent truce. For a fleeting moment, it seemed as if food could heal even the deepest divides.

* * *

Meanwhile, the homeless didn't bother themselves with the ongoing tensions. They had bigger battles to fight, wandering the city center in search of spare change or a warm spot for the night. That day, however, something shifted. Instead of scrounging for pennies at the soup kitchen, they lined up at Hassan's truck, drawn by the smell of roasting chicken and laughter that floated through the air.

For the first time in months, maybe years, these forgotten souls weren't treated as pariahs. They shared in the meal, drank in the fleeting joy, and as they talked and laughed with each other, the weight of their struggles briefly lifted. For a few hours, they reclaimed a bit of their lost dignity.

Standing back, Babou watched the group honour the feast. It reminded him of his own experience of abandonment and foster care. Babou didn't know where he came from and he never wanted to know the truth about his origins. He liked to say "I'm a child of the world, a foundling who finally belongs here in Forrest Hill…"

Bringing the homeless together to eat was Madee's idea. It came to her on the spur of the moment, a burst of kindness that made her forget she wasn't well. She put her own suffering into perspective by devoting herself to others. Babouconsidered Madee his first real friend, someone who shared his sense of displacement, though he could read her like a book and easily guess the reason for her self-forgetfulness. The tiredness in her eyes, the way she avoided talking about herself—he knew what that meant.

Overnight, Tom disappeared from their sad landscape; the bench he occupied every morning had been empty for a month. The familiar sight of his car pulling up outside Elaine's had vanished, leaving a void that Babou couldn't ignore.

Babou questioned Madee at least a hundred times, trying to find out why Tom suddenly left, but he always got the same answer: Tom had suddenly changed his mood and left without explanation. Each time she said it, her voice was flat, as if she had rehearsed the response to avoid emotion. Babou, however, wasn't convinced. His gut told him that there was a wonderful story between Madee and Tom, and it frustrated him that his friend didn't trust him enough to confide in him.

He watched her closely, noting how she tensed up whenever Tom's name came up. Her hands would tighten on the edge of the counter, or she'd suddenly find something to do with her back turned to him. Babou's instincts told him she was pushing Tom away out of fear—fear of loving, of being seen as vulnerable. Maybe she saw herself as unworthy, ugly, or uninteresting. He'd seen that look in people before, the quiet retreat into their own insecurities.

One day, Madee took out her tip jar, which she had hidden under the counter, and slowly, as if trying to steady her shaking hands, she counted the money Tom had left. Babou noticed how her fingers trembled slightly as she touched the banknotes, each one carrying a weight that neither of them could ignore. This money, she said, should be used for good. That was when Madee became even more devoted to the people around her.

Thankfully, there was no shortage of needy people in Forrest Hill, so Madee had plenty to keep her busy. The meal at Hassan's food truck was her latest good deed, and as Babou watched her distribute her small fortune evenly among the needy in the neighborhood, he couldn't help but wonder if she was trying to buy back a piece of her own shattered heart.

The homeless adored Miss Madee, as they called her; everyone appreciated her gentleness and kindness, but the local men also found her captivating, which added to her popularity. Even the young drug dealers at North Station couldn't help but stare whenever she passed by. Yes, Madee was beautiful, though she refused to hear it or accept it. Babou often listened to her repeat that she was abnormal, that happiness was only reserved for the beautiful and popular girls.

From the start of their friendship, Babou had tried to change her mind about herself, to show her what everyone else saw. But the subject was taboo. Madee remained anchored in her maraboutage and her distorted self-image.

Not only did she denigrate herself, but Babou had also watched helplessly as she slowly destroyed herself by starving her body. Madee found excuses to avoid food—claiming she wasn't hungry or had already eaten. Her waistline was shrinking, and her cigarette consumption was becoming worrisome. Babou hated it, watching her fade away while her inner light, paradoxically, shone so brightly to those around her.

No matter what she believed about herself, Madee was radiant and present. Her energy glowed in a thousand colors, even when she tried to fade into the background. Saving others made her feel alive, even if she never admitted it. It was her way of asking the world to forgive her for existing, for what she believed to be her *"mistake of nature."*

With kindness and spontaneity, she moved among the homeless, listening to their stories, encouraging them to eat more chicken. When she was sure they were full, only then did she return to sit beside Babou, placing a tray of potatoes between them.

"The meal of friendship! You've earned your share," she said with a soft smile.

"You know, I hope you'll help me finish it, dear," Babou replied, trying to sound playful.

Madee said, lighting another cigarette to hide behind "I had a good breakfast this morning... as usual,"

"Madee, I'm worried about you..."

"Don't be silly, Babou, everything is fine," she answered, her words quick and dismissive.

Babou watched her inhale deeply, the smoke from her cigarette filling the space between them like a barrier. He wished he could grab her by the shoulders, force her to see herself through his eyes, shake the demon that had latched onto her until it let go. But he knew better. She was trapped in a cycle he couldn't break for her. He glanced at the plate of untouched potatoes. They had cooked together a thousand times, yet they never shared a proper meal, never laughed over a glass of wine or simply enjoyed the food they'd prepared.

Their friendship was lived in a different way, bound by their unspoken understanding. Babou longed for more, but he knew that until Madee found peace within herself, they would remain suspended in this strange, almost melancholic, bond. Babou loved Madee too much to be truly angry with her, but he didn't know how to help her. He had thought about asking Earl to intervene, but the old man was anything but a diplomat. Madee would lose her temper and never speak to him again... Babou decided to give in and postpone the discussion for another time. The best thing was to get back to work and maintain their good relationship. He cleared his throat and stood up; the break was over, and duty called. Madee crushed her cigarette butt into the ashtray, and after a warm goodbye, they went back to work. As they discussed the success of the meal, they walked arm in arm. Madee was proud to have put all the money to good use.

"If I were rich, I could spend my days helping others," she said, her eyes sparkling with joy.

That was Madee, always finding little ways to create joy for herself and savor it... Babou was touched by all the love she had to give.

"Madee, are you feeling better?"

She stopped talking, instinctively arching her back and bowing her head. Babou knew his friend had taken the question as an accusation. Madee was still cautious, always on guard, afraid of doing the wrong thing...

"I don't know what you're talking about, Babou..."

"I know you well, and I see you're avoiding the question again. Let me rephrase: has spending the money made you feel any better?"

"I didn't deserve it..."

"So, you thought that by giving it away, you'd make Tom disappear. Because according to your reasoning, you don't deserve him either, right?"

Madee stared at the ground, her cheeks reddening in embarrassment. She felt exposed. Even though she was angry with him, Babou knew he had to continue.

"Once again, you think happiness is only for others, Madee."

"Tom... that's in the past..."

"Why did he leave?"

"I told you, after our visit to the school, he started acting strange, got in his car, and drove off. I'm not hiding anything from you, Babou. That's really what happened! I didn't throw him out if that's what you think... Life goes on... He's not the first guy to leave me behind... They've all done it to me... Spending the tip money is just my way of warding off bad luck... Turning sadness into joy..."

"But you're not cursed, Madee!"

"Yes, I am. And this curse will follow me until the day I die! I couldn't be happy, even if I wanted to... The problem isn't them, Babou, it's me!"

Babou hadn't known she was so superstitious. Now, he was sure Madee wasn't hiding anything about Tom's departure. She simply couldn't understand, so she preferred to blame herself—it seemed more reassuring that way... How could he help her? They entered the shopping street just as Babou was asking himself this question when the answer appeared before his eyes. He recognized the car parked in front of Elaine's all too well...

"Sweetheart, forget about your curse stories and look straight ahead... It looks like life is giving you a second chance!"

CHAPTER 18

LAURA'S DIARY: A TURNING POINT

Honestly, some people might say I'm crazy. But I say I'm a visionary. After all, how could they ever understand what it's like to shape the perfect love?

Before I continue with my story, I'd like to remind you: I'm not responsible for putting this on paper, and I'll say it loud and clear — I'm innocent! It doesn't make me a bad person to have a dream and do everything I can to make it come true. My ambition is simply misunderstood. Anyone in my position would do the same thing. Most people pride themselves on being like St. Thomas, believing only what they see. But me? I'm like St. Michael, defeating the devil. I'm a strategist defending a noble cause.

I always had the power at home by adjusting my plans and modulating my story. There was no question of eating dinner or going to bed early — I imposed a 'rock' rhythm of life. Dinner couldn't start before 8:30 p.m., and bedtime? Never before midnight. My parents had to understand that an artist's hours are different, and they had no choice but to adapt.

I had to pretend Brandon was coming over several times just to make sure these rules were followed to the letter. They were so proud to welcome their daughter's future husband. A famous future husband, that is. When Brandon didn't show up, I made up absurd stories: He was afraid, or impressed by my family, or his production team forbade him to see us. Once, I even cried and told them Brandon's car had been rigged with a bomb. He was in the hospital, between life and death. Obviously, the media kept it quiet — Brandon's fame had that kind of power. The fact that there was nothing about it online? Of course, it was all part of the cover-up.

The suspense never ended, and my family was captivated by the tragic plot twists I created. It cast me as the brave daughter, the one forced to endure all these terrible trials. Honestly, I loved the suffering. Making myself miserable suited me. Brandon changed my life; thanks to him, I finally felt alive. But more than that — he couldn't be anything other than exactly what I was shaping him to be. I know him better than he knows himself. Sure, I love his physical appearance and the prestige of his career. But beyond that, Brandon is my masterpiece. He's my glamorous version of Frankenstein. Some say I created him. I say I perfected him. He's perfect for me because I built him that way.

As for my mother, Annie? She's even more in love with Brandon than I am. I've turned her into a zombie. She's living out this twisted fantasy — a love triangle between her, Brandon, and me. And Jeff? The blonde? They're pawns. My subjects in a kingdom where I rule. They do my bidding, even if they don't know it yet. I can boast that I'm living the rockstar life. But let's be honest — I'm not just living it. I'm running it.

Mum and I are living it up. I told her that Brandon had taken advantage of our absence one day to install micro-cameras all over the house. He wanted to keep an eye on his little wives in their everyday lives. Annie, thinking Brandon was eavesdropping, started standing in front of the kitchen fan, talking to the wall.

Later, I'd mimic everything Mum said, pretending to be Brandon, in our fake phone calls, where I was the only go-between. I kept the act going, phone glued to my ear, making my fake call to "Brandon" five times a day... Jeff once tried to catch me by checking the phone bill, but I got away with it, telling him Brandon used an encrypted number like all the stars do. Annie's insistence that he leave me alone made him back off, but I could feel Jeff was about to snap, and my peace of mind was on borrowed time.

Some days felt long, but Mum and I kept busy. We talked about our plans, took erotic photos, and got into the habit of kissing each other on the mouth... It shocked Jeff and the blonde. Those losers didn't get it; in rock, there were no limits. Living rock meant living outside the lines, doing what's forbidden...

Jeff and the blonde had to play along with my fake phone calls. Officially, Brandon wanted his whole family with him, even from afar. Unofficially, it was my ego demanding an audience. Those calls were the backbone, the moments where all the plots unfolded. You should've seen Jeff's face when Mum started talking about sex, convinced she was talking to Brandon. He went white when he heard his wife telling her imaginary lover she dreamt of being taken doggy-style or giving him the worst blowjob of his life... You could tell by Annie's frustrated eyes that she'd shut Jeff out for a long time...

The one thing I could never get Mum to do was film herself masturbating. I have to admit, I would've loved to see her fingering herself while moaning Brandon's name. It would've been a great moment. But no, despite her desire to rock, Annie still had her puritan streak...

And what about the blonde? When I wasn't "calling" Brandon, Mum and I would hound her to pass the time. The psychological pressure never let up. Madeleine had to do all the dirty work because Mum refused to lift a finger. She handled everything, solved every problem. And when things went wrong, it was all her fault, even when she did everything right... I had to spice things up a bit, so I told Brandon he had caught her masturbating on camera, just to make her feel ashamed of her non-existent sex life!

Being rock means doing damage, and this bitch was primed to take it all, so I had the right to have some fun. But my extravagant lifestyle came at a price... Jeff was running out of money!

No more shopping sprees, no more restaurants, no more gourmet meals... He was no longer of any use to me, so I started to push him out. Honestly, I didn't have to do much... Mum wanted a divorce. It was great news, except Jeff took it really badly when she broke the news. He started yelling, accusing me of being rotten, of ruining their lives, and tried to convince Mum to get out of this madness. But of course, she didn't listen... Annie loved Brandon too much, she needed him just like I did. She was set on the divorce.

That's when things shifted. Jeff didn't stop there—he cut himself off and started plotting with Madeleine. This new alliance pissed me off more than I could express. The two of them had become a tag team determined to take me down. After everything I had done to them, their need for revenge was understandable... It was now Annie and me on one side, Jeff and the blonde on the other... The tension in the house was suffocating. I used the fake calls to charm Mum, talking as Brandon to twist her mind further. Her hatred toward Jeff grew each day, and I knew a showdown was inevitable.

And sure enough, the fight came. That's when I played the role of Archangel Michael. Mum spat venom at Jeff, accusing him of everything under the sun, and again demanded a divorce. She thought she had all the leverage with "Brandon's" supposed intel, but Jeff hit back, recounting Brandon's public life from the past few years... That bastard just wouldn't shut up... I could see Mum cracking, calling Jeff a liar, but there was no conviction in her voice. If I lost her, my life was over. Madeleine, that little bitch, watched in horror. Jeff knew so much about Brandon because of her!

Mum looked at me, needing reassurance that Jeff was lying. No, of course he wasn't telling the truth! Brandon was with us, he loved us... Mum, the only one who always saw perfection in me... It all unraveled fast. A fit of hysteria overtook me, and I lunged at Jeff with everything I had. I had to shut him up. I managed to push him down, jumped on him, and squeezed, squeezed, squeezed... I watched his eyes roll back... I squeezed harder... I screamed at him to die, to rot in hell...

One final squeeze and it was done—he was dead. I closed his eyes and stood up. That's when Mum realized the enormity of what had just happened. She panicked... I slapped her to snap her out of it... The blonde was ashen, terrified out of her mind... I threatened her, telling her if she spoke or even moved, she'd meet the same fate as her fucking father...

The priority was to protect myself. Killing someone wasn't that hard—I didn't get why people hesitated. When I killed Jeff, I felt like I was draining his life force, and it filled me with energy... It was exhilarating, a fuck you to the moral code of this shitty, hypocritical society! I'm rock, and I'm proud of it! I was risking prison for what I'd done, but breaking the law was so easy... I shook Mum. She had to cover for me—after everything I'd done for her, she owed me. A hundred times over!

Annie cried. I couldn't understand her tears—she should have felt relieved. Why mourn a man she hated? I had to be gentle with Annie, unlike the blonde, whom I'd abused without a second thought. I explained that what I did was necessary because Brandon had confided in me just days earlier that he had proof Jeff had embezzled money from him to support a new lover. Still reeling from that revelation, I let my anger get the best of me when Jeff started tarnishing the purity of our love...

Suddenly, Annie's tears stopped. She stared at Jeff's lifeless body and cursed him one last time. In the end, I was right. Losing Brandon, who truly loved us, was unthinkable. Jeff had been a lying, cheating bastard his entire life—the complete opposite of our Brandon...

We locked Madeleine in her room so she wouldn't witness what was happening. Mum called our GP, an old man who stubbornly refused to retire. His memory was fading, and he often mixed up his patients' illnesses. The moment he arrived, Mum started spinning a tale about her late husband's heart problems. Jeff never had heart issues, but a well-delivered story works wonders... Mum could have been an actress, she was that good!

The old doctor didn't doubt a word she said, even embellishing the story, claiming Jeff had overworked himself. He didn't even bother to examine the body. To him, it was clear: Jeff had died from a heart attack! Without hesitation, he signed the death certificate. A natural death due to the patient's negligence in taking his medication...

To lift our spirits, the old man launched into a series of anecdotes that never happened. He insisted Annie call him if she needed anything. As a thank you, Mum slipped him a wad of cash and asked him to keep everything discreet, counting on his silence. For him, this was a given—part of medical confidentiality, the oath he'd sworn to uphold: the patient, living or dead, always came first! He assured us he'd have the undertakers come to collect the body, and that all Annie and her girls had to do now was mourn. It was a close call, but I did it! For Brandon's honor, I had to. I'd worked too hard for one stupid mistake to ruin everything... Now I could move on. And sleep soundly!

CHAPTER 19

LAURA'S DIARY: A NEW BEGINNING...

Arriving in the city center was a rush. We had to clear the ground quickly after Jeff was buried. The neighbors whispered about Annie Mitchell's husband's sudden death... What had happened to Jeff, that solid, hardworking family man?

Gossip spread like wildfire, even after all these years. At first, people believed my parents without question when they told them I was going to marry Brandon. But time wore them down... All those assholes started giving me sideways looks when we went out, their minds made up: I was just a nasty, mythomaniacal brat. I couldn't stand their warped opinion of me. No, I'm not a pathological liar or crazy—I'm just in love with someone I haven't met yet. And what's so wrong with that? Who gets to judge what's right or wrong?

Anyway, Mum and I couldn't stand the curious onlookers who stopped outside our house, gawking at "the widow's home." There was so much whispering in the congregation at the funeral. People pointed at me like I was some kind of criminal... I wanted to wipe them out, one by one, as they paraded past to offer their fake condolences. The hypocrisy was unbearable... None of them even liked Jeff. They came out of spite, out of jealousy, just to see us suffer... Most of them didn't even speak to me. They avoided me like I had the plague. And it was all because of the blonde... That bitch kept quiet, kept to herself, and that's all we'd asked for... Mum and I warned her before the ceremony that if she said a word, she'd regret it. So why did all the neighbors swarm around her like bees to honey? They all had some comforting gesture, some kind word... I don't care! Wasn't she tired of playing the victim? Why didn't she just tell them to fuck off?

At first, Mum didn't want to leave the house. Jeff had taken out life insurance, but the idiot screwed it up again—the payout was far below my expectations. Mum said it was enough for us to live in our bubble until Brandon arrived... But I had my own needs! On top of that, things were getting too tense with the neighbors. I couldn't risk staying in that suburb any longer. A change of scenery, running away—that was the solution!

Mum is a creature of habit. Despite her stories of an exciting youth filled with travel and parties, she liked her comfort zone. But I had won on one front: Brandon was now her entire world, her only promise of salvation. It was a privilege for her to finally be loved by a man of quality, and she wasn't shocked by the virtual threesome I'd been feeding her. Sharing a man with her daughter felt normal, and she even went so far as to say that Brandon could only be happy because he had both youth and maturity by his side. I was afraid that a nosy neighbor might destroy all my hard work. So, I had to get away, leave it all behind. It was a delicate move, but I pulled it off... Thanks to Brandon. The power of this man works miracles!

"He" was sending messages to Mum through me... The usual routine: to get the message into Annie's head, I pretended to be him. Mum had always seen herself as an extraordinary person, envied by everyone, so I had to craft something powerful enough to make her leave her home. The strength of my lies was in creating a life filled with intrigue, conspiracy, and victimhood. Annie thrived on drama, and the one I was building in my mind was sure to delight her! I felt like I was becoming part of Brandon by pretending to be him. Without flaws, he was the perfect man every girl dreams of—the kind-hearted Prince Charming, with no real personality, entirely devoted to his bride. So "Brandon" told Mum that Jeff's death had completely changed our situation. Jeff used to keep up appearances, but now his staff was giving our threesome dirty looks. It would be a scandal if our story got out. All I had to do was pretend to be scared and convince Mum that our lives were in danger if we stayed in the house. I even told her the producers wanted to get rid of us because we were becoming a problem... Annie became more paranoid than ever... She imagined snipers on the rooftops of neighboring houses, ready to shoot us the moment we stepped outside...

It amazes me how much trust can be built on simple promises. I saw the effects of my psychological manipulation every day, but now... I was shaping Brandon's "speeches" however I wanted. He had to be the brave knight again, ready to protect his "little women" after the devastating news. Mum was to take a flat in the city for now, but it would only be temporary until she could move into the one he'd bought for us. An invisible bodyguard would handle our safety... So, Annie agreed to move. She envisioned herself as powerful, on the cusp of the privileged life she'd always dreamed of... I was safe, my secret was intact! I'd won again, and the neighbors could go to hell...

The plan was in motion. All I needed was to find an apartment in the city center. I wanted comfort and luxury, a stunning place worthy of a magazine spread. With the insurance money, I thought it would be easy... I was wrong!

The real estate market was brutal, something I hadn't anticipated. I naturally guided Mum to the main streets, but the rents were sky-high, and the landlords were picky. I was furious that no one would rent to us!

Mum didn't work, and her income wasn't enough... Any excuse was enough for those bastard landlords to say no! I refused to lower my standards—Brandon didn't belong in a slum! That bitch Madeleine dared to suggest that Brandon should just find us a place since he was so powerful and generous. I wanted to kill her! But what did she care? And to make things worse, Mum agreed with her... Mum sided with the blonde? This wasn't right—it needed to be fixed immediately!

"Brandon" told Mum that she was on her own and that he couldn't help because of the enemies holding a grudge against us. We'd have to sacrifice and go underground if we wanted to reunite quickly... My story was worthy of a spy thriller... Mum unconsciously loved it; small-town nobodies didn't get to have adventures like this. So, the suffering was worth it. The reward would only be greater...

The atmosphere in the neighborhood grew tense as the days passed. I needed to save myself from impending embarrassment... I suggested Mum check out the holiday rental ads. I'd seen online that some landlords offered short-term lets. On a classifieds site, I finally found the perfect place... The owner was heading to his country house for two months but was afraid of burglars and wanted someone to occupy the flat while he was away.

Everything was arranged over the phone, and in exchange for a cash payment, the place would be ours the following week, with a meeting scheduled for the day of our arrival! Mum was euphoric—we had done it, and Brandon would be thrilled! The only problem was Madeleine, but since I still needed her for what was coming, I swallowed my hatred. I had the rest of my life to torment her... The flat was fully furnished; there was no point in cluttering it with useless memories. I convinced Mum that it was time to leave the painful past behind us, to embrace a new life, a new happiness. That meant erasing Jeff...

Annie complied. I took charge of going through Madeleine's things and gleefully tossed everything she cherished into the trash. The bitch cried and begged to keep what she loved... But her tears were useless; she had to sacrifice, to shut her mouth! To be on the safe side, Mum and I locked her in the bathroom without hesitation...

There was another problem: the dog! Bernie, the blonde's little friend... The damn thing pissed and drooled everywhere... I tried to get rid of him, claiming he was ruining the owner's carpets, but Madeleine rebelled. I had never seen her so angry. She even threatened to go to the press if I took her dog. The bitch had been quietly building her case against me, despite everything I'd done to her... I gave in on Bernie. He could come, but his mistress would have to pay me for it... Mum bought me the new StarCall 1 to celebrate our new life. The ultimate phone, expensive and exclusive. With internet access at my fingertips 24/7, I had the perfect tool to keep Annie locked in her fantasy world... It was an adventure living in the city center. I was convinced I'd meet Brandon by chance, he'd fall for me, and I'd finally introduce him officially... I hated all these setbacks; I couldn't wait to become all-powerful and finally get my revenge!

But there was a dark cloud hanging over our arrival. When we saw the flat, it was a crushing disappointment. The street was fine, but inside... My heart still bleeds thinking about it... It was a complete dump! Even Bernie could have caught fleas in that filthy hole!

MYTHOMANIA

Mum and I cried, but we had nowhere else to go. Renting another place was out of the question—it was like an impossible obstacle course, and we were stuck in this nightmare. Madeleine (her again!) decided to go shopping that very day, as if to add to our misery. Since Mum and I were too devastated to leave the flat, this was a rare moment of freedom for her. She came back from the supermarket with one of those free magazines filled with special offers and recipes... I wasn't suspicious—I let Mum take a look... I should never have lowered my guard. It almost destroyed everything... Mum started crying, becoming hysterical, saying, "I want to go home." When I saw the double-page interview with Brandon, my heart sank!

He was talking about his upcoming world tour, his new band members, and how happy he was to be back with his fans... I had been telling Mum for months that Brandon was sick of his career, living in seclusion, refusing to work, waiting for the moment when we could finally live our love out in the open... If he ever had to appear in public, his team would use a lookalike or a hologram to make it seem like he was there... I felt terrible. Absolutely terrible!

Annie had her doubts, and that blonde bitch opened her mouth to say that the family had been fooled, that Brandon had never been a part of our lives. That we'd been duped by some teenage fantasy!

I looked Mum straight in the eyes, indignant, and swore I had no proof other than my good faith. With all the heartache I'd endured, that should be proof enough that I wasn't lying. It was our first fight in the new flat: I pointed at Madeleine and accused her of being in cahoots with Brandon's producers. I screamed that I was the victim of my bitch sister's schemes. I shouted that she'd known what was in the magazine and brought it back to hurt Mum and me, that she'd already destroyed our happiness. That had a magical effect on Mum. She grabbed a knife from the kitchen drawer. Her eyes bulged with fury as she unleashed her rage on Madeleine. She threatened to kill her if she ever messed with her sister again. She walked over to the blonde, pressing the knife against her stomach. It cut right through her clothes...

I stopped Mum, playing the part of the good little girl, and punched Madeleine twice. I held her down and hit her as hard as I could... To assert my supreme authority, I grabbed her slutty hair and ripped out strands of her blonde locks. She cried, but I screamed at her to shut the fuck up, wishing her nothing but misery for the rest of her life... We locked her in the bathroom to calm her down, and Mum and I went out for a meal to forget about the whole mess. It was sweltering... The rules were still the same as they had been in the suburbs: no going out except for essential shopping. No television, but they were allowed limited internet access under my supervision. Mum was never allowed to forget that we were in constant danger!

The big change was Madeleine: Mum declared that from now on, the blonde would take Jeff's place and financially support the family. When Madeleine dared to ask if I was going to work, Mum scornfully replied that Brandon Stevens' wife was never going to be seen working as a supermarket cashier or restaurant waitress. No, I was destined for a grand wedding, not menial jobs. She kept reminding Madeleine that I was in danger and needed to stay safe at home. I piled on by saying that Brandon had told me a thousand times that Madeleine didn't need to worry about the threats—she meant nothing to our future! We were keeping her out of charity, nothing more... I was contradicting myself, but I didn't care... I'd make Mum drive the knife into her gut if the blonde dared raise her voice!

We lived off the last of Jeff's money while waiting for that idiot to find a job. Our savings dwindled fast. So much so that Mum had to pawn her jewelry just to get by. And then there was the problem with the apartment! We were in a precarious situation... We'd have to move out when the landlord returned from his holiday. As for Madeleine, we'd handed her a list of homeless shelters. With that, she shouldn't have any trouble finding a place to sleep... As for us, going back to the suburbs or begging in a soup kitchen was out of the question!

Luckily, I rummaged through the "landlord's" belongings—I'm not one to lack resources. At first, I couldn't find anything useful, but persistence paid off: the guy had been subletting the place to us for a small fortune from the start! I let Mum sink her claws in. She reported the tenant to the rental agency where he paid the rent, crying fraud and breach of trust. Three lonely women at the mercy of a fraud—it was the perfect setup to get the real landlord, who had favored honest tenants, to respond...

One piece of good news followed another, and once the housing situation was sorted, Madeleine found a job as a waitress. Since we'd moved to the city, the blonde had started rebelling more often, reacting to my attacks, and hitting her was no longer enough to keep her in line. If she had money in her hands, she'd leave—she'd run away from us, and I forbade it!

She began losing weight again... The older she got, the more beautiful she became, and that was an insult. No, her money was ours... I edited Mum's bank statement to add the blonde's name because I was skilled with digital tools. Her salary came directly to us, and we used it however we pleased... When the blonde was allowed to go to work, she wasn't allowed to talk to her coworkers, make friends, or go out after her shifts. There was zero tolerance for any delay—we knew exactly how long it should take her to get home! One argument followed another, but I always won. It livened up the house and isolated her even more.

Complain to anyone? No way! People would tell her to leave this toxic environment, saying she was crazy to stay, and that's what they put in her head. That she was just a jealous, disturbed lunatic. Mum and I spent all our time making her understand that her only way out was through us, and that when Brandon arrived, he would declare her dead. Despite her rebelliousness, she was depressed. This cunt dreamed of a normal life, of finding love... She could keep dreaming!

She borrowed self-help books from the library, meditated, wore protective stones, and prayed for a way out...

Did she really think she could escape the blocking energies I'd cast on her? Her worthless talismans wouldn't protect her. It was easy—every time she tried something, I called in the energies to make her fail! She cried and cried. One day she'd kill herself, but in the meantime, she'd be my whipping girl forever.

Enough about that cunt—you're giving her too much importance! How did I spend my days? I watched talk shows on my phone. But most of my time was spent on social media. All my old schoolmates were there, all the people who had humiliated me... I took my mother's maiden name and called myself Laura Wilkins, just to be safe. I didn't want the Mitchell name anymore—it meant unhappiness, shame, and association with Jeff. Why carry that burden when I'd never liked my father? Wilkins sounded prettier, more glamorous... Mrs. Stevens-Wilkins, Mrs. Wilkins-Stevens...

Soon, I discovered you could reach out to celebrities on social media—they were all there! This was going to be a great help in achieving my goal and getting closer to Brandon! Meanwhile, I realized it was possible to become popular online, far beyond my physical location, but I needed friends to do that. I took some suggestive photos of myself—I looked hot—and signed up for a dating game. It was called "Sexy or Ugly," and all you had to do was scroll through users' photos and rate them. I got a lot of likes and friend requests, mostly from guys who wanted to fuck me. I might consider one of them later... But for now, I needed an attractive profile to keep my new "friends" and encourage more to invite me. I had the looks, but I needed to be "perfect" inside too, to make my fans dream. I openly mocked the blonde and her self-help bullshit, but I noticed people loved it. All these sheep, searching for meaning, thought they'd find the answer to their unhappiness through yoga or mantras... Pathetic! But it wasn't a bad idea... Self-help was synonymous with confidence, kindness, and goodwill... I was already the beautiful, unattainable girl, so if I took on the blonde's personality, beliefs, and tastes, I would succeed!

I started by posting quotes from books, so my followers would see I was both original and sophisticated. Then, I began filming myself. In short videos, I gave advice on well-being and self-care. I was simple and smiley on camera, just what people expected from me. The beauty of social media is that people don't know you, so you can invent your life, and they believe every word. They think you're lucky and don't have problems, so they follow you, hoping for a 1% chance of being like you... The more I exploited people's mistakes and their bullshit, the better it worked... My visibility kept growing...

I took the opportunity to start going on dates. I couldn't stand the forced isolation anymore, so I let Mum believe that the danger surrounding the family was easing, and that I was seeing Brandon for some personal time... My dates, however, were strategic. I only went out with people from the entertainment industry to try and make connections. It wasn't about the romance—I was hoping to meet someone who could lead me straight to Brandon. Once I got what I needed, I'd leave all those guys behind. I viewed it as a way to test my ability to charm. These encounters helped me gauge my appeal, and we always parted on good terms. I kept them in my circle, building my network, and my popularity just kept growing... Soon, I'd make our dream a reality for Mum and me.

CHAPTER 20

LAURA'S DIARY: BE BEATEN AT ONE'S OWN GAME...

The blonde is gone! After everything we've done for her, that bitch has the nerve to betray us! To just leave us... so easily, without a single explanation... I wasn't worried—why should I be?

Madeleine was too broken to leave for good. She radiated fear and anxiety, there was no way she could stray from the path she had trapped herself on. I was always right—her feeble attempts to defend herself were futile. Seeing my growing success on social media, I allowed Mum and the blonde to create profiles. The only condition was that I added them to my friends list so I could monitor their posts. I didn't have to worry about Mum—she trusted me blindly and lived between two worlds: reality and Brandon. She liked playing virtual games and didn't interact with anyone except to like my photos and shower me with compliments. But the blonde... I had to be cautious with her!

I tried to read between the lines, drawing conclusions from every quote she posted. To me, they were constant jabs, disguised cries for help, attempts to undermine my credibility. She was jealous of me, but I always turned her pathetic weapons against her. I used her personality to get attention, and for my growing community, I had become exactly what I wanted: the perfect, beautiful, pure-hearted woman. The first rule in dealing with an enemy: strike first. I complained all day about the blonde's lack of personality while she was at work. Madeleine copied everything I did because she was so envious. She couldn't stand being the eternal loser, the last one picked, the girl no one noticed... Mum listened to me sympathetically—after all, she was my only audience. My image as a kind-hearted soul would've been shattered if I attacked the blonde directly on social media. Brandon's fans wanted a mass-adored companion, not a vicious manipulator. By embodying pure goodness, my place would never be threatened... Stars follow what their fans want, and if our relationship sells, Brandon will stay with me!

Men liked the blonde, despite her intelligence. Of course, the guys on the internet aren't exactly the cream of the crop. Ninety-nine percent of them just want sex, but that's no reason for them to start hitting on Madeleine!

Every time I saw a comment where a man called her beautiful, it was like a knife to my heart... Madeleine wasn't allowed to be in a relationship with anyone!

I took control after I found her password. I sent rude messages to the creeps who couldn't understand why "Madeleine" was suddenly acting the way she did. The internet is disposable—these guys didn't waste time on a girl they could never sleep with... One click and they moved on. Their dicks called them to other, more cooperative women... Another issue was that the blonde had joined groups about narcissistic abusers. When I dug into her account, I found out that this bitch was trying to betray me, expose me!

The members of those groups were nothing but weaklings. They spent all day crying about the abuse their *"pervert"*inflicted on them. Depressed, they sought validation and compared their tormentor's behavior to their own misery. Everyone agreed they should leave. But none of them did. These bastards thrived on suffering, satisfied with their misery until something new came along. I've never believed in the concept of a victim, and what I saw confirmed it. All these weak-minded fools should be grateful—they're lucky to have a "torturer" interested in their pathetic lives... What would they be without us? Could they ever live a normal life, full of love and trust? No!

Where ambitious people seek fame, they are nothing but trash, fully aware they will never shine. On the golden platter of social evolution, they lay down their souls. What's more, the system is perfectly designed. What these so-called *"victims"* call psychological harassment is nothing more than persecutory delusions, obsessions, masochism. Proof? The only domestic violence anyone takes seriously is sexual violence!

I'm not a narcissistic pervert... I'm jealous, ambitious, and I won't let anyone outshine me, that's all! You have to eliminate the undesirables to conquer humanity and the world... And I'm the only one who's truly suffered! No one can claim they've suffered as much as I have, sacrificed as much as I have!

The blonde was becoming harder to live with. And this virtual influence wasn't helping her... She started asking for money, wanting to go out, buy new clothes... What's next? Her ego was inflating by the minute. But I didn't give up—I kept putting her down, kept mocking her, kept making her feel guilty, and yet, I had less and less power over her... More than once, she mentioned seeing a psychologist, talked about family toxicity, even a lawsuit... Mum and I used to call her crazy, and it used to make her cry—now it didn't!

I threatened her with Brandon's wrath. She laughed and called my love the invisible man. She looked me dead in the eye and calmly said that Brandon Stevens didn't know me, so I could shove my threats because my power was microscopic... I lashed out at Madeleine during our last argument. But then, she lunged—her hands around my throat. The bitch fought back! I still can't believe it... Not only did she have the audacity to lay a hand on me, but she told me that one day all of this would turn against me, that I'd pay for my cruelty, my lies, and my actions... Who did she think she was? A bitch! I didn't need any lessons from her! Too bad for her—the role of avenger had already been taken, and I'm the only one qualified to judge and direct.

For two weeks, she didn't speak to Mum or me. It was unsettling. Normally, we were the ones who shut her out of everything. But now, she held her head high and kept her lips sealed, her demeanor dignified... She'd come in, take a shower, put on her headphones while I pretended to call Brandon, and go to bed when we left the living room. While she was away, I kept telling Mum that Madeleine was creating a bad atmosphere and that Brandon didn't like knowing his little women were so unhappy. Mum suggested we pack Madeleine's bags and kick her out, but I was against it. How would we live without her wages? Losing our income was terrifying, but I still couldn't stop giving her hell... It didn't matter—Madeleine had returned to the indifferent girl she'd always been... None of my drama got to her anymore.

One night, she didn't come home. As usual, Mum and I watched the clock, waiting for her to walk through the door so we could scold her. Five minutes, ten minutes, an hour... I called her mobile, straight to voicemail... After a hundred calls, Mum and I gave up when we realized the blonde wasn't going to answer... She left us high and dry, the bitch could've at least said goodbye. I was furious she was slipping away, just like that, in silence... The only way I could picture her escaping was through death... Death... But yeah, maybe she was just dead... Mum and I split the calls to the hospitals. None had admitted a "Madeleine Mitchell" that evening...

Mum wanted to call the police, but I got angry—it made no sense! I didn't want the police involved in Madeleine's disappearance; she'd blab about Brandon, Jeff, and everything she'd been through if they got to her... As a last resort, I had Mum call her workplace. Her boss answered. The moment Mum introduced herself and started playing the role of the loving, concerned mother, the boss interrupted. Madeleine had been fired the morning before for using a false bank ID and covering up a scam.

Labour inspectors had come to check everything, going through all the staff and payroll records. They found an anomaly in one of the files—financial fraud hidden as work. The company received a minor fine since it was a first offense, but from that moment on, the boss was under scrutiny. An unknown employee had been receiving a salary. The accountant discovered: Annie Wilkins.

After investigating, they realized that Madeleine hadn't received a single penny for her work because her salary had been going to the infamous Annie... Mum tried to claim her daughter was mentally ill, but the woman wouldn't hear it—she knew Madee and knew she wasn't dishonest. Before hanging up, the boss threatened to sue us if we didn't leave Madee alone... Let the bitch keep her money—it wasn't even enough to buy a luxury handbag!

And that's how she slipped away... Sneakily... I wished she'd just killed herself, ended her suffering... After such a betrayal, which was hard to bear, I needed some consola-

MYTHOMANIA

tion... The hospitals have our number, and I'm waiting for the news of her death... I'm waiting...

CHAPTER 21

FORREST HILL, 7 MONTHS BEFORE THE TRAGEDY...

Tom had practically made a second home out of the empty lot where he parked after leaving Forrest Hill. He, the rich man's son, was no better than the homeless who lingered around Hassan's food truck. A detached wanderer, aimless and lost, he didn't belong anywhere. After a month's absence, he showed up at Elaine's that afternoon. A long, endless month during which he tried to slip back into his meaningless life. A whole month playing the role of "Collins' bitch," a persona he couldn't shake since he was 18. Yet, his thoughts were consumed by Madee... He had convinced himself she'd be there, waiting impatiently for him, by the seductive pull and arrogance of the old days. But finding Earl busy decorating the stage was his first disappointment. Tom dared to ask where Madee was, to which the old man replied with an annoyed, hurried, *"Madee is busy outside."* No matter, Tom decided. He'd wait, whether Earl liked it or not.

Madee arrived moments later, more beautiful than the last time he'd seen her, arm in arm with Babou. No warm greeting. She walked right past his table without even a glance.

"Did you think she'd hug you?"

Earl was watching him closely while polishing the old disco ball. Tom looked up, realizing he was the only customer left. "Yeah, I'm talking to you! What do you want with Madee?"

"Just... talk."

"Talk? To waste her time, bullshit her again? Madee's got better things to do than deal with some little prick like you!"

"It's clear you don't like me, but you're not Madee's mouthpiece! I just want to apologize..."

"Apologize? Shove it up your ass!"

The old fart shook his fist, threatening to grab his bat and show Tom what he could do. Tom was stunned and tried to laugh it off, but if Madee hadn't stepped in between them, it might have escalated. She kissed Earl on the cheek, thanking him for defending her, and her presence calmed them both. Sensing the tension, she pretended to have an errand and took Tom outside. It was better to separate them before things got out of hand.

Alone on the street, Tom started thinking about how to explain his absence to Madee. It wasn't so much about justifying himself, but a desire to be honest with her. However, their conversation was interrupted by locals asking about the evening's theme. Some wanted Madee's opinion on what they'd prepared for dinner, while others just stopped by for a quick chat. The neighbors shifted the conversation.

Forget the awkward argument with Earl—Madee simply asked Tom how he was doing before talking about the community dinner being held at Elaine's that night. She included him in the preparations as a way to break the ice and reintegrate him into the group... sparing him from the explanations she knew he wasn't ready to give yet.

Still, Tom wanted to prove himself. He didn't want Madee to see him as just some jerk playing with her feelings. To show his sincerity, he offered to pay for the entire community meal if needed. Madee smiled; she didn't think it was about money. The remaining errands were no more than ten bucks. If Tom wanted to understand Forrest Hill, he'd have to follow her and let her guide him—because she was taking him to a place he wouldn't forget...

At the entrance to the district, they wove their way through streets lined with abandoned buildings. The same streets that had terrified Tom on his first visit. But Madee showed no fear. She moved with purpose, unbothered by the grime and decay. Tom couldn't help but wonder if she had already figured him out. Maybe she was leading him to some squat full of heroin addicts on the brink of overdose, ready to lecture him about how he would end up just like them—alone, strung out, and hopeless.

"Madee, where are we going?"

"Trust me."

"But... are you sure it's safe here? What if we run into drug dealers or thieves?"

"Tom, the dealers are at North Station! They don't come here. Earl made it clear they're not welcome in his territory. There are no customers for them in Forrest Hill. At best, they'll sell a little weed... nothing more. And as for thieves... well, here we are."

She stopped in front of a building with a soot-covered grey façade and an intricately carved baroque door. After three firm but respectful knocks, the door opened to reveal an old man, his face lighting up at the sight of Madee.

"How nice to see you, Madee, my daughter! You should've told me you were coming. I would've prepared some tea for you and your friend."

"Don't worry, Father. We won't stay long. I just wanted to show Tom the heart of Forrest Hill."

"Come in, my children, make yourselves at home. Madee, I can rest easy now that I know you're here."

"Take care, Father Andrews. I've made a raspberry cheesecake, and I hope you'll join us for dinner tonight."

"I'd love to, if my rheumatism gives me a break. God bless your generous heart."

MYTHOMANIA

Father Andrews settled back into his chair with some effort, barely noticing as the two young people slipped through the doorway. They walked down a narrow hallway, lined with display cases filled with artifacts from around the world. The Koran, a cross, and the Star of David stood side by side with African masks and pagan deities. Photos of a much younger Father Andrews showed him standing beside wells, schools, and smiling locals, no doubt from his missionary days, offering hope to the hopeless.

Tom was overwhelmed. This old building, with its calm and peaceful atmosphere, felt like it was stealing the air from his lungs. A longing washed over him. He wanted to sit beside Father Andrews, to listen to him speak of faraway lands and ancient wisdom. To rediscover the dream he'd had at eighteen—of adventure, of purpose—through this man of God...

Tom joined Madee, who was waiting by the door. She unlocked it and stepped aside, letting him enter first. He found himself in a large room with rough stone walls, lit by hundreds of flickering candles. The faint smell of dampness was masked by the scent of pontifical incense, which lingered in the air. Tom looked up at the starry ceiling, where God, Allah, and Yahweh sat hand in hand, surrounded by halos of white and gold in their divine union. On the floor, cherubs pointed the way, leading visitors to the naked wooden cross of the crucified martyr. In the back, four powerful archangels illuminated Christ, accompanying him in his final trials on earth.

All the secrets, joys, sorrows, and hopes of the people of Forrest Hill seemed to be kept in this holy place, around the rows of pews and under the flickering candles and urns overflowing with papers.

"Madee, it's..."

"Shhh! Let's sit, okay?"

Tom suddenly felt very small among these divine giants, and they sat together on one of the benches. Madee took his hand, squeezing it tightly.

"As you can see, Father Andrews has faith not just in God, but in mankind too."

"Madee, this place... it's beautiful."

"You know, Tom, I don't talk much outside of work. I'm not great at communicating. But here... I can express myself in silence. There's always someone who listens."

"Madee... I'm sorry I didn't come back sooner."

"Let's not talk about that now. Let's just take a moment."

With her hands still clasped together, Tom watched as she closed her eyes. He wasn't comfortable with the ceremony, maybe because he feared the judgment of the divine figures above. But for Madee, it made perfect sense. If humans couldn't forgive themselves, maybe the love of the gods would be strong enough...

The rest of the afternoon was great... until they went to the grocery store and Madee introduced him to Scott. Tom immediately noticed the way the shopkeeper looked at her. This guy wasn't just interested in friendship. The way Scott's eyes lingered on the beautiful blonde was unmistakable. He puffed up his chest, acting as if he wanted to run Tom out of town to claim Madee's attention. Tom hadn't realized Madee had an admirer in the community, and it bothered him more than he expected. He'd naively thought he held a special place in her life... As they left the shop, his mood darkened. It was a reminder that even God's good news couldn't fix everything. Madee didn't seem interested in Scott's flirting, but Tom's insecurities took over. When she asked him to stay for the community dinner that night, he responded coldly, his voice sharp. He refused and ran off again.

* * *

He didn't get far; the wasteland stretched between Forrest Hill and the main road. As usual, he parked the convertible on the side, letting his mental torture run its course. He fought the urge to snort his dose too soon... Madee and Scott... So unlikely, yet somehow logical. They lived in the same neighborhood, shared the same friends. Earl accepted Scott, which was more than he could say for Tom. The thought of Madee with someone like Scott gnawed at him. What could Tom offer her? Nothing. But Scott... Scott could offer stability. A routine. He could marry her, have children with her... The image of that man touching Madee drove Tom mad with jealousy.

"Still thinking about her?"

The snide voice came from the passenger seat. As if by magic, Wayne appeared and vanished. Wayne was no longer part of Tom's life, but his disturbed mind conjured him up anyway.

"My little bitch Collins, talk to your brother..."

There it was again, that nagging voice. Tom clenched his fists. He wanted to be alone, didn't need a hallucination to push him deeper into despair.

"Why chase after that girl? They're all dying to fall into your arms..."

"Shut up! Don't you have someone else to haunt?"

Tom had fallen into the trap again. Every time, he promised himself he'd be strong. But the truth was, he was just a weak, broken man with no willpower.

"Forget her, bro..."

Annoyed, Tom glanced over at the passenger seat. Wayne was still wearing the same clothes. A detail that reminded him this wasn't the real Wayne. The real Wayne cared about his image—changing his outfit several times a day to stay cool at all times...

"Never wear casual clothes in the morning, Collins... You always need to look fresh, like someone with a busy schedule. Tracksuit bottoms and a T-shirt are only acceptable if you're actually going to work out. But if people see you, it's fine. After 1 p.m., you can lose the blazer and unbutton a couple of shirt buttons. And after 4 p.m.? Jeans are allowed. The day's nearly over, so you can indulge a little..."

Tom listened to Wayne's endless fashion rules—how to look sharp, 24 hours a day. It brought him back to the day the tailor made him his first suit.

"It was for your own good, bro. Without me, you'd never become a man of the world…"

"How are you reading my thoughts?"

"Have you forgotten? We're bound by fate. The invincible never die, never separate…"

The wicked smile on Wayne's face never faded. He fed off Tom's suffering, drawing energy from his brother's pain.

"Forget her, brother… She's just like all the others. Probably screwing the grocery boy while waiting to get her claws into you…"

"Stop it! You don't know her! I don't…"

"Oh, I know. You're falling in love… But love doesn't exist, Collins. It's a mirage. Like that powder you've got stashed in the glovebox…"

Images flashed through Tom's mind—Madee and Scott together. The knife of jealousy twisted deeper into his chest. Wayne whistled the tune Babou had sung earlier, the melody haunting and cruel.

"What do we do to calm the storm, bro?" Wayne pointed to the glovebox. "A little brotherly high and all your problems disappear. Just the two of us… We've never done it alone. Get the coke, Collins."

"Get away from me! You're nothing."

"I'm everything, brother. Just like this world. Be a man, Collins. Get the coke."

Tom struggled. He knew one dose wouldn't be enough. He wanted to prove Wayne wrong, to prove he wasn't as weak as Wayne thought. But the pull was strong, and his resolve was crumbling.

"You're no angel, Collins! Everything we did together… All those girls… Let's enjoy what time we have left. Your waitress—Madee—you think you love her, but it's just guilt. You're trying to redeem yourself. But in the end, it's the drugs you love. And right now, while we talk, I bet she's with the grocer, laughing at you…"

Tom's anger flared. He reached out to grab Wayne, but his hands closed on empty air. He couldn't touch him.

"Coke, brother… Coke…"

Maybe Wayne was right. Maybe Madee was playing him. They all seemed innocent at first. What was the point of fighting? He was a worthless piece of shit, and he always would be.

"Yes, that's it. This will be the best high yet, brother."

Tom had no limits. He wanted to feel his body explode, to think of something—anything—other than the jealousy tearing him apart. Wayne disappeared, leaving him alone. Tom poured all five bags of coke onto the passenger seat. The acrid burn of the powder in his nose was drowned out by the scent of leather. Heat flushed his body, spreading from his chest to his fingertips, where his hands began to tremble uncontrollably. His legs felt numb, as if pins and needles were shooting through his muscles. His heart raced, and he lost all sense of place.

Sweating, exhausted, he tore off his jacket. His hands trembled so violently he could barely control his movements. His vision blurred, black spots creeping into the corners of his eyes. Each breath felt shallow, like the air was too thick to fill his lungs. His stomach churned violently, and he vomited into the remaining powder, the acidic taste mixing with the coke. His mouth was dry, his throat burning, but the taste of bile and cocaine clung to his tongue.

His heart pounded in his chest, faster and harder with each beat, as though it might explode. Sounds became muffled, distant—he couldn't tell if what he heard was real or just the blood rushing in his ears. His whole body felt like it was slipping away from him, each muscle moving of its own accord. For a moment, panic seized him. He knew he was losing control. He wanted to call for help, to scream, but his throat tightened, and the words stuck. Sweat poured down his face, mixing with the vomit on his shirt.

His legs wobbled, and he stumbled out of the car, barely holding on. Drenched and trembling, he staggered through the dark. His vision narrowed, and the cool night air couldn't reach his lungs. His heart raced out of control, each beat hammering against his ribcage. He gasped for breath, but nothing seemed to fill his chest. He wouldn't make it...

* * *

There was a festive atmosphere at Elaine's. The community's monthly meals were always filled with laughter and warmth, offering everyone a chance to forget the stresses of work, life, and money. The old cafe buzzed with conversation, and after the main meal, a dessert buffet was set up for those brave enough to indulge after their starter and main course. Madee's pastries awaited them—her famous chocolate cake with raspberry cream was a favorite, especially among the children.

As she sat near the window, watching the kids devour her creations and listening to Babou's rich, soulful voice, Madee allowed herself a moment of peace. Once a month, Babou traded his chef's hat for a microphone, fulfilling his dream of singing in front of an audience. His warm voice filled the room, each word and note steeped in emotion. Madee loved how Babou lived every chord, every lyric. She always encouraged him to share his talent with the world, to take a shot at fame. But Babou resisted.

"If I went pro, my music would lose its soul," he often said. "It wouldn't mean the same if I had to do interviews and post on social media. Here, in Forrest Hill, I can express my creativity by comforting people through food and music."

"You have a thousand ways to be happy," he would tell Madee. "It's up to you to choose the one that suits you."

Babou had found his balance, and in turn, he'd helped Madee find hers. Thanks to him, to Earl, and to the rest of the community, Madee had come alive again. She could enjoy her passions and listen to music, something she hadn't done since Joe... Forrest Hill had become her refuge, a place free of judgment and betrayal, where she could finally feel safe. Her migraines, stress, and chronic pain had disappeared. She was learning to express herself without fear.

MYTHOMANIA

As Babou sang, she didn't notice Betty Harrison take the stage. The old neighbor, still nimble despite her years, performed a few graceful dance steps, a reminder of her days as a revue girl at the Music Hall. Madee smiled, wishing Tom had been there to see it. His presence would have made the evening perfect.

But after their trip to the grocery, something had shifted in Tom. He had withdrawn, refusing to come to dinner. Madeecouldn't understand his mood swings—one moment he seemed fine, the next his head was elsewhere. He was running, but from what? She didn't dare ask, knowing the weight of keeping secrets herself. It wouldn't be fair to push him if he wasn't ready to talk. She forbade herself from growing too attached to him, trying to protect herself from disappointment. But his absence left her feeling hollow. Even in the midst of laughter and music, she couldn't shake the melancholy that clung to her.

As the evening wore on, she felt the urge to retreat, to be alone with her sewing machine, where her hands could work and her mind could be free of distracting thoughts. Rising to say her goodbyes, she glanced out the window and noticed Eddy and Dave standing outside, waving. It was strange—they were usually the first to come inside for a meal, but never this late. Why hadn't they come in? Jazz, Eddy, Dave... They all knew they were always welcome.

Having spent so much time with the homeless, Madee had learned to read their signals. They communicated with gestures, a survival tactic from the streets. And Eddy's frantic hand movements—his fists pumping in the air—meant one thing: emergency. Madee rushed outside, her heart pounding as she saw Tom lying unconscious on the pavement. Eddy and Dave were panicking, talking over each other, but Madee quickly realized they had found him near the wasteland and brought him here. Doc had taught her how to handle emergencies, but she had never imagined her first real case would involve someone she cared about. Pushing her emotions aside, she ordered her friends to carry Tom into the cafe.

As soon as they entered, she shouted for Doc. The room fell silent, all eyes on her as they saw Eddy and Dave struggling with Tom's limp body. Doc grabbed his briefcase and hurried over. Earl, ever the leader, clapped his hands and announced the evening was over, sending everyone home quickly.

Seeing Tom like that made Madee's stomach churn. She felt sick, her composure slipping. Doc noticed her panic, and his voice softened as he spoke. "Madee, I need you to stay calm. I need your help. Focus on Tom, not on your fear. He's the priority now."

Eddy and Dave hovered nearby, nervously explaining what had happened.

"We found him by the dump, Doc. His car was parked nearby... He was already out cold when we got there."

"I checked the car too," Dave added, hesitating. "At first, I thought he'd been mugged by the North Station scum, but no... um... I'm not sure I should say this in front of Miss Madee..."

MYTHOMANIA

Doc kept working, unphased by their hesitations. He carefully examined Tom, his face grave.

"Madee, fetch me a vial and a syringe from my case, please."

Madee did as she was told, her hands shaking as she handed him the items. She dreaded what was coming next, but she had to hear it.

"I'm afraid this will only confirm my diagnosis..." Doc began gently, his eyes full of concern. "Madee, are you ready for this?"

She feared the worst, but she nodded. She had no choice.

"The City Prince is on drugs..."

Dave turned red with embarrassment, glancing at Madee. He didn't want to hurt her, but the truth was unavoidable. Tom's condition spoke for itself.

"Overdose," Doc said, his tone grim. "It explains the erratic breathing, the sweating, and his weak pulse."

He could see the worry etched on Madee's face. No one could hide anything from Doc.

"He's in a bad way, dear... I've given him a shot and administered first aid, but it's going to be a long, difficult night. I'll take him to the clinic."

"No!" Madee said sharply. "We'll take him to my house. It's closer!"

"Madee, that's not a good idea... At the clinic, I can keep an eye on him the whole night."

"We'll take turns watching him. He's coming home. I'll take care of him."

Doc hesitated, his eyes softening. "If he pulls through, he's going to rehab, Madee. It's what's best for him."

"Let me take care of him tonight," she insisted, her voice stronger than she expected. "Please."

The room fell silent. Five pairs of eyes turned toward her, surprised at the intensity in her voice. Madee couldn't believe how determined she was, how sure she felt. Tom wouldn't be in this state if she had pushed him to talk about his unhappiness. She blamed herself, her past weaknesses, her quiet acceptance of her family's horrors. For Tom's sake, she would never give up again. Doc sighed, giving in. "Alright, sweetheart. Babou, Eddy, Dave, take him to Madee's house carefully. I'll head to the pharmacy and bring back everything I need. After that... it's in God's hands."

* * *

Tom felt completely drained. He couldn't remember anything, didn't know where he was. All around him, the desert stretched endlessly, not a soul in sight. The sun beat down on him mercilessly, burning his skin, yet despite the searing heat, his body shivered. His jacket was gone, leaving him defenseless against the icy cold that rattled through his bones. His only option was to dig—dig and dig deeper into the sand, burying himself. Maybe he would find warmth in the depths, maybe he could await death in his makeshift grave... or perhaps a miracle.

Flashes of Madee bending over him interrupted his efforts. Her lips moved, but no sound reached him. He let himself sink further into the sand, pulled toward the center of the world... When Tom opened his eyes, the desert had vanished. He was lying in a soft bed, wrapped in white sheets that smelled faintly of laundry detergent. The cold was gone, replaced by the warmth of a thick duvet. Somewhere nearby, the scent of warm bread and pancakes lingered in the air. The room around him was small, modest, with one door and one window facing each other.

He wondered if the sand had led him here—to some kind of waiting room for the condemned, where a redeeming angel would appear and offer him an ultimatum: live or leap. But the room was far from supernatural. The furnishings were simple, almost homely. Two small bedside tables, carved from white wood, stood on either side of the bed, each with an art deco lamp. On the right table, he noticed his wallet and watch neatly placed.

The rest of the room was filled with tastefully chosen furniture. A massive wardrobe, reminiscent of oriental cabinets found in flea markets, loomed against the wall, alongside a chest of drawers topped with a large mirror framed in gold. Three wise monkeys—see no evil, hear no evil, speak no evil—decorated the top. A cheerful collection of trinkets cluttered two small shelves: African giraffes, a small wooden carousel, statues of Shiva and Ganesh meditating quietly among black, white, and gold elephants. An angel holding a lily seemed to offer a promise of renewal. On the curtains, a vibrant jungle scene depicted a panther lazily resting on a branch during the hottest hours of the day.

Whoever lived here saw the world beyond the ordinary path.

"You're awake!"

The voice pulled him from his thoughts. The angel was none other than Madee, who entered the room quietly. She looked like a teenage heroine, dressed in high-waisted jeans and a candy-pink sweater. Her appearance, so light and carefree, made Tom's heart skip a beat.

"How are you feeling this morning?" she asked softly.

The question confused him. His mind was still clouded, struggling to piece together the fragments of what had happened. Madee approached, sensing his agitation, and placed a calming hand on his shoulder.

"Eddy and Dave found you by your car, unconscious," she explained gently. "They brought you to Elaine's, and Doc took care of you. Then we brought you here... to my house. Doc and I took turns looking after you through the night."

Reality hit Tom like a punch to the gut. Gone were the fleeting dreams of redemption. Everything came rushing back—his jealousy over Scott, his insecurities, the ghost of Wayne, and the cocaine he had snorted to numb it all. He felt a wave of shame crash over him. Madee had seen him in the lowest state imaginable, teetering on the edge of death from an overdose.

Doc must have told her the truth, and Tom wished desperately that she had learned it some other way—any other way. If only he had had the courage to tell her himself. He opened his mouth, trying to find the words to apologize, to explain that he wasn't the broken man she had seen the night before. But Madee wouldn't let him.

"I've asked Jimmy, our local mechanic, to collect your car from the wasteland," Madee said softly. "He's happy to help. He'll keep it in the garage while you recover, and he promised to have it serviced and cleaned for you. Oh, and... I had to undress you to get you into bed. Your watch and wallet are right there on the bedside table. I didn't go through your things, but your wallet fell out when I took off your trousers... Nothing's missing. You can check if you want."

"Madee! I would never think of accusing you of stealing," Tom replied, a little stunned by her comment.

"I'm poor, you're rich... I just don't want that kind of misunderstanding between us. We had to act quickly last night, and... well, the circumstances."

"Madee, I'm so sorry... I wanted to tell you, I was just... scared."

"Now I know. But I'm not here to blame you, Tom. I have no right to do that. We all have our demons to fight. You need to rest now. We'll talk about it when you're feeling better. Doc will be here soon to check on you and discuss what comes next. I made you some breakfast. Just make yourself at home. It's not much, but you'll find everything you need. Doc will bring you some clothes so you can change later."

"Thank you, Madee."

"You're welcome." She smiled, glancing at the shelf filled with her collection of statuettes. "Oh, and you're safe here. My treasures will protect you."

Madee's face lit up as she proudly gestured toward her beloved figurines. Tom could see the faith she had in them. Her belief, so innocent and pure, was endearing. He knew it would take more than the gods of the universe to fix his mess, but somehow, Madee's certainty gave him hope, even if it was fleeting. With the quick, shy kiss of a child, she leaned forward and kissed him gently on the forehead.

"I'll be back later during my break," she promised. Doc entered just as Madee was about to leave.

"Hello, Madee. I knocked, but you didn't hear me, so I let myself in."

"You did the right thing, Doc," she replied. "Make yourself at home. Boys, there's food in the fridge if you need anything. Call me if you do. See you later!"

The room felt colder as soon as she left. Tom was suddenly aware of how much he already missed her presence, her warmth. Doc was still there, of course, but it wasn't the same. He knew the old doctor would get to the heart of the matter—Tom's shameful reality. The whole community probably knew by now. After all, the homeless had found him and brought him to Elaine's, which meant everyone had seen him at his lowest.

People probably wondered why someone like him—a man with everything—would choose to self-destruct. And Madee... how could she not be shocked? Yet, here he was, lying in her bed. The bed she might share with Scott.

The thought twisted in his gut. Doc watched him quietly, perhaps sensing that Tom needed a moment. Then, deciding the rest had lasted long enough, he opened his briefcase and took out his stethoscope.

"How's my patient today?" Doc asked, his tone light and cheerful.

Tom had braced himself for a lecture, but it never came. He was surprised by Doc's calm demeanor. In his youth, Tom had rarely gone to the doctor. He'd never had any major health issues, and the few doctors he had seen had always been cold and distant. But Doc was different. He took his time, examining Tom with care, his movements precise and efficient, his focus unwavering. Doc wasn't like the high-priced doctors who saw patients as little more than dollar signs. He was hands-on, used to dealing with the unexpected and the extreme.

"Heart rate's good. Blood pressure normal. Reflexes are fine," Doc said, his voice steady. "Everything looks encouraging, but I think we should do some follow-up tests, just to be safe. We don't want any complications sneaking up on us. Madee's done a great job, though. She's a Master of Emergency procedures."

"Madee?"

"I've been teaching her a few things," Doc explained. "Sometimes I don't have enough help at the clinic, so she's picked up some skills. When Eddy and Dave brought you to Elaine's, she's the one who brought you inside. She did everything right until I took over. She's a good girl, that one."

Tom swallowed hard. "Doc, do you think... do you think she blames me for not telling her about my problem?"

Doc considered the question for a moment.

"I can't speak for her, son. But I can tell you this—she's the one who insisted on bringing you here. Until last night, I'd never set foot in this apartment. The only one from the community who comes here is Babou. So no, I don't think she blames you."

Tom's ridiculous jealousy made him feel even more ashamed. Doc had no reason to lie to him. If Madee didn't let even her closest friends into her home, there was no way she was welcoming Scott into her bed...

"She's got you, buddy! That bitch is strong!"

Wayne's voice slithered into Tom's thoughts. He glanced around the room, and there was Wayne, lounging on the dresser, sneering.

"This decor sucks. It's like a brothel in here. I told you to forget it... but no, you just had to throw yourself into the lion's den! You're so damn naive. That old fart of a doctor's full of shit..."

Wayne moved around, his fingers grazing the trinkets on the shelves.

"Look at this garbage—a collection of little superstitious shit. Like the good Lord cares... He didn't make us to believe in Him. He made us to win! And none of this crap is gonna save you, Collins."

With a swift, careless motion, Wayne grabbed the angel with the lily and smashed it to the floor.

"No! Don't touch that! Get away from me! Leave me alone! Stop following me!"

Tom's voice cracked as he struggled to get out of bed, but he didn't have the strength to stop Wayne. He could only watch in horror as the angel lay shattered on the floor, its delicate wings broken, the lily crushed beneath it.

"Bad luck, my bitch..." Wayne sneered, his voice dripping with malice.

Tom felt tears sting his eyes. All he could think about was what Madee would say when she saw the destruction. She'd be furious, throw him out, and he'd lose her forever.

"Tom! Tom! Calm down, son!"

Doc's voice broke through the chaos. He leaned over Tom, gripping his shoulders firmly, his voice steady and reassuring. Tom struggled, his mind still focused on the broken angel, on the peace that seemed forever out of reach. He wanted to get back in his car, plunge his face into the powder, and let the sand swallow him whole. He could almost feel the water rising in his throat, threatening to drown him from the inside. But Doc was still there, talking to him, grounding him. "It's going to be all right, son. I've got you."

"I broke the angel. It's my fault... I'm bad luck."

"It's over now," Doc said gently. "You're going to feel better in no time."

Doc's calm voice began to break through the fog, and Tom closed his eyes, trying to focus on the only steady presence in the room. He mumbled that he needed a broom to clean up the pieces. He didn't want Madee to be angry with him. He didn't want to leave. He had nowhere else to go.

As the weight of his exhaustion settled over him, his desire for the powder slipped away. His eyelids grew heavy, his body sinking deeper into the mattress. He could no longer move his lips, no longer fight. For the first time in what felt like forever, he allowed himself to drift into sleep—a sleep where, for now, Wayne couldn't reach him.

* * *

Doc remained calm. He had seen the devastating effects of drugs too many times to count. There was little he could do but watch helplessly as the cravings took over. He administered medication to Tom, substituting one substance for another to appease the demon that would return regularly over the next few months. For Tom, this was just the first of many battles. Now, locked in a war with himself, his withdrawal had begun. Only time would tell who would win.

Doc's thoughts drifted back to his own mother. A seemingly normal woman who drowned her pain and paranoia in illegal substances—no one would have guessed. The first time he saw her use cocaine, he was five. She thought she was alone in the kitchen, taking a moment for herself to escape the monotony of being a housewife.

From his hiding place, Doc had watched her cry as she prepared dinner, only to pull a bag of powder from beneath the sink, draw a line on the cutting board, and snort it quickly. When she caught his eye, she had scooped him into her arms and hugged him, saying that Mommy just needed her medicine to feel better. Her tears dried up, her face brightened with a smile, and soon, she was laughing.

But when the "medicine" wore off, she forgot to pick him up from school. When he found her at home, sprawled on the couch, she didn't recognize her son. She thought he had broken into the house. So Doc would give her the "medicine," and sometimes, he'd be the one to fetch money from the jewelry box to pay the strange man who brought the bags. His mother called him "the chemist" and swore her son to secrecy—she didn't want the neighbors to know she was sick.

As a child, Doc had admired what he saw as his mother's strength. He had been there for every overdose, right up until the last one, the one that took her life. Too young to understand that his beloved mother, Ethel, had a problem, there was nothing Doc could have done to save her.

Drugs became the catalyst for his calling. He wanted to save lives. Doc spent years studying addiction, diving into the psychological mechanisms behind it. He even created his own detox protocol, which he tested voluntarily at drug rehabilitation centers. The results were promising, and Doc felt confident in the validity of his thesis. But the medical establishment didn't share his enthusiasm. His colleagues scoffed at him, telling him to stick to standard treatments.

Disheartened, Doc gave up his passion and went where he was truly needed. He turned to humanitarian medicine, treating anyone who asked for help. During his missions, he faced the horrors of war-torn countries, the massacre of innocents, famine, and poverty. He saw both the cruelty and the miracle of life as he tried to save those who were dying or watched as they recovered against all odds. Each experience only enriched his expertise, though he knew he was capable of more.

Back home, he turned down prestigious job offers. Traditional medicine had laughed at him, and he refused to compromise his values to join a system he didn't believe in. So he settled in Forrest Hill, dedicating himself to the small community. In his spare time, he continued perfecting his alternative method of treating addiction, all while living his remarkable human story.

Doc felt too old to believe he could change a world that no longer made sense to him. Despite prevention efforts, drugs were now a trendy pastime, consumed as easily as any other product. Who would listen to an old man who still thought he could detox users in denial, convinced they weren't addicts?

He glanced at Tom, now asleep. Doc had immediately liked this polite, modest young man. Beneath the marble facade and fine suits, Doc saw an intelligent boy in search of something real. His addiction didn't seem to fit his character. What could have driven him to self-destruction? In his delirium, Tom had said he had nowhere to go... Wealth didn't shield anyone from tragedy, but what was Tom's tragedy?

Listening, understanding, helping to release what was hidden... Doc was convinced that his therapy could work on someone like Tom. The withdrawal wouldn't be easy, but he could be clean in record time. It meant Tom would stay in Forrest Hill for a while longer. Perhaps he'd opt for treatment at the clinic, or perhaps he'd return to his old life.

Then there was Madee... There was undeniable chemistry between her and Tom. They got along well, but the girl had her own struggles to face. Doc was already helping her with her eating disorders and insomnia, but could she find the strength to fight multiple battles at once? He worried that the feelings growing in her heart might shatter under the weight of Tom's detox. Love was so fragile...

Tired, the old doctor let his patient sleep and went into the kitchen to make coffee. He smiled when he saw the tin of shortbread on the table—one of his favorite treats, especially the ones with orange zest. He admired Madee's ability to think of everything, even in the midst of a storm. That girl had something for everyone. Next to the tin was a note saying that Tom's breakfast was in the fridge.

The kitchen was small but well-kept, everything in its place and logically organized, just like the rest of the apartment. Doc hadn't explored the whole place, but what he had seen reflected Madee's need for security and stability. Apart from the issues he was helping her with, Doc didn't know much about her. During their conversations, Madee had shared very little about her life before Forrest Hill.

Whenever Doc asked about it, she skillfully deflected, talking instead about the books she was reading. He had tried to unravel the mystery, to encourage her to confront the wounds she kept buried, but she kept certain doors locked tight. Madee ate little, worked a lot, and kept herself on an intense schedule. Her involvement in last night's events made it clear that she was more attached to Tom than she let on. The young woman's fragile balance could easily be shattered by disappointment or grief.

The aroma of fresh coffee filled the kitchen, and Doc felt its soothing effect. Why dwell on the worst? Light often shone brightest in adversity, and only God knew the plans for each of them. His role now was to help his patient, to ensure Tom made it through. That was what God wanted from him, and that was enough. God's secrets were not for him to question.

* * *

Tom woke with a start, unsure how long he had been asleep. It was still light, and from the brightness in the room, he guessed he had been out for an hour or two. His mind immediately went to the broken statue, wondering how he would explain it to Madee. He didn't dare look at the shelves. She'd never believe such an absurd story—ghosts didn't exist.

And Doc... he was probably already at Elaine's, warning Madee about his deteriorating mental health. Tom didn't want to seem crazy, but he also didn't want to lie. He would tell the truth about Wayne, no matter how ridiculous it sounded. Gathering his courage, Tom finally glanced at the shelf. To his astonishment, the angel with the lily stood there, untouched and proud. The messenger remained whole, transmitting its power through time and space to those it chose.

Something stirred deep inside Tom, something he couldn't explain. A new resolve. He wanted to heal. He wanted to be free of drugs forever. The powder, the excess—it disgusted him now. The broken angel symbolized the end of his old life, the life he'd lived under Wayne's shadow, a life of sex, aimless wandering, and inherited expectations. This was his chance. He had to take it. Tom would finally discover who he was.

Pleased to see his patient awake, and making no mention of the delirium, Doc poked his head through the door.

"How are you feeling?" he asked.

"My head's playing tricks on me, Doc..." Tom admitted.

"It'll pass," Doc reassured him. "You're going through a tough period, but it'll get better soon."

"Doc... am I going to make it?"

"When did you start using?" Doc asked.

"I was 18..."

"Then you're experienced! If I can give you some advice, it's this: you know drugs. They don't surprise you anymore. They don't give you any illusions. You can look at them for what they are, with full awareness. That's why it'll be easy to let them go. Take it one day at a time. Madee will keep an eye on you tonight, and tomorrow you'll be free to go to the hospital and choose the treatment you want."

Tom withdrew into himself. He had thought Doc would suggest he stay in Forrest Hill, but his last words were clear: tomorrow, he would be leaving to seek treatment elsewhere. He didn't protest when Doc mentioned other patients; he just wanted to be left alone. Tom wanted to create as many memories as possible, knowing he might never return to Madee'sapartment.

Before leaving, Doc handed him his mobile number and some pills in case of another attack. He advised Tom to eat and rest, and reassured him that if anything happened, he'd be there in no time. Tom listened absently, already thinking of the hours he'd spend alone until Madee returned. In his eyes, the doctor was no longer a friendly figure—just an obstacle to overcome. He wondered if Madee knew what awaited him. He had to talk to her as soon as she came home. He had to plead his case at all costs...

He was surprised he had managed to stand at all, though his first steps out of the bedroom were shaky. A bag of clothes had been left for him beside the wardrobe, and the community had done their best to provide something for him to wear. But his height was a disadvantage. As Tom sifted through the items, he noticed most of the trousers were too short, and the T-shirts too tight. The only outfit that seemed to fit was a pair of navy-blue tracksuit bottoms and a yellow sweatshirt with a hot chocolate brand mascot on it. He laughed when he saw himself in the mirror. Strangely, he felt good dressed like this. It made him feel like the wild teenager he used to be.

Tom went into the bathroom to freshen up. It was the smallest bathroom he had ever seen. A blue mosaic adorned the corner walk-in shower, and an antique washbasin served as the sink on the same side. There was only a toothbrush in the cup, which brought a smile to Tom's face. Doc wasn't lying—Madee really did live alone. The bathroom contained only the essentials, though it was unmistakably feminine with its mosaic tiles and carved mirror frame. Without unnecessary frills or extravagance, Madee seemed content with just what was useful for her hygiene and beauty. Tom had imagined her spending hours getting ready, perfecting her natural charm, but this wasn't the case. Madee was satisfied with what she had.

The apartment wasn't very large, so after a quick look around the kitchen, Tom moved into the living room to eat. There was so much to take in that his attention quickly shifted away from the large plate of pancakes. The living room was the heart of the apartment, a spacious square with a single window facing the building opposite. Positioned by the window, where the light was best, were Madee's sewing machine and a dress form wearing an unfinished garment. Bright prints and colorful fabrics adorned racks of clothes scattered around the room.

Brushes, paints, glue, and glitter were spread across the dining table alongside vases, plates, and broken bric-a-brac. A life-sized picture frame leaned against a large leather trunk. Beneath the glass, an image of an old-fashioned funfair displayed candy stalls and archery booths. Children laughed as they rode the merry-go-round and bumper cars. At the center, the Ferris wheel carried passengers skyward in its colorful gondolas, towering like the matriarch of this boulevard of dreams.

No technology—no TV, no stereo, no telephone—just books. A turquoise wooden bookshelf overflowed with them, with more stacked on the floor, patiently waiting to reveal their stories. Tom wanted to touch everything, to study every detail, to understand the decor, this extension of Madee's personality.

On the wall opposite the sofa, a painting of two African goddesses offering jugs of water to heaven and earth captivated him. The white, purple, blue, and gold in the painting were an ode to the beauty of life. Tom felt transported, as though he were part of the infinite cycle of the universe. The same emotion he had felt the day before at Father Andrews' came flooding back. His neglected heart felt at home, part of something larger. Tom realized he didn't need to travel the world. His ideal was here.

He picked up the book lying on the coffee table: *Vita Nova by Dante*. The worn cover suggested it had passed through many hands before ending up with Madee. The corners were torn, and the pages well-used. Flipping through, Tom noticed notes scribbled in the margins and highlighted passages. Which ones held meaning for Madee?

"And when they asked me, 'Who did you spend all that love on?' I looked at them with a smile and said nothing."

Beside this sentence, in Madee's handwriting, were the words: *"Session with Doc, 11 November."* Tom closed the book and pressed it to his chest. Dante's words became Madee's, and Tom took them as a declaration of love, though he wasn't sure. She looked at him with a smile and said nothing. Just like him—silent, keeping her inner world hidden. Madee lived hers in the alleys of a funfair, vibrant with music and neon lights, while Tom let drugs destroy the silence of his own. She said nothing... Pulling the leopard-print throw from the armrest, Tom lay back on the sofa. He smiled and said nothing, holding Vita Nova against his heart.

* * *

As he devoured a giant candyfloss, his cheeks sticky with sugar, the little boy marveled at each of the rides. He'd never been to a funfair before. Too shy to try the merry-go-round and too timid for the loops of the roller coaster, he contented himself with watching the families enjoying their day.

A little blonde girl, about his age, was also alone. The boy thought about offering to share his pink candy with her, but he wasn't sociable enough to do it. He followed her along the sandy path, not wanting to lose sight of her. She stopped in front of the caterpillar ride once, and then later at the lottery booth. The boy kept his distance but stayed close, his curiosity growing.

While a magician was turning handkerchiefs into doves, the little blonde girl disappeared into a tent. The audience erupted into applause. The boy scanned the crowd for her almost-white blonde hair but couldn't find her. Then, dressed in a blue bodysuit and a sequined top hat, she reappeared on stage. The boy edged closer. The next trick was the highlight of the show, and the magician asked for silence. With only her head sticking out of a box, the little girl stepped inside.

The magician held the audience in suspense for a moment before grabbing an axe and lifting it high. A spotlight shone on the boy, and the magician winked at him. Before the boy could scream, the sound of the axe slicing through the girl's head filled the air. Tom wept helplessly as the crowd roared with laughter, watching the girl's head roll across the stage. He tried to escape, but a group of old women surrounded him, pulling his hair, while men stomped on his candyfloss...

"No! No! Stop it! Leave me alone! The head, the head... The magician killed her..."

A hand gently caressed his cheek, and Tom recognized the soothing voice speaking to him. Back in Madee's apartment, Tom opened his eyes. Madee was sitting on the edge of the sofa, wiping his forehead with a towel.

"It's all right... Take it easy... Just breathe," she said softly.

"Madee! You're finally here!"

Tom hid his face, not wanting her to see him cry, and threw himself into her arms.

"It's OK, Tom. Just breathe, relax. You were asleep when I got home from work. Doc said it might happen, but it's over now."

Madee's calm voice helped bring him back to reality, easing the terror of the nightmare. There had been no magician, no trick, no decapitation. The little blonde girl still had her head. Madee encouraged him to take deep breaths, to clear his mind.

"The worst is over now... You're safe, Tom. You need to eat something—you haven't had anything today. But nobody can resist my pancakes! And I hope my cannelloni will make you proud."

Tom lied, saying he was fine, though he didn't want to be left alone. He followed her into the kitchen. The table was already set, and Madee was pulling a dish from the oven. The smell of cheese-crusted cannelloni made Tom's stomach growl. He sat down at the table as Madee served him a generous plate. She didn't take any for herself. Anticipating his question, she smiled and explained that she'd already eaten a sandwich before coming home.

"Enjoy!"

"Are you sure you don't want to eat with me?" Tom asked.

"I'd rather not," she replied.

Tom noticed a momentary flicker of unease on Madee's face. Apparently, he wasn't the only one struggling with inner conflicts. While he devoured the gratin, she settled for coffee and a cigarette. Watching him eat made her smile again, and they made small talk, carefully avoiding the delicate subjects that hung between them.

"Dessert? I saved you a slice of chocolate cake and cheesecake!"

Tom thought he was full, but the temptation was too strong. Madee was spoiling him, and he wasn't sure he deserved so much attention after everything he'd put the community through.

"Madee, I don't have the words to thank you..."

"You just did," she replied, smiling softly.

"No, really... Thank you so much."

"It's nothing."

"You didn't have to take care of me like this."

"Doc did most of it, I was the one panicking... Did you talk to him today?"

"He told me to go back to the city for proper care."

"And what do you want to do?"

"I want to get clean, Madee. But I know I can't do that in rehab..."

Tom carefully explained that he wanted to stay in Forrest Hill. He didn't want to impose on her, but the thought of leaving was unbearable.

"Madee, I should have been honest..."

"Doc's the best. He'll help you... and I will too. You can have my bedroom. I'll sleep on the sofa... I'll be here for you, Tom."

In her own awkward way, Madee was inviting him into her life. Tom felt both foolish and happy—foolish for ever suspecting she had feelings for Scott, but still needing confirmation. Casually, he asked if Scott would mind them living together. Madee laughed and told him Scott was the one person in the community she couldn't stand. He was uneducated, talked too much, and she did her best to avoid him.

Once the moment of awkwardness passed, it was agreed—Tom could stay if he needed time to recover. Madee took charge, sending him off to shower while she called Doc to let him know she'd be housing a long-term patient and to help prepare the room to make him feel at home.

"Tomorrow is another day, Tom. Focus on the successes to come. Don't dwell on yesterday."

When Tom returned from the bathroom, Madee had changed the sheets, and he noticed a small child's night light on the dresser. She pressed the button, and glowing stars began to swirl across the ceiling. Pleased that it still worked, she jumped up and down like a little girl. She was afraid of the dark, so she thought he might appreciate a little light.

She lay down next to him, both of them on their backs, mesmerized by the magical display on the ceiling. Tom let his mind wander, imagining he was driving a colorful go-kart through the clouds on a rainbow road. The demon of desire tried to hitch a ride, lurking between the bombs and grenades scattered along the track, but Tom ignored it, focusing on the finish line.

"Your apartment is fantastic..." he murmured.

Madee turned her head to look at him. "I'm glad you like it. You know, I did it all myself."

"You mean the decorations and stuff?"

"Among other things, yes. But I also did some of the work, like the bathroom."

"So, the flat didn't match your style when you moved in?"

"When I arrived, I had nothing, Tom. Just my handbag. I had to take out credit at the grocery just to buy a toothbrush and some toiletries. For the first two months, I lived in an almost empty flat until I discovered where the treasure was..."

Her story was tinged with sadness, but she told it with a resilience that impressed Tom.

"Treasure?"

"That's right! Ever since I was a child, I've learned how to make the little I have last. It's important to me. I remember one day, I was shopping with my mom—I was about five years old—and I saw this battered teddy bear lying abandoned on the pavement. It was dirty, full of holes, and missing an eye. I didn't dare pick it up, and I regretted leaving it there for days. I cried about it... It's silly, but I fell in love with that bear at first sight. I wondered where it came from, what it had done to make its owner throw it away... It's not the happiest story, I'm sorry..."

Madee's eyes welled with tears, but she held them back.

"I'd like to know what happened next."

"With the bear? There's no next. But I did discover a real passion for lost things. You wouldn't know this, but there's a dump here in Forrest Hill. Several times a week, trucks bring in everything people don't want anymore. Society is fickle, Tom. Everything becomes disposable, interchangeable. People forget their connections and move on to something else before they've even had time to appreciate it.

People don't know how to love anymore, caught in this cycle of mass consumption... I rescue things from oblivion, try to imagine their past lives, and in my free time, I give them a second chance. Everything in my home, even my clothes, is something someone else discarded. I give them the love they deserve. I may be broke, but I don't lack imagination."

Tom was moved. He thought of his mother—Margaretha, the millionaire businesswoman obsessed with the trinkets she jealously guarded in her workshop. She and Madee had more in common than he had realized.

"Madee, have you ever thought of promoting this hobby?"

"Let's be real, Tom. Who would care about a girl from Forrest Hill who rescues things from the trash? No one would! I've never been popular, never had friends around me. I've always been judged too harshly, and I'm afraid of what people think. Popularity comes with a price, anyway—it requires compromise. People would try to "shape" me. I'd lose my authenticity, and the message I want to send wouldn't have the same power. Get rich, get out... I hated my life in the city. The cruelty, the superficiality. Here, we're all discarded objects, Tom. Babou, Doc, Father Andrews, me, the others—and now you. We're all living our second lives. Each of us has found our place, and the balance has been restored."

"Madee, I miss my old life so much..."

"Then maybe it's time for a new beginning. Everything will be okay. I believe in you, Tom."

Lying side by side in the bed, the silence between them was charged with an energy Tom couldn't ignore. He could feel the warmth of Madee's body beside him, her presence so close yet so distant. Every subtle movement she made—the rise and fall of her chest, the quiet sound of her breathing—drew him deeper into his own longing.

He turned his head slightly, stealing a glance at her. The soft glow of the night light cast a delicate shadow on her face, making her seem ethereal. His pulse quickened. He wanted to reach out, to brush a strand of hair away from her face, to feel her skin under his fingertips. The need to be close to her, to have her, was almost unbearable.

Her wisdom, her quiet strength, everything about her pulled him in. He wanted to be the one to protect her, to understand her in a way no one else did. The connection they shared felt sacred, yet his desire was raw, primal. His whole body ached with the urge to close the distance between them.

But he knew it wasn't the right time. Not here, not now. It was too soon, too fragile. He clenched his fists, forcing himself to stay still, his breath shallow as he fought the overwhelming desire that surged within him. He couldn't ruin this moment, couldn't risk breaking the bond they were building.

Instead, he closed his eyes and pretended to fall asleep, though the ache in his chest and the heat in his veins lingered. He listened to Madee's quiet movements as she slipped out of the bed, wishing for nothing more than to call her back, to tell her not to leave. But he let her go.

CHAPTER 22

LAURA'S DIARY: FATE AND JEALOUSY

Fortune favors the bold. Or rather, those who know how to be in the right place at the right time. I needed to escape the suffocating atmosphere at home, so I wandered through the streets of downtown. I had a new video to prepare for my followers, but Mum's constant babbling was driving me mad. She must ask me about Brandon at least 100 times a day—what's he doing, where is he, when is he coming home... Think Brandon, breathe Brandon, live Brandon. I should've thought twice before putting her on a pedestal; she steals my secret love from me every single day. She thinks I'm too young—he likes experienced women, apparently. Instead of obsessing over her daughter's future boyfriend, why doesn't she find someone her own age?

What she loves about Brandon is all the lies I've spun to earn myself a place of honor at home. But still, she should learn to stay in her lane! I got my revenge for her constant nagging by telling her that Brandon had invited me on a shopping spree through the luxury boutiques downtown. That shut her up. She started crying, of course—pathetic, really. We're both Brandon's little wives in her mind, so she can't understand why I get to see him and she doesn't. Not a single day passes without her having another breakdown. Her crocodile tears are insufferable. And I don't even have Madeleine anymore to take out my frustration on... If I ever find her again, I swear I'll strangle her!

I still need Mum for a roof over my head and to pay for the things I can't be bothered with. Sure, my social media partnerships bring in decent money, but who knows what tomorrow will bring? It's smart to save. I hate working, I'm not built for it, so why waste the money I've had to sacrifice for? Once I'm with Brandon, I won't have to worry about any of this. I'll have a chauffeur to open the car door for me, I'll dine at the best restaurants, and I'll be living off designer brands, all courtesy of his record label. I can't wait. I can't wait for people to finally call me Mrs Stevens, for them to recognize me on the street. My life will finally be perfect...

To escape my shitty life, I drowned myself in dreams of a bright future. Sometimes I'd watch those people who had never known what it's like to struggle, who had never faced the humiliation of scraping by at the end of the month. As I grew older, my jealousy twisted into resentment toward the rich. I'd sell my soul to the devil to join their ranks, but deep down, I know I'll never be one of them. I'll never forget how I've begged for favors...

I watch a woman and her son step out of their luxury car, casually handing the keys to the valet and leaving a generous tip. Twenty notes for some idiot to drive their car back and forth. They must have money to burn. How I envy that... Not being afraid of tomorrow, being able to spend without a second thought. Throwing down the equivalent of three lowly workers' salaries just to buy a shirt. Never having to say, *"I can't, I'm broke."* My poverty makes me miserable, and it's getting worse. I'm tired of being the penniless little princess. I was born for luxury.

I drifted away from the main shopping street and into the upscale residential area. I'd kill to have an apartment in one of those buildings with a doorman—it would mean I had made it. I imagined Brandon and me living there, hosting trendy parties, our friends all rich and famous like us. A sleek convertible passed by. If I had that car, I'd speed through the streets, daring the police to stop me. I'd be untouchable, invincible. The convertible predictably stopped outside one of the buildings further down the avenue. I moved closer to watch as the couple stepped out. The driver was a handsome man in his thirties, perfectly at home in this posh neighborhood. The blonde with him looked uncomfortable. Maybe she was some hooker he'd picked up on the sidewalk... No, she didn't look the part. Besides, men like him don't take prostitutes home, even high-end ones.

Cindi and her prince... They proved that a man like Brandon could love an ordinary girl, and that gave me hope. Maybe I still had a chance. I followed them at a distance. There was something about the girl that drew me in. I didn't know her, but in my mind, she was already a rival. I needed to know her secret—how she'd seduced the driver. She probably knew how to work it in bed, using her ass to keep the guy coming back. I hoped it wouldn't last, because she didn't belong here. I could tell she wasn't a prostitute; they carry themselves differently, like they own the world. The sidewalk is their kingdom, and woe to anyone who crosses into their territory...

Then she turned around, and my heart stopped. I quickly lowered my sunglasses, pulling my phone out of my pocket. I wanted to rip her apart, right there in front of her "boyfriend," but it was too risky. The smarter play was to blend in. So, I pretended to be a tourist, snapping pictures of the buildings, feigning awe. I switched to burst mode and captured every movement. What a bitch... Abandoning us, leaving us to drown in the shit she created... The convertible's Cindi was Madeleine.

The bitch was still alive! I was convinced she had killed herself, that she'd die alone, rotting in some forgotten corner. But I was so wrong! Not only is she alive, but she's radiant. And, as if that weren't enough, she's hit the jackpot—a beautiful man that every mother dreams of for her daughter. Does she live in this building? God, I hope not. Jesus,

Madeleine with a guy like that? The world's gone insane, a dimension where ugliness reigns!

Does he take her to cocktail parties and galas? Parade her around in public? Shower her with expensive gifts? Has he proposed to her? I went through all the things she must have, all the things I desperately wanted. It was a curse! Madeleine... Madeleine, the fat girl who can't fit into sexy clothes because she can't show off her chubby legs at parties... Madeleine, with that guy... It's absurd, unnatural—a complete inversion of the future I had planned for her.

Her Prince Charming took her hand and led her inside... Disgusting. Unjust. She was going to sully those sheets with her fat, repulsive body. Before I left, I almost slashed the tyres on his car—just to rain on her little parade. But the stupid doorman stepped out for some fresh air, stopping me in my tracks.

All the way home, I couldn't stop thinking about her. I had to know everything: who, what, where, when, how long... I had programmed Madeleine to be weak, vulnerable, a nobody. She was never meant to have a happily ever after or be parading around on that guy's arm!

I stormed home, furious. When Mum asked where Brandon was, I cruelly told her he didn't want to see her. She started crying again, so I slapped her twice to shut her up. It wasn't the day or the time for her whining. She'd come crawling back later, begging for forgiveness. I held her leash tight—she needed her dose of Brandon, and I was the only one who could give it to her. That was enough to keep her in line.

Madeleine and her Prince had just given me the inspiration for my next video. My social media needed a boost, anyway. Some idiot blogger had recently published a scathing article about my content. According to him, I was a decent person, but I talked too much about myself. The bastard was wrong, obviously—narcissistic, me? Absolutely not! There's nothing wrong with putting yourself first. After all, my well-being is my business, and I have to represent the image I project. But fine, I'll admit, I didn't interact much with my followers. They weren't participating enough in my content. I used to give these losers moral lessons, making them feel good about themselves, but now I had bigger things to deal with. I was their virtual *"good friend."*

I had to make them feel like I was a real friend, someone they could reach out to. Of course, I'd never tell them the truth—I'd twist the facts, make dramatic stories they could relate to, something they could identify with. If I played my cards right, the contracts would multiply. And with that money, I'd hire a professional to finally take care of my bitch sister.

CHAPTER 23

LAURA'S DIARY: MY ENTRY INTO THE WORLD

Influencing is more than just making dreamlike videos or posts that give desperate followers a sense of inadequacy. Whether you're invited or not, being an influencer also means going to all the parties. To get favors, opportunities, free food and drink, networking, sex, and fun, this step is essential. I've gained enough clout to get plenty of invites, but it's still hard to access the most prestigious events. I usually end up at promotional parties where the reality TV and internet crowd gather. I hate them—those fat hicks who've stumbled into fame by accident.

I'm the king of hypocrisy, so to them I'm Laura the good, the nice, the supportive friend. It has its perks though. They confide in me, and I store their secrets away for the day when a rivalry emerges... No one likes their reputation tarnished. I've built enough of a profile to imagine Brandon would have heard of me by now, at least in the early days of my influencer career. But, like all stars, he's elusive. Fortunately, I don't just go out for work. A long time ago, I realized I needed to branch out and move in the circles where I'd have the best chance of meeting my Brandon.

Getting into exclusive clubs doesn't require connections. Being a sexy, beautiful girl who isn't shy and is draped head to toe in luxury brands is your ticket in. Confidence does the rest. You just have to be bold and switch up your approach each time. One night, I'm meeting friends. The next, I'm a celebrity's new protégé. If a bouncer knows you, it's even easier—he won't ask questions, and you become a regular. Sometimes, if one gets too pushy, I make a scene and demand to see the owner. Fresh meat doesn't bother most club owners... A quick blowjob in a dark corner or a rougher fuck in the manager's office solves the problem. Always use pussy for good...

Parties are a zoo—a place for souls waiting for their moment of glory. It's where losers come to find their style. Everyone's an aspiring singer, model, actor, or influencer. It's like a talent show for the rejected. They're failed artists, clinging to the hope that the right connection will change their lives. These parasites would kill their own mothers for the chance to sip champagne in the VIP lounge. All hell breaks loose the second a starlet appears. The bees swarm the honeypot, desperate for a moment in the spotlight. But many are called, and few are chosen. Nocturnal friendships are fleeting. Those left unchosen console themselves with drugs, alcohol, or cheap sex. Sometimes, I feel like one of them—adored by the masses, but still closed off from the world.

Building a network requires being opportunistic without looking desperate. You have to pretend to be indifferent, slipping away at just the right moment. Always be one step ahead, like a chameleon, feigning interest in the latest trends, armed with business cards that give you credibility. Make them believe they're talking to someone of quality, and they'll lower their guard. But always keep the upper hand. Stay mysterious enough to spark curiosity. If someone has nothing to offer, promise them just enough to keep them hooked, or don't offer anything at all. Time is money. My goal is Brandon. And sometimes I regret that Lou isn't in my life anymore. If she were here, I wouldn't have to drag my ass to these shitty parties... Celebrities are the hardest prey. When I say celebrities, I mean the real stars, not the small-town nobodies with fleeting fame.

There are two kinds of celebrities: the arrogant ones with inflated egos who despise everyone, and the depressed ones who are easy to manipulate. It's the second category that needs to be infiltrated. But before claiming victory, you have to get past the gatekeepers—the agents, assistants, and producers. These vultures jealously guard their cash cows and have an uncanny ability to sniff out parasites. I've kept my profile low. They see me, they know me, but I act like I don't care. The safest bet is with daddy's boys—the rich kids lurking in the shadows, with less media exposure. They're ideal prey because they have their fingers in all the pies. The others are easily reassured by a stranger with a fat wallet. Dreaming of being Brandon's wife has taken years of sacrifice and hard work, but now it's time to finally step into the light. I'm tired of wading through shit...

* * *

That night, I looked sexy as hell in my short red dress. I should have been thrilled—I'd managed to get into the White Club, the ultimate temple of glamour. Just getting your picture taken here was a step up the social ladder. And the best part? I didn't even have to suck anyone off to get in. My looks and outfit were enough to impress the meatheads at the door... I was in the Holy of Holies, but my mood was foul. All I could think about was that bitch Madeleine and her Prince Charming. My sister always managed to ruin everything, even when she wasn't around. She was the reason I couldn't enjoy my evening!

What could she be doing right now? My jealousy gnawed at me. I imagined her in bed with her Apollo, and it made me sick. That chubby bitch, getting her hands on a hot guy? Unacceptable. I sat at the bar, shooting down every guy who approached. Brandon is the love of my life, but tonight, I wanted to hurt that whore by stealing the man she'd fought so hard to get. I was so lost in my thoughts, I hadn't noticed the woman who'd been watching me for a while. For her to come sit beside me, I must've looked like shit.

"Dany, get me another one... and pour my friend here another drink, too!"

This woman had confidence. She knew the bartender and seemed like a regular. My instincts told me not to let her slip away. I turned my head, and she was staring at me, full of desire. Her eyes didn't lie—she liked what she saw. My ego swelled. I'd chosen the right look tonight. Fucking her? Why not. It would be a distraction.

"Hi! You don't look like you're having much fun," she said.

"This place sucks."

I deliberately lied to keep her attention.

"I've never seen you here before..."

"It's my first time. Definitely my last—this place is so overrated."

She leaned in closer, our knees brushing. The touch excited me, but I stayed cool. Her hand rested on my thigh, gently stroking it. Heat crept into my pussy, desire flaring... Now I wanted sex, which only frustrated me more.

"I'm Angela. I come here often with my husband. What's your name?"

"I'm Laura."

"Gorgeous name. I've got a table in the VIP lounge. Want to come finish our drinks there? We can chat..."

I couldn't believe my luck. A beautiful stranger inviting me to the VIP area?

"VIP lounges aren't really my thing, you know?"

I played it cool. She threw her head back and laughed, leaning in to whisper in my ear.

"You haven't seen mine yet. It's quite comfortable."

Her hand pressed harder against my skin. If she kept this up, I'd have to sneak off to the bathroom for a quick release.

"Come take a look."

"Okay, but just for five minutes."

I wanted to finish my drink, the one she'd so generously offered. Seeing me down it, Angela laughed again.

"Forget it. There's a bottle waiting for us downstairs!"

"I haven't even touched it..."

"Who cares?"

She tossed a one hundred banknote on the bar, telling Dany to keep the change. He flashed her a grateful smile. We pushed our way through the crowd of five-star partiers, bodies moving under the lights, the atmosphere pulsing with heat. Angela pressed herself against me, and it made me wet. I wanted to drag her into the bathroom, lift my dress, and eat her out. This place, though refined, was a den of vice. Everything—sex, sensuality, beauty—was palpable in the music, the people, the decor. The common folk will never understand how the elite live, but now I finally had access to the world my mother had idolized all her life.

Angela led me to a door guarded by four bouncers. They smiled as they let us into the VIP area. The music was quieter here, and the soft lighting created a warm, intimate atmosphere. A white marble bar dominated the center of the room, and on the leather sofas, I spotted a few stars casually flirting or sipping champagne. I was mesmerized by the aquariums set into the walls, watching exotic fish swim in peaceful circles. Angela interrupted my thoughts, explaining that it was a quiet night because all her friends had gone to bed early. I was lucky. My lucky star had brought me here.

We stopped in front of a red brocade curtain, and Angela casually asked the doorman to bring us two bottles of Grand Cruchampagne, some cocaine, and to not disturb us. The private room was similar to the lobby—large aquarium, white marble table, and luxury leather sofa. A man sat there, around thirty, with blonde hair and tanned skin. He looked like a typical rich daddy's boy, the kind who never had to fight for anything. My eyes were drawn to the white suit he was wearing; I was sure Brandon had worn the same one in one of his promo shoots... But the guy didn't even notice us, too busy snorting a line of coke.

"This coke is fucking shit!"

There was still white powder caked around his nostrils. To show his displeasure, he slammed the table. Angela looked at me and smiled. Clearly, I'd missed something—her husband was in a bad mood tonight.

"As usual, sweetheart," she said, without a care.

"You bet! They charge us the same price, but it's like fucking sugar! I can't get high... I'll shut this place down if they start giving us poor people's drugs!"

Angela sat next to him and snorted another line.

"Fucking good! I'm so horny, I swear it's the same stuff."

"You're always horny, Angela. Coke or not."

Without any shame, Angela pulled down the top of her dress. I wanted her asshole husband to get off me and suck on his wife's perfect tits...

"Who's she?"

"That's my friend, Laura. Laura, this is Wayne, my husband. Don't just stand there, come join us."

I happily accepted her invitation. She didn't need to stroke her nipples to encourage me. As soon as I sat down, Angela pulled me against her, kissing me. Her tongue in my mouth intensified my desire. I could already imagine the pleasure of her tongue on my pussy... Excited, I pulled up my dress, ready to spread my thighs and offer myself to her. Her junkie husband just had to watch...

"Enough bullshit, stop!"

Angela was cut off mid-passion by Wayne's booming voice. Surprised by the outburst, she looked at him.

"Since when are you a jealous husband? Wayne, baby, we're here to have fun..."

"Shut up, Angela! You bring some girl I don't know into our place... I know you, I know the others, but I don't know her!"

"Don't be so paranoid, honey... Laura and I are just having a good time."

"Not until she tells me what the hell she's doing here!"

"You're being ridiculous, baby... We've never interrogated anyone we've fucked before."

"Well, maybe we should've... Some were grateful, but others... especially that little bitch Collins... He abandoned his brother!"

"Forget him, baby... I've told you a million times, he was never worth it."

But Wayne wasn't listening. With a note stuck in his nostril, he snorted another line. The rush seemed to amp him up even more as he swept the remaining coke off the table, sending it flying through the air before it landed on the carpet.

"What the hell are you doing here?" Wayne demanded, glaring at me with his beady, menacing eyes. He wasn't letting go until I told him something.

"Who do you think you are, asshole? You know what? Fuck you! I didn't come here to get interrogated. I'm out."

"Shut the fuck up, bitch! You're not going anywhere. If you try to leave, security will call the cops, and I'll just tell them you came here to cause trouble... I've got connections, so I'd advise you to obey without making a scene, sweetheart. Otherwise..."

The threatening tone in his voice told me he wouldn't hesitate to carry out his threat. I was out of ideas, no lies left in my arsenal that could get me out of this mess. I didn't trust Wayne. My usual tricks wouldn't work on a guy like him—he was a deadly snake, too smart to fool. My brief moment of happiness shattered. I felt trapped.

"I just went out to clear my head, and your wife approached me at the bar—"

"Save your innocent little-girl act for someone else. How many times were you turned away from this club before tonight?"

"I don't know what you're talking about. I can get in anywhere I want."

"Maybe in Hicksville, Princess, but here? You're nobody. If Angela hadn't been feeling generous, you'd have had zero chance of getting into the VIP. So, what do you do, Laura?"

"Well... I'm an influencer. My last video got 100,000 views."

"Wow, so you're a poor man's celebrity. Nothing to be proud of. What are you peddling? Cheap clothes? Budget cosmetics? Discount vacations? You're just a walking billboard, sweetheart. The last link in the marketing chain—cheap labor."

Wayne's laughter chilled me to the bone. He loved humiliating me, reminding me of my place. It felt like high school all over again when Joy plastered the truth on my locker... He wanted me to crack, but I wasn't going to give him that satisfaction. I stood up, keeping my head high.

"I'm not here to be insulted."

"Sit down! We're not finished yet."

Wayne snorted another line, which only made things worse. He took sadistic pleasure in messing with me. Angela stayed silent, her confidence gone the moment her husband started his interrogation. I wouldn't get any help from her. I was just a one-night stand. I tried to remember how my mother would've handled this. Playing the strong girl backfired, so why not play the victim? That's what

Mum would do, of course. Wayne's bad mood was triggered by this Collins guy, and mine by Madeleine. There's my way out. I smiled to myself—everyone has a weakness, even spoiled bastards like Wayne.

"Why are you smiling?"

His voice was slurred. I wasn't sure he could even see straight. Now was my chance.

"You want to know what I'm doing here? Fine. But you have to promise not to judge me."

"I'll judge you if I want. I have every right. I'm invincible."

"My sister betrayed me."

"And we're supposed to care?"

"You don't get it. My boyfriend left me because of her."

"That's life! People use you. You do them a favor, and they take what they want before ditching you."

This bastard was ruthless... I had no problem using people to satisfy my need for control, but hearing it from someone else hit me like a punch. It felt like Wayne could see right through me. This guy could've been my double... or my soulmate. Hard, unforgiving, with no faith in anyone. I needed to think fast. Wayne and Angela weren't the kind of couple to believe in "inner beauty," so I grabbed my phone from my bag, pulling up the photo of Madeleine and her Prince Charming. Wayne was lost in a frenzy, his pupils dilated as he zoomed in on the photo with trembling fingers.

"I don't fucking believe it! Angela, look at this!" His voice was filled with disbelief, but something else—an excitement that made my skin crawl.

"You should've told me right away you were fucking Collins," he growled.

I blinked, trying to keep my composure. Collins? Madeleine's Prince Charming and Wayne's enemy were the same person? My heart raced. Too good to be true.

"What would it have changed?" I asked, forcing my voice to stay calm.

"Everything, Laura. Everything..." His voice was laced with venom, a hatred that mirrored my own feelings for Madeleine. He couldn't tear his eyes away from the photo, as if he were seeing a reflection of his own resentment.

"He dumped you for this chick?"

"Yes..."

Wayne burst into laughter, but it wasn't out of amusement. There was something dangerous in it, a crack in his facade.

"So my Collins bitch is in a relationship now, huh?"

I nodded, biting my lip.

"Despite all his money, the guy was always a slob. In college, if it wasn't for me, he wouldn't have survived... But now, with this chick? He's lowered his standards... She must fuck like a goddess to make up for being that ugly."

I felt a flicker of rage. How could anyone find Madeleine attractive when I was right here—better than her in every way?

Wayne, still in a frenzy, seemed to have found a new target to destroy. His excitement was palpable, in stark contrast to the rising tension inside me, but I had to play along. Angela, on her part, smiled, satisfied, patiently waiting her turn in this twisted game that was their marriage.

"Laura, you're officially our new bestie! We're going to get revenge, and we're going to destroy Collins. But you have to do exactly what I say..."

"Explain your plan."

"You'll know soon enough," Wayne muttered, his eyes piercing as his mind raced to orchestrate his revenge. "I need some information to pass on to my network. We need to be prepared before we strike. What's your sister's name?"

"Madeleine Mitchell, but I've always called her Madee..."

I quickly told him how Madee had disappeared, running away to be with Collins. A part of me hoped he would really hurt her. Another, weaker part wondered what kind of mess I was getting into.

"Don't worry, we'll find her and Collins. I've got contacts everywhere." He gave me a predatory smile. "Just give me your number, and I'll call you when we're ready. Now, let's drink to lovers and relax. Time to have fun. You can fuck my wife if you want."

Angela squealed with delight, eager to begin. Without hesitation, she started undressing me with the expert hands of someone who knew exactly what they were doing. Her fingers moved across my body with disarming precision, awakening deep desires. She knew where to press, how to make me respond. I wasn't her first one-night stand, but she wanted to make me the most memorable.

Wayne, sitting nearby, watched with a perverse interest, his gaze burning with a twisted desire. Far from being embarrassed, I was aroused. I felt at the height of my power, relishing every second of pleasure, letting the tension build. Angela and I rubbed against each other, our fingers slipping into each other's wet pussies, our bodies moving in perfect sync. She lay back on the sofa, legs wide open, ready for me to devour her. But the thrill of power surged even higher; I wanted to feel her inside me while I gave her pleasure. Just as I was about to come, Wayne, aroused by the spectacle, stood up. His eyes glinted with lust, and I could see his desire growing. His cock, hard and ready, stood at attention.

"On your knees, bitches. You've warmed up nicely. Now, let your man take care of you."

Neither of us protested. We knelt on the sofa, arms resting on the backrest, ready to be taken. Wayne walked over to me first, that twisted smile on his lips. "Guests first," he laughed, his hand gripping his cock. He slapped my ass with it, asking if I was ready for him. I nodded eagerly, offering my body without hesitation.

Wayne took us both, Angela and me, relentlessly, switching between us. Every thrust was a release, a mix of pain and pleasure. He knew how to keep us on the edge, drawing out every second. I wanted more and more. I screamed for him to go faster, harder, to bury his hatred inside me like a weapon. It was the ultimate revenge, and

MYTHOMANIA

I savored every second of it. When the night finally ended, exhausted but satisfied, Wayne got dressed and promised to call me soon. Angela, half-naked, fell asleep on the sofa. As for me, I went home with a satisfied smile, hoping this twisted alliance with Wayne and Angela would mark the beginning of the end for Collins and Madee.

CHAPTER 24

LAURA'S DIARY: LIFE CHANGE

My life changed... A week after we met at the White, Wayne finally showed up. I had been desperate for him to call; all I could think about was getting my revenge, and every second of waiting felt like torture. When the phone finally rang, I breathed a sigh of relief—satisfaction was just within reach.

Wayne assured me the plan would go off without a hitch. His contacts had tracked down Madee. Forrest Hill, the most wretched slum suburb imaginable, was where the bitch was hiding. Apparently, she was working as a waitress in some dingy cafe frequented by the lowest of the low. Of course, I should've known. Madeleine had always gravitated toward the poor; she was never cut out to be a lady. It was only logical she'd return to her natural state... A weed can never bloom into a refined and delicate flower.

Wayne's informant had also discovered that Tom Collins was living with her. I couldn't help but laugh at the image—Tom, the son of property tycoons, slumming it in some godforsaken dump with Madeleine. Wayne, with a straight face, warned me that Tom wasn't the prince charming he appeared to be. In fact, Tom was as much of a junkie as Wayne, hooked on cocaine and endless nights of debauchery.

Apparently, Tom Collins' dick had been passed around nearly every hot girl in Sun Valley. The more Wayne described him, the more I reveled in it. I'd bet my life that sweet little Madee had no idea her *"beloved"* was just another bored, rich asshole using her as a distraction. She probably thought they were in some fairy-tale romance, but in reality, she was just a piece of meat for him to chew up and spit out.

Wayne was seething with jealousy, furious that his former "brother" had supposedly cleaned up his act. He couldn't fathom why Collins would let some goody-two-shoes like Madee control him, why he'd stay trapped in a cage with a girl who sucked all the fun out of life. Wayne already despised her without even meeting her, convinced she was force-feeding Tom her naive moral lessons. He couldn't understand why Tom hadn't already bolted, why he'd let some small-town waitress drag him down when he could be out living the high life again.

MYTHOMANIA

But Wayne gave me hope. Once we got rid of Madeleine, Tom would come back to me. We'd be a family, just like I'd always dreamed. First, though, we had to get her out of the picture. There was a press conference coming up where the Collins family planned to announce that Tom would be taking over the family business. Wayne was confident that once Tom had his hands full with that, there'd be no room left for her. We just needed to lure her out of her little bubble in Forrest Hill—get her alone. Wayne already had an idea. The plan seemed foolproof, but I couldn't shake the fear of getting caught. What if someone traced it back to us? What if things went wrong?

Wayne, though, was unconcerned. His father had powerful connections in the legal world, and Angela's influence meant they had plenty of shady people in their corner. If anything went south, Wayne assured me, we were untouchable. His father, a courtroom shark, had bailed them out of trouble more than once, and he had dangerous people in his debt. Wayne had already found the perfect guy for the job. A brutal, elite kidnapper fresh out of prison, desperate for money to disappear and start a new life. Ruthless, efficient, and accustomed to this kind of work. If things went wrong, he'd be the one rotting in a cell, not us.

I couldn't help but admire the sheer power that came with having money and connections. Mum had always said, if you have wealth, you can do anything—even eliminate those who stand in your way. Wayne, Angela, and I went to The White every night, fueling our anticipation for revenge.

I was part of their world now, no more waiting in line, as I was officially on the VIP list. I would meet up with either of them during the day, sometimes to talk, other times to release tension. Our connection grew stronger as I listened to their secrets. Angela had known Wayne since they were 15, their fathers had been close, and it seemed inevitable they'd end up together.

Angela sometimes grew weary of their fast life—drugs, casual encounters—but every time she tried to stop, the pull of their world sucked her back in. With me around, Wayne was in good spirits again, and that brought Angela some relief. She confided in me her frustrations about Tom Collins, still bitter that he'd only been interested in her once. She hated how he avoided her at parties, always acting as if no woman was good enough for him. Once he was done with them, they were discarded. Angela was sure Madee would face the same fate. "Serves her right," she'd say.

Then came the revelation that changed everything. Angela mentioned casually that she was Brandon Stevens' producer. My heart leapt. Her father had discovered Brandon and launched his career, and now she was managing him. I played it cool, acting like just another casual fan. It worked. Angela promised to introduce me to him, even texting him to set up a private evening at her place. I was overjoyed. Finally, the moment I had worked so hard for was within reach. Everything I had sacrificed had led to this. One day, Brandon would be mine. For appearances' sake, I'd still need to seduce Tom Collins, but that didn't mean

I couldn't have a relationship with Brandon at the same time. In my mind, Tom was the challenge, but Brandon was my true goal.

Amidst all the happiness, one thing was gnawing at me: Mum. She used to be useful, always supporting my lies and fantasies, but lately, she'd become unbearable. She was more obsessed with Brandon than I was, constantly asking questions, demanding more details. It didn't matter what I told her—nothing satisfied her anymore. She no longer saw me as her precious daughter, but as a rival. She thought Brandon was hers, as if she deserved him after the mess she had made of her life with Dad.

At first, I didn't care about her growing obsession. I even enjoyed watching her torment Madeleine with her emotional pressure. But now, Mum was getting in my way. She had crossed a line. She wanted to meet Brandon, to take part in my life, imagining some fantasy love affair with him. Ridiculous! If anyone was going to be with Brandon, it would be me. I had worked too hard for this. Mum was supposed to support me, torment Madeleine, and stay out of my way. Now she complained constantly about me going out every night, asking to join me, saying it wasn't fair. I couldn't stand it anymore. Her role was to believe me, support me, and let me handle things. Falling in love with someone she had never even met? That was something only foolish teenagers did. I was suffocating... Always having to answer to her... That bitch should never have run away... I hated Madee even more for leaving me alone with Mum... Last night Annie and I had a fight, and she gave me an ultimatum: either I introduced her to Brandon or she'd go to the police and tell them about my dad. I threatened her not to do that, I played the powerful girl with her connections, but she wouldn't listen. She thought I was hurting her too much by putting myself between her and Brandon all the time. It was delirium, pure madness... I never forced her to build up some kind of imaginary romance... If she suffers, it's her fault and mine alone! Brandon is mine, whether she likes it or not! I felt a little uneasy, if she carried out her threat and dug up some bodies, that would be the end of it for me! I calmed down, sent a message to the fake number I usually used to "call Brandon" and wished her good night. I waited patiently for her to fall asleep, sneaked into her room and wrapped my hands around her neck until she stopped breathing... At least she didn't suffer and never will again...

I was free to live as I pleased. I called Wayne for help and told him that Mum had listened in on our phone calls and was going to talk to the police. He was relieved to know that I'd acted in time... I didn't have to worry; he would send his man over to the house to get rid of the body... One less thing to worry about... I got ready, I wanted to go and celebrate... I'd done it, I was invincible too... Once again Madeleine thought she'd escaped me, but she'd lost, I always win against her... The bitch should know that I've got her in my sights... She's already dead...

CHAPTER 25

LAURA'S DIARY: SO CLOSE TO THE GOAL...

I'm losing my patience! I thought that once Wayne's plan was set in motion, it would come to fruition very quickly, but nothing has happened. Madee is still out there... I can't stand it when I have no control over people and their fates. The waiting is driving me insane. I'm completely at the mercy of Wayne, his moods, and his decisions. Why is it taking so long? He has the power, the contacts, the resources, and yet he does nothing. If I push, he gets angry. If I want satisfaction, I have to shut up and wait. I feel like a dog he's kicked aside when he's bored. My ego is struggling... Rich bastard who thinks he owns the world...

A small camera was installed in Madee's apartment by Wayne's men. Every day I get the video of the day, showing my stupid sister in her pathetic little paradise. Forrest Hill, a dump where she's playing at being happy. Apparently, it's a tight-knit community, so we only managed to get one camera in the living room. If it had been up to me, we'd have cameras everywhere. But Wayne's man had limited time and botched the job. At first, Wayne wanted to follow Tom and Madee everywhere, but the mole warned us: Blondie's boss, Earl, is a paranoid, trigger-happy old man who runs Forrest Hill like a dictator. If we overstep, we could lose it all. So, I'm stuck watching this one pathetic room, day after day.

Wayne and I spend hours dissecting every detail, every gesture, every shitty part of their lives. It's become our ritual. Wayne keeps telling me how much Tom has changed—how he's become this boring, obedient man who no longer parties, no longer fucks around, all because of Madee.

"She's fattening him up like some fucking pig," Wayne says, disgusted. "A guy like Collins should be in clubs, living it up, not rotting with some plain girl who feeds him junk."

Wayne's wrong, though. Madee, sucking? Please. My sister thinks she's too good for that. She's one of those holier-than-thou bitches who thinks being a slut is beneath her, even though she is one. She's probably waiting for Tom to make some grand declaration of love, but all she's getting is cold air. They don't even sleep together—she's on the couch, like a servant, while he's in the bedroom. And that makes me laugh. She's already in love with him, and he doesn't even care.

That can't happen. It won't happen... at least I hope not. Otherwise, I'll lose it. I'm confident, but at the same time, there's this gnawing doubt. They don't have sex, I know that much. But what I do see is Tom being all soft and caring with her, like he's trying too hard to figure out what makes her happy. They laugh, they chat, they share drinks... but there's no chemistry. There can't be. If there were, he'd want to fuck her. Tom can't love Madee. He can't be swayed by her so-called "heart." As soon as he steps back into his real life, into his world, she'll just be another forgotten memory. When I come into his life, I'll be the one he desires. I'm like Madee, but better—socially acceptable, worthy of a man like him.

Brandon is the love of my life, and I'll never stop loving him. But right now? Tom Collins is my challenge. I want him to look at me the way he looks at her. I want her to vanish from his mind, erased by the reality of what I can give him. Once he's in my bed, he'll wonder what he ever saw in her. We'll be together, living the life he was meant for... all I need is for Madee to disappear. And fast.

CHAPTER 26

FORREST HILL, THE DAY BEFORE THE TRAGEDY...

Tom had never been happier. The past few months in the Forgotten District had passed at an astonishing speed. Detoxing under Doc's care had initially seemed impossible—an insurmountable task that Tom thought would break him. But looking back now, Tom couldn't deny that the old doctor's unconventional method had worked wonders. Rather than fighting drugs as an enemy, Doc taught him to see them as a key to unlock the hidden parts of himself, forcing Tom to face his innermost demons. Through the wisdom and guidance of Doc, Tom transitioned from dependence to independence, rediscovering pieces of himself he had long forgotten. His new sobriety was a source of pride, yet Tom knew that the secret to his salvation had little to do with his own strength. Alone, he would have relapsed within days.

Madee... She had been his saving grace, his anchor in the storm. From the night of his overdose, she had never left his side. She opened not just the door of her home but the door to her heart, supporting him through every agonizing moment of withdrawal. The nights were the worst. Tom remembers her coming home from work to find him curled up in the corner of his room, trembling and drenched in cold sweat. She'd hold his hand, helping him to bed, wiping his forehead with gentle hands that carried both strength and kindness. In her presence, he felt human again—alive in ways he hadn't in years. Together, they found joy in the simplest routines—quiet dinners, soft conversations, and nights where she worked on her sewing machine while he read *La Vita Nova* for what felt like the hundredth time. It was those moments that stitched his broken pieces back together.

Tom marveled at Madee's quiet resilience, her way of breathing new life into forgotten things—just as she had done for him. Her creativity extended far beyond the treasures she rescued from the dump. She had given him a second chance. In her care, the shattered fragments of his soul were slowly, patiently reassembled. And secretly, Tom wished he could become part of the world she cherished so dearly, to be one of the many small wonders she nurtured into something beautiful again.

MYTHOMANIA

In Forrest Hill, hidden beneath the surface of decay and desolation, Tom had found an unexpected paradise—a place where simplicity offered salvation. Where once he had wandered aimlessly through a hollow, superficial existence, now he felt like a man reborn. Madee had restored his faith in life, in himself. And with every passing day, Tom realized just how much he had come to rely on her—not only for the care she provided but for the quiet companionship that had transformed his darkest moments into something resembling hope.

* * *

That evening, they were invited to the monthly community meal. As usual, it was held at Elaine's, and for the first time, Tom had decided to take part in the preparations. He wanted to give something back to all these people—his friends—who had welcomed him so openly and without judgment. In his previous life, he might have just made a donation, imagining that money could fill whatever gap was needed. But he had learned now that money, while it could ease certain worries, would never replace the richness that came from real human connection. So, with one of Madee's cookbooks in hand, Tom had poured his heart into making a lasagna. As he brought the dish to Elaine's, his cheeks flushed when Madeeand Babou praised it. It was a small victory, a simple but meaningful gesture that made him feel like he was finally contributing something good to the world.

He had been ready for over half an hour, waiting for Madee to finish getting ready. A new kind of nervous energy coursed through him. Tom didn't know how to move past their friendship. Every time he was near her, his heart raced, yet he felt paralyzed, unable to bridge the distance between them. His desire for her had grown steadily over the past few months, and it was torture to retreat to his room each night, falling asleep alone in the large bed while she was just on the other side of the wall. His body was waking up in ways it hadn't in years. In the past, he had relied on drugs to heighten his physical responses, but now, sober, he found himself struggling to control the sudden surges of lust that would hit him without warning.

He would retreat in secret to take care of his needs, but no matter how much he tried to quench his desire, it only seemed to intensify. He imagined her—soft, naked, vulnerable—caught between the fantasies of his mind and the restraint he forced upon himself. Without the crutch of drugs to dull his senses, his longing felt overwhelming. And yet, in front of Madee, all his confidence vanished. As a man, he had always been defined by meaningless encounters—fleeting, passionless sex that left him feeling emptier with each passing moment. The rush of it all had been hollow, a cycle he could never escape. Now, here he was, in love with someone who represented everything pure and true. But that made him feel even more unworthy.

He didn't dare confess these feelings to Doc, despite the trust he had in the old man. Forrest Hill had its way of sharing secrets, and Tom feared that anything he told Doc would eventually make its way back to Madee. He wasn't willing to risk their friendship, not for the sake of his own desire. Besides, she had never given him any clear indication that she felt the same way. She was nothing like the women he had known before—the ones who were all too eager to exploit his body, driven by their own selfish needs. With Madee, everything was different, and that terrified him.

Madee stood before him, radiant as ever... She looked like one of those ancient goddesses in a navy blue and white silk blouse embroidered with gold sequins and a long-pleated skirt... This strength, this delicacy emanated from her unawares... So touching, so spontaneous, so natural, Tom was captivated by her beauty... His thoughts wandered, together they would make such a beautiful couple... He would be so proud to be able to present Madee to his parents, to flaunt himself on her arm, to shout out to the world: "This is the woman I love!"

"Tom? What's wrong?"

She looked at him, worried... What if that look was the sign he was waiting for?

Pretend to be tired, be alone with her, forget the community... Earl and the others would understand...

"You don't look too good, Tom, do you want me to get Doc?"

"No, I'll be fine, I just need to sit down for a bit."

Tom ached to tell her he loved her. She had become his new addiction, the drug he craved, the obsession that occupied every moment of his thoughts. He wanted her so badly it hurt. But he had to keep quiet. For Madee, he was just a burden, an ex-junkie barely holding himself together. She didn't need someone as damaged as him...

"Come on..."

When she took his hand to help him onto the couch, Tom felt the same electric thrill he had felt the very first time. Her touch sent shivers down his spine. He remembered the day Madee came to pick him up after school and trembled at the thought of what might come next...

"Take your time, breathe... Doc said it could be a long time... Don't give up, you can be proud of what you've already achieved..."

She was sitting next to him, so close... Her perfume, subtle but intoxicating, filled his lungs. His eyes wandered down to the delicate neckline of her blouse. She wasn't wearing a bra. He could see the soft outline of her breasts, the faint trace of her nipples peeking through the silk...

They had an unspoken agreement: they didn't talk much about the past or their personal lives. Their bond flowed naturally without the weight of their histories getting in the way. Madee supported Tom in his battle against his demons, and both seemed to understand that digging up old wounds wouldn't help either of them heal. They lived in the present, discovering each other anew every day...

"Madee... You're so beautiful..."

Her gaze shifted away from his. Their hands still clasped, but now her expression was different. A sadness crept into her eyes, a sorrow he hadn't seen before. She was in pain... He could feel it, a quiet agony she carried within. Tom moved closer, heart pounding, unsure of whether to push forward or retreat. His hesitation only lasted a moment before desire took over. He kissed her, giving in to the overwhelming need he'd been holding back for so long. It was an awkward, fervent kiss, charged with the kind of passion that comes from months of restraint. His lips pressed against hers, his hands trembling as they found their place on her waist.

Her lips were so soft, warmer than he had imagined, and their tongues danced together as if they had always belonged. Tom's mind was racing, yet his body knew exactly what it wanted. He could feel his pulse racing in his chest, his heart pounding louder than his thoughts. He wanted to go further, to lose himself in her completely. But something stopped him. He wanted her with every part of his being, but he couldn't break the fragile moment. Not yet.

"I love you, Madee." His voice was raw, barely above a whisper.

Tom breathlessly uttered the words with barely contained emotion. Madee wrapped her arms around his neck. Their second kiss was even more intense, more passionate. Tom leaned over her, his hands exploring the shape of her body under her clothes. He could barely control his desire. What if his body betrayed him? He had given himself to others so many times... He was just a sex machine, nothing more. He feared not being able to give the woman he loved any pleasure, of disappointing her.

"Do you think you can fuck her, Collins?"

No. This was not the time to think about Wayne Beckett. He needed to focus on the moment, on the happiness of being here with her, safe. Gently, he unbuttoned Madee's blouse, revealing her round, voluptuous breasts.

"Stop wasting time, Collins. Shove your dick in her ass. They like men who get straight to the point."

Wayne's voice echoed in Tom's head. But Tom decided to block it out and concentrate on his growing lust. He still doubted his ability to satisfy her, to be enough, but he had the right to love her. Everything would be fine. Madee arched her back, responding to his caresses, and with her, he felt like he was freefalling. Unlike the others, where there was no tomorrow. What would she think of his performance? What if he was too rough? What if he hurt her?

Tom was navigating the unknown. For the first time, he wanted a tomorrow that would repeat itself, over and over again. He wanted everything to be perfect. He wanted her so much, but he kept delaying the moment of grace when they would finally become one. His caresses became more insistent, his mouth playing with her nipples, now red with desire. She smelled so good, and he kissed every inch of her bare skin. He noticed a tattoo on her side, a skull surrounded by the cosmos. Just above her navel was a fine scar. The wound must have been five centimeters long before time healed it. Tom was mad about Madee's body—natural, alive, warm. He lost himself in the discovery of her generous curves, drunk with love. Consumed by jealousy and regret, Tom wondered how many men had loved her before him. Why hadn't he met her sooner? She could have gone to Garland; he could have met her on campus. They could have talked for hours, walked hand in hand, flirted. They would have decided to lose their virginity together, after six months or much later, it wouldn't have mattered. They would have never known anyone else—just him and her, growing up together, growing old together.

"Make love to me, Tom."

Tom felt his heart racing when he heard those words from Madee, like a soft invitation to lose himself in her. His breath became shorter, his hands trembled slightly as he brushed against her skin. He had always seen himself as a broken man, unworthy of the love he felt for her, but in that moment, everything seemed to change. Their breaths mingled, their bodies drawing closer inexorably, and Tom felt his desire rise like a crashing wave.

He gently stroked her cheek, searching her eyes for permission. Are you sure? Her eyes sparkled with a brightness he had never seen before, as if she was finally entrusting her heart to him. Their lips met again, but this time, he took his time, savoring every second, every sensation. Their mouths barely touched, hesitant at first, before coming together in a deeper, more languorous kiss, where every movement seemed to bring them back to life. Tom closed his eyes, letting himself be carried away by the softness and warmth of their embrace.

His fingers traced a line down her spine, drawing invisible patterns on her bare skin. He could feel the shivers coursing through her body, and that excited him even more. Each of Madee's touches, each movement of her body against his, was a silent response to his desire. He took his time, savoring each moment, afraid that the dream would fade away.

"You're so beautiful, Madee... I don't want to rush anything."

She sighed softly, and he felt her fingers intertwine with his, as if urging him to continue. His caresses became more intense but still gentle, exploring every corner of her body with a reverence that felt almost sacred. His lips followed the line of her collarbone, then slowly descended to the curve of her breasts. He paused for a moment, watching the slight rise and fall of her chest, her nipples hardening with desire, and he let himself be swept away by a wave of passion.

He kissed her belly, just above the thin scar. What hurt you like this, Madee? he wondered with a hint of sadness. But he didn't dare ask the question. In that moment, all that mattered was her, her hands on him, her warm breath on his skin. He wanted to know her, to understand her in all her humanity, but most of all, he wanted to love her.

Madee ran her fingers through his hair, and Tom felt her body tense beneath him. He moved up toward her lips, meeting her gaze, seeking confirmation in her eyes. His body responded with such intensity that he felt overwhelmed by an emotion he had never known before. He felt whole, as if with her, he was finally becoming the man he wanted to be.

"I love you, Madee... I never want to lose you."

She responded with another kiss, even more passionate, and Tom knew that everything was right, that she wanted him as much as he desired her. Their bodies intertwined with slow sensuality, each movement a silent confession of their growing love. Tom knew this night would be different from all the others because with Madee, it wasn't just sex. It was the communion of their souls, a promise of a future together. He had waited so long for this... A wave of shock coursed through his pelvis as he entered her. He was no longer in control, no longer passive nor a mere spectator, the sensation of pleasure growing with each thrust, deeper, more intense... His heart pounded at a frantic pace, and with every movement, he inched closer to the point of no return, yearning for a new, unknown ecstasy. Madee's moans, soft and intoxicating, resonated like an intimate melody, urging him to go faster. She tightened her grip around his thighs, her fingers digging into his skin, as if to hold him close forever. Her voice, breathless and burning with desire, whispered in his ear, "Don't stop..."

The osmosis between them was complete. Their bodies melded into each other, impatient, hungry for pleasure, connection, release. Every sensation, every shiver amplified their need to possess each other, beyond the flesh, as if their souls were brushing against one another. Then, at that climactic moment, their bodies tensed in perfect synchronization. Their sexes contracted together in an explosion of searing pleasure that swept through them like a wave. Their breaths intertwined as they reached the peak, and the bliss they shared was not just physical but emotional, almost sacred. It wasn't just an orgasm; it was a release of everything they had held back, a union beyond words.

In this ecstatic embrace, where their love seemed frozen in time, Tom buried his face in Madee's neck, trembling, overwhelmed by the intensity of the moment. They remained like this, breathless, exhausted but fulfilled, lulled by the quiet complicity of their union. Holding her close, a realization slowly dawned on him. Never before had he felt anything so deep. It wasn't just desire; it was a connection he never thought possible. Every embrace with Madee erased the weight of the years spent in darkness. With her, he felt whole, finally free from the chains of his past. For the first time in his life, love and desire intertwined, creating a new identity, one he could finally believe in... The time that had paused during the act resumed its course, but the night passed in a flash. They made love again and again, their bodies never tiring of each other, endlessly seeking the same magic, the same embrace that consumed them. Tom didn't sleep, choosing instead to savor every second by her side, watching her, her peaceful face asleep, a smile still lingering on her lips... On the small couch, too narrow for the two of them, he nestled against her. He couldn't stop watching her sleep. Her silence was punctuated by twitches, she trembled and cried, surely descending into the depths of her subconscious. Madee's body revealed the hidden suffering she was trying to forget, and he could feel the tragedies she kept buried inside... Tom stroked her hair, held her even closer to warm and protect her... This wasn't just pleasure; it was healing. Every kiss, every caress made it feel as though the invisible scars of his soul were slowly closing. For the first time in years, he felt alive, truly alive, ready to rebuild what had once been destroyed. He loved her too much to see her suffer, and at that moment, Tom realized he was no longer a man lost in the darkness but a man reborn in the light of their love.

* * *

She seemed to have forgotten the dark places she was trapped in when she awoke in the early hours of the morning... Tom kissed her forehead and looked at her tenderly.

"Hello, my love..."

"Um... What time is it?"

"6:45."

"Oh no, I'm late! I have to get to work!"

She jolted awake at the thought of neglecting her responsibilities as a devoted employee. She quickly straddled Tom to free herself from the couch, but he held her by the waist, wanting to keep her close just a little longer. The sight of her in that position stirred his desire once again...

"Stay with me... Earl can wait..."

Madee smiled, leaning in to kiss him. She wanted it too, he knew it, he could feel it...

"I'd like to stay with you..."

He was trying to sway her decision, and Madee didn't resist. She surrendered to her lover's touch, unaware of her own beauty and sensuality. Living fully in her femininity, it made her even more extraordinary. This time, it was she who set the pace, controlling the rhythm of her hips, sometimes pausing to feel Tom inside her, savoring every moment. Never before had a woman made love to him like this... Attentive to both the pleasure she gave and received, Madee was in tune with their bodies.

They lost themselves in each other, nothing else mattered but the two of them... The world could have crumbled around them, yet trapped in their love, they would have noticed nothing, carried away by their passion. It wasn't until the moment of orgasm, when their bodies trembled in unison, that they were brought back from the ecstasy that consumed them.

Tom busied himself with breakfast while Madee got ready. He felt stronger and more relaxed than ever before. Though he didn't have her culinary skills, he did his best to take care of her, making coffee and trying not to burn the toast. The kitchen lit up when she appeared, her smile instantly warming the room.

"Madee, darling, I've made coffee, but... I think I burnt the toast."

She laughed softly, and despite the small mishap, Tom couldn't help but feel a deep connection growing between them. Just like his parents had cherished the small, imperfect moments, Tom realized that love wasn't about perfection—it was about being present, just like now.

However, the soft glow of the morning was dimmed by a sudden, harsh reminder of reality. His phone had buzzed earlier, yanking him from his serene moment with Madee. The cursed message announced that today was the day—the Collins family press conference. The day his family had chosen him to be the sole heir.

For months, Tom had thought he was forgotten, replaced by someone more deserving, more eager to play the part. But now, the weight of expectations crushed him again. Why him? Why now? He was determined to let go of the life his family had imprisoned him in, to break free from their grasp and live his own life, with Madee. His rebirth into the man he wanted to become was so close, and he couldn't let anyone pull him back.

"Tom, honey, what are you thinking?"

Madee's voice brought him back, her soft touch pulling him out of his thoughts. She sat on his lap, her fingers gently brushing his cheek. Tom looked up at her, his heart aching with the love he felt for her. All he wanted was to stay in this bubble with her, safe from the world.

"I'm happy with you, Madee..."

Her eyes twinkled with curiosity, but also with a hint of fear, as if she sensed the struggle within him.

"I don't know how to take that when you say it with such a serious face!"

Her teasing brought a smile to his lips, but Tom knew he couldn't escape the reality of what awaited him. He kissed her, holding her tightly as if to absorb her strength.

"I have to go into the city today... Family business."

Madee's smile faltered, and her brows furrowed with worry.

"Tom, if you have any regrets about last night... you can tell me."

Tom shook his head, his heart breaking a little at her doubt.

"Darling, it's not that at all. I love you, Madee. It's just... I don't want this legacy that they're trying to force on me. I want to stay here, with you, build something real. Money won't ever make me as happy as I am with you."

Madee's eyes softened with understanding, but Tom could see the flicker of concern she tried to hide.

"Tom, we can love each other without you having to make any drastic decisions..."

"My family's money destroyed me, Madee. It made me into someone I hated. I want to rebuild myself, with you by my side. Trust me, this is what I need to do."

They sat in silence for a moment, listening to the rhythm of their hearts, beating in sync. Madee kissed him softly, then looked into his eyes with unwavering trust.

"I trust you, Tom. But promise me you'll act with respect for yourself and everyone else... okay, love?"

"I promise, sweetheart. And afterward, we'll go away. Just the two of us. Somewhere far away where I can have you all to myself."

"I'm already yours, Tom."

"We'll go somewhere where we don't have to worry about anything. Just us, making love whenever we feel like it... I'll love you madly, every moment."

Madee laughed softly, pressing a tender kiss to his lips.

"I can't wait for that. But I really have to go to work... Just send me a message, okay? I'll be thinking of you all day."

Tom kissed her one last time, his heart heavy as she walked out the door. He couldn't shake the subconscious fear that tugged at him—the fear that something would happen, and he'd never see her again. The weight of the upcoming press conference loomed over him, but when they dined together tonight, he knew one thing for sure—he'd be saying goodbye to the old Tom Collins for good.

CHAPTER 27

LAURA'S DIARY: PERFECT TIMING

He fucked her! And not only once! The words loop in my head, my rage bubbling up, threatening to boil over. If I could, I'd smash everything around me. They don't deserve happiness—no, they aren't allowed to be happy. Not ever.

Wayne called me. The second I heard his voice, I knew he was on something. Again. He had something important to say, but not over the phone. He was holed up in some downtown hotel room, finalizing details with the guy in charge of "housekeeping". Today was the day—the perfect moment, the point where destiny would strike. I got there as fast as I could. Unlike the glitzy hotels, this one was stripped down—no fancy suites, no room service, no polite bellboys. Just the kind of place where cheating husbands pay by the hour to fuck their mistresses. When Wayne opened the door, he was all relaxed, laughing about everything. The coke had him riding high, but it made him unpredictable, and that's when I couldn't stand him. At that moment, I got it—why Angela fantasized about getting rid of him sometimes.

Between bursts of laughter, he rambled on about how everything was going perfectly, how we were blessed by the gods. His incoherent nonsense made my skin crawl. Why the hell couldn't he just tell me what the big news was? I was too wired for this. He dragged things out, making me lie on the bed, on those disgusting, sweaty sheets. Did he really think I was in the mood? One look from me, and he knew better. I wasn't here to play his games. He snapped out of it, grabbed the tablet from the nightstand, and opened a file. I recognized the room on the screen. It was Madee's living room. The latest video. Wayne ordered me to watch it because this time we were in for a real treat.

Tom and my sister were sitting on the couch. Why was Wayne so euphoric? There was nothing worth watching—just those two losers stuck to each other. My patience was thinning fast. I shoved the tablet back at him, irritated that he'd dragged me out of bed for this trash. But Wayne, as usual, insisted. He fast-forwarded the video a few seconds... Then it hit me like a punch to the gut. My worst fear. Tom was kissing Madee. And not just any kiss—it was the kind that lingered, the kind that seemed full of some resigned tenderness. It made me sick. He didn't mean it. It wasn't real. It couldn't be. It was just a kiss of someone who'd settled for less, nothing more. But the next shot showed him undressing her, his hands too eager, sliding over her limp body, his tongue lingering too long on her breasts, on those nipples standing at attention.

I couldn't stand it. I moved past the foreplay, convinced it wouldn't go further. Tom would stop. He had to stop. He wasn't capable of this, not with her. They were naked, and I saw him hesitate. Yes, that hesitation was there. He looked into her eyes, kissed her... He was going to tell her he couldn't do it, that it was over, that he felt ashamed to have sunk so low. He'd run from her, lock himself in the bathroom, sick to his stomach. Madee would cry, humiliated, rejected. But that didn't happen...

Wayne laughed beside me, grating on my nerves, making it impossible to think straight. I watched, heart pounding, as Madee spread her legs wider, inviting him in. And Tom... he entered her. Gently. Respectfully. The way his body moved against hers, the look of pleasure on her face—it disgusted me to my core. She enjoyed it. Every stroke, every lick, she reveled in it. How could she? After all I'd done to crush her, to make her feel like the worthless piece of shit she was—she still found pleasure. Life is unfair.

Their first fuck was boring as hell. Tom stayed on top of her the whole time, trapped between her thighs, as she gripped his hips. They came together, and he stayed inside her, lingering in that disgusting embrace as if he didn't want it to end. I hated it. I'd seen enough, but I couldn't look away. I kept hoping—praying—that he'd snap out of it. That he'd run, realize it was all a mistake. But he didn't.

Wayne kept talking, his voice a nauseating commentary over the video. He was convinced things would heat up, that there was more to come. He was wrong about her. She hid it all so well behind that innocent facade. Even Wayne, that pig, was mesmerized by her naked body curled up in Tom's arms. Despite her imperfections, even he found something to admire. And I hated her more for it. Despite everything, no one had ever looked at me like that... When Wayne confided in me that he'd jerked off watching them fuck, I told him to shut up. Wayne—the man who sodomized the most beautiful women—was turned on by my sister. It was an insult. What power did she have? What was it about her?

The next images on the screen showed Madee transformed, confident, daring. She took control, and I never thought she had it in her. Giving a man like Tom a blow job? Her? My stomach churned as I watched the smug look on Tom's face, his eyes glazing over as she sucked him. They melted into each other, their bodies shifting, bending, changing positions to heighten the pleasure. I didn't think Madee could move like that—so lithe, so fluid, her body contorting gracefully to take him deeper into her. It was disgusting. And it was beautiful. It wasn't just fucking. It was love. And I wanted to cry. My sister—my rival for so many years—had just won a victory I couldn't ever claim. People loved her for who she was. Me? I was only loved with violence, or lies. That bastard Wayne saw how disturbed I was. And he seized the opportunity to twist the knife. No mercy.

He said things were serious between Madee and Tom. Serious. Because Tom Collins never fucked the same woman twice. He had rules: never see her again, never kiss her, always use a condom. No risks. No diseases. No babies. And yet, there was something about Madee that broke all his rules. He'd made love to her that night. No condom. He came inside her—inside her—several times. He didn't hold back. And the worst part? Madee couldn't have children. At least, that's what she had been led to believe for years, a lie meant to crush her dreams of ever having a family.

I couldn't take it. I was shaking, seething. I couldn't just stand by and do nothing. I wanted to be there when Wayne's thugs came for her. I wanted to destroy every last trace of Tom's cum still inside her. I wanted her to never have sex again. Not with anyone. I wanted her gone. Dead. Erased from the face of the Earth. I lost control. Screaming, raging, cursing her name, vowing that my sister would pay for everything she'd ever done to me. Wayne had to slap me to calm me down. He told me to focus. If I behaved, if I was good, I'd get my prize—I'd get to set fire to Madee's apartment. But only if I kept my head. I had to put my personal grudges aside. Tom was in love. That made the plan even more perfect. Nothing I did now would ruin it. In a few hours, it would all be over.

CHAPTER 28

LAURA'S DIARY: SHOW TIME

It's done... at last! Wayne's henchman has taken her to her final resting place. I don't know where—Wayne keeps that secret locked tight. But it doesn't matter. What matters is that Madee's new life no longer exists. For those who knew her, she's already dead. And now, all that's left is Tom Collins. My turn to seduce him. I left before the fire started, but not without taking everything I wanted. Everything I loved. This gold leather blazer, this red mermaid dress, these retro pumps, this pendant... And this shirt. The one that still smells of the last passion. The one Tom Collins so delicately removed when he undressed her, when he made love to her. No, I didn't steal it. I took back what belonged to me. These things are my trophies, the material proof of my triumph over Madee.

The informer—Scott, I learned his name today—came with me to the apartment. He's the one who carried the homeless woman's body into the kitchen. He even pulled out her teeth, ensuring no forensic tests could be done. I was honestly surprised that a grocer from Forrest Hill had it in him to do something like that in cold blood. He was always a show-off, calling Tom a troublemaker just because Madee rejected his advances. Idiot. If he wasn't careful with his mouth, he'd get us all into trouble.

I wanted to knock him out, leave him there to burn. It would've been perfect—Madee and Scott, caught in the flames together. The perfect alibi to frame Tom. I imagined it clearly: the rich lover walks in on his sweet Madee having an affair with the little grocery clerk. In a fit of rage, he kills them both, sets the apartment on fire, then speeds off in his luxury convertible. A crime of passion. The case would close, Tom Collins would rot in prison, and resume his role as a little whore behind bars. But this time, I doubt he'd be king of the orgy... Wayne refused to eliminate Scott. First time I'd ever heard his name. Said he'd keep his mouth shut, and he'd better if he wanted to enjoy the nice little sum that magically appeared in his bank account. I didn't argue. One day, Wayne would meet his end too. Patience.

There's no CCTV around here, which is one of the perks of living in a slum. No one wants to spend money on pariahs, so the council keeps the gangrene away from the security measures in place elsewhere. I made it to Madee's apartment without a trace. No one will ever know I'm the one who left the kettle on. Before I left, I lit one of the incense sticks she had lying around. Not to repent—what do I have to be sorry for? But to give the whole thing a mystical touch. Purifying fire with fire. A farewell gift for my dear sister, for her great journey into the 9th circle of hell. With my bag of belongings under my arm, I left as if nothing had happened. Who's going to miss that dump anyway? Scott and I exchanged a handshake—our little collaboration was over. Now, the ball was in my court. The next phase was up to me. I had to transform myself into the perfect bait for Tom Collins. Wayne had been clear: Tom's a sucker for blondes. He even joked that the color of my pubic hair wouldn't matter to Monsignor Collins. I still don't know how Angela put up with that bastard for so long.

I made an appointment with the hairdresser. Going from brunette to a bright blonde shouldn't have been difficult. But when he solemnly informed me that I'd have to cut my hair to shoulder length to avoid breakage, I nearly fainted. I'd been dying my hair black since I was fifteen—it's not like bleach couldn't handle it. I tried to tell him how to do his job, to explain that I could be as blonde as Marilyn Monroe in two hours without losing any length, but he wouldn't budge. I wanted to shove those damn scissors down his throat.

But in the end, I gave in. One hour and one scandal later. Why didn't I just go somewhere else? Because this asshole hairdresser works on all the rich women in town.

He's the best, and I needed spectacular blonde hair—better than Madee's. Still, his name's on my list now. One day, he'll pay for his arrogance. Don't mess with the future Mrs. Stevens.

Me, as a blonde... I didn't recognize myself. I looked like a dumb bimbo. But my followers? They loved it. I made a video, posted some shallow crap about how change makes you feel good, giggling in front of the camera like an idiot. They ate it up. Another thousand followers, all thrilled to see every step of my hair transformation (except for the cut—too humiliating). I have to admit, I looked a bit like Madee. Except, of course, I was better. Stronger.

That night, I went to the White to meet Angela and Wayne. Angela's eyes popped out of her head when she saw me, and Wayne laughed, saying he'd teach me how to fuck like a blonde. The night was... unforgettable. I wasn't worried about Tom Collins. It was a done deal.

To get to know his habits, I lingered around his neighborhood. There was no reason for him to stay in Forrest Hill now that his Cinderella was gone. The only time he ventured out of his gilded prison was to buy booze from the corner store. Physically, he was a shadow of the man he'd been. Devastated. There was nothing left of the handsome guy who'd made love to my sister. He'd forget her. He had to. She was an illusion. A mistake. It was scientifically impossible for him to love her.

Back in the shabby flat where Mum and I used to live, I stopped paying rent. The landlord kicked me out, not that

I cared. When I collected my things, I told him to fuck off. But for the first time, I found myself on the street. I called Wayne, and he set me up in a hotel. A luxury one, of course. Not too far from Tom's place. I needed to keep an eye on him.

I'd been putting off our "meeting" for days, waiting for the perfect moment. Choosing the ideal setting wasn't easy, so I asked Wayne for advice. He said I should play innocent. And with my blonde hair, it would be easy. Tom would melt at the sight of a naive young woman, all sweet and helpless. Wayne was right. I managed to drag Tom into a cafe, and it worked.

He was distant, strange. Hardly spoke. But those impenetrable blue-grey eyes of his—they fascinated me. He wasn't really listening. I talked for both of us, terrified the silence would expose the real Laura hiding under all that blonde hair. I wanted him to fuck me like he fucked Madee. I imagined his cock, the orgasms it would give me. The camera was ready. All I needed was to get him back to the hotel...

When he finally came, I pulled out all the stops. I gave him the best of my body, fucked him like a savage, and... nothing. He was there, but he wasn't. I moved on his cock, but I couldn't get any pleasure out of it. It was like fucking a corpse. My vibrator had more warmth. Tom had shut down completely, blocking me out of his heart, out of his mind. I was fucking him, but he didn't care. None of my slutty tricks worked. He hardly even moaned when I blew him. He just let it happen—passively, like a toy. He was Collins' bitch, making his cock available to the slut in need. I hated him for it. He was supposed to love me, not her.

But he never said he wanted me. Not once. It felt like my kisses disgusted him. He was indifferent to my perfect body, and no matter how inventive I was in bed, I couldn't shake him out of his torpor. It wasn't me turning him on—it was her. He was still reliving that one night with her. I've always believed that beauty compensates for a lack of spirit or personality. Thinness and beauty guarantee success. But with Tom Collins, I realized my perfection was a curse. He was so cold. Without saying a word, he reduced me to nothing more than vulgar, disposable trash. Angela had warned me… I was suffering the backlash of my own lie.

I could feel him tiring of me, of the whole act. But I didn't give up. To trap him, I took a photo of us in bed and posted it on my social media. He wasn't happy about it—not that his opinion mattered. He was in my network now, and he had to play by my rules. Too weak, too devastated by his "loss" of Madee, Tom tried to escape downtown—and more importantly, get rid of me. He didn't understand that he couldn't just throw me out. So when he said he was heading to his country house, I went with him. Obviously, I wasn't part of his plan, but I didn't care. I used the mob to force his hand. Manipulating my followers was easy. They loved my sob stories, so I played the little victim. I cried on command, telling them I didn't understand why Tom didn't want to move in with me when we were so happy. My audience was furious at the heartless bastard breaking my heart. The support hashtag went viral. People are so easy to control—you just have to tell the right story. Fed up, Tom took me with him. He was forced to do something he didn't want, but it didn't matter. It was my will, not his.

His country house looked like something out of a magazine. Perfect. I wasn't thrilled about being so far from the city, though. If he didn't change his attitude soon, I'd go mad with boredom. I needed sex and money to make it worth my while. Once we arrived, I took over. Immediately. I rearranged the furniture, redecorated, and made sure everything reflected me, not her. If he ever planned to bring Madee here, I had to erase her spirit from the place completely. Tom said nothing. His silence was both sublime and pathetic. A rich idiot, the perfect prey to take out my frustrations on...

I wanted him to fuck me in every room of the house. My goal was to shatter whatever dreams he had left of a life with my sister. I needed to defile this Temple of Love, to let the echoes of my pleasure reverberate through these pristine walls. But it didn't go as planned. Tom didn't want me anymore. I tried to force him, but he resisted, pulling away like I was some dangerous monster he needed to guard himself from.

This rich man didn't live like others. I had imagined myself on his arm at glamorous parties, photographers capturing every moment as journalists screamed my name. I couldn't have been more wrong. Tom let his beard grow out, spent hours wandering in the forest. He refused to go out, refused to attend events. I was furious. How had I been so stupid? How had I let him deceive me like this? No wonder he fell for someone like Madee. They were as dull as each other.

I can't imagine life without conflict. When I'm bored, I need chaos. And Tom, refusing to fuck me, refusing to take me out—he was asking for trouble. So I made his life hell. I followed the same procedure as I did with sweet little Madee: shut him up, contradict him, belittle and dehumanize him at every turn. I criticized everything—his clothes, his silence, his endless imperfections. Tom Collins is the perfect example of a man without a personality. Take away his good looks, his money, his status, and he's nothing. Just another invisible man you can shove in a corner.

But Tom threw me off balance. Most of the people I torment cry, break down in pain. But not Tom. He was tough. I did everything to provoke him—picking at every little detail, shouting, giving orders, getting hysterical—but he wouldn't react. He'd let me rage, then lace up his trainers and go for a run. His indifference drove me insane. The only good thing about him? He wasn't cheap. He thought handing me his credit card would make up for ignoring me. I bought everything I wanted, spent his money lavishly, but it wasn't enough. He didn't know me. Money isn't enough. Not for me.

Sometimes, his phone would light up with messages. He never answered. Most of them were from someone named Margaretha, a woman who seemed worried about him. After some internet digging, I found out she was his mother. The woman who had conceived him. One day, I saw a message from her, *"My darling, this girl you're seeing is not for you. Come home. Your father and I are worried. Mum."* Who does this old hag think she is? That I'm not good enough for her son? Does she think Madee, the elephant, is the ideal daughter-in-law?

Before she could convince her precious son to leave me, I had to deal with her. I pretended to be Tom and sent her a message: *"Don't contact me again. I'm happy with my life. I don't want to hear from you or Dad ever again."* I can only imagine the look on that old bitch's face when she read it. The thought thrilled me.

But no matter what I did, Tom wasn't interested in me. He couldn't see my beauty. He couldn't forget that bitch. Madeewould always be between us. I thought her death would solve my problems, but it only created more. Meanwhile, I was still seeing Wayne and Angela, partying harder than ever—drinking, fucking, spiraling. I was about to meet Brandon, who had just finished recording his new album. Angela told me he was in a tight spot—he needed money, and Wayne and she were his saviors. They held his career in their hands. Without their help, he was bankrupt. So what was I supposed to do with a bankrupt Brandon?

Apart from the black cloud of Tom Collins, my life was getting better. Wayne kept me updated on Madee's situation. He admired her toughness, her strength of character. He didn't go into too much detail about the treatment she was receiving, but I knew it was bad. She was locked in a cage, barely surviving, reduced to starvation, lying in her own filth. Wayne couldn't understand how she was still alive—how she kept hanging on when others would have given up long ago. But no matter. She'd be ready for the big night. And I'd be there to witness her pitiful end.

I was already planning what to wear to her death. Maybe I'd put on the blouse I'd stolen from her apartment. I'd watch her die wearing it, sinking the final dagger into her heart. I'd make her wandering soul suffer, one last time. Emotional death always comes before physical death. I would be her grim reaper, her chaos, her horseman of death. And I'd savor every second of it. There was still time.

CHAPTER 29

IN THE DEN OF VICE, SIX FEET UNDER...

In the den of vice, the blue light still shines. Despite the crackling neon, it spreads its brightness repeatedly, casting its sickly glow over everything it touches. They'll have to change the damn bulbs soon, Death Face thinks, slumped in his chair. The dim light is beginning to lull him into sleep. Time doesn't matter to him anymore—it's just something for others to care about.

The boss has been spending more time with Sandra, enjoying his twisted games of control. Wayne draws it out, tormenting her, watching her break. Death Face doesn't like watching, but the money keeps him silent. So he films, does his job, and waits.

It'll all be over soon. He'll leave this behind—start a new life on some faraway island, maybe take Sandra with him if she survives. If. But Wayne's cruelty won't let her last long. Still, she has to live until the ceremony. The boss is vague about the details, but he's proud. It'll be a spectacle, a finale for the girl who doesn't even have a real name anymore. Madee.That's what they call her now, but it doesn't matter. Her past is gone, her identity crushed. Wayne took it all.

But Sandra was different to Death Face. He had cared for her, watered her like a flower, hoping she'd bloom. But the flower was wilting. Just like Grandma...

At night, she would come into his room, peeling off her nightdress to reveal her sagging body. She'd lie next to him, pressing herself close, telling him how much she needed him, how much she desired his touch. Evan never penetrated her—Grandma didn't allow it. She said she was too old for that, but that didn't stop her from making him touch himself. He had to control his youthful erections, and if he came too quickly, she'd scold him. Not cruelly, but just enough to make him try harder next time. She collected his seed, guarding it like something precious. She loved it.

And when he pleased her, she'd reward him, reading him stories or letting him suckle at her breasts, her sagging skin reminding him of his mother. Sandra—the doll—was always there, watching them, smiling her silent approval. She never interfered, never judged. Evan could train with her, but it was always Grandma's approval that mattered most. She held the power.

When Grandma died, everything changed. Evan was alone. He wandered the streets, grew up in foster care, and no one ever asked him for his seed again. No one controlled him the way Grandma did. Later, he met women. He bought them flowers, took them out to dinner, tried to be gallant. But when things turned serious, they never did it the right way. They never touched him like Grandma did. They wanted him inside them. Evan refused, and when they realized he wouldn't, they left, calling him names—faggot, impotent.

When he met Craig in a bar, Evan was ready to give up on everything. He drank and cursed the world, complaining about how much he hated it, how much he wanted to destroy it. Craig saw something in him—what Grandma had seen. A potential for violence, for control. He offered Evan a way out, a chance to become someone powerful. And so Death Face was born. He became the thing he had been trained to be, using violence in the service of men like Wayne. Evan ceased to exist. Until Sandra.

She was alive, but the smile she once had was gone. She was like the doll he used to know, but now broken, lifeless. Frustration and anger gnawed at him. He had found her, but she didn't love him the way she was supposed to.

Sandra didn't love him anymore. She had been crying non-stop since the boss showed her the video. Death Face had cared for her—feeding her, giving her water, washing her. But now, Sandra refused to eat, vomiting what little she managed to swallow. She had lost her color, her shape, even the beauty of her blonde hair. But to Death Face, none of that mattered. He still loved her. But Sandra—ungrateful—cried for that man, the redhead from the video... Tom Collins.

She had betrayed him. She had been defiled by that man, and worse, she had liked it. She had enjoyed it when Collins took her, penetrated her. She betrayed him and everything Grandma had taught him. Watering her, caring for her, wasn't enough anymore. She wanted something more. The little bitch. The wise doll had gone wild. Death Face's frustration grew into something darker. He wanted to take back what was his. Maybe if he claimed her, maybe if he took her like the other man had, she'd stop crying. Maybe she'd love him again. Maybe she'd forget about Tom.

His mind racing, Death Face turned on the camera. He needed to remember this moment. He needed proof of what was about to happen. He walked over to where Sandra lay, near the bag of rubble, and grabbed her by the ankles, pulling her into the middle of the room. She struggled, weakly, but she was too exhausted to fight back for long. She gave up, letting him position her as he wanted.

Death Face spread her thighs as wide as he could, staring down at her, his eyes fixed on the place that had been taken from him by his rival. Sandra turned her head, her face streaked with tears. She refused to look at him, and that only made him angrier. She would learn.

He unbuttoned his trousers with shaking hands, his mind clouded by the lessons Grandma had taught him—lessons about control, about taking what was his. His virgin cock was ready, aching to claim her. No preliminaries, no tenderness. He pushed into her, the warmth of her body enveloping him as he forced himself inside her.

It was awkward, clumsy. He moaned like an animal, pushing deeper, harder, desperate for some kind of release. But Sandra made no sound. She didn't react. She didn't enjoy it, didn't moan like she had for the other man. She lay still, silent, letting it happen. Letting him use her.

Frustration boiled over. Death Face gripped her tighter, pushing himself as deep as he could go, thrusting wildly, needing to feel something, anything. His body convulsed as he finally released inside her, filling her with everything he had. But as he pulled out, it wasn't enough.

His gaze fell on her as his seed dripped from her, sliding down between her legs. He stared at the sacred place he had tried to reclaim, but all he felt was rejection. She was spitting him out.

Rage overtook him. He slapped her hard, the sound echoing in the room. He hated her for keeping the other man's seed, for betraying him and his love. Furious, he got up, pulling his trousers back on, and returned to his chair, leaving her lying there—broken and used. There was nothing left.

* * *

"No boy will ever love you if you stay fat." This memory surged back into Madee's mind, triggered by the shock of the assault she had just suffered. Often, when the four

of them sat down to eat together as a "family", and Madee glanced hungrily at the leftovers, hoping for a second helping, her parents would lecture her on the importance of being normal. In the Mitchell family, being normal meant being thin.

Love was measured by the number on the scales and the level of beauty. Her parents kept insisting it was for her own good, that boys only dated skinny girls, and if they ever slept with a fat girl, they did it in secret, too ashamed to face the social consequences. Thinness equaled success, and nothing else mattered. Madee had to change, had to shrink herself to fit in, or she'd never be loved.

She remembers the moments of humiliation when the entire family looked down at her with disapproval. Her gluttony made her feel guilty, and she'd cry alone in her room afterward. Laura would laugh at her, sometimes even pinching her thigh discreetly under the table, just to make her feel worse. *You're overweight, and no boy will ever love you.*

At fifteen, Madee believed that. She believed it when she met Joe, the first boy who ever paid her any attention. She was just a teenager, head full of dreams, knowing nothing about love or flirtation. Nobody ever looked at her at school. In the hallways, she was known simply as "Fat Madee."

Boys stayed away from her, but thanks to the diet Annie had forced her to follow, she had already lost 45 pounds. She still wasn't thin enough for the boys, though. So, she isolated herself. That was always how she coped when things got bad—by disappearing, by retreating into her own world. And it worked.

Madee remembers her first cigarette. She had read in a magazine that smoking helped you lose weight, so she started. Not to fit in socially, but to shrink. Alone in her corner, she'd light a cigarette, put on her headphones, and read. To everyone else, she was just the weird, fat, ugly girl, easily ignored.

She skipped school often, preferring to learn outside the classroom. She already knew what she wanted to do with her life—either open her own restaurant or work in the music industry. She could cook, but she had no real talent for singing. The few times she'd tried humming a song, her parents burst out laughing, telling her she sounded like a rusty saucepan. And as Annie, the self-proclaimed expert on showbiz, liked to remind her, to make it in the music industry, you had to be beautiful and thin.

Madee didn't really care if she could sing. What excited her was guessing which songs would become hits. Nine times out of ten, she got it right. She had a knack for it—she could feel a hit in her bones. During her days of lonely truancy, she'd spend her little pocket money in record shops, buying blank tapes to make her own compilations. At night, she'd plug her headphones into her CD player, listening to the radio, waiting for a track to catch her ear, ready to hit record. Madee was on a quest for the perfect connection between songs. She spent her free time crafting playlists, inspired by the vibrant voices and instruments, weaving stories through music. In those moments, she could escape, lose herself in a world she controlled.

Some of the record shops began to recognize her—the strange girl who hung around for hours, sometimes leaving with a record or a tape. No one asked for her opinion, but she'd come back to share her thoughts anyway. Her favorite shop was Paradise Records. Not just for the neon palm tree sign or the colorful décor, but because there was someone there who treated her differently.

Joe Russo. He was tall, skinny, and had a shy smile that Madee found endearing. Joe was 25, working at Paradise and another job at The Set Club. He'd talk to her every time she came in, and Madee—awkward and nervous—pretended to know more than she did, not wanting to look like a kid in front of him. The Set Club was just another suburban nightclub, the kind of place her mother, Annie, would call a den of debauchery. But to Madee, it sounded like freedom. Her mother had her own idea of fun, and anything that wasn't glamorous or prestigious was beneath her. Excess was only acceptable for the rich.

Joe wanted to be a DJ, and just like Madee, music was his life. They spent hours talking about artists they loved, albums they obsessed over. Joe didn't treat Madee like the others did. He didn't mock her or ignore her. With him, she finally felt seen, like she could be herself.

He had a key to The Set Club, and sometimes after his shift at Paradise, he'd take her there. The blue lights, the mixer, the empty dance floor—it all mesmerized Madee. She half expected to see some pop star from her childhood in a leopard print suit, making her the queen of the party. But instead, it was just Joe, playing one of her favorite records.

No one would have believed her if she told them. Fat Madee, interested in a boy, and an older one at that? Impossible. But it was real, and she kept those moments with Joe to herself, protecting them like secrets.

With time, Madee's confidence grew. Joe called her baby, and she found herself falling for him. He wanted her by his side when he DJed at The Set Club, and although she was terrified of getting caught sneaking out, the pull of his affection was stronger. If Jeff or Annie found out, they'd punish her for sure, but for the first time, someone cared about her. The choice was clear—between heart and duty, between a place where she was loved and a home where she was hated.

One night, she made her decision. At 11 p.m., she snuck out to meet Joe at The Set Club. Being underage, she was terrified she'd be thrown out at the door. But the club was on the brink of bankruptcy, and security had been told to let anyone in. Inside, the place was nearly empty. A few lonely souls hovered at the bar, trying to forget their misery. Joe was behind the mixing desk, barely visible, playing music that was flat, lifeless. There was more energy in a lift. Disappointment crept into Madee's young heart.

Joe knew a lot about music, but when it came to mixing, he wasn't as good as he claimed. To impress her, he'd boasted about his connections in the music industry, but now that she was here, it was clear to Madee that Joe had been lying. Still, she said nothing. She didn't want to embarrass him. Joe was thrilled she had come and proudly introduced her to Ricky, the owner of the club, before offering her a soda.

Ricky was exactly the kind of person Jeff and Annie would look down on—a tenant, a schemer, the type they loved to mock. But Madee didn't care. She liked the old Italian man with his Hawaiian shirt, safari hat, and sunny accent. He accepted her immediately, even sharing the club's financial struggles with her. For the first time, Madee felt welcomed. So, she felt she had to do something for her new friends. Joe asked her if she liked the music, and Madee, ever gentle, told him she had expected more. He seemed crushed, admitting that he was struggling, that the club crowd wasn't responding to his sets. That's when Madee decided to help. The club could be saved, and she could stay with her new "family" if they could attract a crowd with the right music.

Together, they started working on new mixes for The Set Club. At home, no one noticed her absence, and no one asked where she was. One day, the school called Annie to inform her that Madee hadn't been attending classes. Her mother's reply was cold: "It's the education system's job to deal with lost children."

Madee spent every night at the club. At first, the new mixes weren't working. Most nightclubs were riding the Eurodancewave, while others stuck to disco, attracting an older crowd. But Madee and Joe saw music differently—they wanted it to break down social barriers. Madee encouraged him to remix old disco hits, giving them a modern twist. Slowly, the strategy worked. The club's attendance grew, the queue at the door stretching longer each night. People flocked to see Joe, the young DJ who knew how to make them dance.

Ricky was over the moon. He always said Madee was a treasure, a kid Joe needed to take care of. "None of this would have happened without her," he'd say. But despite everything, Madee wasn't sure where she stood with Joe. They kissed sometimes, but he never publicly acknowledged her as his girlfriend. Now that he was gaining popularity, other girls hung around him, often coming up to the DJ booth to request songs. They looked at Madee with disdain, as if she were the fat little sister tagging along. But at the end of the night, it was Madee who Joe went home with.

While Joe smoked weed and passed out, Madee cleaned up the house, made breakfast, and worked on his career. She was the one who prepared his demo tapes for record companies. She knew he needed a memorable artist name, something that would make him stand out. Every DJ had a generic stage name—DJ this or DJ that—but Joe needed something special. Madee spent hours scribbling potential names in one of her old course books, but none of them felt quite right. Joe was reserved, shy, and his music was his only focus. Nothing else seemed to matter to him. As Madee watched him sleep, the name "Echidna" came to her mind. Like the Emerald Keeper she used to play with on her video game console, Echidna could fly and smash through walls—just like Joe did at the Set Club, trancing the crowd and breaking down barriers with his music.

For a while, things were good between them. Their artistic routine flowed smoothly, and then the day came: Madee made love to Joe for the first time. But it wasn't how she had imagined it. Joe didn't even undress her fully. He offered her his erect penis to suck, then swiftly put on a condom, pulling down her jeans and panties before penetrating her. Within minutes, it was over. In the end, people always embellished sex—it wasn't as good as they said. Madee tried not to lose hope; Joe was tired, and she convinced herself it would be better next time.

But sex became rare after that first time. Joe's mind was elsewhere, lost in his ambitions, spending less and less time with her. When they did have sex, Madee pretended to enjoy it, to feel satisfied, but inside, she felt alone and neglected. When the moment came, anxiety would seize her. Joe was not gentle, suddenly thrusting into her with no warning, leaving Madee feeling torn apart. She stayed silent, afraid he would leave her if she said anything. Sometimes he promised he would take her away from the suburbs with the money he was going to make. Clinging to that dream, Madee held on to her fantasy—an escape from home, her parents, her sister, and the sadness that haunted her life. She believed Joe would be her way out.

And Joe did leave the suburbs... but without her. A producer had heard the demo Joe had sent and showed up at the Set Club with a contract and a fat check. Joe thought he was talented enough to make it on his own. He took everything with him—all of Madee's work, her ideas, everything—and packed his bags. The harsh law of showbiz.

Joe, now known as Echidna, became a top DJ, and his album Loneliness Island soared. Madee never saw him again. Left with nothing but her suffering and a silence where music once thrived, she stayed behind in the suburbs. Without Joe, music lost all meaning. Every song she once loved only reminded her of him. He was the only one with whom she had ever shared her passion for it. At home, Laura would mock her endlessly, tearing apart her taste in music. Only rock was allowed once the Brandon Stevens lie took over their household. Madee thought rock was dumb and grimy, the music of losers who hated themselves but pretended to be better than everyone else...

* * *

Tom wasn't so different from Joe—he took what he wanted and then discarded her. Joe left her for fame, and Tom replaced her with Laura. The dagger of betrayal twisted deep in Madee's heart. She had told Babou that she was cursed... She never truly understood Laura's obsession with taking away what little she had. Madee's indifference had been her armor, a shield against the injustice and cruelty of her family, but she never showed open hostility towards her sister.

What would have been the point? Fighting a losing battle was futile. Yet, she could have taken revenge when Laura started spinning her lies about Brandon Stevens.

With just a little research online, she could have exposed the truth, torn Laura's credibility to shreds, and stopped the madness. If she had had any backbone at all, she could have halted the plague before it spread. Maybe that would have prevented her family's downfall…

No, she had no right to hold a grudge against Laura. Her own cowardice had made her an accomplice to her sister's diabolical schemes. Silent, docile, afraid—she had done nothing to stop her. And now she was paying the price for her weakness. Her rare rebellions had meant nothing, and in the end, Madee had to run away just to find some fleeting peace. Laura had taken everything from her. Annie had been right: a man of status can't stay with a fat woman—no, the thin one always wins the social battle.

Fate had caught up with her. The fleeting pleasure she'd felt when Tom made love to her had evaporated, leaving only the bitter truth: she was just a receptacle, the fat girl no one would ever truly love…

Now, Madee lay on the cold floor, at the mercy of the scum who held her captive. She had to stop crying—not to prove she was strong, but to say no to the abuse she didn't deserve. If no one cared about her, why did she keep changing for them? Anger rumbled deep in her tired heart. She was so done being nice…

"This child is bad," "She's so selfish," "You should sacrifice yourself for your sister, she's a woman now," "You buy clothes for yourself when your sister has nothing to wear…"

All the thoughts, all the accusations, all the violence these monsters had inflicted on her flooded back. She rolled onto her side in agony. Even if it meant dying, she had to defend herself... She had to reach out to the skeleton man, strike him, she could do it... Destroy the curse at its root. The monster's laughter echoed, disturbing, but she didn't hear it—too obsessed with avenging the rape...

"Very bad idea, beauty."

Before the light went out, the sharp glare of a titanium fist smashed into her face...

CHAPTER 30

LAURA'S DIARY: MY LAST WISHES...

He'll never love me... I hate it when people resist me, and Tom Collins has done exactly that. Why he loves Madee so much is beyond my comprehension. This rich, superficial man—I thought I had him all figured out. I was convinced he would quickly choose between the beautiful and the nice. Love... love without beauty is nothing. The enraptured glances of those first moments might hide the ugliness, but once the magic fades, reality always catches up with the illusion. It wouldn't have lasted with Madee—she didn't meet the criteria. When he has me, why does he love the dead girl? It's a cruel world out there, where the dominant crushes the dominated. I've got the looks, the sexual prowess, the public recognition, and yet, despite all these assets, he still rejects me...

When I woke up this morning, he wasn't beside me. I lay alone in the big, empty bed, in this hollow house. I drank more alcohol than usual—I've developed a taste for the dizzying haze at those lavish parties. My body still reeked of the vices of the flesh. I went out with Angela, happy that Wayne was busy in his "whore trap," as he calls it. While he was raping Madee, I was fucking his wife...

I loved the debauchery with Angela, her soft hands on my skin, her tongue lapping at my pussy. We were equals, two exhausted bodies, tired of playing roles, tired of being men's dolls. With her, everything was fluid, easy. We gave each other pleasure without a care in the world—we were finally in control of our bodies. No more strategy, no more power games, no more men... I experienced softness, freedom—I saw myself in a new light. For once, I wasn't fucking to gain favors, recognition, or some fleeting sense of validation. It felt like resting after an endless marathon.

Angela wanted to end it all, run away with me, leave behind our dirty little games. She asked if getting Tom back, if having Madee disappear, had calmed me. I didn't think she was capable of such intelligent thought... Angela, the drug-addicted nymphomaniac who became a music producer thanks to Dad. My deepest desires were none of her business—we had our fun, but I didn't owe her answers. Wayne and I will finish what we started...

I dragged myself out of bed, hair a mess, eyes like a panda, and wandered through the house like a zombie.

MYTHOMANIA

Fucking hangover! That'll teach me to drink more than I can handle. I needed aspirin—fast! I started rummaging through the bathroom, opening drawer after drawer. The hidden cupboards in this cursed house were driving me insane. That old witch Margaretha must have been a total control freak. Who puts cupboards in the most absurd places?

Frustrated, starving, and cursing myself for living in the middle of nowhere, I heard the doorbell ring. I ran down the stairs, certain it was the delivery man with the limited-edition pumps I had fought so hard to get. After two scandalous calls to the brand's customer service—who swore the shoes would arrive within 48 hours—the package had finally come. The fleeting joy of owning something other girls would kill for made me forget my loneliness. Tom could go fuck himself. I was one of the lucky few who would wear these on my feet!

Before opening the door, I glanced at the mirror—pretty good for a girl who'd been drinking all night. I loved seeing the admiration in men's eyes. Of course, I'd never stoop so low as to fuck a delivery boy, but I liked making them dream a little... The bell rang a second time, insistently. This idiot was clearly in a hurry to drop off his parcel and scurry back to his pathetic little life... Annoyed, I decided to open the door so he could hear me and learn his place. But the man on the stoop wasn't your average delivery boy. There was no van, no package. His scruffy appearance meant nothing to me at first. He looked to be in his late forties, of average height, with close-cropped brown hair and beady little eyes staring straight at me. He wasn't here for a courtesy call... I could feel panic slowly creeping in.

I scornfully asked what he was doing on private property. He smiled—a smile that told me he was used to dealing with women like me. Without a word, he reached into his leather jacket, pulled out a card holder, and flashed a badge. Detective Donahue, CID. For a moment, I thought my heart would stop. But I couldn't show it. I had to believe I was strong, that everything was fine. I glared at him with disdain, asking why he was here. He wanted to talk to Tom Collins, he said—ask him a few questions. My confidence was slipping, but I kept my composure.

In a breezy tone, I replied, "Tom hasn't returned from his morning jog yet, but if I can be of any help, I'd be delighted."

My charm had no effect on him. He kept his gaze steady, unflinching. He needed to speak to Tom about an ongoing investigation. I tried to pry more information from him, but he wouldn't budge. He just handed me his card, his eyes scanning me from head to toe, then repeated that he needed to speak to Tom as soon as possible.

I wished him a good day and shut the door. But I didn't move. I stood by the window, watching him. What if that bastard had walked around the garden, looking for something? My heart pounded as he finally returned to his car. He sat there for a moment, checking his rearview mirror. Those few seconds felt like an eternity. I was pale. I was scared. What if Tom had betrayed me? What if his sadness had been a cover to set me up? What if he knew I was related to Madee?

A million questions raced through my mind. I grabbed my phone and called Wayne, shouting at him the moment he picked up. We were in trouble. We had to act fast before the cops caught up with us. Wayne laughed, unconcerned. He didn't believe for a second that the detective had any real suspicions. He tried to calm me down, telling me Collins was an ex-drug addict—he probably just had some old trouble catching up to him. I was panicking for nothing, he said...

My instinct screamed at me to get out of there as fast as I could. The thought of the police showing up at my door so early in the morning made my skin crawl. *"Hysterical, crazy,"* Wayne had called me. I had to keep my head down—the meeting with Brandon was already arranged. I needed to find him and Angela, fast. Donahue's visit felt like a distant memory now, barely worth worrying about. Just the mention of Brandon's name gave me hope. Wayne was right—Tom hadn't told me he was in trouble, that's all. Nothing more to it. I wanted to cut off this dead weight and start my life with Brandon, free at last. But before I left, Tom owed me. One last fight, one last fuck. I was going to make that bastard pay, drag him through hell one final time...

CHAPTER 31

THESE DAYS, IN THE HERE AND NOW...

Tom hadn't even realized it had been dark for hours. Mechanically, he reached over and turned on the lamp beside the bed. Lost in Laura's despicable confession, the world outside didn't matter. Page after page, her words sent shivers down his spine. Slowly, the pieces began to fall into place. He finally understood why Madee had been so terrified of downtown, why she had hidden herself away in Forrest Hill... She had been safe there, she would have stayed if he hadn't insisted she come with him to the loft.

Tom's anger grew with every passing thought. He and Madee had been cruelly manipulated—just collateral damage in the twisted mind of a jealous woman. He had no idea jealousy could lead to such atrocities. For what? Some fanatic obsession, a delusional hope for fame, platonic love, an inferiority complex... It was clear now that Laura lived in a parallel dimension, completely disconnected from reality. She had no idea what love really was, no concept of life beyond her own twisted fantasies. Madee didn't need to be perfect or fit some ideal. She was perfect for him just as she was. He didn't care about her weight, her money—none of it mattered.

Wayne and Angela's influence had only made things worse, feeding Laura's vice and her destructive quest. Laura wasn't just misguided—she was a monster, an evil soul. She had been right about one thing, though: it was hard to believe she and Madee were sisters. How could they be? Their personalities couldn't have been more different. Thinking of Madeenow, the suffering she had endured in silence, Tom's heart ached. Just a few months with Laura had drained him completely—he couldn't even begin to imagine what it must have been like to grow up with her, alongside abusive parents.

His grief had blinded him. He had been selfish, consumed by his own misery, never thinking of what others were going through. He had fallen into Laura's trap, let her poison his mind. He had dragged Madee down with him, stolen the freedom she had fought so hard to earn. He would never forgive himself for that.

Tom was panicking now. He knew Wayne. He knew what that enemy brother was capable of. Madee was still alive, somewhere, but she was in Wayne's hands, alone, defenseless. Laura had mentioned a celebration... Brandon Stevens... He had to find her. He had to save her before it was too late!

With trembling hands, Tom opened the gift Laura had left him. Maybe the twisted woman had left him some clue, though he had little hope. As he lifted the silk blouse from the box, Madee's scent filled the room. The delicate fabric slipped through his fingers, bringing with it memories of their time together. He buried his face in it, seeing himself unbuttoning it, revealing her soft, round breasts, feeling the warmth of her skin under his touch. Tears welled up in his eyes. The happiness they'd shared had been stolen from them.

"Forgive me, my love... Forgive me..."

Where to start? Tom had to act, and act fast. There was no time for self-pity, no time to wallow in the guilt of a privileged man. At the bottom of the box, a USB stick gleamed—a night of love stolen, violated by Wayne and Laura, who had no qualms about desecrating such intimacy.

Tom stood up, his heart pounding, and walked down the corridor to the room now serving as an office. The computer sat there, waiting, but his hand hesitated over the power button. What if it was worse than he imagined? What if seeing the truth broke him completely? But he had to know. With a deep breath, he entered the password, his fingers trembling. Laura's last open tabs flashed before him—luxury clothing sites, a ridiculous shopping spree.

Anger bubbled to the surface. So much money, wasted on vanity and illusion. What a damn waste!

He forced himself to focus. As expected, the USB contained only one file. Typical. Wayne and Laura's bloated egos hadn't even bothered to give it a name. To them, it was probably just another anonymous moment, a twisted game, part of their collection of stolen lives.

The video was in high definition—cruelly clear. Blue neon lights illuminated a naked body in a windowless room, shadows dancing around the edges. With his back to the camera, Tom instantly recognized that bastard Wayne. He was violently sodomizing a barely conscious body. Tom's fists clenched, his teeth grinding in reflex. He watched in horror as his old college roommate groaned loudly and motioned for the camera to come closer. Wayne hadn't changed—still the same orange tan, the same gleaming white teeth in the garish light.

The camera zoomed in on the victim's emaciated buttocks, exposing a gaping anus dripping with blood and semen. Wayne's voice pierced the silence, ordering someone to clean him up because *"the bitch's ass is bleeding."* Tom's whole body shook with rage. If Wayne had been standing in front of him, he'd have killed him on the spot.

A close-up followed—Madee's face, suffocating beneath a plastic bag. Tom had dreaded this moment. Madee wasn't smiling anymore. Her once bright eyes were hollow, her cheeks gaunt, her breath labored. She had given up, resigned to her fate. There was no more fight left in her. Wayne disappeared from view, only to return moments later with his phone in hand, waving it like a trophy, showing her images she never should have seen.

"Collins never loved you," he jeered. "He's been fucking Laura."

Tom felt it—the exact moment when Madee's heart shattered. He could see it in her eyes, hear it in her silence. Wayne wasn't just hurting her physically—he was destroying her soul, piece by piece.

The video froze on Madee's look of despair. Tom exploded. Grabbing a paperweight, he hurled it across the room, the shattering glass echoing his own heartbreak. He couldn't hold back the tears. Wayne had dared to touch the woman he loved, dared to tear her apart. That son of a bitch had to be stopped. And fast. He glanced at the video's timestamp—recent. Madee was still alive, she had to be.

"Hang in there, my love," he whispered, choking on the words. "I'll move heaven and earth if I have to, but I'm coming to get you. I promise."

Sitting back at the desk, Tom folded his hands, praying to the God who had long since turned His back on him. Desperately, he hoped Madee could hear him, that somehow she would find the strength to hold on just a little longer. That she would know, beyond any doubt, how much he loved her.

Tom returned to the bedroom and picked up Laura's diaries again. Flipping through the last few pages, he found an entry about a policeman showing up that morning. Finally, it all made sense—this was what had triggered their last fight.

Laura had also mentioned the business card the officer had left. Tom frantically turned the notebooks over, but of course, there was nothing. Laura wouldn't have made things that easy for him. He clenched his fists in frustration. He needed that damn card. He wouldn't get far without help, and Madee's life depended on it. His mind wandered to his parents. How ashamed they would be if they knew the truth. For so long, he had taken them for granted, always dreaming of spitting his flaws in their perfect faces. John and Margaretha, the loving couple, who had done everything to help their son succeed... They were the opposite of Annie and Jeff, who had given everything to the daughter who ultimately betrayed them. And now, Tom realized how much he needed his parents, even if he couldn't bring himself to admit it.

For Madee's sake, he had to stop running away. He had to make amends, to offer her the family love he had always missed. It was just after midnight—his parents would still be awake, probably sharing a drink in the library like they always did. Maybe he could at least get his mother on the phone. Margaretha would understand the situation better than John... He had never quite known how to communicate with his enigmatic father. But there was no time for hesitation. Not now. Madee's life was on the line. He swallowed his pride, wasted a few more precious moments, then finally pressed the button to dial his mother's number. One ring, two rings, three... The screen remained black. His heart sank. Maybe this was a mistake. Maybe he should let it go. But just as he was about to hang up, Margaretha's face appeared, radiant as always. She never took her eyes off the screen, as if she wanted to make sure it was really him.

"Tom? Sweetie?"

"Mummy... Sorry to come back like this..."

"What's wrong, Tom?"

"I'm in trouble, Mum. I need help."

Margaretha's expression changed instantly. She turned away from the screen, calling for John. Moments later, his father appeared, wearing his usual indoor jumper.

"Your dad's here, darling... You look so sad. Tell us what's happening."

"Not over the phone, Mum... I need to see you."

"Where are you, dear?"

"At the villa."

"We're getting the car out of the garage right now," Margaretha replied.

John's voice cut in, firm and steady: "Son, it's Dad. We'll be there in 30 minutes."

The screen went black, leaving Tom in silence. The countdown had begun. There was nothing more he could do but wait. His mind was a mess, torn between remorse and hope. He needed to clear his head. He needed to prepare himself. A shower. He'd clean up, tidy the place. His parents' support would be crucial for what came next.

* * *

Tom had just finished tidying up the living room when the doorbell rang. John must have been speeding—driving well over the limit to have arrived so quickly. Tom rushed to open the door and fell into his parents' arms before they even crossed the threshold. For a brief moment, he savored the joy of being their little boy again, of finally feeling like part of their family.

Over a cup of coffee, Tom told them everything. His misfortunes at school, the chaos of college—drugs, parties, sex, his toxic friendship with Wayne, and his entanglement with Laura. They listened without interrupting, their faces solemn, their eyes full of sadness for their son's decline. Tom could see the regret in their eyes—anger that they hadn't noticed, guilt that he hadn't confided in them sooner.

Then he told them about Madee. He described Forrest Hill, Elaine's, Earl, Babou, Doc, Father Andrews, and the children. How he had fallen in love with Madee the moment he met her. His perseverance in trying to build a life with her, the overdose, the circumstances that led him to move in with her.

"That's why I turned down the company," he continued. "Madee told me not to do something I'd regret... I was blinded by my emotions. I wanted to spend every day with her... Dad, Mama, Madee made me born again. I can't live without her!"

John and Margaretha exchanged a glance, holding hands, overwhelmed with emotion. Tom thought they were touched by his story. There was a softness in Margaretha's voice that he hadn't heard in years. Her blue eyes sparkled with a youthful glow, a flicker of nostalgia.

"Sweetheart, we have something to tell you... Your father and I never told you this, but we met at Forrest Hill."

"Mum, you don't have to do this..."

"Tom, it's true!" Margaretha insisted. "I was an art student, and your father worked in construction. Our apartments were connected, and we fell in love."

John nodded. "Your mother's right, son. Old Earl was our landlord. The Collins Company was born in Forrest Hill. Our first regeneration project was in that area."

Tears welled in John's eyes as he recalled those happy memories. Tom could barely believe it. His parents? From Forrest Hill? In his mind, John and Margaretha had always been wealthy, untouched by the difficulties of everyday life. He had never imagined them anywhere but on the family estate.

"Forrest Hill seems to bring good fortune to our family!" John said, his usual stoic demeanor softened by the past.

But Tom couldn't share his father's optimism.

"Dad, Mum, you never left each other. I lost Madee..."

"A Collins never gives up, son!" John declared firmly. "It's no coincidence that your GPS led you there, that you met that young woman..."

Margaretha chimed in. "Your father's right. And you're forgetting Earl..."

John chuckled. "That's true. And God knows what a tough old bird he is!"

They laughed at John's remark, a brief moment of lightness in the midst of so much tension. It was clear that

Collins Senior had felt the wrath of Earl's temper back in the day.

"Earl's still as sharp as ever," Tom confirmed.

"What we're trying to tell you, my love," Margaretha said, her voice tender, "is that you can count on us. We're sorry we didn't understand each other before..."

Tom's voice broke. "What should I do, Mum?"

"We'll activate our networks," Margaretha assured him, "and you'll tell the cop everything you know."

"What if I don't have time? What if the detective doesn't believe me? If Madee dies, I'll never recover..."

"It'll be all right, darling! Have faith!"

John and Margaretha immediately began making phone calls, sending messages to their assistants and anyone who might help locate Detective Donahue. The three of them searched the house together, hoping to find the business card Laura had mentioned. To save time, they excluded the locked rooms. After 30 minutes of frantic searching, still nothing. Tom's hope was starting to waver when John's phone buzzed.

"Son, I've got it! Detective Phil Donahue, Downtown Central. Take down the number."

Tom's heart raced, his hands trembling as he dialed the number. One ring... two rings... three... No answer. His pulse quickened with every ring. Why wasn't Donahue answering?

Exasperated, Tom hung up and immediately called back. If he had to harass the detective all night, so be it. On the third attempt, a groggy voice finally answered.

"Donahue!"

"Detective Donahue... I'm Tom Collins, you came to my house earlier..."

"Do you realize it's the middle of the night? Call back tomorrow!"

"Don't hang up! I need to report a kidnapping, and if no one helps me, there's going to be a murder..."

"You're crazy."

"Wayne Beckett will kill her!"

Silence. Tom's heart pounded. Had Donahue hung up? That first contact had been a disaster. The detective clearly didn't take him seriously—until he mentioned Wayne Beckett's name. Suddenly, the cop's tone shifted, sharp and alert. Tom could almost hear Donahue's mind whirring to life. He seized the moment, explaining everything as quickly as he could.

"Collins, report to Downtown Central in 20 minutes."

"I'll be there!"

"Bring everything you've got. I'll see you there."

John and Margaretha had stayed silent throughout the call, hanging on their son's every word. When Tom finally hung up, they exhaled in unison, relief flooding the room as he told them Donahue was waiting for him at Downtown Central. Tom gathered his "evidence," kissed his parents goodbye, and headed for the door.

"You're going to make it, darling," Margaretha said softly. "Your father and I believe in you."

There was no time to waste. Tom's heart raced as he rushed out of the house, determined to save Madee, no matter the cost.

CHAPTER 32

DOWNTOWN CENTRAL: FIRST MEETING

Downtown Central was nothing like a local police station. Tom had expected to find officers stuffed with coffee and doughnuts, working the night shift with the relaxed smiles of people dealing with nothing more than a single drunk in custody, exchanging jokes with their colleagues. But stepping inside Downtown Central shattered that illusion. The movies had lied—there was nothing glamorous about this place.

The entrance was guarded by two overworked officers, barely managing to regulate the chaos in the complaints office. People squeezed in, dozens at a time, taking tickets like they were waiting for their turn at a crowded train station. Whatever their problems—speeding, pickpocketing, neighborhood disputes, fights—they all had to be patient. At nearly 3 a.m., Downtown Central looked more like a frenzied terminal than a center of justice.

Reception duty had been left to the rookies, fresh out of the academy. Before they could arrest criminals, they had to earn their stripes by enduring the complaints of the common man. Their faces were tight with exhaustion, listening with one ear as people demanded justice for every slight and misfortune. Complaints about speeding, fights, minor thefts—all filtered through the haze of a long night shift. Those lucky enough to make it past the waiting crowd weren't much better off. They wore handcuffs, guarded by officers who looked equally tired from a night of patrolling the city streets. No one here could be taken lightly—the stress and tension radiated from every corner of the room. Tom felt it creeping under his skin. How was he supposed to find Donahue in this mess?

The officer at the entrance barely glanced at him, told him to take a number, and walked away. When Tom tried to explain why he was there, the cop cut him off and rushed to help two colleagues restrain an aggressive taxi driver. This wasn't what Tom had expected. He'd assumed Donahue would meet him as soon as he arrived—not that he'd be left to wait among the masses like everyone else.

Frustrated, Tom pulled out his phone and called Donahue. No answer. Swearing under his breath, he left a message, telling the detective he was waiting in the lobby of Downtown Central. He paced back and forth, growing more impatient by the minute. Ten minutes later, a tall man with a moustache approached him.

"Collins?"

Tom looked up. The man introduced himself as Officer Harvey.

"Come with me. Detective Donahue's waiting for you on the third floor."

As he stepped out of the lift, Officer Harvey handed Tom a plastic box.

"Put your personal belongings in here—keys, wallet, phone," the mustachioed officer instructed. "Just standard security measures."

Tom hesitated. "I have important documents for the detective. I don't want to part with them."

Harvey's expression hardened. He didn't appreciate his authority being questioned, but he swallowed his ego and nodded.

"You'll keep them, but follow the rules. The boss will decide what happens next."

Harvey led Tom down the corridor and into the interrogation room. The walls were grey and bare, the room furnished with nothing but a table, two chairs, and a camera. The atmosphere was cold, sterile. Tom couldn't help but speak up.

"There's been a misunderstanding. Detective Donahue is expecting me in his office. This isn't supposed to be official."

Harvey gave him a slight smile but said nothing. He simply closed the door behind him, leaving Tom alone with his impatience.

* * *

From behind the one-way glass, Donahue watched Tom closely. Collins was calm, but the detective didn't miss a thing. He could see the tension in the man's body, the nervous energy bubbling just beneath the surface. Donahue liked to make them wait. If they were guilty, it helped them crack. If they were innocent, the waiting built pressure, coaxing out confessions about their own vices—or someone else's.

Phil Donahue wasn't in a good mood. He'd been on the Wayne and Angela Beckett case for two years, and every day it felt like he was hitting a brick wall. It had all started with Jess Finnigam, a young aspiring singer. Her story was painfully ordinary—an ambitious girl with big dreams, working small-time gigs until, one night, a music producer approached her after a show.

Jess was beautiful, incredibly talented, and Angela Beckett, the name on the card, was a star producer. She worked with Brandon Stevens and other big names. Jess thought it was her big break. But when she agreed to spend a week at Angela's house to *"work on her career,"* she had no idea what awaited her.

Wayne, Angela's husband, put Jess at ease with lavish parties. But what Jess thought was her ticket to stardom turned into a descent into hell. A little booze, a little dope, and before she knew it, she was at the center of a threesome. Fifteen men, including Wayne, raped her while she was barely conscious. They filmed and photographed her, despite her refusals. She had no choice. Donahue hadn't believed her at first. Stories like Jess's were everywhere in the entertainment industry—tragic but common.

Jess Finnigam never became a star. Traumatized, she hanged herself with an electrical cord. After that, more women came forward, each with the same story: rape and assault at the hands of Wayne Beckett. But none of them pressed charges. They were terrified of what it would do to their careers. They feared reprisals, and worse, being discredited.

Still, Donahue had quietly pushed for an investigation. Wayne Beckett was one of the most powerful men in the country. Exposing him had to be done carefully. The girls' testimonies weren't enough—without official charges, he had no legal grounds. And Wayne and Angela Beckett's money and social standing made them untouchable. To the public, they were "good people." If the case went public, the girls would be vilified—seen as opportunists trying to extort money from the rich and famous.

Even as the stories piled up, Donahue had nothing solid. These girls had been reduced to commodities—bought and sold for promises of fame and fortune. Some had tried to move on, throwing themselves into the spotlight to forget the past. But in the end, they all faded into anonymity, maintaining the law of silence. Wayne Beckett remained untouchable, and Donahue was left chasing shadows.

The case was stalling, and Donahue's superiors had him cornered. If there were no results soon, they'd be forced to close it. But Donahue wasn't giving up. He focused on the victims, the facts, their stories. So far, his attempts to dig into Wayne Beckett's life hadn't yielded much. Angela Beckett had been the face of their operation, using her status as a music producer to lure girls into their web, while Wayne kept his hands clean—at least in public.

Wayne Beckett was well-liked in his social circle. To everyone on the outside, he and Angela were the perfect couple—successful, charitable, living the high life. It was hard to unmask a man with two faces.

But Donahue persevered. He started looking into Wayne Beckett's youth. The son of Douglas Beckett, a feared and respected attorney, Wayne had grown up surrounded by wealth and privilege. He'd attended the best schools, including Garland University, where he had been the undisputed leader of his fraternity: Invictus. When Donahue questioned the former dean, he was met with a familiar story: "Invictus is for the elite. Brilliant young men, victims of others' jealousy..." Wayne's fraternity "brothers" gave the same rehearsed speech, portraying themselves as victims of class envy. They all claimed to have lived under the same roof as Wayne but were too focused on their studies to be involved in any of the wild parties rumored to take place. Their statements were too polished, too perfect. Wolves don't eat their own.

Wayne had learned well from his father. He maintained a spotless public record, not even a parking ticket to his name. If he was a king of mischief, it would be nearly impossible to prove. But one name kept coming up in Donahue's interviews with Wayne's old "brothers": Tom Collins. He and Wayne had been inseparable, best friends, life and death. And yet, strangely, Tom Collins was nowhere to be found in Wayne's current circle. This piqued Donahue's curiosity. Who was this "phantom brother"?

Tom Collins, the son of real estate tycoons, had always been destined to take over the family business. Unlike Wayne, he was easier to track. Donahue found everything he needed to build a profile on him. Tom had lived a life of excess—sleeping by day, partying by night. He was a regular in all the city's high-end bars, known for charming women and offering his "services" for their pleasure, without asking for anything in return. Some described him as a gentleman, polite and well-mannered, but not particularly talkative. In a way, he was the Good Samaritan of sex. But there was more. Tom had a serious drug problem. He regularly bought from the same dealer, ordering large amounts of cocaine four times a week. Donahue could have arrested him for possession alone. Yet one detail stood out: despite his life of debauchery, there was no trace of Wayne Beckett in Tom's recent history. Why hadn't they seen each other? What had caused the rift between them?

Something didn't add up, and Donahue was determined to find out what it was. Donahue had kept tabs on Tom Collins for months—until the man vanished completely. It was as if he had dropped off the face of the earth. He'd left his loft, disappeared from his usual bars, abandoned his libertine lifestyle. No records in hospitals or rehabs. No official statement from the family announcing his death. Nothing. Just a black hole, a void where the heir had once been.

And then, as if out of nowhere, the ghost reappeared. When Collins refused to take over the family business, it made headlines, but instead of returning to his old habits, he locked himself away—first in his loft, then in the countryside. Donahue had been patient, but now his curiosity had paid off. He had thought about questioning Collins, even if it meant risking the case. But Collins hadn't been home. Instead, a strange girl had answered the door, and Donahue was certain she was hiding something. It only deepened the mystery.

And now, here Collins was, sitting in an interrogation room, supposedly in possession of vital information about the man Donahue had been chasing for two years.

"Who are you, Collins?" Donahue muttered to himself. His instincts were off—he couldn't get a clear read on the man waiting behind the glass.

"What's going on, boss?"

Donahue hadn't heard Harvey approach. He nodded toward Collins, still staring through the one-way glass.

"What do you think of that guy?"

"He's weird, boss. My gut says he's not a criminal, but he's got nerve."

"You think he's bluffing?"

"We can't trust anyone in this business anymore, boss. They're good at that game. But he seemed sincere when he talked about the documents."

"I'll know soon enough." Donahue sighed. "He's had enough time to stew. Let's throw him in the frying pan."

"Good luck, boss."

CHAPTER 33

LAURA, EARLIER IN THE DAY...

The cop's surprise visit had set my nerves on edge. I was furious that I hadn't figured out why he'd come. Wayne's certainties weren't enough to calm me. The feeling of being trapped was growing by the minute, and my headache wasn't helping. I couldn't think straight, couldn't come up with a Machiavellian plan to fix this. Where the hell was the aspirin?

My head pounded, each throb making my anger flare. And that bastard Tom wasn't there. He was never there when I needed him. I needed to release this frustration, channel my helplessness into something. I had to focus, so I went hunting for the aspirin, slamming open cupboard doors in the kitchen. Each slam echoed my frustration. I wanted to break everything. Destroy everything, just to scare him. Just to remind him of what I was capable of. I didn't hear him come in. He was always careful not to be noticed. Coward. He avoided me. After a while, I grew tired of abusing Mama Margaretha's perfect cupboards. I paused, breathing heavily, when the ghost finally appeared in the kitchen. While I was falling apart, Madee had somehow gotten the best of him.

I don't think I'd ever seen him in a proper suit. Those old sports clothes were enough for me to know what kind of man he was. His disheveled look, that caveman beard, the messy hair... It disgusted me. Could he ever be sophisticated? Wayne was right. No amount of money could hide the slob in him. He didn't even glance at me. Everything about his posture screamed contempt. He made his coffee like I wasn't even there, like nothing had happened. We had done Madee a favor—she would never have been happy with him. Happy. What a joke. She didn't deserve happiness. It was time for me to make a scene. Tom wouldn't escape so easily this time. I needed to keep up the pressure. He couldn't run anymore.

I started slow, dropping little hints, weaving subplots into the conversation. I was the heroine, the one who had the courage to stand by a man like him. To be honest, and contrary to the legend, Tom Collins was a terrible lover. It didn't bother me that he stuck his dick wherever he could. He'd learned to live with his shame, despite what people said. But I knew where to strike. Mentioning Madee would hit a nerve. I slipped away, preparing for round two.

I went upstairs, isolating myself in my bedroom. I wrote the last pages of my diary. Confession time was over. My big day had come, and it was time to end my old life of hardship, to forget everything. Wayne had sent me a short video with instructions. I was to give this to Collins to keep him from talking. If he refused, something would happen to his precious Madee. Empty threats, of course—Madee's fate was already sealed.

The video was short, barely five minutes long. Wayne was in action, completely naked, in a windowless room bathed in blue light. His buttocks clenched, and I knew, from the countless times I'd fucked him, that he was about to come, spraying his sperm all over my sister's body. He groaned and pulled out, calling for his henchman to get closer with the camera, zooming in on Madee's gaping, cum-soaked bum.

I wondered for a moment if those emaciated buttocks really belonged to my sister. The camera panned around her trembling figure, crouched on the floor like a broken doll. Wayne, with careful precision, wiped her sex with a handkerchief, as if to erase any trace of his vile pleasure. His voice was filled with fury. The bitch was bleeding, and it angered him. He barked orders at the cameraman to zoom in on her face, covered in a plastic bag. Wayne yanked it off, revealing a corpse-like Madee, her red face slowly turning blue. Wayne shouted at her, calling her a worthless, two-bit whore, a disappointment who had ruined his fun. For a moment, I thought he might hit her, finish her off with a single slap. She lay there, helpless. He could have ended her right then and there. But instead, Wayne disappeared from the frame for thirty seconds, only to return with his phone in hand. He knelt before what was left of my sister, grabbed her hair, and yanked her head up, forcing her to look.

The sound of my own cum, my fucks in the hotel with Tom, filled the air. Madee's face turned livid, but she made no effort to defend herself. She was broken. Wayne told her that she was trapped, that Collins would never come for her. He was happy to be rid of her because now he could live freely in his love with Laura. The camera zoomed in one last time on her defeated face before the video ended.

I transferred the file to a USB stick and slipped it into the little gift I had prepared for Tom. With that distraction out of the way, I had a million things to do—packing, for one. I couldn't afford to forget anything. I didn't know what outfit Brandon would like, so I needed options. If everything went according to plan, I'd never want to be seen wearing the same thing twice. I also began crafting the perfect farewell speech for my final video. My followers would understand that Brandon Stevens' wife could no longer afford to be on the internet. Soon, I'd have a press agent to handle all of that for me. My farewell would be touching, and I'd be remembered as the woman who lived the modern fairy tale.

MYTHOMANIA

A pungent smell of smoke caught my attention. I'd left that bastard Tom in the kitchen, and now this—he was breaking my rules. Of course, he'd dare. He always dared. I'd found the pack of cigarettes in one of the bar drawers. He could die of lung cancer for all I cared, but if he thought he could yellow my walls with his filth, he had another thing coming.

For the second time that day, I stormed downstairs, and there he was, caught in the act. The ashtray was full. My rage surged, the hatred and desire mixing into a lethal cocktail. I wanted him to fuck me like a real man, not like some high-class whore. I thought of Madee's arse, the way she lay helpless in that video. I wanted Tom to do the same to me—stick his cock in me, dilate my hole, flood me with his cum. But the bastard pushed me away.

He had no right. His body was mine to use. I flew at him, hitting him with everything I had until I was out of breath. The coward, the weakling—he fled from my dominance. If he even thought about going to the police, the macho men in uniform would laugh him out of the station. Hit by a tiny woman? What a joke. All I had to do was cry and complain about domestic violence, and the ball would be in my court. No one would know who had started the fire. And besides, you don't mess with Mrs. Stevens. Maybe Wayne's henchman wouldn't mind earning a little extra. I could hire him to take care of dear Tom. People will do anything for money. Tom would be back soon, if my predictions were right. Unless the coward drove himself into a ravine. But his fate wasn't my concern anymore. His little gift would be waiting for him on the bed.

I hesitated with my diary. I didn't want to drag this remnant of my past into the glorious future that awaited me. I should have burned all traces of my youth, but there was a part of me that wanted to finish destroying Tom. He would never be able to use my story against me. Everyone goes through a rebellious phase. Who would believe the words of a troubled teenager uncomfortable in her own skin? People would just shrug it off and say, "It's her age."

And if it came to the worst, I'd sue them for libel. Claim that Wayne and Angela manipulated me, that the diary was a forgery. Between the son of a real estate mogul and the wife of the great Brandon Stevens, we'd see who wins. I took a deep breath as the taxi sped away from that deserted countryside. For the first time in my life, I didn't have to worry about anything but my own happiness. As if by magic, all the troublesome people were disappearing from my path. There was only one person left to settle a score with, and she would apologize profusely for humiliating me in public.

I pushed my hatred aside, just for now. I was tired of thinking. In front of Brandon, I had to look perfect—fit, rested, relaxed. I'd already made an appointment at the beauty salon at the President Hotel. No more blonde. I was done with that look. When I told the stylist to darken my hair, the idiot who had turned me into a bimbo nearly had a stroke. He warned me that bleaching wasn't something to be taken lightly, that I wasn't ready to go blonde. Blah,

blah, blah. I didn't get angry. I called Angela. Within five minutes, she had the top stylist on the phone, and the idiot was falling over himself to apologize. The power was incredible, and it felt good—so satisfying. It was official. I was now part of the upper echelons. No one would ever question me again.

CHAPTER 34

DOWNTOWN CENTRAL, INTERROGATION ROOM

Donahue burst into the interrogation room, coffee in one hand, files in the other, without a trace of unnecessary politeness. It was his signature move, meant to unnerve Tom: entering without knocking, looking rushed, pretending to hold incriminating evidence The files had nothing to do with Tom Collins, but Donahue knew he had to play the game—impress him, pressure him. Collins was here voluntarily, alone, no lawyer in sight. A rarity for someone like him... Daddy's boys usually have a lawyer by their side, even when they just want to chat. But the stakes were high, and Donahue couldn't afford any mistakes. One complaint and he'd be stuck behind a desk or, worse, patrolling the streets with a rookie. As he entered, Tom shook off the weariness from waiting, rising to greet him. The gesture grated on Donahue; the kid was trying to level the playing field. But this was his room, his interrogation.

"Tom Patrick Collins, I'm Detective Phil Donahue. Sit down."

His tone was firm, direct, the kind that left no room for negotiation.

"You asked for me. Some kind of emergency..."

"Detective... my girlfriend... she's been kidnapped. He's going to kill her. You have to see this!"

Donahue watched as Collins struggled to maintain his composure, but his words tumbled out in a chaotic rush. The man wasn't built for this kind of pressure. Maybe he was just acting. Stay sharp.

"Alright, but before we jump to conclusions, let's start from the beginning, okay?"

The detective softened his voice, playing the part of the calm, rational guide. He had to keep Tom talking, ease him into the trap.

"When you say your girlfriend, you mean the woman who was at your house this morning?"

"No."

"Who was she, then?"

"Laura... Laura Wilkins..."

"And who is Laura to you?"

"Detective, I'm here for Madee!"

Collins' avoidance of the question set off warning bells in Donahue's mind. The pieces weren't adding up.

"Who's Madee?"

"My girlfriend."

"Who isn't the woman at your house this morning… Laura, right?"

"That's right."

"And Laura is…?"

Donahue watched as Tom cradled his head in his hands, his voice cracking on Madee's name. Fragile. He was starting to fall apart. The detective knew pushing too hard now would just shut him down completely. Time to keep things calm… for now.

"Collins, if you want my help, you need to help me too! Who's Laura?"

"My girlfriend… well, the one who pretended to be my girlfriend. She tricked me… She took Madee. Her and Wayne Beckett!"

"Wayne Beckett? How long have you known him?"

"We met at university, but I cut ties with him years ago! I hate that son of a bitch!"

"Why do you hate him?"

"Help Madee, Detective! It's all in here, look!"

Tom shoved the documents toward him, but Donahue barely glanced at them. From this spoiled, junkie son of a rich man, the detective didn't expect anything solid. He needed to keep his approach steady, the traditional method of pressure before locking Collins away for 24 hours just for the pleasure of exercising power.

"Listen, Collins, Wayne Beckett is already under investigation for sexual assault and pimping. His entire life, and the lives of those around him, are under scrutiny. You, in particular! The party boy, the addict, the seducer. The invisible brother who cuts ties with Beckett from one day to the next. Doesn't that seem suspicious? You abandon this "brother," live a dissolute life until a few months ago, then vanish without a trace. Now you're living with a woman who you claim is your girlfriend but... isn't really. Then, suddenly, you accuse Wayne Beckett of kidnapping another woman, someone no one has ever seen. You fit the profile of a suspect, Collins, and I think you're part of the same scam as your buddy. So either answer my questions, or I'll have you arrested and wait for a full confession."

The weight of Donahue's words hung in the air. After all this pressure, Collins would either call for a lawyer or crack open. Donahue dreaded the first option—if a lawyer stepped in, his case would be dead in the water. Back to square one, and those poor girls would remain lost in the system.

Collins gathered the scattered documents, his face hardening as he stood. Silent. Defiant. Donahue couldn't hold him without concrete evidence, and he knew it. But nothing riled him more than having his authority questioned.

"Where are you going, Collins?"

"You're wasting my time, Detective. If you won't listen to me, I'll find Madee myself, because she needs me!"

"Collins! The interview isn't over!"

"Yes, it is! And for the record, don't overstep your bounds, Detective... You've got nothing on me, and you know it! I'm not proud of the way my life turned out. I take responsibility for my mistakes. But I would never, ever, sink to the horrors that Wayne Beckett is putting Madee through. She means everything to me, and right now, she could be dead... but I'll fight to find her, to give her back her dignity! You want Wayne Beckett? I want to see Madee again, hold her, love her... So, save your police tactics for the real criminals and do your job. Open your eyes and ears, damn it! With what I'm giving you, you've got enough to lock Wayne Beckett away for the rest of his life! I'm not your enemy, Detective... The choice is yours, but I know what I have to do."

Donahue hadn't expected Collins to push back. He quickly weighed his options. If Collins was telling the truth about the papers, the key to bringing Beckett down could be right in front of him. The girls wouldn't have to live in fear anymore, Beckett would finally answer for his crimes... And this woman, Madee... The number of victims, the shattered lives, weighed heavily on him. His past failures haunted him, clouding his judgment.

"Collins! Wait..."

Tom was already in the hallway, collecting his things. Harvey glanced at him, unsure if he should intervene. He exhaled in relief when Donahue arrived, preferring the detective to handle this kind of situation. Donahue motioned for Harvey to back off. Grateful, Harvey returned to his reports, happy to avoid being caught in the middle of an argument.

"Your personal effects..."

"You mean the stuff you confiscated, Detective?"

"Collins…"

"You treat everyone who needs your help like a criminal?"

"Try living my life…"

"Are you going to help me or not?"

"If what you're saying holds up, yes. But you need to understand, we might not be able to save her… I can't promise anything, but I'll do what I can."

"Your job is to arrest people who break the law!"

"I'm not a superhero, Collins… Madee might not be with us anymore…"

"I don't want to hear that!"

"But you must face it. You must accept the possibility."

"She's alive! Madee can't die… She just can't…"

"Collins… let's talk in my office."

CHAPTER 35

LAURA, EARLIER IN THE EVENING...

The limousine crept slowly through the city streets. Angela had warned me that a car would come to pick me up, but I didn't expect it to be this extravagant. I couldn't help but feel impressed—she and Wayne never did things halfway when they took control. Yet another undeniable proof of the power of money. As I caught my reflection in the rearview mirror, I barely recognized myself. The blonde phase was over. No more of that pathetic act where I had to play the sweet, innocent girl. I was back—fiery brunette, wild and untamed, the rock girl with no limits. On the phone, Angela had told me to look stunning because the evening would be unforgettable. I took her seriously—spa treatments, massage, waxing, makeup, manicure. I spared no expense. Perfection was non-negotiable for my big night.

I behaved horribly, treating the staff like they were nothing more than dirt under my feet, just there to serve me. I hunted for mistakes, demanded they redo even the smallest imperfection, and I loved watching their faces tense with the anger they couldn't show. They had no choice but to bow to me, the demanding, wealthy client. In that moment, I finally understood Annie's pride, the way she used to talk about being treated like a queen, the way it thrilled her to have people who were beneath her bend to her will. Now, that was my life, and all those pathetic losers who couldn't stand me would have no choice but to shut up in my presence. Money was no longer an issue, and these expenses were just the start of building my public image. All I had to do was show up, and people would be in awe. Where others slaved away in their cheap uniforms, I would walk in and command the room. I was now part of the 0.1% of girls who had it all.

But when I started going through the clothes I had packed after my makeover, a surge of rage hit me. Nothing looked right. All those overpriced designer rags made me look fat, and I felt the panic rising. Desperate, I called room service and demanded garbage bags. I needed to purge these blonde clothes, rid myself of the disgusting memory of Tom Collins. That little Veridi skirt—trash! The Poesia blouse—trash! The Enric Dan blazer I had once wanted so badly—trash! Trash, trash, trash! I couldn't stop the fury building inside me—anger at myself, at what I had put myself through to get here.

Why do men sacrifice so little? Why do they just have to exist to be loved? I looked at the pile of bags on the floor and realized I had thrown almost everything away. It didn't calm me down, though. It didn't fix my problem: I had nothing to wear. Well, no need to panic. Tomorrow, I'll just go shopping with Angela and refresh my wardrobe. I left the bags scattered across the room—let the hotel staff divvy up the spoils once I was gone. I didn't want to see those clothes again, clothes these hicks could never dream of affording. The clock was ticking, and I still wasn't ready. I needed an incredible outfit for tonight—something I didn't have. The lack, always the lack. It was unbearable. The few clothes I had left were for a casual lunch, not for meeting Brandon Stevens.

That's when I noticed it—a bag on the sofa in the living room. It was labeled 'second-hand' with the name of the shop. I could swear it wasn't mine. I would never buy second-hand clothes. Recycling someone else's rags? I had suffered enough of that as a child. Still, curiosity got the better of me. I knew who it was for, of course. My jealousy kicked in. While I'd been using his bank card, that bastard Tom had gone and bought her a gift. I rationalized. It was second-hand, so he couldn't have spent a fortune. Typical—stingy to the core, even with the woman he supposedly loved the most.

I opened the bag and unwrapped the contents. I hoped it would be something hideous, but I was disappointed. Inside was the perfect silk dress for the perfect occasion. An old Cascade piece, once worn by a famous model, making my jealousy spike even higher. A dress almost impossible to find. Tom Collins was a fool—fantasizing about Madee, comparing her to models who made millions. Just the feel of the silk made me want her.

What a letdown it would be for Tom when his precious princess didn't fit into the dress. Too beautiful for her. Madee'smisfortune was my triumph, and thanks to her, I now had the stunning outfit I needed. In that moment, I wasn't Laura. I was Cindy, Alexia, Shannon—a woman of undeniable beauty and power.

As I walked through the hotel lobby to the limousine, heads turned. The question on everyone's lips was clear: Who is this magnificent woman? I basked in it, the magnetic pull I seemed to have over everyone. This was the ultimate revenge for all those high school days, for all the bastards who had dared to look down on me. They had no idea how far I'd come, how well I'd succeeded. I couldn't wait to shove it in their faces, to make them choke on their words. The injustice was almost over. Just a few more hours, and I'd settle the score.

CHAPTER 36

DOWNTOWN CENTRAL, CRISIS UNIT

"Harvey! Check your emails and get the team together, now! I need to know if there are any CCTV cameras around Forrest Hill and North Station. Get the footage from six months ago. Have Johnson compile a list of all the properties owned by Wayne and Angela Beckett. And tell him to dig up everything on Douglas Beckett too—that bastard knows the law inside out, probably hiding assets with ghost companies. I also want a list of anyone released from prison seven months ago—long sentences, anyone with enemies. Wayne Beckett has a woman hostage: Madee Mitchell. And get Forensics to track down the source of that video. Beckett isn't working alone—Laura Wilkins is his accomplice. I need a detailed report on her movements in the last 24 hours. I want an arrest warrant on my desk! Wake up the boss if you have to!"

On the third floor of Downtown Central, the air buzzed with activity. After barking his orders, Donahue hung up the phone before Harvey could get a word in edgewise. Normally, Donahue would take time to go over theories with his partner. They always joked about being the "cerebral cops," different from the adrenaline junkies in the department who loved the heat of the moment. It was their way of coping with the reality that they'd never be profilers or feds, just detectives figuring things out one puzzle at a time.

Alone in his office, Donahue stared at the confession of the property tycoon's son, his mind swirling with possibilities. He had sent Collins out for coffee, needing space to think. His eyes drifted between the photo of two teenagers on his desk and the frozen image of a woman on his computer screen. Laura and Madee Mitchell—the hostile sisters. One dominant, the other submissive. One a liar, the other silent. One a killer, the other innocent.

And between them, there was Wayne Beckett and Tom Collins. Four lives tangled together, their fates intersecting in ways too strange to be coincidence. If Donahue believed in anything mystical, he'd see this as a modern-day apocalypse, a battle between good and evil, with God and the devil incarnate in the mix. Two years. Two years of investigation, filled with grey areas, and finally, by sheer chance, the pieces were starting to fall into place. Donahue had seen his fair share of criminals—people with unstable personalities, broken by miserable lives.

But this case? This was something different. Money, power, and revenge—they were often the drivers behind these crimes, but this new facet of human nature was still a surprise to him. Wayne Beckett and Laura Wilkins, two people who had it all, yet were consumed by envy. They were the tragic child kings, trapped in their ruthless pursuit to protect their thrones. No limits, no regard for others. To madness, to death.

Laura Wilkins didn't see herself as a criminal—like all fanatics, she saw herself as a victim, even as she played the role of executioner. She was fueled by a warped conscience, twisting right and wrong to suit her needs. She had killed her father, ruined her parents, and now, she was trying to kill her sister.

All to protect an adolescent lie, a fantasy romance that only existed in her twisted mind. Jealousy. A desperate need for recognition. Everyone else had moved on, grown up. But Laura was still 15, convinced that seducing Brandon Stevens would finally let her walk through the gates of high school with her head held high.

"You'll get your headlines soon enough, sweetheart," Donahue muttered to himself. "Don't worry. Your face will be on every front page in the country. And as for you, Beckett, not even daddy's money is going to save you this time."

The ringing of the phone interrupted his thoughts. Harvey better have some good news.

"Yeah?"

"Boss, we've got something."

"I'm on my way."

Two coffees in hand, Collins returned, offering one to Donahue.

"We don't have time for that, Collins. We've got news."

Tom's face hardened, but he followed Donahue silently into the crisis room. Donahue knew he'd get a reprimand from the boss for involving a civilian in an investigation. He had no right. But he'd deal with that later.

The priority now was to nail Beckett and Wilkins—and to find Madee Mitchell.

* * *

The crisis room was about the size of a small bedroom. For his persistence in investigating Wayne Beckett, Donahue had been severely punished. Digging into the affairs of the son of the city's elite didn't sit well with the higher-ups. The bureaucracy found other ways to make him pay, though his spotless service record kept them from sidelining him entirely.

Gone were the spacious offices from the days of tracking down *"The Package Killer."* Al Moore had talent, but he wasn't lucky enough to be the son of a well-connected lawyer. Much easier to cover things up that way... Those days of high-profile cases were long gone, and now Donahue and his team were tucked away in the forgotten corner between the fire escape and the coffee machine.

The dimly lit room smelled of cold tobacco. Harvey and Johnson sat at the large round table, an ashtray overflowing with cigarette butts between their laptops. They were exhausted, worn down by months of setbacks and the toll of Donahue's shifting moods. The failures had made Donahue increasingly bitter. Once this was all over, he'd be asking for a bonus and a week's vacation.

"Sit down, Collins, and keep quiet," Donahue ordered as he entered the room. "Whatever you see or hear is confidential. Don't interfere and let us do our job."

The overhead projector was already on, which gave Donahue a small flicker of hope—Harvey must have found something worthwhile.

"Well, what have we got?" Donahue asked, eyes sharp.

"First, Forrest Hill," Harvey began. "Johnson and I checked, but there's no CCTV in the area. The last cameras were taken out five years ago."

"Why?" Donahue's voice was clipped.

"Old guy with a baseball bat destroyed them," Harvey replied. "Name's Earl Stone. Lives in Forrest Hill, runs a coffee shop. Anti-authority, but no criminal record."

Donahue turned to Collins for confirmation.

Tom nodded. "Yeah, he runs Elaine's Cafe. Bit paranoid, but harmless."

"Alright, what's next?"

"You don't like suspense, boss?"

"Harvey, cut the crap. What else?"

"Look at this."

Seconds later, the wall lit up with a grainy video. Madee Mitchell, walking quickly down the street, unaware of the man creeping up behind her until he knocked her out cold. "We widened the search perimeter and found one active camera at North Station," Harvey explained. "It's near the new railway line. The girl is Madee Mitchell. We've confirmed it using facial recognition. We're still piecing together why she was there, but the guy—"

Harvey paused, freezing the video and zooming in on the attacker's face. The image sharpened, revealing a gaunt, deathly man. Donahue stared at the face, unfamiliar, but unsettling nonetheless.

"He's well-known to our department," Harvey added.

But Donahue couldn't place him. The face was distinct, like a ghost, but somehow, he had never crossed paths with him before.

"Evan Briggs, boss," Harvey began. "He was part of a criminal organization called The Guardians. When the wealthy need to indulge their worst vices, they call these guys to kidnap and "educate" their victims. Briggs climbed the ranks quickly, proving his loyalty. His stage name was Death Face. He made millions from high-profile contracts, but eventually, he got caught. A sham trial, no jury, no lawyer—he never stood a chance. Spent ten years in GranfoxMaximum Security. Released for good behavior seven months ago. The prison guards were relieved to see him go. He terrified them. Same with the inmates. Rumor has it, Death Face is a bloodthirsty psychopath. The few bigwigs who tried to mess with him in prison regretted it. Since his release, his probation officer hasn't heard from him once."

"Have you tracked him down?" Donahue's voice was tight with frustration.

"Briggs is smart. He doesn't use a phone—or if he does, it's a burner, impossible to trace. We spotted a black car on the CCTV, but the angle's bad. Can't make out the plates."

"Damn it! What about witnesses? Maybe someone saw something?"

"In North Station? Not likely..."

Donahue felt the sweat beading on his forehead, the heat of the room and the dead ends testing his patience. They had the henchman—Evan Briggs, a significant lead. Laura Wilkins' diary was starting to look more credible. Her Machiavellian plan to eliminate her sister, the "rival," seemed all too real. Taking advantage of the brief silence, Harvey nodded at Johnson, passing him the baton.

"I've been analyzing the video," Johnson said, "Didn't want to wait for forensics. I used an algorithm I've been developing to triangulate the position of the digital camera used to record the rape. It's still experimental, but in the meantime, I found something else. The software cross-referenced images... Madee's become a sort of mascot on the Dark Web. There's a platform for extreme pornography where a user named BrokeAngel has been posting rape videos. Madee'scaptivity has been split into episodes, like a sick reality show. I can't believe people are paying to watch this filth... Briggs appears in one of the videos. And Beckett—he's the star when Briggs isn't on camera..."

"We've got them," Donahue growled. "Good work, guys. What about Laura Wilkins?"

"She hasn't posted anything on her social media in two days. But I ran a trace on her mobile signal. She stayed at the President Hotel, but her last location puts her in Sun Valley—though not in the residential area."

"So, in other words, we've got nothing," Donahue spat.

"The algorithm's still running, boss. It's comparing her signal with BrokeAngel's IP address. But I do have some good news..."

"Then lead with that next time, Johnson," Donahue snapped.

"Madee Mitchell is still alive. The last video was uploaded yesterday morning."

Donahue's eyes flickered with a glimmer of hope.

"So, we still have a chance."

Tom's unease was palpable. Donahue could see it in the way he stared, transfixed, at the thumbnails of the videos. His face had gone pale, tension radiating from his rigid posture. Thousands of views, likes, and comments had accumulated over hours of torture and rape. Donahue could imagine the pain Tom felt, watching the woman he loved reduced to a helpless victim, a sexual commodity. He signaled to Johnson to turn off the projector before Collins lost it entirely. This kind of thing wasn't for the faint of heart.

"Collins!" Donahue barked, trying to snap him out of it. "We're going to nail these bastards. We can't give up now!"

Dazed, Tom nodded, but no sound came from his mouth.

"Do you need a minute, Collins? You want to step outside?" Donahue asked, his tone softening slightly.

"No," Tom croaked. "I'm staying."

His hands trembled as he raised the cup of cold coffee to his lips. Donahue exchanged glances with his colleagues, signaling that they should hold off on discussing the rest of the investigation for the moment. Collins needed results, something concrete, and they couldn't afford to push him too far. The fact that Madee Mitchell appeared alive in the latest video meant little—what mattered was how much longer Wayne and his gang would keep her that way.

"Harvey, what about the warrant?" Donahue pressed.

"I filed it as an emergency, boss, but there's been no response from the DA's office. It's late."

"I need that damn warrant. If I have to drag Ron Simons out of bed myself, I will!"

Donahue's history with District Attorney Simons wasn't great. A dispute over an old case had soured their relationship, leaving them more inclined to avoid each other than work together.

"I can help!"

Tom's voice cut through the tension as he suddenly jumped to his feet, his eyes blazing with newfound determination. Without waiting for permission, he yanked his phone out of his pocket and dialed a number, putting the call on speaker.

"What the hell are you doing, Collins?" Donahue snapped.

"Shh!" Tom waved him off. "You want your warrant? Let me do this. Dad? Dad, can you hear me?"

Donahue grumbled under his breath. Of course. The rich kid calling Daddy for help. These people always had a trick up their sleeve. Always one step ahead.

"Dad, I'm here with Detective Donahue. Madee is alive, at least for now."

"Thank God," came the relieved voice on the other end.

"Dad, do you and Ron Simons still do karaoke on Tuesdays?"

"Of course! Ron's got a great voice. Beat me last week with *"Love Me Tender"*... but why are you—?"

"Dad, Detective Donahue needs an arrest warrant for Laura and Wayne Beckett. The team's request hasn't been answered."

"I'm on it, Tom."

"Thanks, Dad."

"Hang in there, son. I'll call Ron right now and sort this out. Love you."

Harvey and Johnson couldn't help but snicker, lowering their heads to hide their laughter. The idea of Ron Simons, the tough-as-nails DA, crooning into a karaoke mic, was an amusing contrast to his reputation as a pitbull of justice. Even Donahue, usually stoic, couldn't bring himself to scold them. He would've paid to see Simons belting out Elvis.

Still, a shadow of doubt crept over Donahue. Simons had a reputation for being incorruptible. Would he really do a favor for a friend, even one as well-connected as Tom's father? Donahue's ego stung. It was his job to get that warrant, not Tom Collins' job to pull strings with the DA. He hated feeling useless... His phone buzzed, snapping him out of his thoughts. His pulse quickened when he saw the name: District Attorney Ron Simons.

"Hello?" Donahue answered cautiously.

"I can't say it's a pleasure to hear from you, Donahue," Simons grumbled.

"I'd like to return the compliment, Mr. Attorney," Donahue replied, his sarcasm barely concealed.

"Still the comedian, I see. Let's cut the crap. You know why I'm calling."

"I need the warrant, Simons."

"And you'll get it, Donahue. John and Margaretha Collins are close friends of mine, and I've known Tom since he was a kid. I won't tolerate any screw-ups. Got it?"

"Crystal clear, DA."

"No showboating. Follow protocol, make the arrests by the book. Douglas Beckett will pounce on any mistake. His son's involved, and he'll use any loophole he can find. Am I understood?"

"Loud and clear, DA."

"Good luck, Inspector. I want your preliminary report on my desk tomorrow morning. I'll review the evidence and prepare the indictment. You've got five hours to get this done. Don't screw it up."

Donahue motioned for Johnson to check his inbox while he finished speaking with the DA. His teammate gave a quick thumbs up. As soon as the call ended, Harvey burst back into the crisis room, holding the precious warrant in his hand. Meanwhile, Johnson's computer beeped several times—the software had results.

"I've got it, boss! I entered the GPS coordinates for comparison and... bingo! The address that stands out is 1333 Seaway, up in the Sun Valley hills."

"Wayne Beckett owns property there?"

"I'm checking... Give me a second... Officially, no. Not under his name, anyway. The property is registered to a Swiss real estate company called Langford Corporation. Partners? Douglas, Wayne, and Angela Beckett. But technically, they don't own anything in the country except their money."

"We'll deal with their tax evasion later. Are we sure they're at the house? Simons gave us the green light."

"Laura Wilkins' phone is still pinging from the nearby cell tower."

"Call the SWAT team."

"There's a complication with the house," Johnson said, zooming in on the satellite images. "These villas are built on sloping land. 1333 Seaway only has one entrance from the main road. As soon as SWAT moves in, they'll see it coming, and things could go south fast."

"What's your suggestion, Johnson?"

"See this patch of land above the Becketts' villa? It's downhill, unfenced, and overgrown with palms. If we send a drone to scout, our team could approach the garden from there and make the operation more discreet."

"What are the odds of success?"

MYTHOMANIA

"I don't want to give you false hope, but I'd say we have a 90% chance of arresting Beckett and Laura. As for Madee Mitchell... she could be hidden anywhere. I'll check the maps for any tunnels or cellars connected to the property."

"Good work, guys. When this is over, remind me to buy you both a drink."

Donahue couldn't wait to slap the cuffs on Wayne Beckett and Laura Wilkins. This case had come too close to ending up as a cold file. And for that, he had Tom Collins to thank. Without his help, they wouldn't be this far.

* * *

Thirty minutes later, Chief Walters of the SWAT team arrived for the briefing. Walters and his team were the best Downtown Central had—former soldiers, experts in tactical operations, ready for anything. Donahue had chosen them not just for their skill but for their medical experience. If they found Madee alive, they'd need to stabilize her quickly before the paramedics arrived.

The hardest part was dealing with Tom Collins. The lover had made up his mind that he was going to accompany them on the raid. Donahue had to shut that down quickly. Simons didn't want any unnecessary attention, and the orders from above were clear: no civilians on site.

But Tom wouldn't let go. He was determined to be there when they found Madee. He wasn't prepared for the worst. It wasn't negotiable. No untrained civilian could be part of a police operation—it was out of the question.

Donahue's patience snapped. He threatened to throw Collins in a holding cell until the raid was over if he didn't stop with his ridiculous demand. Reluctantly, Tom backed down, but not before making his own demands: he wanted to be kept informed of everything. As if Donahue had time to send him constant updates during a high-stakes operation. Without giving him another choice, Donahue sent Collins home with an officer to keep an eye on him. With that setup, he was confident the developer's son would be out of the way.

Adrenaline surged through Donahue's veins. He retreated to his office to mentally prepare for the operation. This was part of his ritual before every major arrest. Whether the operation would be successful or not? He left that to his favorite pair of dice. Before rolling the two green plastic cubes on his desk, he blew on his palm. A five and a four—completion and transformation. It was time to move.

CHAPTER 37

LAURA: IN THE PALACE OF THE GODS...

To calm my impatience, I sipped a glass of champagne, tapping on the window separating me from the driver now and then. Each time, his pitiful voice replied the same: the traffic was clearing up, and we would arrive at Sun Valley Heights as Mrs. Beckett had arranged.

Sun Valley Heights... Only the privileged few could call it home. The stories about it were endless—mansions rising high, dominating the town from their lofty, sloping grounds. Even among the rich, there were castes.

The lower part of Sun Valley housed the wealthy, but from Green Way upwards, the land belonged to billionaires, people with estates all over the world. In summer, the crème de la crème and the stars hosted ultra-private parties, the kind even a name on the guest list couldn't guarantee entry to. But tonight, I had my chance. I was going.

Suddenly, a wave of doubt washed over me. Would the Cascade dress be too modest for such a temple of excess? I'd never doubted myself, but in this moment, my confidence wavered. This dress was supposed to be the pinnacle of everything I'd worked for. The invisible Laura no longer existed. I was Madee, I was Joy. I was better than all of those people I had once envied. In this moment, I was the elite—I wasn't dreaming the dream, I was living it. I smiled at my reflection in the window, closing my eyes. Everything was perfect.

When we arrived, Angela greeted me with her sculpted figure wrapped in a tight leather dress. She set the tone for the night with a passionate kiss, pulling me close. I knew her well enough to know what that meant—before the evening was over, we'd sneak away for something dirty, and I wouldn't mind. She took my hand, leading me into the villa, telling me over and over to treat it as my own, to make myself at home. Her confidence in me was intoxicating. I was in, I belonged here. With Brandon, it was only a matter of time. I could already picture tomorrow's post—me, triumphant, with Brandon naked beside me in bed. The apologies from old classmates would flood in for days.

As we entered the living room, I let go of Angela's hand abruptly. The luxury around me blurred because all I could see was them, standing by the French windows, locked in an embrace. Wayne and Brandon. Kissing. MY Brandon.

No. It couldn't be. There had to be a mistake. The real Brandon Stevens hadn't arrived yet. The man with Wayne had to be some hired escort for the night, someone playing a part.

"Brandon, darling, I'd like you to meet a friend of mine," Angela said, calling him by his first name with ease.

They were playing a cruel joke on me. The man standing in front of me was nothing like the one who had graced the posters in my bedroom. Where was the eternal Peter Pan? This man was nothing but a poor imitation—paunchy, with short hair, brown eyes, weathered skin, and clothes that looked shabby and dated. This couldn't be my Brandon, the one who had bewitched me all these years.

Brandon barely glanced my way, dismissing me with a haughty wave and a snobbish voice before turning back to Wayne. The man I had worshipped in that old teenage video had vanished. This Brandon was a tired, decrepit version of the flamboyant rocker I had idolized. Sensing my discomfort, Angela leaned in.

"Brandon lost his hair a year ago," she said matter-of-factly. "He wears wigs for public appearances. He never had blue eyes either. That was Langford Senior's idea, to give him a romantic air. Brandon Stevens is a construct, a persona. But you know how the industry is."

Her words hit me like a slap. What about the video? The one that had defined my teenage years? My pride was shattered, and I didn't dare ask Angela any more questions.

This older, worn-out version of Brandon wasn't what I had expected. I felt revulsion and rage bubbling under the surface, but I forced myself to smile. I couldn't let myself lose.

With a strained smile, I asked, "So, do Brandon's girlfriends approve of all his... adventures?"

Angela was too eager to gossip.

"Girlfriends?" she laughed. "They're all just props, a cover for the public. He has to keep up the image—rebellious rock star, the dream guy for insecure teenage girls. But behind the scenes? Brandon's always been gay. He's been with Wayne for years. He never came out. It's part of the game. Privacy is everything."

I felt betrayed, humiliated. I wanted to scream, to rip them apart one by one. But then I thought of Annie. She used to say that a man is still a man, and I had plenty of charm. Maybe I didn't like Brandon anymore—reality had doused my fantasies in cold water—but I wasn't going to admit defeat. I needed to win, no matter the cost. And I had a plan.

A lot of alcohol would help. I'd turn on the charm, be sensual, clever, make a few witty remarks, embellish my life. I'd make Brandon forget Wayne in an instant. All I had to do was be magnetic, and once we were living together, I'd have the name and the fortune. He'd beg me to love him. My plan was perfect. My smile became more genuine as I pictured stealing Brandon away from Wayne before the night was over. After all, I had managed to land Tom Collins—Brandon Stevens would be easy.

Eternité Cuvée Spéciale champagne awaited us by the dozen, lined up near the Japanese buffet Angela had ordered from an overpriced, trendy caterer.

"Sushi's light," she explained. "You can eat it without feeling stuffed."

The chef had followed Wayne's trainer's instructions to the letter, substituting konjac for rice in a calorie-free recipe. I dreamt of seafood and caviar. Next time, for my receptions, I'd serve only the most expensive dishes, even if I didn't care for them myself.

During dinner, I desperately tried to amuse everyone to catch Brandon's attention. I tried to act like Madee, remembering how natural and funny she was, but in my mouth, her jokes sounded fake.

Angela and Wayne laughed, but Brandon barely acknowledged me. Every time he glanced my way, I could feel his judgment: his silence screamed, *"Oh God, make her stop talking!"*

To hide my anger at being invisible, I became even more exuberant. But I didn't give up hope— the night wasn't over yet. If Brandon hadn't responded to my looks or my humor, he wouldn't be able to resist sex. I was very good at it... after all, I had been well-trained. A man never says no to a woman who knows how to please him.

At the end of the meal, Wayne suddenly demanded silence. Apparently, I wasn't the only one tired of my babbling because he cut me off mid-story. I took the opportunity to down my glass of champagne in one gulp as Wayne raised his own glass and hit me with the truth like a sledgehammer. Angela wasn't alone anymore, he said, and he thanked me for coming into their lives. A sudden heat rushed through me, and I didn't see the betrayal coming, even though it was obvious. He took Brandon's hand and kissed it, announcing they were going to make their relationship official. Brandon would come out at the press conference for the release of his new album. We were now a family... Angela had me, Brandon had Wayne... He no longer needed to hide anything, nor share anything. Rage boiled inside me. I wanted to punch Wayne right in his smug face. I poured myself another glass of champagne and toasted, "Cheers, to the happy couple!"

I felt pathetic, betraying my own values. I had mentally slapped myself. Here I was, strong enough to crush the weak, but now nothing more than a little hypocrite, forced to put on a smile. I was once again the unpopular girl from high school, the disheveled Laura with the redneck look. Everything I had built—my rock culture, my beauty—it was all just a smokescreen. I would never be Joy or Madee, those real personalities I had worked so hard to destroy. There was no going back. I was stuck in this dream house of despair, surrounded by smoke and mirrors. I was part of this *"family"* now, but far from its leading member. I wondered where Madee was...

I remembered when I was four, climbing onto her back, stammering *"Madee, Madee"* because I couldn't say Madeleine... My silent sister, in her recycled clothes and cheap books... She never wanted fame, only happiness, and I managed to ruin that for her.

MYTHOMANIA

Angela took my hand with a vacant smile. It was the coke talking. After years of pandering to her asshole boyfriend's whims, the drugs had helped her accept becoming the woman she once rejected. The pile of powder on the table was enough to satisfy an army of junkies, but I hadn't even noticed it. Of all my vices, drugs weren't one of them. They scared me, and besides, I was too cheap to spend money on them. I was stung to the core when Brandon asked me if it was normal for me not to do drugs. Wayne, already on his third line, laughed and said I was *"healthy,"* Saint Laura. He mimed lighting an imaginary candle in my honor, thinking it was hilarious. Brandon laughed so hard he cried, openly showing his disdain for me. Why did he hate me so much?

I was about to find out. In a desperate move, I grabbed Angela's straw and snorted a line of powder. I didn't feel its effects immediately, but to perfect my act, I sat on Angela's lap, brushing my fingers across her chest to turn her on. My body was on fire, but my mind wanted something else. Angela responded eagerly, her tongue slipping across her lips, her drug-fueled eyes inviting me to go further. But when I glanced at Wayne and Brandon, hoping for their attention, I was disappointed again. They were kissing lazily, without the slightest interest in us.

Angela, on the other hand, was relentless. Her hands searched for the zipper on my dress. I thought of Tom Collins dreaming of doing the same to Madee. But instead of excitement, it only left me feeling bitter. She stripped me bare, her filthy words pouring over me even though I was already soaked. She was relentless, hitting every sensitive spot like a pro, but all I craved was a hard cock pounding inside me. Across the room, Wayne was going down on Brandon, and the sight of it made my blood boil. That cock was mine in my fantasies, and now someone else was devouring it. The unfairness of it all. I wanted to wedge myself between them. It wouldn't have been weird – it was an orgy after all – but Angela had her own plans for my pussy. She dove between my legs as I spread them wide, hungry for her touch. She was on fire, fingering both my holes while her tongue danced over my clit. Every nerve was buzzing, the drugs cranking my senses into overdrive.

As for the boys, Brandon was leading, driving into Wayne with a passion I hadn't seen in him before. Wayne, always so dominant, was letting himself be taken. Proof that you never truly know what someone wants. Angela finished me off, but I was too distracted to enjoy it. I had to join them. Wayne barked at me to fuck off, but Brandon, ever the gentleman, agreed to some time with me.

When Wayne left, I slid onto Brandon's lap, my heart racing as his eyes locked onto mine, making my skin prickle. His stare froze me in place – something in his gaze told me not to move. He leaned in, his breath hot against my ear, and I instantly regretted the drugs. Tomorrow, I wouldn't remember what he said. But then his words cut through the haze, each one landing like a punch

"I know what you did to my niece. And I know you fucked Troy. We've been watching you for a long time, bitch. Hurt anyone I care about, and you're dead."

My whole body tensed. He recognized me. Despite the makeup, the hair, the drugs – he saw right through it. That's why he'd been so cold, so distant. He wasn't just disgusted by me. He was here to settle a score, to make me pay for betraying his niece. He wasn't done. His voice was sharp, brutal

"You think you can cover up your stupidity and emptiness with that fake image? You're nothing. A stupid girl hiding behind a mask."

I felt sick. The shame, the anger, the humiliation... I couldn't take it. Brandon shoved me off his lap and dismissed me like I was nothing. I stumbled out, tears burning my eyes, as someone whispered, "Leave her alone, she can't handle the drugs."

But it wasn't the drugs that crushed me. It was Brandon.

CHAPTER 38

TOM, JOURNEY TO THE CENTER OF THE EARTH...

To ensure he wasn't being followed, Tom kept glancing at his rearview mirror. Donahue wasn't going to like this. The cop would be furious when he realized Tom had slipped through their grasp.

The third-floor squad at Downtown Central had worked miracles finding Wayne's secret hideout. Tom had thought his help would earn him a pass to join the SWAT team on the scene, but the orders were clear: Tom Collins is just a civilian—go home and wait for news. The cops were too focused on catching Wayne and Laura. They hadn't given a thought to how terrified Madee would be, seeing an army of officers storming the villa after months of isolation and abuse. She was treated as a mere afterthought, a victim who would soon be nothing more than a macabre footnote. But Tom refused to accept that. Protocol be damned! Do nothing? Impossible. He had managed to sneak away without the officer assigned to keep an eye on him noticing a thing. God bless whoever invented emergency exits.

Along the way, he detoured through the tourist area, knowing the late-night shops there would still be open. Acting on instinct, he bought a bottle of Madee's favorite perfume and some comfortable clothes for her. She wouldn't notice, maybe, but Tom wanted to restore some semblance of dignity and femininity to her. As he drove, the scent of roses filled the car, calming him. Inhaling deeply, he felt her presence beside him, a source of strength, a soft caress on his cheek.

* * *

The hum of the engine broke the silence. This was Tom's first time in this part of Sun Valley. Almost every villa in the area had been built by his parents—priceless, luxurious, and only inhabited by celebrities or the ultra-rich during the summer months. These mansions dominated the landscape, scattered far apart on the sloping hills. Hidden from prying eyes and the noise of the city, they were perfect venues for extravagant, hedonistic parties.

Tom considered whether he should continue on foot. The property he needed to pass through to reach Wayne's land was about two kilometers away, but he feared making too much noise. What if that bastard had surveillance cameras installed everywhere? Wayne Beckett could afford anything, and Tom cursed himself for giving Wayne so much power in his mind. The guy had limits—money couldn't cover up his crimes forever.

Stick to the plan: Find Madee, carry her to the car, get her to safety. Escape this nightmare for good. He had to move quickly and carefully. Daylight was coming, and his window of opportunity was closing fast. Tom knew he couldn't afford any mistakes.

He finally reached his destination—the last stop before crossing into enemy territory. He assessed the risk of being spotted and judged it to be minimal. There was no fence around the garden, and the villa appeared unoccupied, almost abandoned. It resembled a multi-story yacht, with portholes and metal railings, as if it had run aground in a sea of palm trees. The square, imposing building stood lifeless, a shipwreck without a crew. The place felt like a ghost ship, an ideal haunt for thrill-seeking teenagers or urbex adventurers.

The atmosphere weighed heavily in the lingering shadows of the night. A stagnant pool of water, now home to croaking frogs, surrounded the teak terrace. Up close, the majestic "ship" seemed soulless, a hollow shell of former grandeur. Tom half-expected ghosts to rise from the depths and drag him down with them. His heart raced when the automatic sprinklers suddenly hissed to life, spraying water in every direction. Panicking, Tom clutched his backpack and sprinted to avoid the jets shooting up from the ground. After a few meters, he realized there were no sea monsters chasing him, just sprinklers—likely an old trick from the villa's owner to scare off unwanted visitors.

Reassured, Tom continued down the sloping part of the property, walking carefully to avoid losing his balance or stepping into a hidden hole. Harvey's warning about Wayne's employee echoed in his mind—a ruthless, blood-thirsty man with a criminal record as long as his arm. Tom didn't dare turn on his flashlight. That brute would take his job seriously, ensuring no curious onlookers disturbed his boss. Tom knew that if he crossed paths with him, he wouldn't make it out alive.

The descent was less steep than he had imagined, though the lack of visibility slowed him down. Despite his caution, Tom didn't see the tree root jutting out of the ground. His foot caught on it, sending him tumbling down the slope, rolling like a rag doll and landing headfirst into a neatly trimmed bush.

For a moment, Tom wasn't sure where he was. His body felt numb, and he lay there, disoriented. His forearms and face were covered in scratches, but other than the shock of the fall, there was no significant pain. Slowly, he realized how lucky he was not to have broken a bone. He took his time getting to his feet, his head still spinning from the tumble.

A few more steps, and he reached Wayne's estate. The back of the white villa, with its Roman columns, was eerily familiar—an exact replica of the Invictus residence. Tom felt as if he had stepped back in time to his first day at Garland, half-expecting to see a golden car parked nearby. But those university days were long gone, and now he stood at the home of Mr. and Mrs. Beckett. The showy car had likely been replaced by a more discreet car, fitting the new life of excess and secrecy Wayne and Angela led.

Tom wasn't surprised to learn that Wayne and Angela had married. In fact, it was inevitable. What kind of sane person would willingly bind their future to someone like them? He wondered which one had proposed. Back in the day, Wayne was terrified of commitment, while Angela was busy supplying them with a constant stream of girls ready to party. Love was never part of the equation—neither of them believed in it. Their life was made of parties, sex, and drugs, with marriage merely a convenient facade for appearances.

The lights were still on in the villa, and the terrace was littered with empty champagne bottles. Tom's hatred for them boiled over. These scumbags were celebrating while leaving a trail of shattered lives behind them. It sickened him that people like Wayne, Laura, and Angela could cause so much damage with impunity. They belonged in prison. His anger blinded him, and all he could think about was making them suffer—seeing them scream in pain and shame. He wanted to break everything, strip away their masks, and watch them agonize, slow and excruciating. Sure, there would be a trial, but human justice would never be enough.

In the silence of the night, Tom's phone rang. Swearing under his breath, he yanked it out of his pocket and rejected the call, quickly switching it to airplane mode. Donahue. The cop had sounded the alarm. Tom was glad he hadn't run into a smarter officer, or he'd never have made it this far. The buzzing phone felt like a siren in the night, and Tom stood frozen, holding his breath, listening for any sign of movement. He expected Wayne or his henchman to appear at any moment. Donahue could have ruined everything. Tom wasn't here to be cautious—he was here to dive headfirst into the lion's den.

Still nothing after a few tense minutes. Relieved, Tom moved further into the shadows. The videos had shown a dark room, windowless, probably a basement, but he had no idea where exactly Madee was being held. Safety regulations required all properties like this to have underground corridors leading to the outside, in case of fire. The entrance had to be somewhere near the road, especially on a sloped site like this. Tom hoped Wayne hadn't sealed it off. That bastard was so convinced of his own invincibility, he probably thought he was immune to everything—even natural disasters.

Tom crept around the unlit part of the garden. There were no manicured flowerbeds here, just gravel paths and overgrown bushes—the servant's paths, he thought bitterly. Typical of Wayne, always reminding his underlings of their place. The leaves crunched softly under Tom's feet, and he barely had time to crouch down when a noise reached his ears—a creak, just a few meters away.

Through a small gap in the bushes, Tom spotted a faint blue light reflecting off the ground. A figure slowly emerged from beneath the earth—a tall man, rising like a corpse from its grave on Halloween night. Under any other circumstances, Tom might have smiled at the comparison. But not now. Now, he knew the truth: this zombie was real. Violent, cruel, and meticulous. Evan Briggs. Death Face.

Madee was right below him. Tom's heart pounded in his chest. According to the cops, Briggs' job was to "guard" her, to discipline her. That meant the jailer had probably heard Tom's phone ring. That's why he'd emerged from his hideout. Tom's pulse quickened. He knew if Briggs decided to search the area, it would be over. He was nothing to the jailer—just another trespasser to be disposed of.

In the middle of the path, Briggs stood motionless, like a predator sniffing the air for prey. Tom froze, trying to make himself as small and invisible as possible. He couldn't hold this position for long—just a few more seconds, he told himself. 10... 9... 8... 7... His legs trembled with the effort of staying still. 6... 5... 4... Sweat beaded on his forehead. 3... 2... 1... Satisfied that the area was safe, Briggs finally turned and walked toward the house.

Tom exhaled slowly, heart still hammering in his chest. Now was his chance. Briggs wouldn't be gone for long—he needed to find the entrance quickly. Staying low, Tom rushed across the gravel driveway, moving like a shadow. He scanned the ground with his hands, crawling on all fours, letting instinct and memory guide him. No stray thoughts. Just focus. Then, his fingers brushed against something wooden—a trapdoor. Hope surged inside him. He had found the way in. He was going to free Madee.

CHAPTER 39

LAURA: THE OTHER SIDE OF THE COIN...

Looking for a place to hide, I wandered naked through the ostentatious, luxurious villa. My conscience had awakened, and all my bearings had been turned upside down. Earlier tonight, I had been so sure of myself... Now, this cold, soulless display of wealth disgusted me. I realized I was utterly alone—everything familiar had vanished. Desperately, I opened doors at random, hoping to find Madee, to run into the arms of the sister I had hurt so much. Maybe she'd hold me, maybe she'd forgive me... But I didn't know her well enough to imagine how she would react. Would she have ever gotten herself mixed up in something like this? Probably not.

I thought back to my teenage room, to the comfort of the home I had patiently worked to destroy—all for nothing. All to relive the torment of my high school years. The surgery, the manipulation, none of it had changed a thing. My certainties had crumbled, and now I was surrounded by people who didn't want me. Everything was a lie, nothing was real. I was drowning in a delirium, trapped in a reality where I was nothing. I wasn't the queen of the chessboard anymore—I was the pawn knocked off in one swift move.

I'd gone too far, and now I was paying for it. I finally understood that I couldn't control everyone's free will. Maybe people had tolerated me for so long—Joy, Lou, Troy, Madee, Annie, Jeff—because they felt sorry for me. My wounded ego still hoped Brandon would change his mind, would beg and plead for my love. Why hadn't this situation turned to my advantage like it always did?

I stepped into a room with the initials W.B. embroidered on the curtains and monogrammed on the sheets. The master's crest told me I had entered the royal suite. Disgusting Wayne—self-centered and vile to the core. I looked around but found nothing of interest, except for a vibrator and a tube of lube in the bedside drawer. Typical.

My curiosity led me to the adjacent bathroom. More marble, more excess. Everything in this house screamed indulgence. In a display case, lit like a museum exhibit, Wayne's cosmetics were perfectly arranged. Among the anti-wrinkle creams and hair-loss products, I spotted a razor—a barber's razor, its blade sharp and gleaming.

MYTHOMANIA

I could take it. I could lie down in the enormous bathtub and slit my wrists, end my life, and claim my place in heaven... as Annie used to say, *"You'll get over it, girl!"* No. I wouldn't let anyone win. Death was a surrender, a recognition of my enemies' superiority. I stole the razor instead, laughing at the thought. Wayne hated facial hair. Without his precious tool, he'd be forced to grow a beard like Tom Collins. I emptied his shampoos and creams into the sink, leaving the empty jars in plain sight. It wouldn't matter—he could buy more without batting an eyelash.

Satisfied with my little rebellion, I left the royal suite—the lair of a rival I had never suspected. I couldn't stand Wayne. To me, he was a domineering, sadistic macho who hurt others for fun. But to be fair, he was a thousand times worse than me. This bastard was far ahead of me, and we shared the same goal in the shadows. I clung to the hope that he was on the verge of making a fatal mistake—and when he did, I'd be there to seize my chance.

Looking for a place to hide, I wandered naked through the ostentatious, luxurious villa. My conscience had awakened, and all my bearings had been turned upside down. Earlier tonight, I had been so sure of myself... Now, this cold, soulless display of wealth disgusted me. I realized I was utterly alone—everything familiar had vanished. Desperately, I opened doors at random, hoping to find Madee, to run into the arms of the sister I had hurt so much. Maybe she'd hold me, maybe she'd forgive me... But I didn't know her well enough to imagine how she would react.

Would she have ever gotten herself mixed up in something like this? Probably not.

I thought back to my teenage room, to the comfort of the home I had patiently worked to destroy—all for nothing. All to relive the torment of my high school years. The surgery, the manipulation, none of it had changed a thing. My certainties had crumbled, and now I was surrounded by people who didn't want me. Everything was a lie, nothing was real. I was drowning in a delirium, trapped in a reality where I was nothing. I wasn't the queen of the chessboard anymore—I was the pawn knocked off in one swift move.

I'd gone too far, and now I was paying for it. I finally understood that I couldn't control everyone's free will. Maybe people had tolerated me for so long—Joy, Lou, Troy, Madee, Annie, Jeff—because they felt sorry for me. My wounded ego still hoped Brandon would change his mind, would beg and plead for my love. Why hadn't this situation turned to my advantage like it always did?

I stepped into a room with the initials W.B. embroidered on the curtains and monogrammed on the sheets. The master's crest told me I had entered the royal suite. Disgusting Wayne—self-centered and vile to the core. I looked around but found nothing of interest, except for a vibrator and a tube of lube in the bedside drawer. Typical. My curiosity led me to the adjacent bathroom. More marble, more excess. Everything in this house screamed indulgence. In a display case, lit like a museum exhibit, Wayne's cosmetics were perfectly arranged. Among the anti-wrinkle creams and hair-loss products, I spotted a razor—a barber's razor, its blade sharp and gleaming.

I could take it. I could lie down in the enormous bathtub and slit my wrists, end my life, and claim my place in heaven... as Annie used to say, "You'll get over it, girl!" No. I wouldn't let anyone win. Death was a surrender, a recognition of my enemies' superiority. I stole the razor instead, laughing at the thought. Wayne hated facial hair. Without his precious tool, he'd be forced to grow a beard like Tom Collins. I emptied his shampoos and creams into the sink, leaving the empty jars in plain sight. It wouldn't matter—he could buy more without batting an eyelash.

Satisfied with my little rebellion, I left the royal suite—the lair of a rival I had never suspected. I couldn't stand Wayne. To me, he was a domineering, sadistic macho who hurt others for fun. But to be fair, he was a thousand times worse than me. This bastard was far ahead of me, and we shared the same goal in the shadows. I clung to the hope that he was on the verge of making a fatal mistake—and when he did, I'd be there to seize my chance.

The pristine decor of Wayne's room made me sick, like a space too perfect to be real. There was nothing left to see, just a lifeless emptiness that choked me. Instinctively, I walked into the adjoining room, which I assumed was Angela's. The stark contrast hit me immediately. The soft duvet of Angela's bed welcomed me as I collapsed into it, exhausted. I recognized her clothes, carelessly tossed across the room. I tucked the stolen razor under the pillow and closed my eyes, trying to shut out the chaos in my mind.

Moments later, I heard the door creak open and close, and Angela slid into bed beside me, wrapping her arms around my body. I pretended to be asleep. I couldn't face her—her touch disgusted me. The shame of it all was unbearable. Her lips grazed my neck as she whispered, "I love you." I cursed life for putting this girl in my path. Now she "loved" me, but it was a mockery. I was trapped in a life that wasn't mine, and it only deepened my self-loathing. What had become of me? The only goal I had left was to be recognized, respected, as the wife of Brandon Stevens. Yet, here I was, lost, clinging to a fleeting illusion.

***

I closed my eyes and, when I opened them again, I was no longer in bed. I stared down at my hands and feet. I was wearing platform boots, my nails painted black—my teenage look, the one that had made me popular. An endless corridor of student lockers stretched out before me. Muffled laughter echoed from inside them, and through the gaps, I could see yellow eyes spying on me. I tried to turn, to run, but I couldn't. I was floating forward, pulled down this hellish corridor. Metal doors slammed behind me, and from them emerged demons, jeering at me, their spit sizzling as it hit the ground.

"*Mythomaniac, mythomaniac, mythomaniac...*"

The word followed me, the label that had been branded on me forever. The demons spat fireballs at me, their voices echoing down the corridor. I recognized the song playing in the distance. Brandon's hit. But now, in this distorted reality, it was terrifying. A prophecy of my doom.

"Every day I risk my life,
In this shitty world I'd like to escape,
But at the end of the corridor, she's waiting for me,
Death, my sweet friend.
And I dance with her, oh yes, I dance with her..."

The devils' laughter grew louder. I stumbled past a stall selling T-shirts with my picture on them. Beneath the image of me, vulgar and exposed, were the words in bold red letters: *Mythomaniac.* The demons began to shape-shift, taking the forms of people I had known—Joy, Troy, Lou, Jeff, Annie, even Madee. Their eyes swelled grotesquely, popping out of their sockets and splattering me with acid. Others plucked out their glass eyes and hurled them at my feet, trying to trip me, to make me fall.

I was trapped in this delirious, hellish nightmare, surrounded by malevolent spirits mocking me. I wasn't strong—I was just a victim. I wanted to scream, to escape, but I was powerless. Then, an angel appeared before me, holding a delicate flower in his hand. My savior, my only hope. But the flower twisted in his grip, transforming into a flamethrower. His serene face remained calm as he pointed it at me. The flames erupted, but before they could touch me, the devils laughed and pissed on me, putting out the fire. Their sexes stretched out like lassos, wrapping around my wrists, ankles, waist, and neck. They tied me up, their grotesque bodies pulling me tight as they paraded their victory. The mad escort chanted in unison: *"Mythomaniac, Mythomaniac, Mythomaniac."*

They led me forward, still bound by their endless ropes, until we reached the end of the corridor. The devils knelt before their master, a shadowed figure standing amidst a giant spider's web. Slowly, he stepped into the light, his entrance accompanied by flickering multicolored lights. He wore a purple velvet robe, and his long, jet-black hair was twisted into a turban, giving him the air of an ancient alchemist. The devils chanted his name, encouraging him. Calmly, the Master pulled a gun from beneath his robe and pointed it at me.

"The only bullet is for you, Laura."

I begged for my life, tears streaming down my face before I even realized I was crying. He smiled, his teeth sharp and dripping with blood.

"Those you have broken deserve their revenge."

The song's haunting refrain echoed in my ears:

"But at the end of the corridor, she's waiting for me,
Death, my sweet friend.
And I dance with her, oh yes, I dance with her..."

The Master pulled the trigger.

CHAPTER 40

BEFORE THE BELL TOLLS, IN THE DEN OF VICE...

After the particularly gruesome session he had been forced to witness, Death Face needed a break. The boss had doubled down on his cruelty towards Sandra. Where he once would just come in, rape her, and leave, now sex wasn't his main focus. For two weeks, he had escalated his torment. Wayne would circle around her, inspecting her from every angle as soon as he descended into the cellar.

Sandra had grown so thin there was hardly anything left of her. The boss liked it that way. He took her weight loss very seriously. Armed with measuring tongs, he would pinch the loose skin, his lips curling into a sneer.

"Still too fat," he would mutter, his voice dripping with disdain. He accused her of eating like a pig, calling her filthy, telling her she was nothing compared to the model-sized girls he admired. He would drag in large buckets of ice water, dousing her, saying it was to purify her—claiming the cold would burn calories and cleanse her soul.

"You'll never be like them," he'd hiss, pointing at the posters of perfect women on the wall. "You'll never be respectable."

Sandra had been strong up to this point, but the last session had shattered her. Wayne had raped her violently while delivering electric shocks with a taser, demanding she contract her muscles to trap his cock inside her. The agony had pushed her beyond the edge. Wayne, dissatisfied with her compliance, had squatted over her, shitting on her after ejaculating in her mouth. He smeared the feces across her skin with his foot before scrubbing her body with a brush, stripping away flesh in the process. Death Face had looked away, unable to watch.

Accustomed to short, restless nights, the jailer now needed sleep. He could hear laughter and music from the garden—champagne corks popping, voices carefree. Inside the cellar, Sandra trembled uncontrollably, her teeth chattering between coughs. Death Face had stopped touching her after the boss discovered his *"moment of weakness."* The reprimand he'd received had been enough to scare him straight. The boss had made it clear: if he disobeyed again, he'd be sent to prison. Death Face didn't mind the punishment—he had learned his lesson. He didn't like fucking her anyway. She was tainted, contaminated by the redhead she cried for so often.

Sandra's presence had become unbearable. She was dirty, inside and out. She soiled everything she touched, even preventing him from sleeping with her pitiful sobs. If it weren't for the boss's orders, Death Face would have ended it himself—suffocated her in her sleep. The bitch deserved nothing less.

Even while dozing, Death Face remained ever vigilant, attuned to every sound. He had trained himself to pick up even the slightest disturbance, ready to react at a moment's notice. Upstairs, the party was in full swing. Nothing unusual. Soon, it would devolve into an orgy, like always. Sex was a part of the business. They hired Death Face for his skills, but also for the atmosphere of controlled chaos he brought with him. Social power thrived on repressed desires, on indulging in what was forbidden. In this world, everything was allowed—no matter how extreme.

Death Face had taken the job out of necessity, a chance to restore his reputation in a field that had turned its back on him. A final performance before he vanished into obscurity. After this, his name would be on everyone's lips. He could raise his prices when the wealthy and powerful called on him during his peaceful retirement. It was all he knew how to do—he had been born for this, not to rot in a prison cell.

In the distance, he heard the faint ringing of a telephone, likely the boss receiving one of his late-night calls. Wayne was like a vampire, his thirst for sex insatiable until the early hours. By day, his coffin was the UV booth that maintained his absurd tan.

Sandra's labored breathing filled the cellar, each breath sounding like it could be her last. Death Face had seen too many in agony to be moved by it now. She was close. He tried not to pay attention, but if she died before the *"grand finale,"* the boss would send him straight back to prison. She had to live long enough to meet the end they had decided for her. Her death wasn't his to choose.

Curled up in the corner, Sandra shook uncontrollably, her body wracked with violent shivers. It was forbidden to cover her—she had come into this world naked and bloody, and she would leave it the same way. As Death Face approached, he noticed froth collecting at the corners of her mouth. She was drooling like a rabid dog. A bad sign. She was dying.

No mercy. She had chosen her side. Once, when she was still Sandra, she had been cared for by him, by granny. But now, Death Face had made it personal. Sandra didn't love him anymore. She didn't deserve sympathy.

In her condition, it would be easy to strangle her, to end her misery. Or he could finish her with an electric shock, make her heart stop, feel the last beats fade under his fingers. He could take her soul before it slipped away. Then, he'd dismember her—keep her head and her pussy as trophies, dump the rest in the sea. His ego, bruised and battered from years of rejection, weighed heavier than the promise of profit.

The dilemma gnawed at him: honor versus freedom. He held her life in his hands, ready to deliver the final blow. But instead, he let her go. He would leave the dirty work to the boss. Rescue wasn't his concern anymore. This revenge scheme... it would end in disaster. His instincts screamed at him to take his money and disappear before the empire fell.

* * *

Being outside felt strange. Death Face had almost forgotten what the world looked like from the surface, after being locked away in the decay and vice below. Since the night he'd brought the girl here six months ago, he hadn't set foot in the garden. Standing in the middle of the driveway, he wondered how Wayne would react. The boss would likely see this initiative as arrogance—after all, Death Face had never been allowed inside the house before. These perverts were all the same, using guys like him to clean up their dirty business. He couldn't afford to get lost in pointless thoughts now.

Returning to the shadows meant accepting the blame if things went wrong. Death Face let his legs move mechanically: ring the bell, talk about the girl, demand his dough. Ring the bell, talk about the girl, demand the dough... The mantra echoed in his mind as his finger pressed the bell.

Wayne opened the door, naked, his face flushed. In the light, Death Face barely recognized him. The orange tan was riddled with deep wrinkles, despite its artificiality. His bleached hair had thinned, turning yellow, and the implants couldn't disguise his premature baldness. Powder had ravaged him from the inside out. The self-proclaimed living god was aging, and no amount of wealth or power could make him immortal—not even his devoted followers.

"What are you doing here?" Wayne snapped, his voice sharp, aggressive. Clearly, this unexpected visit had startled him.

"It's about the girl, boss."

Wayne sighed in frustration, annoyed at being disturbed over something so trivial.

"Not here! Don't just stand there like an idiot, get inside!"

Who could have possibly heard them? The property was isolated, perched on the hill. But Wayne's paranoia was heightened, his loud sniffles betraying that he was in the middle of a comedown, making him nastier and more volatile than usual.

Inside the luxurious foyer, Death Face felt a strange pull of memory—granny always made him wipe his feet. But here, the Becketts didn't have a rug for that. A rug would ruin the aesthetic, distorting the carefully curated display of expensive furniture and artwork. Death Face, who felt like a sewer rat, was embarrassed by such opulence. He'd been allowed into the god's house, but he still knew his place—the bad boy no one wanted to be seen with.

He followed Wayne in silence, noting how the boss didn't bother to cover himself, as if nothing unusual was happening. Wayne, seemingly oblivious to the tension, boasted about the riches they passed.

"These tables," he said, "were made by the finest marble-maker in Italy. And those paintings—bought by my father for next to nothing from some formerly rich drunks, desperate to pay off their debts." He laughed, shaking his head.

"Who would waste money on art made by poor losers? Not me. It's charity, really."

They reached the living room, where Wayne poured two glasses of gin. Death Face watched him closely, repeating his mantra in his head. Talk about the girl, demand the dough. Wayne, meanwhile, downed his first glass in one gulp, his mind elsewhere, still basking in his own grandeur.

"So, what's so urgent?"

"The girl... she's sick. She's dying."

"What do I care?"

"I thought you'd want to know."

Death Face hadn't even touched his glass, but Wayne was already on his third. His laughter rang out, sharp and mocking, as if Death Face's concern was the punchline of a joke.

"You thought, huh? Buddy, you're not paid to think."

Wayne's words dripped with condescension, his tone bored, dismissive. But Death Face pressed on.

"There's a problem. I thought you'd want to hear about it. I'm paid to watch over her, but if she dies, the deal's off."

Wayne poured himself another drink, slower this time, swirling the liquid in his glass before taking a long, loud sip.

"The deal is off," he repeated, almost to himself.

Death Face could sense the trap tightening. Wayne wouldn't pay without a fight—men like him never did. The powerful never feared repercussions, not even from the Guardians. And Death Face knew he no longer had their backing. He was on his own.

"You want your dough, don't you?" Wayne's voice had taken on an oily, taunting quality, each word dripping with false sincerity.

Death Face kept his guard up. One wrong word, and Wayne would use it to his advantage. He didn't answer, letting the silence stretch, calculating his next move. Wayne stood up, his movements sluggish, and stumbled to a sideboard. He opened the drawers, pulling out wads of cash, his arms full of money. Standing before Death Face, Wayne grinned wide and opened his hands, letting the bills cascade to the floor like some obscene parody of charity.

As Wayne sat back down, finishing the rest of the gin, his laughter turned darker, more erratic. A gunshot exploded through the room, the deafening crack of the bullet reverberating off the ceiling. Death Face's body tensed—Wayne was holding a gun now, the barrel pointed straight at him. Wayne's laughter grew louder, wilder. He was beyond reasoning. The gun's barrel remained locked on Death Face, and he knew that at any moment, Wayne could pull the trigger. He'd seen the look before—the unhinged glint of a man too far gone to care about consequences.

"What the hell is going on, Wayne?"

A woman's voice broke through the madness. A beautiful brunette rushed down the stairs, her eyes widening in horror. Death Face felt her terror as she avoided meeting his gaze. She knew exactly what kind of man Wayne was, but seeing him like this was something else entirely.

"None of your business, Angela! Get back to bed!" Wayne barked, his irritation flaring as the gun wavered in his hand.

"Who is this guy? Where did you get that gun?" Angela demanded, her voice shaking.

"I said get back to bed!" Wayne was losing patience, his rage simmering just below the surface.

Angela didn't move, her defiance hanging in the air.

"You're pissing me off, Angela! You want to stay? Fine! Make yourself useful. Fuck my guest!"

The shock registered on her face, but Angela wasn't shy. Her disgust was clear, but she still stood her ground.

"Wayne, you're insane! No. Not that."

"Fuck him!"

"That's enough. I'm leaving!"

"You're not going anywhere, babe. I've got the money, I've got the power... and I've still got those videos of your dear old daddy fucking little girls."

"You're disgusting!"

"Shut up! Fuck our guest, bitch!"

"Never."

The gunshot came without warning. Angela crumpled to the floor, her lifeless body collapsing onto the carpet. A single bullet through the head. Wayne didn't even blink. He glanced at the blood splattered across the walls, the bits of brain staining the expensive furniture, and he smirked.

Wayne scratched his cheek with the gun barrel, toying with danger. One wrong move, one stray bullet, and it could all be over for Death Face.

"Don't get me wrong, I'm a generous boss. I know the worth of my people. Madee's lasted this long because of your stellar care... So, here's what I'll do. Consider it a tip, a big bonus for excellent service. You fucked her, right? That moment you came inside her... wow, that was something, mate! Now, go ahead, I saw the way you looked at Angela before..."

"No thanks. Not my style."

Wayne laughed darkly, shaking his head.

"Oh, you don't get it, mate. You don't have a choice. Go on, she's only missing her head. She's still warm... fuck her, and the money is yours."

Wayne gestured with the gun, forcing Death Face into compliance. He started telling dirty stories about his wife, playing on the frustration of a man who always stood on the sidelines, watching others indulge. Wayne wasn't mad at him for Madee—the bitch was there to be used, and the video had been a hit.

While Wayne masturbated, gun in one hand, cock in the other, Death Face gave in. His pants came off, and he climbed on top of the corpse, following Wayne's every instruction.

"Yeah, that's it, mate. Spread her legs more... she liked it deep, remember?"

Death Face followed through, pounding the body as Wayne cheered him on. But it all stopped when the shot rang out. A bullet pierced his back, straight through his heart.

Calmly, Wayne blew on the barrel of the gun. Without a second glance at the two corpses, he picked up the cash and stuffed it back into the drawer. He'd deal with Madee later. The bitch could wait. Her death would be livestreamed—people had paid, and they deserved the grand finale.

CHAPTER 41

TOM, IN THE DEN OF VICE...

It didn't take Tom long to find the opening to the trap door, made of cheap wood. Mounted on two hinges and adorned with a simple metal handle, the pine plank was by no means a secure door—any child could open it with ease. Tom wondered if it wasn't a booby trap, some trick Wayne had left. His heart was pounding, but he had no time to hesitate. Death Face could return at any moment, and Tom had to hurry Tom cast a quick glance at the trap door. Every second spent in this room reduced their chances of getting out alive. Light sounds occasionally echoed above his head. He couldn't be certain—were those footsteps? Or was it simply the house creaking under the weight of time? He bit his lip. If Death Face came back now, it would be over before he even had time to react. Sweat trickled down his back.

The storage room, likely an extension of the pool's utility room, was neither a shelter nor a passageway. Used to store cleaning products, or perhaps more illicit goods... Death was queen in this filthy space, the unbearable stench of decay draining the life from anyone who entered. Tom covered his nose, fighting the urge to gag. There was no other way out, just the hole he had come through. His eyes scanned the room, absorbing the grotesque display of photos on the walls—women used and discarded, their stories told in snapshots of shame and suffering.

Past, present, indifference, and love—all clashing in Tom's mind, a brutal reminder of how a man's choices can change his life forever. But he had no time to linger on these thoughts. With his flashlight, he swept the room with the beam of light. And there, near a pile of rubble swarming with flies, he found what he had come for.

Seeing her there, huddled and trembling on the damp ground, tore his heart apart. Pain gripped him as he knelt beside her. Madee weighed no more than 80 pounds, her lungs wheezing, collapsing like balloons deflating. Blood had clotted on her scratched skin, her face was barely recognizable—bloodied, shapeless, beaten beyond comprehension. The face Laura had so often wished would disappear was now swollen and disfigured by the violence. Her wavy blonde hair had turned into a colorless, tangled mess, soaked in urine, semen, and dirt.

Tom forced himself to ignore the putrid smell emanating from her broken body. He caressed her face, whispering reassuring words.

"You're safe now, I'm here."

Yet his heart clenched, seeing her cracked lips, her greyish complexion. Scabs covered her frail arms, some of them still bleeding. How could such suffering exist?

Still, despite all of this, Tom could see her light. They had tried to destroy her, to erase her, but they could never take away the purity of her soul. That was something they could never break.

Her forehead was burning with fever, her pulse weak and erratic. She was barely conscious, deathly close. Tom lay down beside her, pulling her into his arms. Despite the danger, despite everything, he had finally found her—his Madee, his love, the comforting presence that had given him strength when he had none left.

"I'm getting you out of here, darling, I promise," he whispered.

He was sure she heard him. He kissed her gently, whispering soft reassurances, making sure she knew she wasn't alone anymore. She was no longer forgotten, no longer unloved.

He looked at her face, twisted in pain, her breathing uneven. He hesitated for a moment, his heart pounding in his chest. Moving her might kill her. But staying here? It was a death sentence. Every second spent in this sordid cellar brought Madee closer to the point of no return. He closed his eyes for a moment, calling to mind the image of Ganesh and the protective angel. There was no room for fear. No more time to waste. She had to survive. They had to make it out together. With great care, he laid her down and pulled the clothes from his backpack. His hands trembled as he dressed her, careful not to hurt her further. First the trousers, then the sweatshirt. But even with gentle movements, Madee's trembling doubled in intensity. He looked sadly at the bottle of perfume he had bought for her. What foolishness, what naivety—the indiscretion of a man ignorant of the brutal reality.

"I'll pick you up gently, my love, just stay with me... everything will be fine," he whispered, more to himself than to her.

Tom's fear wasn't about what was coming, but about this very moment. He could feel the thin thread of life still tying her to this world, so fragile, so tenuous. Moving her was madness—she had already endured too much, fought too hard. Trying to save her now might kill her. But staying here was a death sentence. He had promised her. He couldn't fail her.

A muffled bang startled him. Staying here would mean certain death. He remembered the day after his overdose, the vision of Ganesh, Shiva, the elephants, and the angel with the lily. Madee had faith, she believed. Now was not the time for doubt, not the time for fear. He would no longer resign himself to failure, no more delaying for tomorrow, no more waiting for it to pass. He called upon the angel for protection, holding Madee close to his chest as he prepared to pull her towards the exit.

Before lifting her to the surface, he placed one last kiss on her forehead.

"I'm taking you home, my love," he said softly.

The rustling of the wind through the trees seemed to echo his words, urging him forward. With each step toward the exit, the weight of the world bore down on him. He would save her. He had to save her.

CHAPTER 42

LAURA: CHECKMATE!

The bang snapped me out of my nightmare. The devils and the Master were gone, and I was no longer in my teenage clothes. Back in the bedroom, I felt a gnawing suspicion crawl over me. I got up to check the wardrobe, half expecting to find some lurking evil spirit. But no, there were no hidden doorways to the underworld—just Angela's clothes hanging on the racks, untouched.

Angela wasn't there anymore. She had probably gone to the next room for sex. I slipped into one of her satin nighties, ready to join her. Maybe her carefree spirit could make me forget the sting of last night's defeat. Before leaving, I retrieved the razor I'd hidden under the pillow. That's how I was—I liked to keep stolen objects for a while, letting them soak up my energy until they fully belonged to me. And when I got bored, I'd toss them aside like everything else in my life.

The door to Wayne's room was slightly ajar. I only had to push it open to step inside. But instead of the expected scene, only Brandon lay there, fast asleep in the massive bed. There was no orgy in sight, no debauchery—just him, ugly, naked, and vulnerable, abandoned by his lover.

I had offered him the world, the chance to shine, to conquer it all—and he rejected me. It wasn't supposed to end like this. I couldn't bear the insult. Me or no one! Brandon had to pay for his disdain. I had to teach him that fame didn't make him untouchable. It was my will, not his, that mattered. He belonged to me, his most devoted fan. For two decades, I had adored him, worshipped him—and this is how he repaid me?

The razor in my hand felt heavy, alive with Wayne's lingering energy. A wild idea bloomed in my mind. Attack when they're defenseless—always. The opportunity was right there, waiting. I couldn't let it slip by. This was my victory, the moment where I reclaimed my power. All I had to do was get close enough to slit his throat. But no, that was too simple. Too merciful.

No, Brandon didn't deserve death. He deserved suffering. He had to lose everything, be stripped of what mattered most to him. The public would mourn him if I killed him, they'd glorify him in the media. That wasn't good enough. I needed him to suffer privately, to be denied the one thing that gave him power.

MYTHOMANIA

I held the razor tight. My hands trembled, but my mind was sharp. He refused to fuck me, so I'd make sure he'd never fuck anyone again. Be ruthless, show no mercy. Let him feel the weight of my power. I had sacrificed my life for him; I wasn't just another fan. I would take my reward by force.

I watched him for a moment. Without makeup, his face was crisscrossed with wrinkles, his skin weathered and sagging. If things had gone my way, I might have looked at those imperfections with affection. But now? Now they disgusted me. They were the symbols of his decay, his vulnerability.

"Too bad for you, Brandon. No one resists Laura Wilkins."

My steps were slow, calculated. The razor glistened in the dim light as I approached the bed. He looked so peaceful, so oblivious to the storm about to break. For a moment, I hesitated. Not out of mercy, but because I realized I was no longer the victim here. I was the predator. And he, my prey.

I thought back to the countless nights I had dreamed of him—dreams where he was mine, where we were inseparable, where I was his queen. But reality was crueler, harsher. He rejected me, chose to humiliate me. And now, I would make sure he paid.

Just a few more steps, and I could mark him forever. The razor gleamed in the moonlight streaming through the window. My heart raced. All I needed to do was slice it across his skin, and he would never be the same. Never be the man the world adored. I would take that from him, strip him of his power, and leave him broken.

But even as I raised the razor, I could feel the weight of my obsession. This wasn't about Brandon anymore. This was about control. About reminding the world that I, Laura Wilkins, could never be discarded or ignored.

Excited by the thought of what I was about to do, I frantically pulled back the bed sheet. My heart raced with anticipation as I unfolded the razor blade, its sharpness catching the dim light. Would it hurt him? Perhaps. But the pleasure I would feel from this act would far surpass any pain. I grasped his cock with my left hand—my heart's hand, a symbol of all the love I had ever felt for him.

The razor moved closer, sharp and clean. A kitchen knife would have been quicker, but I worked with what I had. Blood flowed instantly, fast and thick, painting the sheets in a deep crimson. Brandon Stevens emptied himself before my eyes. His vulnerability made him mine in a way he had never been before.

When I was done, I stood back to admire my work, holding his severed manhood like a trophy. I laughed—an uncontrolled, maddened laugh. I had finally made him pay. For all the humiliation, the rejection, I was now the victor. A second shot echoed in the distance, but I paid it no mind. Clutching his cock in my hand, I felt powerful, unstoppable. Nothing frightened me anymore.

I grabbed one of Angela's bathrobes and carefully wrapped the bloody trophy in a towel. Without a second glance at the man who once consumed my every thought,

I left the room. I descended the stairs in silence, the weight of what I had done sinking in with every step. In the living room, I caught sight of two bodies on the floor. One of them was Angela. Her pretty head had been blown apart. What a waste, I thought, of such beauty.

Wayne was nearby, picking up wads of cash. I wasn't surprised. It was typical of that scumbag to be more concerned about money than the people he killed. He didn't notice me slip into the kitchen, where the knife rack sat like an absurd decoration. No one here would have ever used it; I doubted Angela even knew how to cook. The stupidity of the rich overwhelmed me. They felt invincible, always believing they were safe.

Another gunshot, followed by a scream from upstairs. "Showtime," I thought, smirking. I picked the largest knife from the rack, my grip steady. There was no need to rush. Wayne would come to me on his own, his rage making him reckless. All I had to do was wait. His anger would blind him, make him careless. I placed the severed cock on the bar, prominently displayed like a centerpiece. A final mockery.

More gunshots, doors slamming, and Wayne's voice bellowing insults. I smiled as I listened to his desperate shouts.

"Bitch!" he screamed, and worse.

His anger only made the moment sweeter. He was a fool if he thought he could bait me out with such childish taunts. I was the queen of manipulation, the master of psychological warfare. Wayne was no match for me.

"You think you can lay down the law in my house?" he roared, his voice cracking with frustration.

The answer was simple: I didn't need to explain myself to him. I had no desire to justify my actions. Wayne had used me to get to Tom Collins, to destroy Madee. But I was the law now, in his house or anywhere else. He owned nothing—not even his own fate.

I heard his footsteps getting closer, his voice losing its echo. He was running out of steam, his threats becoming more desperate. I knew, deep down, he was afraid. Who wouldn't be afraid of me?

"You ruined my family, bitch!"

Ruined his family? What family? Family didn't exist! I was Laura, the dominant one, the one who had always kept Madee, Jeff, and Annie trapped in a cage. Playing their pathetic roles in Wayne's pretend family? That was never an option. He was alone now, against me, his weapon powerless. One day, they would all find themselves alone against me. I saw his gun aimed at the door. One step, two steps, three steps... Wayne's eyes fell on the cock, displayed there on the bar like a grotesque trophy. He lunged for it, proving his stupidity by falling into my trap.

The knife was already in his back before he could even turn around. I watched him stagger, his strength fading as he collapsed face-first onto the floor, unconscious, without ever getting the chance to see my triumph. He was as good as dead. His money, his plans—they couldn't save him now.

As I pulled the blade from between his shoulder blades, blood spurted out in violent bursts. Blood of war, blood of sacrifice, blood of conquest. But it wasn't enough to wash away the years of torment I'd suffered. The hardest part is always the first kill, and once you've done it, the taste lingers. This was even better than sex. As the knife sliced through his flesh, the sound was like music to my ears. I wanted more—more blood, more power, more life to absorb.

"But at the end of the corridor, she's waiting for me, Death, my sweet friend, And I dance with her, oh yes, I dance with her..."

The cursed words of Dancing with Death hummed on my lips as I moved with the rhythm of the kill. I was dancing, dancing with death herself, and I wouldn't stop until the final step was complete. Death's dance card was full tonight, and I had claimed the lead.

Grabbing Wayne's bleached hair, I yanked his head back, forcing his neck to expose itself. I could feel the tension in his limp body, the last vestiges of life clinging to him. The blade met his throat—quick, precise. Checkmate. His blood gushed out, warm and sticky against my skin, and I reveled in the sensation. I had silenced Wayne Beckett forever.

But this wasn't just a victory over him—it was a dance, a macabre waltz where I was the lead. Each cut, each spurt of blood was a step in the ritual, and I was no longer just Laura Wilkins. I was death incarnate, a specter, a force that consumed everything in its path. And like the devils in my dreams, I hummed, swaying gently as I watched the life leave Wayne's body.

"But at the end of the corridor, she's waiting for me... death, my sweet friend."

I held the knife up, gleaming in the dim light, and twirled it in my fingers like a dancer's ribbon. The last act of the night had been played, and I was the star.

CHAPTER 43

MEANWHILE, ON THE OTHER SIDE OF THE MIRROR...

Tom dreaded reaching his destination. After six months, the thought of returning to square one filled him with dread. He knew Forrest Hill would be anything but welcoming. His eyes shifted to Madee in the passenger seat. Leaving Wayne's estate had been a nightmare. Gunshots echoed from inside the villa as Tom shielded Madee with his body, his heart racing. He feared being spotted, chased by Wayne and his thugs. Climbing up the steep slope with Madee in his arms, he could feel her limp body, unconscious and feverish. He tried to steady her, but the rough ascent made her shake uncontrollably. Yet Tom kept moving. Weakness meant death. Twice, he had to stop, his legs trembling, his breath short. He wasn't sure he'd make it to the car.

Each step up the slope was a battle, the sounds behind him amplifying his fear. He dreaded the appearance of the ghost from his nightmares, whispering, *"Say hello to your wife,"* before ripping Madee from him. In that moment, Tom felt a deep connection to the suffering of the Son on the cross. He prayed fervently that his plea had reached the angels, that they were by his side, guiding him.

"A Collins never gives up," John's words echoed in his mind, fueling him to push forward. He and Madee would survive this. When the villa yacht came into view, he quickened his pace, dodging the sprinkler, sprinting across the garden to the car. Breathless, he climbed in, started the engine, and took off, eager to leave this nightmare behind. The phone in his pocket buzzed with missed calls and messages. Most were from Donahue, furious over the botched operation. As he sped down Sun Valley, a saloon car caught his attention, heading toward the SWAT vans. When they reached the same altitude, Tom saw Donahue and Harvey inside. The cop made a move to cut him off, but Tom veered sharply, narrowly avoiding a collision as he sped ahead. He knew Donahue would be right behind him. The car didn't follow, but the phone rang. Tom hesitated, not wanting to make things worse, but he answered. Donahue's voice erupted on the other end.

"I'll have you arrested, Collins. Obstruction and kidnapping—you're in serious trouble."

"Are you done, Donahue?" Tom's voice remained steady.

"Mock me all you want, Collins. You won't be laughing when we cuff you!"

"On what grounds, Detective? Because I did your job for you?"

"Quit playing games. What were you doing in Sun Valley? I told you to stay home."

"I've been straight with you from the beginning. Wayne and Laura are your problem. My priority is Madee. I found her, Donahue. She's here with me."

There was a pause. Donahue's fury seemed to fade, replaced by silence. Tom knew the detective was calculating his next move. Then, a violent coughing fit broke through the tension. Madee, pale as a ghost, was coughing up blood.

"Collins, stay where you are. I'll send an ambulance."

"No. I'm taking Madee home."

"She needs a doctor, Collins."

"And I know exactly who to call. I'll be in Forrest Hill soon."

"Forrest... Are you out of your mind? Madee Mitchell needs a hospital, not some backwater retreat. St. Michael's intensive care team is ready for her."

"You don't give a damn about Madee, Donahue. She needs to be with people who love her."

"You'll be the one to blame if she dies in that car!"

"I'm sorry, Donahue, but I'm taking her to Forrest Hill. Goodbye."

Tom hung up, his heart racing. Anger surged through him. Donahue didn't know Madee, didn't understand what she needed. But as he glanced at her frail, unconscious body beside him, doubt crept in. Maybe Donahue was right—Madee was in worse shape than he wanted to admit. The car ride was taking its toll on her.

"My love," he whispered, his voice trembling. "I should have taken you with me, or stayed behind. You'd never have gone to North Station on your own. I'm sorry... so sorry. Please, give me a sign. I've made mistakes, but I swear I'll never leave you again. Please fight, Madee. I can't live without you. I love you."

His words hung in the air, unanswered. She remained still, her breathing shallow. Tom gripped the wheel tightly, his eyes darting to the rearview mirror. Flashing lights appeared behind him. That bastard Donahue had sent backup. Two police cars were closing in. Tom's mind raced. Calling the detective would only escalate things. He'd be torn away from Madee, possibly even barred from seeing her again. He couldn't let that happen.

It was impossible to shake off the cops on this stretch of the dual carriageway. Tom's only hope was to reach the Forrest Hill exit, four kilometers ahead. He knew where he was going, unlike the cops, who rarely patrolled the Forgotten District. The road ahead blurred in the distance. He worried the cops might call for backup. As the landscape shifted, signaling the city's edge, the police cars inched closer. Then, a slow-moving lorry loomed in front of him. Without hesitation, Tom floored the accelerator, swerved around the lorry, and veered sharply into the Forrest Hill exit. Glancing in the rearview mirror, he saw the police had missed the turn. There was no going back. He'd made it.

The entrance to the Forgotten District was a familiar sight, the buildings still battered and bruised. One day, these rundown houses would be torn down, replaced by homes with gardens and playgrounds for children. Tom envisioned green spaces, community bus routes. The neighborhood would be reborn. Madee would smile to see Forrest Hill brought back to life. Together, they would rebuild it, finish what his parents had started.

"I'll give you back everything you've lost, my love. We'll find treasures together..."

His voice cracked as he glanced at Madee beside him. But something was wrong—her chest wasn't rising. Panic shot through him. They were nearing the oasis. Doc's clinic was just ahead.

"No, no, no, not now, darling! Stay with me!"

Tom slammed on the gas, skidding to a halt in front of the clinic. Madee's body was ice-cold when he lifted her from the car. Racing down the alley and up the steps, his legs burned with the effort. Inside, he shouted, "Doc! Doc!" hoping the doctor could hear him.

Old faces peeked out from the recreation room, their eyes wide with surprise at the disturbance. They stared at Tom as if they weren't sure he was real. He pleaded for help, but no one moved. Rage bubbled up inside him—this wise generation had seen it all, but Madee might never get the chance to live. Adrenaline pushed him forward, wings on his feet, until he burst into Doc's practice. The door was ajar, and Tom barged in without knocking. Doc was measuring Father Andrews' blood pressure when they both froze at the sight of Madee's lifeless body in his arms.

"Doc, help her!" Tom's voice was hoarse.

"Tom, calm down. I'll take care of her."

"Save her, Doc! Please, save her!"

"Leave."

"But—"

"Tom, leave! Go sit with Father Andrews."

Through the closing door, Tom saw Doc attaching Madee to a set of old medical equipment before shutting it in his face.

Left standing in the hallway, Tom turned to Father Andrews, who was seated, gripping a rosary, quietly invoking the Virgin and Saint Raphael to pray for Madee. The priest motioned for Tom to sit beside him.

"Come, my son, let's pray."

"I'm not good at this, Father," Tom muttered, his voice tense.

"But God is with you, and you and Madee were meant to meet. You did what God wanted."

"I'm afraid, Father…"

"Those who believe can do anything. Let's pray."

Tom wanted to argue but kept silent out of respect for the priest. How could Father Andrews be so sure, so confident, when Madee was dying on the other side of that door? Tom clenched his fists, struggling to focus on the words of prayer. He tried to pray, tried to believe in a miracle, but the closed door stood like a barrier between him and faith. His thoughts spun in frustration. Why hadn't

Doc let him stay? He should be in there, fighting alongside Madee, not out here.

There was no clock in the room, which only added to his anxiety. Doc never kept clocks—he believed in giving time to his patients, refusing to be a slave to the ticking hands. "People waste their lives rushing," Doc had once said. He wasn't wrong. Time slipped through their fingers while they ran in circles...

Tom couldn't sit still. Father Andrews' prayers, whispered quietly beside him, did nothing to calm his nerves. He stood, pacing the small room, his steps restless and uneven. Every few minutes, he pressed his ear to the door, straining to catch any sound, but there was only silence. And silence felt like the worst kind of punishment.

If something had happened to Madee, surely Doc would have come out by now, wouldn't he? Tom forced himself to cling to that thought. The longer the wait, the better the chance. Yet the waiting gnawed at him, each passing second an agony he couldn't escape.

CHAPTER 44

FORREST HILL, A FEW STREETS FROM THE CLINIC...

Another gloomy day began at Elaine's, curtains drawn back at 5 a.m. Earl had always been an early riser, but since Madee's death, he had little left but his morning coffee. He worked to forget his failure to protect her. His days were spent trying to keep his community safe, helping the young, the old, the forgotten. But people were just passing through. The walls stayed standing.

After the funeral, Earl had turned his office into his home, waiting, listening for the bells, in case Madee ever walked through the door again. Shame weighed on him. He had seen her burned body on the fire brigade stretcher, arranged the mass, thrown the first flower and the first clod of earth onto the coffin. The smell of cakes lingered in his memory. Sometimes, he thought he could smell chocolate in the kitchen. He would rush to see, only to find Babou asking how he was. Earl would grunt, tell the cook to check everything, then walk away, leaving the ebony giant behind at his stove.

Since the fire, the cafe owner's luck had only worsened. Losing Madee was the worst, but the fire brigade and cops made it unbearable. The investigation was botched; they blamed an electrical fault. Someone had to be responsible, and Earl, as landlord, became the obvious scapegoat. They accused him of renting out dangerous accommodation, claiming he profited from the misery of others. Forrest Hill might be poor, but Earl took care of his buildings. He would never endanger his family. When he called the cops morons, they slapped him with a fine.

That's when it all began. Sanitation officers came next, inspecting everything, but found nothing illegal. Forrest Hill and its buildings were intact—no rats, no mold. They left empty-handed. Then the tax officers descended, demanding forty years' worth of accounts, scrutinizing every purchase, even a pair of toilet glasses. It was a nightmare. The bureaucrats were like vultures, picking apart what little was left. And finally, the planning officers arrived, announcing plans to turn Forrest Hill into a residential area. They told Earl his *"open dump"* was ruining the view from Sun Valley. He'd lost his temper. If Sun Valley folks didn't like the view, they could move to another hill.

But the town planners were relentless. They returned with bad offers, lowballing him at every turn. What followed was a legal battle, a David versus Goliath struggle that drained Earl and the community of their morale. Their world was crumbling around them. Then came the threat of collective expropriation. Earl was at his breaking point. He held back the tears by changing Elaine's opening hours.

Earl busied himself with cleaning, trying to fill the silence. There were no customers. Tom was the only one who ever came at opening these days, he thought. Sometimes, he missed the *"city prince,"* but at least Madee had been happy with him. Earl turned away from the door when the bell rang. Probably Babou, arriving early. The giant never liked leaving his boss alone, always saying, "I'm watching you, boss. I can feel when you're about to do something stupid." Earl appreciated the support but also cherished his moments of solitude.

He waited for Babou's usual greeting, but there was only silence. Earl turned, half-expecting he'd imagined the sound of the bell. Instead, a man in his sixties stood near the stage. His tailored suit screamed politician. Earl's stomach tightened with suspicion. Forrest Hill was already hanging by a thread—he needed to stay calm. Madee's doctrine, he reminded himself. He's a customer, treat him like one.

"Can I help you?" Earl asked, surprised by how polite he sounded.

The man turned from the stage and nodded.

"This stage is impressive. The acoustics must be something, especially with this wall paneling?"

Earl blinked, not expecting that. If even the politicians were starting to show up at his door, he wasn't safe yet.

"Is that Zak Gamble?"

The man's eyes fixed on a photo of Earl with the old 70's singer. Earl's chest swelled with a mix of pride and nostalgia. Few people remembered Zak.

"Zak's from Forrest Hill," Earl said, unable to resist. "Had rhythm, a voice like no other. Not like these artists today, screaming or getting remixed."

The man began humming *"Goodbye Summer,"* Zak's one and only hit from 1972. Earl couldn't help but join in, clapping along. For a moment, the man seemed less intimidating. Their duet was cut short by the doorbell ringing again.

Babou entered first, followed by a man and a woman.

"John? Margaretha?"

Earl's eyes widened. The Collinses? After all this time? And at this hour? They embraced him warmly, happy to see him again. Babou eyed the newcomers, puzzled by their polished appearance. John Collins shook hands with the man in the suit. That's when Earl's heart sank. Forrest Hill was still in jeopardy, and this visit wasn't just a friendly reunion. Margaretha spoke, breaking the moment.

"Earl, you've met Ron. Ron, this is Earl Stone. We told you about him on the phone. Earl, this is Ron Simons, the District Attorney."

"District Attorney?"

Earl's gaze hardened, suspicion flooding back. The politician extended his hand, but Earl didn't take it.

"Mr. Stone, it's a pleasure to meet you."

Earl's pulse quickened. "So, this is it then? Are they going to demolish the neighborhood? And you two," he said, looking at the Collinses, "you've taken over the construction site, haven't you?"

The confusion on their faces did nothing to calm him. Earl's stomach churned. Everything felt like an inevitable failure, one he hadn't seen coming.

"Mr. Stone, I'm not here to decide Forrest Hill's fate. I'm looking for someone, and I was hoping you could help me."

Earl stood frozen. How could he possibly help this prosecutor he had just met?

"Mr. Stone, do you know Madee Mitchell?"

"What kind of question is that?"

"Have you seen Madee Mitchell recently?"

"Prosecutor, get your facts straight. Madee died six months ago. She's not coming back from the dead!"

"Madee is alive, Mr. Stone. I thought she might be here."

Earl felt a wave of disbelief wash over him.

"You're out of your mind!"

Babou stepped closer, sensing the shift in the atmosphere, ready to support his boss. But the prosecutor pressed on.

"Mr. Stone, Madee didn't die in that fire. The body was that of a homeless woman. Madee was kidnapped that same day and held captive for six months...until tonight."

Earl's voice rose with anger. "This is bullshit! I don't want to hear any more lies!"

"I'm not lying, Mr. Stone. I fight for justice. The truth is, Madee is alive. We have a problem. A few hours ago, her boyfriend told Detective Donahue everything—about the evidence and the people responsible. He rescued her, but she needs medical attention. Her boyfriend brought her back here, to Forrest Hill. Mr. Stone, Madee's boyfriend is Tom Collins. Has he come to you?"

"Collins...? Is this some kind of joke? John? Margaretha? Is this a joke? Your son?"

John and Margaretha showed Earl and Babou photos on their phones. The boy in the pictures was the same one who had lived in the community, the same one who had been close to Madee. Earl's heart sank. He didn't want to hope—he was still mourning.

"Did you help Tom Collins, Mr. Stone?"

"No, I didn't! I didn't know he was John and Margaretha's son. I thought he was one of those city council workers here to make a report. He was arrogant, and I didn't trust him. Then he got close to Madee, and I didn't want her getting hurt. We didn't get along. He left after the fire, and I never saw him again. I'm sorry, John and Margaretha."

"If he didn't come to you for help, where did he go?"

"Is what you're saying about Madee true?"

"Her condition is serious, Mr. Stone. She needs medical attention."

"If it's true... I think I know where Tom went. We're going to check it out. Let's go!"

MYTHOMANIA

They set off through Forrest Hill together, moving like a band of survivors. Earl and Babou led the way, tense, their thoughts swirling. They didn't dare speak, in case the District Attorney or the Collins family overheard. But Simons' words had shaken them. Earl's mind raced. Who would hate Madee enough to kidnap her? The pact between the districts had kept the riff-raff in check. None of them would have dared to break it.

Earl didn't know what to believe. He almost hoped they wouldn't find anything when they arrived. The prosecutor's revelations challenged everything. Could Madee really be alive? And could Tom actually be the hero in this story? It seemed absurd, surreal. As they walked through the neighborhood, Earl found himself wanting to believe, even as doubt gnawed at him.

Earl half-listened as John and Margaretha spoke to Simons, recounting memories of their youth. He couldn't believe Tom was their son. He had been too suspicious, too wary, to dig deeper. Tom had always seemed dangerous, disrupting the order of things simply by showing up.

"Boss, look!"

Babou's voice pulled him from his thoughts. The giant was restless, shaking Earl's arm and pointing to a car parked in front of the building. Earl's mind raced, but there was no time for reflection now. They hurried inside. In the children's corridor, the old folks were murmuring about the event that had disrupted their quiet breakfast. Earl's temper flared—none of these half-senile remnants had thought to inform him. Wasn't he supposed to know what went on at Forrest Hill?

"Silence!"

He clapped his hands sharply, snapping the elders out of their gossip. They looked at him sheepishly, pointing toward Doc's door. "Tom's back. He wasn't alone," one muttered.

Earl waved them off, ordering them to return to their breakfast. His voice echoed down the corridor. "I'll tell you what's going on!" Anger coursed through him as he marched toward the door, followed closely by John, Margaretha, Ron Simons, and Babou. Inside, Tom was pacing anxiously, while Father Andrews knelt in prayer. Earl's eyes widened, disbelief mixing with fury.

"You too, Father?" Earl shouted. "This is a conspiracy! It's disgraceful!"

"Calm down, Earl!" Father Andrews responded softly. "I don't know what you're thinking."

"I'm not imagining anything. I'm seeing Father Andrews!"

Earl's voice trembled with a mix of anger and confusion, but he stopped short of attacking the priest directly. Even though he wasn't much of a churchgoer, he knew better than to challenge a man of God. The last thing he needed was divine wrath. But deep down, Earl's anger was directed at Tom. He couldn't forget the night of the fire, when Tom had appeared out of nowhere with his new fiancée, disrupting everything. Madee had given Tom everything, and for what? Earl still couldn't forgive him. Why should he?

Tom might be John and Margaretha's son, but he had wrecked Madee's life.

Earl was being hostile, and Tom was trying his best to explain what had happened to him and Madee, but it was like talking to a wall. Earl wasn't listening. He didn't want to listen. All he wanted was to lash out, to hurt Tom—perhaps in some twisted way, to defend the surrogate father who had lost his daughter.

Earl took two steps forward, still keeping a measured distance from Tom. The silent message was clear: he would never be part of their family. He didn't even need to think about his next words; they spilled out, filled with bitterness.

"You think you're the hero here, but maybe you're the one who caused all this."

The room went cold. The group was stunned by Earl's accusation, the absurdity of it. John, Margaretha, and even Baboutried to reason with him, but Earl brushed them off.

"This is between me and him," he snapped. "None of your business."

"If Madee dies, it'll be your fault! You ruined her life!"

Earl knew he had crossed a line, but in his anger, he didn't care. Tom's face darkened, and in a split second, his fist connected with Earl's jaw. The fight broke out like a storm, raw and childish. The two men wrestled, throwing punches, struggling like two animals defending their territory. Old and young clashed in a whirlwind of resentment.

The others tried to pull them apart, but the fury was too intense. And then, the door burst open.

"What the hell?"

Doc's voice cut through the chaos like a whip. He stood in the doorway, his expression a mix of anger and disappointment, blood staining his smock—Madee's blood.

"You're both acting like fools!" Doc barked. "Shame on you!"

Earl and Tom froze, both lowering their heads as if scolded children, forgetting their grudge for the moment. All eyes turned to Doc, who was still framed in the doorway, his voice commanding the room.

"You can settle your scores later, like civilized men," he said, his tone cold. "But for now, the priority is Madee. I've done all I can. She's stable, but her body needs time to recover. If I hear one more word, I'll throw every one of you out—no exceptions. My patient needs rest, so shut up and stick together, dammit!"

Without waiting for a response, Doc turned and slammed the door behind him, leaving them all standing there in frustrated silence. Earl had never seen his friend like that. And deep down, he knew why—it was his fault. He had let his impulsiveness get the better of him.

Earl slowly walked over to Tom, his anger dissipating, replaced by shame and regret. He held out his hand.

"Let's make peace," he muttered, barely able to meet Tom's eyes. "For Madee."

CHAPTER 45

TIME FOR THE TRUTH...

It had been six days... The news of Tom and Madee's return had spread throughout the community. Friends and family came with flowers, gifts, and words of support. The children's corridor was lined with tables where people left their offerings. Only Doc, Tom, Earl, and Babou were allowed into Madee's room. They remained by her bedside, waiting for her to wake up. Madee was too severely injured to be moved. Even a short ambulance ride could worsen her condition. Ron Simons had arranged for medical care to be set up within Forrest Hill, avoiding the risk of transporting her further.

The caregivers from St Michael's were eager to help, curious about this critically ill patient who had never been admitted to their ward. They were even more intrigued when they learned about the doctor responsible for her survival. Doc had performed what seemed like a miracle with outdated equipment. What Tom didn't know was that Doc had once been offered the position of head of emergency at St Michael's but had turned it down to stay in Forrest Hill. The entire medical team was eager to learn from this experienced doctor who had chosen to dedicate his talents to helping the forgotten. Yet opinions about Madee's chances of recovery were divided. The doctors from St Michael's saw her as a soul trapped in a vegetative state. If she woke up, they believed she would suffer permanent, life-altering damage.

Tom tried not to let their grim predictions affect him. Whenever he was by her side, he would hold her frail hand tightly, his eyes fixed on the monitor, hoping to catch a sign of life that no one else had noticed. He whispered to her, begging her to come back, sometimes feeling a faint twitch in her palm. Each time, he would call the medical team over, only to be told that such spasms were common in unconscious patients. But Tom clung to hope. He replayed memories in his mind—their first meeting, the conversations that had sparked their connection, the life they had shared, and that one night of love. He told himself over and over that they would pick up right where they left off.

Six days had passed, and Madee was still unconscious. She seemed so small in the white hospital bed, her emaciated face half-hidden under an oxygen mask, her bruised arms the only parts visible. Tom sat beside her, hoping that by now Wayne, Laura, and Angela were behind bars, awaiting trial. But even justice wasn't enough to erase what had happened. Tom would give anything to see Madee smile again, to restore her health, but human cruelty had already taken its toll on their happiness.

"Are you okay, boy?"

Tom hadn't heard Doc enter the room. The old man had a way of moving unnoticed.

"It's my turn to watch over Madee," Doc said softly. "You need to rest."

Tom didn't respond, his grip tightening on Madee's frail hand. Letting go felt like surrendering, like accepting the bleak prognosis the caregivers at St. Michael's had given. He couldn't admit what he was feeling, not even to Doc, who knew him better than anyone.

"Madee is going to die..."

The words slipped out before he could stop them, his gaze fixed on the machines that were keeping her alive. He felt ashamed for saying it out loud. Doc sighed heavily, and Tom braced himself for the doctor's response.

"You're giving up on her."

"Giving up on her?" Tom snapped, his voice shaking. "I'll never give up on her!"

"Yes, you will. You're killing her in your mind while her heart is still beating."

"You don't understand, Doc. She won't wake up! Right now, she's just waiting for her body to give out."

"Madee wouldn't have given up on you like this."

"I'm trying to accept that I'm losing her. Again. You can't fight death."

"Leave death where it belongs," Doc said quietly. "Try to see this differently."

Tom's frustration boiled over. It felt like Doc was lecturing him, and he hated it. He didn't want to be treated like a child who didn't understand life's realities.

"Why do you think it's over, Tom?" Doc pressed.

"Look at her," Tom whispered, his voice breaking. "It's been six days. Doesn't that scare you?"

Doc didn't flinch. "I've seen war, worked in humanitarian crises. I've lost patients. You're right, you can't fight death when the time comes."

Tom nodded, resigned. "Then I should start accepting it now, before it destroys me."

"You're not letting me finish. Yes, sometimes death is inevitable. But there are people with worse injuries than hers who have recovered."

"But they're never the same. They're disabled for life."

"Madee will recover," Doc said firmly. "I'm not saying that to give you false hope. I know it. She's come a long way. Stop focusing on the machines. Look at the bigger picture. Madee is protecting herself. Coma is still a mystery to modern medicine, but I believe it's a way for the mind and body to disconnect from the pain. Madee has been through hell—her heart may have stopped, but her mind withdrew so she wouldn't have to suffer anymore. She's not dead, Tom. She's hiding. Her body's here, but her mind is somewhere safe. She knows you're here. Give her time to stop being afraid."

Doc's theory would have sounded far-fetched to anyone else, but Tom knew the man too well to dismiss it. Yet, even with Doc's wisdom, the question gnawed at him: Did Madee even want to wake up? She was the only one who could decide whether to stay or leave.

"She needs you, Tom," Doc said softly. "And you can't help her if you're lost in your own doubts."

Doc's words were full of wisdom, as always, but they brought Tom no comfort. He leaned over and kissed Madee'sforehead gently before standing up to leave. Being alone was supposed to help him clear his head, but instead, it made him anxious. He didn't know what to do with himself. For a brief moment, he thought about going to Earl's—they had buried the hatchet, after all—but he wasn't in the mood for company. He felt locked in his own bubble, with no news about the investigation or the aftermath of the assault. Knowing the truth would help him move forward, but Simons and Donahue were nowhere to be found.

Tom left the clinic, stepping into the outside world, hoping to find answers on his own. If the authorities couldn't help him, he would seek the truth himself. He needed to understand what had happened six months ago... The place to start was North Station. Maybe, just maybe, he'd find out that none of it had really happened. He imagined Madee walking toward him, her light, elegant gait, and taking his hand. Together, they would go home, leaving this nightmare behind. But no matter how much he clung to that fantasy, he couldn't shake the question that had haunted him for months—why had she gone to North Station alone? She called it the Streets of Rage and avoided it like the plague. Hassan's food truck was always her limit. Beyond that point, Earl's protection ended, and she never ventured past it.

* * *

Tom walked quickly through Forrest Hill, passing familiar landmarks: Elaine's Cafe, the grocery shop, the garage... Each step felt like retracing the route of his memories. He quickened his pace, eager to reach the beginning of this pilgrimage. At the corner of Fleet Street, he hesitated. It would only take a few minutes to detour to Bell Street, where happier memories lived. But he decided to save that stop for last, as if finishing with those memories would bring closure.

Five hundred meters further on, he crossed into the neutral zone. Hassan's food truck was gone. The *"truck of happiness,"* as Madee had called it, had disappeared, likely moving on to other horizons. Tom felt a lump form in his throat. Madee would have been devastated to learn that Hassan was no longer there. She loved his food, even if she never allowed herself to enjoy it fully.

Tom's chest tightened as he thought about how much he had tried to nurture her, to feed her. Madee had always had a complicated relationship with food. She refused to find pleasure in eating because she still saw herself as the obese girl everyone had called ugly. Even now, as she lay unconscious, hooked up to a drip, she might never eat again. The thought overwhelmed him with grief.

The large wooden tables were the only remnants left in the neutral zone. A few homeless people sat around, drinking beer and talking about the hardships of life on the streets. Alcohol didn't heal wounds, but it helped numb them for a while. Tom knew a thing or two about that... As he walked by, some of the tramps recognized him as Miss Madee's friend and waved half-heartedly before returning to their conversations. For them, people just came and went, like ghosts passing through.

A few meters ahead, Tom crossed into pagan territory. North Station was in a far worse state than Forrest Hill. The towering concrete buildings blocked out the sunlight, casting the area into an unnatural gloom. Urban music blared from old transistors left on the pavement. The streets were littered with used syringes, condoms, and greasy wrappers. Groups of young crack, weed, and heroin dealers lurked in the doorways, waiting for desperate customers. The police hadn't ventured here in years, and the air was thick with danger. Sensing a potential customer, a young man in a brightly colored sweatshirt approached Tom, his eyes scanning him for any sign of weakness.

"You looking for something?" he asked casually.

In the past, Tom might have bought the kid's stash of weed for a few crumpled bills. But those days were long gone. Instead, Tom pulled out a hundred and handed it to the boy.

"I'm just looking for directions to the station."

The kid eyed the money greedily, hesitating at first, then snatched it. He pointed down Church Street, just a block away.

"Turn right at the end."

Tom nodded his thanks, but before he could walk away, the boy leaned in. "Watch out for the *Sheitan*. Creepy guy showed up around here... snatched some girl from Forrest Hill a while back. No one does business on that street anymore. Cursed place."

Tom's heart clenched. He didn't need to hear the rest of the story—he knew it too well. The boy's attempt to scare him fell flat. Tom's face hardened, and he continued walking, ignoring the dealer's disappointed look as he slunk back to his corner, happy with the easy hundred.

Visually, Church Street wasn't much worse than the rest of North Station. Same concrete buildings, same kids with no future—the specter of misery was everywhere in these slums. But for Tom, this place carried a darker weight. He stood exactly where the CCTV footage had captured the moment Madee's life had spiraled into horror.

Tom paused, closing his eyes. He could almost feel the predator's excitement, the thrill before the act, when Death Face had trailed her. Death Face was just a pawn—weak, expendable, drawn by the promise of money. He went where he was told, did what he was told... and he had destroyed everything.

Opening his eyes, Tom realized there was nothing more to find here. This place held no answers, only shadows. As he turned to leave, he noticed the drug dealers watching him more closely now, their hostility palpable. One spat in his direction, calling him a *"shitty cop,"* ordering him to get lost or they'd make sure he disappeared. The tension thickened around him. Just as Tom braced himself, the boy from earlier appeared by his side, gesturing for him to follow. He escorted Tom back to the Neutral Zone, away from the rising threat.

* * *

The rest of the journey passed without incident. Back in Forrest Hill, Tom felt the familiar comfort of being home. He walked down a narrow alley that led directly to Bell Street, where Madee's building—their building—stood. The scent of smoke still lingered in the air, even after all these months. As he stepped onto Bell Street, the sight of the charred remains of number 15 hit him like a punch to the gut. The fire had ravaged the building, leaving behind a blackened skeleton. Surrounding structures were covered in thick layers of soot, and yellow fire brigade banners cordoned off every entrance. The damage had been so severe that the authorities had deemed it unsafe for the remaining residents.

As Tom approached, he noticed a figure standing in front of the building, staring intently at the scorched walls. The man scribbled in a notebook. Tom recognized him instantly—Donahue. The detective, lost in thought, was still piecing together the puzzle of that night.

"Hello, Detective…"

Donahue looked exhausted, dark circles under his eyes. The pressure from D.A. Simons was taking its toll, and it was clear he wasn't going to let the detective off the hook.

"Hello, Collins. What brings you here?"

"I'll ask you again, Detective! You never called me back..."

"Do I look like your secretary, Collins?" Donahue snapped.

"No, but I expected you to keep me informed about the case. Have you arrested them yet?"

"It's more complicated than you think, Collins..."

Something in Donahue's tone was off, and Tom felt a knot form in his stomach.

"Collins... we haven't arrested anyone."

"What do you mean?"

"When we got there, they were all dead. The Becketts, Briggs, Brandon Stevens... Laura. Look, you need to see this."

Donahue pulled out his phone, tapping a few keys before handing it to Tom. On the screen, a video was paused on a close-up of Laura's face—her smile smeared with blood, no makeup, wild eyes staring back.

"This was the last video before we stormed the villa. By the time we managed to take it down, it had reached 4 million views."

Tom's pulse quickened. He wanted to throw the phone back at Donahue and refuse to watch, but he had to know what twisted rant Laura had unleashed. For Madee's sake, he couldn't turn away. He pressed play. Laura's voice crackled through the speakers as she addressed her fans, a twisted grin on her face. *"Hey, my darlings, today's lesson is all about winning..."* Her face disappeared from the frame, replaced by Wayne's mutilated body lying in a pool of blood. *"This here is my dear old friend Wayne,"* Laura's voice mocked, lifting his head by the hair to show his slit throat to the camera. *"Say hello, Wayne,"* she cooed, bringing the camera closer so her viewers could admire the gory details. Tom clenched his fists as Laura's laughter echoed through the video. She left Wayne's body and strolled over to the bar, her tone casual, as if nothing had happened. *"But first, let's talk about me."* She rambled through lies, half-truths, and delusions, blaming her school friends, Joy, her parents, and of course, Madee—the *"bitch sister who made my life hell."* Laura walked through the villa, making sure her fans saw the bodies of Angela and Death Face. She didn't want her *"darlings"* to miss any part of her gruesome handiwork.

"Here's Angela, the only one who could eat me out properly," she jeered. *"And here's the guy I hired to kill my slut of a sister, Madee, who's still hiding somewhere."*

Tom's throat tightened as Laura climbed the stairs, revealing Brandon's bloodied body on the bed. *"I didn't lie about him, you know. Brandon was mine... I just knew it before he did."* She giggled, running her fingers over his blood-streaked face. *"I just wanted him to love me, to see me."*

She turned back to the camera, her eyes wide, her voice trembling with fury. *"I wanted to be recognized. I wanted to make those bastards pay."*

Without warning, Laura raised a gun to her temple and pulled the trigger. The screen went black as shocked comments flooded in, but Tom couldn't read them. His mind was too numb with disgust. He handed the phone back to Donahue, unable to bear it any longer. Laura had escaped justice, and Madee would never get the closure she deserved.

"The case is closed, Detective, isn't it?"

Tom's voice was tight with frustration. Donahue, his face lined with exhaustion, shook his head slowly.

"I'm sorry, Collins... I wanted to catch those bastards as much as you did."

"What about Scott?"

"No one's found him. He's probably changed countries, changed his identity. There's an arrest warrant out for him..."

Tom's heart sank. "What am I supposed to tell Madee when she wakes up? That her torturers are dead and they won't have to face justice? That they'll never have to pay for what they did?"

"Collins, you're intransigent—"

"No, Donahue, I'm not. I'm going to fight to restore her dignity. To give her back some faith in life. She deserves, at the very least, a symbolic sentence. Without that, she'll never recover."

Donahue lowered his gaze, the weight of his own helplessness heavy on his shoulders.

"I'm sorry, Collins, but I don't have that kind of power... It was a massacre when we got there, and the worst part is the media is all over it. This case is a disaster. My team, my superiors, Simons, we're all trying to deal with Douglas Beckett, who's screaming conspiracy. Legally, there's nothing more we can do. But you, Collins... you have the power to protect Madee. She's going to need that, despite all our precautions."

Tom's chest tightened as he looked up at the second floor of 15 Bell Street. The remnants of Madee's life had been destroyed in the fire. Her African goddesses, her funfair trinkets, her vintage clothes—all of it was gone. The fragile semblance of freedom she had fought so hard to create was reduced to ashes. Those objects, those hours spent restoring them, now lived only in memories. Without a word, Tom turned and started walking away, leaving Donahue standing alone on the pavement.

"Collins! Where are you going?"

"Near the one I love, Donahue."

"Collins, wait!" Donahue called after him. "Can I ask you something?"

Tom paused but didn't turn around. "Make it quick."

"What happened to Wayne Beckett?"

Tom's pulse quickened, and he slowly turned to face Donahue.

"Why do you want to know? Need it to counter Douglas Beckett's accusations?"

"Collins... I've been investigating this case for two years. I've looked into you, but I never understood why you disappeared. It has nothing to do with the case, it's personal..."

Donahue's question cut deeper than Tom expected. It awakened something he had tried so hard to bury—a trauma he didn't want to relive. Memories of Wayne flooded back, of the moments that had torn at his self-esteem, the guilt he carried. Tom hated everything Wayne had been. And worse, he hated himself for never being able to say no.

"Donahue, I'm not sure you need to know that..."

"You're a puzzle, Collins... I think it's time to find out what made you who you are."

Tom lowered his head, his hands deep in his pockets, teeth clenched. A wave of unease washed over him.

"Did you know that Wayne Beckett was having a relationship with Brandon Stevens?" Donahue asked.

"I didn't... but I knew he was attracted to men. Everything he did to Madee was to punish me."

Donahue's eyes narrowed.

"What happened, Collins?"

Tom hesitated, a knot forming in his throat. "It's been so long... Why dredge up the past?"

"For you and Madee, to build a new life."

Tom shook his head, his voice low. "Do you really think we can survive this?"

"You must."

Tom wasn't convinced. Revealing another trauma would only make him look more broken in the eyes of the detective. He glanced up at the second floor, the burnt-out ruins of Madee's life staring back at him. What more did he have to lose?

He sighed heavily, the weight of the confession pressing down on him.

"All right... On the day of Garland's graduation, Wayne threw a huge party at the Invictus house. Nothing out of the ordinary—drugs, girls... We got stoned, we drank, we fucked. I can't even remember how many girls went down on me that night... it doesn't matter. I was just a fucking asshole looking for an identity, and I regret it more than anything now."

Tom paused, his breath catching in his throat. He had never said these words out loud, and it felt like they were tearing through him as he continued.

"It was about three in the morning; we were out of cocaine, and I had some left in my room. I went upstairs to get it, and Wayne followed me. We were both naked. He closed the door behind us... pushed me against the wall and kissed me. I pushed him away."

Tom's voice trembled, and he stopped, swallowing hard.

"He thought I was playing hard to get, trying to excite him. He started confessing—telling me that he had chosen me at Invictus because he liked me, that we'd be some kind of unofficial couple outside the orgies. I knew Wayne's temper, how volatile he could be, and I got scared. I told him I wasn't interested, but he didn't listen."

Tom's hands clenched into fists, the memory of that night crashing back.

"He got angry, threw himself at me, turned me over... I was too stunned to react. I couldn't stop him."

A bitter silence followed. Tom's breath was shallow, his voice barely a whisper as he finished.

"He raped me, Donahue. And then he went back to the party like nothing happened."

Tom's eyes were glassy with the weight of the confession. He wiped his face, ashamed "I packed my bags and left Garland early the next morning. I became a ghost. Collins' little bitch, continuing my life as a sex object, until I ended up in Forrest Hill... and Madee came into my life. Apart from the parties and the excesses, sex terrified me. I thought I'd never know love. But Madee... she saved me. Without her, I'd be dead. And Wayne Beckett took everything from her... because of me."

Donahue's face softened, his voice gentle.

"Collins... you could've gone to the police, reported this."

Tom scoffed. "Who would've believed me? A man, raped by another man? They would've called me a liar. I came home angry at my parents for sending me to university, rejected them, and destroyed myself. All the privileges I had in life didn't protect me from that."

He paused, his voice lowering again. "I've never told anyone, Detective. So I'm trusting you with this."

Donahue remained silent for a moment, his eyes full of understanding. "Collins..."

"Just pretend you don't know anything," Tom cut in, his voice sharp. "That's all I ask."

Before Donahue could respond, Tom's phone rang, saving him from having to say more. He glanced at the screen, and his heart skipped a beat when he saw Doc's message: *Come back soon, Madee's awake.*

Tom's pulse raced as he looked at Donahue. "She's awake. Madee's awake."

Donahue gave a nod, understanding the urgency. "I'm coming with you. It's probably too soon, but we'll need to interview her when she's ready."

Tom's mind was already on Madee, but he knew procedure would demand it. He just hoped that the questions wouldn't break her again.

Tom and Donahue arrived quickly at the clinic. In the hallway, the neighborhood children were playing quietly, aware that they shouldn't *"disturb Madee who was sleeping."* Even though it was school vacation, these children spent their days here while their parents worked. They didn't have the latest computers or game consoles, but they gathered in this place where they could play and be together. They didn't need more to be happy. Were these children wrong? They had their whole lives ahead of them to conform to outside expectations.

The children's muffled laughter echoed softly down the hallway, as gentle light illuminated the murals painted on the walls. Donahue paused for a moment, gazing at the innocent drawings. He seemed moved, and Tom, touched by this sudden vulnerability in the detective, pointed out one painting in particular: an angel riding a unicorn, ready to fly off into the sun.

"After my overdose, when I was well enough to go out, Madee brought me here... We painted this mural together. She said we would always be children and always have the right to dream..."

Donahue, usually so tough and pragmatic, suddenly seemed softened by what he was seeing. He didn't hide his admiration for this enchanted world. There was a time, long before he became the jaded detective he was today, when he too had been a child.

"Collins, I didn't understand... Who you were, your suffering, your disappearance... This is where you lived..."

They continued walking down the hallway until they reached Doc's office. As they were about to enter, Donahue stopped Tom with a gesture.

"Collins, Madee may never be the same... But I think you should tell her what you've been through."

Tom hesitated, his eyes fixed on the door that separated him from Madee.

"I'm not sure it will help me, Donahue..."

The detective placed a fatherly hand on Tom's shoulder, his gaze full of understanding.

"Time will tell, Collins... You and Madee, don't let the dead haunt you... Now, let's go in."

* * *

They had difficulty making their way through the St. Michael's staff, witnesses to the miracle of life. The nurses were blocking the entrance to the room, all eager to see the survivor and ready to assist Doc if necessary. But Doc paid them no attention, focused solely on his patient as he carefully removed the oxygen mask. Madee's eyes were open, her gaze fixed on Doc, who was speaking to her softly, helping her regain awareness of the world around her. Surrounded by strangers staring at her, she seemed lost. She smiled at Doc, as if reassuring herself that after months in the dark, the daylight was not a mirage.

Tom approached the bed, eager to see her more clearly, to sit by her side and take her hand. The moment she sensed his presence, Madee began to cry. Tom understood the violence of her emotional shock, the horror of the repeated rapes, Wayne's cruelty, and now, her second chance at life... Doc finished his examination and declared that she needed rest. The old doctor, too wise not to see, realized that the two lovers needed to be alone. He firmly ordered everyone to leave, instituting a rule that only one visitor would be allowed in the room at a time. Tom thanked Doc warmly, and the doctor wished him good luck before quietly slipping out.

Left alone, Tom felt helpless in the face of Madee's tears. He didn't know how to express just how happy he was to finally be with her, despite the distance created by her harrowing ordeal. Madee had always been the one to take the first step toward him, but now it was up to him to go further, to prove to her that she could count on him. She turned her head toward the window to avoid looking at him as he sat in the chair beside her bed. When he took her hand in his, he felt the familiar warmth that electrified him every time he touched her. Happy memories, a kaleidoscope of their moments together, rushed back to him all at once. He knew she hadn't forgotten him; Tom felt the fusion of their souls...

"My love, I've missed you so much..."

In a tender whisper, he murmured words of love to her, covering her hand with kisses like the insatiable lover he had been on their first night together.

"I'm here... I'll always be here, my love... I love you so much..."

But the magic between them shattered abruptly when Madee pulled her hand away. Tom, confused, wondered if he had moved too quickly. She slowly turned her head toward him, sadness in her eyes more eloquent than words. She opened her mouth to speak but immediately fell silent. Tom waited patiently, hoping to hear her first words to him. She hesitated several times before finally speaking in a weak voice.

"Tom, I can't..."

"My love... let me explain... nothing can separate us now..."

"You should have let me die... I'm sorry, Tom... I can't... I need time..."

"Madee... No!"

Tom tried everything to convince her, but she had already gone quiet, her tears falling silently. He understood that she had made her decision, and he had no choice but to go along with it. He waited, hoping she would change her mind, that she would scream that she hated him, but instead, she cried. Tom wasn't going to give up. He would stay by her side, no matter the cost. He got up to leave her alone when a memory flashed before him—the blonde girl at the fair and *La Vita Nova*. Madee needed to understand, she had to know.

"Madee... The first time I saw you, I knew you were meant for me... My life has never been the same. I thought about you every moment... You are the only woman who has this effect on me, Madee... I waited patiently for you to come to me, and when that day came, I felt blessed. Thanks to you, I realized I had taken the wrong path, that I wasn't the man I thought I was... When I overdosed, I was afraid you would tell me it was over, that you would judge me, but I was wrong. You brought me back to life... I made so many mistakes. One of them was believing you were dead instead of listening to my heart that beats only for you... I'm not proud of what I've done, and I'm terribly angry with myself, but believe me, when I found out about Laura and Wayne's dirty plan, I would have gone straight to hell to find you. Because I'm in love with you, Madee! I love you to death, and whether you like it or not, I'm not giving up on you!"

Although it was heartbreaking, Tom left the room without another word. He ignored Doc and Donahue, who asked him how things had gone between them—what was there to tell them anyway? Madee's reaction had been predictable, but he was determined to show her what he was capable of.

As he walked down the hallway, his thoughts heavy with emotion, Tom pulled out his phone and called his mother. She answered immediately.

"Tom, darling, how's Madee?"

"She's awake, Mum..."

"And?"

"I don't want to talk about it, Mum..."

"Tom, darling, she's traumatized. Give her time to heal..."

"Mum, I've made a decision. I'm going to join the company. There might not be room for me, but I want to finish what you and Dad started when you were young. I'm going to rehabilitate Forrest Hill. My only conditions: no other projects, and I need time to take care of Madee..."

"I'm so proud of you, Tom."

"Does that mean yes?"

"It means that your father and I will support you, but for the rest of the project, you're on your own. The lawyers will handle the official documents."

"Thank you, Mum!"

"Tom... Are you sure you have the strength for this project?"

"I love Madee, Mum. I'll do anything to make her happy. And even if she doesn't change her mind and doesn't want me in her life, I want to give her this gift."

"Well then, your father and I will be waiting for you at the office tomorrow morning. You've got work to do, so roll up your sleeves! And bring Earl with you—you'll need him to succeed!"

"See you tomorrow, Mum. Love you."

Tom hung up, a smile tugging at his lips, eager to get started. He wasn't afraid of the enormity of the task ahead because he was certain it was his calling. A flash of memory brought him back to a conversation with Father Andrews about faith and vocation. At the time, the priest's words had seemed old-fashioned, but now he understood. Destiny could call at any moment, and all he had to do was believe in it—everything would change. With a light heart, ready to embrace the work ahead, Tom left the clinic and headed toward Elaine's.

CHAPTER 46

EPILOGUE

"Could you keep it down a bit?"

"We've got deadlines, Mr. Earl!"

"Slow down, kids, we can't hear ourselves think!"

Standing just outside the door, Earl took his role as the neighborhood gossip to heart. He had a front-row seat to watch the progress of the work, observing the construction chaos with a mix of grumbling and pride. The place was a mess, but deep down, he couldn't help but feel a sense of satisfaction at the fresh air the project was bringing to Forrest Hill.

Forrest Hill had never been busier. An army of workers had taken over since the redevelopment had been approved by the politicians Earl had always openly despised. It had to be said that Tom Collins was no stranger to this chaos. But if he hadn't been so relentless, Earl knew that by now, he'd be watching his life's work get bulldozed with nothing but tears in his eyes. At first, Earl was suspicious. He didn't believe Tom when he talked about his plan to regenerate the Forgotten District. The old man thought it was all talk, but Tom had kept his promise. He had even asked each resident how they envisioned the new Forrest Hill, with the goal of making it a community project where everyone would feel at home once the work was finished. Such determination commanded respect, but more than anything, Tom's effort reflected the unconditional love he felt for Madee. It was for her that he had mobilized his energy. City Hall had been more than happy to hand over Forrest Hill to the Collins family, burying the administrative hatchet. Of course, the media frenzy had helped sway things in the community's favor...

Poor Madee... Her tragedy had made national headlines. The *"Mythomania/Brandon Stevens"* case was on everyone's lips, and it hadn't died down yet. Earl couldn't understand people's fascination with the sordid. They fed on and reveled in misery and violence from dawn to dusk, filling the pockets of those who knew how to sell sensationalism. A horde of journalists, TV vans, and curious onlookers had swarmed Elaine's when news of Madee's whereabouts leaked. Everyone wanted to speak to, or even catch a glimpse of, the survivor. The vultures...

Madee received thousands of offers. She could have been rich by now if she wanted to. Write a book, make podcasts, tell her story on TV—they all came rushing in with their sharp claws and well-padded wallets. But Madee didn't need any of that. She wasn't some sideshow attraction. All she needed was to return to a normal life, not to be crushed by the relentless media machine. She had already had more than her share of bad luck. Earl was more than happy to rid his district of the vultures. He didn't want those kinds of people around Forrest Hill. He even hired a new waiter just to throw them off. The young fool didn't know a thing about the business, but his presence alone was enough to disappoint anyone hoping for a chance to bother Madee at her workplace. For the more persistent types, Earl had another trick up his sleeve: his old pellet gun. Faced with the sight of a barrel aimed their way, even the most determined of them thought twice and turned around...

Earl spotted John and Tom arriving from his vantage point. Father and son were walking together toward Elaine's for their usual breakfast. The kid seemed to be thriving in his new daily routine—work was going well for him, and he had a knack for leading and motivating his teams. Soon enough, Tom would be more talented than John Senior...

"Time for a break?"

"It's well deserved, Earl! Could you get us a thermos of coffee for breakfast?"

"Sure, John!"

John Collins Senior was in a good mood. The man always stayed composed, no matter the situation. Earl had laughed when he read the article dubbing John *"the Ice-*

berg"—a fitting nickname for the businessman who could cool down an erupting volcano with a simple puff of air. But on the other hand, Tom wasn't looking as well, despite his victory with City Hall and the construction site progressing faster than expected. By day, he was Tom the Savior, the man who had brought Forrest Hill back to life. He smiled, chatted with people, and directed the workers, but there was no joy in his heart.

His relationship with Madee was stuck, despite his best efforts. They were still inseparable, of course, but whenever Tom tried to show her affection, she kept her distance. The kid was struggling—Madee was slipping away from him, not as part of any strategy, but because the love story between her and her Prince Charming had been battered by everything she'd been through. Anyone in her position would have reacted the same way, but Earl knew one thing for certain: Laura didn't count in Tom's heart anymore. He finally understood.

Tom took care of Madee, catered to her every wish, pampered her like a queen. But still, she refused to let herself be happy. She couldn't see the difference between what had happened and what could still be… Earl didn't understand young people anymore. Back in his day, people didn't make life so complicated for themselves. Earl could tell that Tom's mental health was spiraling. The boy wanted more than just a loving friendship with the woman he adored. They loved each other deeply, that much was clear, and Earl felt sorry for them. He hadn't wanted to get involved before—he respected Madee too much, considered her like a daughter—but now he didn't have a choice. These two young people needed to stop hurting each other and get on with their lives. With nothing more to see outside, Earl decided he had earned his morning break in his office. He limped across the dining room, berating his new recruit as he went, when Tom suddenly joined him.

"Earl, is Madee coming in today? I sent her messages last night and this morning... No reply... I've got something for her."

Earl felt the urge to mess with him—not out of spite, but because, well, he was still Earl, the old man who couldn't resist teasing. But at the same time, he pitied the young Collins. His mind was made up—he was going to fix things between those two.

"She's not usually expected. Her session with the shrink yesterday was tough... Don't worry, my boy, I'll take care of it! You'll see your Madee today, I swear on my life!"

"Thanks, Earl!"

"Yeah, yeah, right..."

The old man made his way to his office, grumbling about how large Elaine's seemed to his tired legs. When he finally reached his den, he collapsed into his chair and began searching for the old telephone buried under a pile of papers. Earl didn't know if that prehistoric machine even worked anymore, but he hated mobile phones and technology. You never got a signal when you needed it, and you were spied on 24/7—damn modern world!

At least with a corded phone, he could be sure of getting a dial tone. As he hovered his hand over the receiver, Earl hesitated. He was about to go straight to hell for lying to Madee... When he was a kid, the parish priest had always said lying was a cardinal sin, the kind that opened the gates of Satan's fiery home.

"Fuck it, I don't care what the preacher said!"

Earl dialed Madee's number. He'd make his peace with the devil later. Right now, the lovebirds needed to be reconciled, and quickly. After three rings, Madee picked up. Her voice was soft, like someone who had cried too much through the night.

"Yes, Earl?"

"How the hell do you always know it's me?"

"When you call me, your number pops up on my screen."

"Bandits! We're being spied on all the time! Damn this lost generation..."

"Earl..."

"Sorry, sweetheart, just thinking out loud! My leg's killing me, could you come help me at the cafe?"

"Earl, you're overdoing it. I'll call Doc to have a look, but in the meantime, stay put!"

"You're too kind, but I'm really struggling to get out of this chair..."

"I'm on my way, don't worry!"

Madee had already hung up before Earl could say another word. He leaned back in his chair, a wave of guilt washing over him. Sure, his leg hurt, but not enough to stop him from moving. Still, he justified it to himself—it was for a good cause, after all. The kid needed his girl, and someone had to make sure these two stopped torturing each other.

Ten minutes later, she walked into the office like a ray of sunshine. In her floral dress and gold shoes, she looked beautiful. No wonder Tom fell in love with her... This girl had it all, both morally and physically. Unlike others, her suffering had made her even more beautiful. After the same tragedy, some people would have withered away, but not Madee. She didn't let it destroy her, though she seemed to have lost her way when it came to Tom. By accepting her light, by taking her place in the world, she had turned her misfortune into strength.

"Earl, don't move! You're going to lean on me, and on the count of three, you'll stand up slowly..."

"As if your bird-like frame could support an old fart like me! Sit down, darling, we need to talk."

"You sound like you're about to sue me."

"Maybe I am... Have you seen him?"

"Yes, I saw him. He's with his father. I stopped by their table to say hello."

"Madee, don't let happiness slip away."

"I thought you didn't like Tom very much..."

"It doesn't matter whether I like him or not—he's lovesick for you."

"Oh yes, he loves me so much that he had sex with my sister as soon as I disappeared! And what do I have to offer him?"

"You've got everything to give him, honey, everything he's never had. Listen, sweetheart, you're wrong. Yes, he slept with your sister, but she put him through hell. Once she realized Tom would never love her, Laura quickly showed her true colors."

"I don't know what to think, Earl... He was free to say no to Laura..."

"She could be persuasive, you of all people should know that!"

"She was very good at it..."

"Then why are you pushing Tom away?"

"Because I'm scared, Earl! I'm scared he'll leave me and go back to his old life when he's tired of me. I don't want to trap him—he already feels sorry for me. I'm not even a real woman anymore..."

"If he was going to leave, we wouldn't be having this conversation, darling! He moved heaven and earth to find you the moment he learned about your sister's games. He loves you, damn it. And do you love him?"

"I can't imagine my life without him..."

"Then stop pushing him away and let him in. You've both been hurt too much. Only together can you get through this."

"I'll think about it... I just don't know if I'm ready..."

"Yes, you are! Your body has healed, stop letting your mind take over. And Tom... Tom is a gentleman."

She tried to hide the tears welling up in her beautiful blue eyes. She moved toward Earl and wrapped her arms around him like a lost child... He was the only father figure she had left. How sad was that?

MYTHOMANIA

Their moment of tenderness was interrupted by a noise coming from the dining room. Madee started to panic—the crowd, the oppressive feeling, the anxiety attacks creeping in...

"Earl, it's happening again..."

"You can hide in here, girl. I'll gladly take care of these assholes myself!"

"No! I'm tired of being the eternal victim. And you're right, I can't keep running away from life. It's up to me to face them once and for all."

Madee took Earl's arm and helped him walk, using the movement as motivation to confront these frightening strangers. With a good idea of what awaited them behind the door, they took their time leaving the office. But with Earl by her side, Madee felt safe. As soon as they stepped into the dining room, a group of people moved toward them, phones out, cameras rolling, ready to capture her every move. What a burden to bear—learning to live as the sister of Laura, the fanatical, crazy, lying influencer. Once again, Laura had escaped the consequences of her cruelty. In her eternal rest, she didn't have to suffer the torment of these amateur paparazzi, this modern plague...

The group stepped aside to let two men pass. The first one raised his arms to the sky, demanding to be noticed. Madeedidn't like his filthy, hypocritical face—he was shallow and seemed to have an oversized ego. A kind of Wayne Beckett alter ego... Madee shuddered at the thought of her torturer. Even if he was no longer in this world, it felt like he could return from beyond the grave...

She recognized the second man—the Star. He had changed so much since she'd last seen him. Two decades later, he must have made a fortune for his plastic surgeon, his fitness coach, his tattoo artist, and his dentist. His brown hair now reached the middle of his back, and he looked like one of those partygoers from Ibiza or some other extravagant paradise. Completely detached from reality, he had transformed into the ultimate version of his public persona—Echidna, the king of the night. Far from the unknown DJ Madee had hung out with in her teens... She had long since filed their story away in the archives of her past. She had only thought of him during her captivity...

"Baby? Jesus, baby, is that you? I almost didn't recognize you! When I saw the news in the media, you can't imagine my surprise! Brandon Stevens... Wow... Naturally, I started a big support campaign on my socials: #supportmadee #echidna. I told all my followers about you—we got a million views, can you believe it? Anyway, here I am!"

Confused, Madee didn't know what to say to her first boyfriend, who now felt like a complete stranger. She felt so far removed from him, from the love-struck teenager she had been, flattered that someone was finally paying attention to her.

"Aren't you going to say anything? If your trauma left any lasting damage, you can tell us. Everyone will understand—you're in a friendly environment! Oh, by the way, I haven't introduced you to Tim, my manager! Tim, this is Madee. Madee, Tim."

No sound came out. She wanted to speak, but the words were stuck in her throat. Her body felt like it was tearing apart, the sensation reminding her of the months of abuse. She wanted to scream, to let out the fury of her rejected teenage self, to tell him to leave her alone. Her hands turned clammy, her limbs stiffened, and her anxiety rose like a wave crashing over her. All those phones pointed at her... Her ears rang, her pulse quickened... Echidna still saw her as a child, a broken child at that. She felt like nothing—just a piece of trash trampled on without mercy.

Her arm tensed completely, and Earl could feel her faltering. Whoever this jerk was, he didn't need to be here, and Earl would make sure he got the message.

"Okay, Madee and I were thrilled about your visit, but now it's time for you to go. We're expecting people! Get out, or I'll blow your ass away with my gun!"

Earl's threat had an immediate effect on the idiot's followers. They grabbed their phones and scurried off like rats, realizing this wasn't the publicity stunt they had been promised. It would be a social disaster for the star to lose his fan base like this. But Echidna and Tim stood their ground, blatantly ignoring Earl's orders... an attitude that was enough to annoy the old man even more.

"Are you still here? Scram, scram! Leave Madee alone!"

Tim didn't budge. Instead, he extended his hand to Earl in a show of peace.

"I assume you're the agent for... what's her name again? Oh yes, Madee! We must discuss business."

"Boy, do you not understand that the only business you'll be doing here is getting yourself sent to the hospital?"

"Ah ah, hard bargaining, I love it! I love this old grump! Now, is there anyone around who can get us some coffee? It's bad enough we came all the way to this swamp..."

"How about an extra dose of arsenic in your coffee?"

"I love him! I absolutely love him!"

Tim's talkative style, asking and answering himself, was clearly meant to confuse his opponents—his way of negotiating. But Earl wasn't the kind of man to be confused by cheap tricks. He just rubbed his hands together, thinking he might as well let these two clowns waste their time because they weren't going to get anything out of him.

Echidna, looking disdainful, found a seat near the window, always the narcissist. He struck a pose, waving at the few people passing by Elaine's at this early hour. He seemed disappointed that no one came in to ask for a selfie or an autograph. The hard truth for an artist clinging to the spotlight—desperate to avoid slipping back into obscurity.

With an air of authority, Tim grabbed Madee's arm, pulling her toward their table. She wanted to pull away, but he held on tight, refusing to let go until he got what he wanted. Earl brought over the coffees, taking the opportunity to warn the two jerks that he was watching them closely. He took a seat with Tom and John, keeping a sharp eye on the scene. Madee wasn't ready to face the past, even with her loved ones nearby. Joe had always been a coward, and after two decades in the shark-infested waters of showbiz, he'd probably tear her to pieces. But Joe remained silent, letting Tim do the talking, convinced that his words were all that was needed to sway her.

"Madee, I've got a job offer for you. A golden opportunity for someone like you..."

"Someone like me?"

"I misspoke... Sorry... What I mean is, this is your chance to get out of this hole for good! You know Joe—well, Echidna—you're in the perfect position to know his first album, *Loneliness Island*, was a worldwide success. Nowadays, his albums still sell, but he's been labeled commercial. We've surrounded ourselves with the best producers, but Echidna'screativity has hit a wall. The early fans, the specialized press, the clubs—they're all waiting for him to rise again."

"And what does that have to do with me?"

"It's all about you, Madee! From the very start, you're the head, you're the inspiration, you're the muse."

"But what else?"

"Here's how I see it: You're beautiful, so the makeover won't be much work—maybe swap those granny clothes for some designer pieces. You've got an ear for music, but your biggest asset is that you've got a story to sell. Imagine it—two music-obsessed young lovers, separated by life. He's the international DJ, and you... the battered sister of Laura, the psychopathic influencer. They reunite, fall in love all over again, and produce tracks that make record sales history. I've already got clubs lined up, wanting you exclusively! Picture this—a two-and-a-half-year world tour, culminating in a live album in Ibiza. Money rolling in, everyone gets rich, life is good."

"Wow..."

Madee was at a loss for words. Ten years ago, if Tim had come to her with this offer, she might have accepted without hesitation, just to escape the tyranny of her family. But now... Echidna watched her closely, sensing none of the enthusiasm he had expected from the woman who had once helped him rise to stardom. Blinded by the lure of money, he stepped in to support his manager's pitch.

"Baby, I'm sorry! I thought about you all the time, but I was a coward, I didn't have the guts to come back after I left you... Please don't get me wrong... I had dreams back then, and when the label offered me the chance to produce Loneliness Island, I had to jump on it. Opportunities like that don't come around every day... I had to make a choice... And honestly, you weren't exactly the person I wanted to become. But I know you have a good heart, baby, so I'm asking you to forgive me and accept Tim's proposal... For me, for us..."

From his table, Tom didn't have to strain his ears to catch the conversation. The two clowns were talking so loudly that even a deaf person could hear them! Echidna and his manager were unbearable... Jealousy gnawed at Tom's heart. What if Madee chose this guy? Who wouldn't jump at such an opportunity? Tom's hands trembled as he nervously twisted his napkin. He couldn't understand why

Earl, usually so quick to act, wasn't stepping in to chase them off.

John the Iceberg smiled at his son with the calm wisdom of a father and a seasoned businessman who knew exactly when the right cards would fall.

"Son, let them play their game and watch them wallow in it."

Echidna, sure of himself, thought Madee would fall into his arms after his declaration. She used to be more malleable, easier to convince... But now, he could sense her hesitation. His mind raced—he had to come up with something fast, or he could kiss his career goodbye. His fame was fading, like all passing trends. The younger generation of DJs was rising, pushing him closer to the exit. No, he wouldn't let it end like this—not after so many years of glory. He'd reclaim Madee, and with her by his side, he'd reclaim his place at the top. He couldn't bear the thought of playing small village parties for the rest of his life because of her!

All he had to do was play the role of the charming, repentant lover, and she wouldn't know the difference. Women... you just had to feed them the right lines, give them a few gifts, and they'd overlook everything. Madee had become so beautiful—his friends would be green with envy when they saw her on his arm, this stunning woman who had reappeared out of nowhere. His plan was foolproof. As Echidna spoke, Madee remained still, but her hand trembled ever so slightly. Her eyes darted away from his, as if she could sense the falsehood in his words, the manipulation behind his charm. She hesitated, her mind torn between the allure of what he promised and the bitter taste of who he really was. The weight of his words pressed on her chest, bringing back the memories of how he had left her behind before.

From across the room, Tom felt his heart pounding in his chest, the panic rising with each passing second. The thought of losing her, of seeing her taken in by Echidna's lies, filled him with dread. He clenched his fists under the table, his pulse quickening. How could he fight against someone offering her the world?

"Baby, I love you, I've never stopped loving you... I've been a big jerk, so I'm begging you, give us a chance to start again. Take Tim up on his offer, you'll see..."

Madee's fists clenched under the table, her nails digging into her palms. Her patience, which had already been thin, was now gone. Her heart raced as the anger swelled inside her, but she was done being silent.

"Shut up, Joe!"

"What?"

"I said shut the fuck up, all right? I'm the reason you're successful, and you have the nerve to treat me like some girl you've come to rescue."

She stood up now, her hands flat on the table as she leaned toward him.

"I thought I was in love with you, but it was all an act. I moved on a long time ago. You're just a silly, complex opportunist, so you, your manager, your declarations of love, and your job offer can all be fucked! End of interview!"

"Baby..."

"Oh, and I forgot—famous or not, you pay for your coffee! And we charge extra for morons here, so that's 50! Now get out!"

Madee stared at Echidna, who finally lowered his head, realizing he'd lost. Mad with rage, he yanked a 50 from his pocket and stood up, casting one last glance back at her.

"You'll regret it, baby!"

"You can stick your threats up your arse, Joe! I won't say it twice—get out of here, and don't forget the tip!"

Madee burst out laughing, flipping him off with a raised middle finger. It was over. A chapter of her life was finally closed, and for the first time in a long while, she could think about the future. Her shoulders relaxed, and the weight of it all seemed to lift as she let out another laugh. She was free.

John Collins glanced at his watch, satisfied with the defeat of the two intruders. It was time to return to the building site, and then he and Margaretha would head back to the city for lunch.

"Earl, put our breakfasts on my bill, will you?"

"No problem, John!"

Before leaving, John ran his hand through Tom's hair, a gesture that reminded him of when Tom was just a boy. There was a glimmer of emotion in his eyes—being reunited with his son, seeing the man he had become, filled him with pride. He would forever be grateful to Madee for bringing Tom back to the right path. His beloved son was now a strong, responsible man, and John knew all he needed now was a final push of encouragement.

"Madee has the soul of a Collins, my son! It's your turn now... marry her!"

John gave his son a firm pat on the back, a smile playing on his lips, and then walked out of the cafe, whistling one of those old tunes only he knew.

Tom watched his father walk away, still puzzled by the enigma that was John the Iceberg. He was a strange man, but Margaretha was the only one who truly understood him, the only one who could decipher every nuance and subtlety. That was the power of love—to be the one who sees what the other never reveals to the world. Tom's gaze shifted to Madee, who stood by the window, her eyes lost in the sight of the changing street outside. Nothing ever stayed the same—except the regrets of lost moments.

Tom joined her at the table, pulling something awkwardly from his pocket and placing it in front of her.

"The workmen found it when they were clearing the rubble of our old building..."

It was the angel with the lily, miraculously untouched by the flames, waiting in the wreckage for someone to find it. Madee gently wiped the soot from the small statue, her fingers delicate as she held it close to her heart.

"I messed up, Tom," she whispered, her voice soft but steady. "I was convinced you only pitied me, that you stayed out of obligation... I pushed you away, and that was deeply unfair. I'm so sorry... I let jealousy and my own insecurities blind me... I love you, my darling. I can't imagine my life without you."

Her face glowed with a newfound serenity, her eyes bright and clear, free of fear and doubt. With a soft smile, she placed the angel back on the table, then left her chair to curl up in Tom's lap. She wrapped her arms around him, and for the first time in what felt like forever, she allowed herself to kiss him—the man she had been afraid to love.

Tom savoured every second of that kiss, deep and passionate, the kind that made the world disappear around them. Their happiness was palpable, but as they pulled away, Tom knew there was one final step to take to make their reconciliation complete. Tom took a deep breath, clearing his throat as he held her hands in his.

"Madeleine Mitchell... will you marry me? Will you take my name, share my life, wake up with me every morning, grow old with me? Will you do me the honor of being my wife?"

Madee's eyes filled with tears—not of sadness, but of pure joy. She smiled, her heart racing as she replied.

"I want nothing more than to be by your side, Tom Collins. Yes, I want to be your wife, and you do me the honor of being my husband."

"For the rest of my life," Tom whispered, pulling her close.

Applause erupted from the other side of the room. Earl and Babou had been watching the entire scene unfold, beaming with happiness as they witnessed the couple's long-awaited reunion. Earl grinned and raised his glass, while Babouclapped louder than anyone.

"Well, lovebirds, I hope we're invited to the wedding! Shall we toast to the good news?" Earl chuckled.

Tom and Madee exchanged a glance, their smiles bright as they shared another kiss before joining their friends. Earl had already prepared the champagne, pulling out his best bottle—the special cuvée he had saved for a truly momentous occasion. As the glasses were filled, the room was alive with chatter and laughter. Together, they raised their glasses to friendship, to love, to new beginnings, and to the many years ahead of them. As they stood together, a calm settled over them, and Tom's mind drifted back to a day that had changed everything.

It was in Father Andrews' chapel, that peaceful sanctuary where they sat side by side, their hands intertwined as they prayed. He remembered the flickering candles, and the deep sense of peace that had enveloped them both.

That day, they had found comfort in their prayers, asking the angels to guide them. Tom could still feel the warmth of Madee's hand in his. Those hadn't been just words—they were a promise. A silent vow that no matter what trials came their way, they would always find their way back to each other. And now, with Madee in his arms once more, Tom knew they had followed that path faithfully to this very moment.

*"And lead us not into temptation,
But deliver us from evil.
For thine is the kingdom, the power and the glory for ever and ever.
Amen."*

To extend the immersion into Mythomania, here is the playlist that inspired and accompanied me throughout the writing of this book.

Anthropology (Official Music Video) – Vladimir Cauchemar
Aulos – Vladimir Cauchemar
(G)rave – Vladimir Cauchemar
4:30 - Danger
Street Life – The Crusaders
Stormy Weather – Etta James
Oh Love – Emilie Nicolas
Unnskyld – Yomi
Anthropology 2, the final – Vladimir Cauchemar

Did you enjoy *Mythomania*? Follow me on social media to dive deeper into the world of the novel, discover writing insights, and stay tuned for my next literary adventures!

Instagram: @lhopeauthor
Facebook: LaurenHopeAuthor
X :@LaurenHopeAuth

Printed in UK by Lghtning Source UK Ltd. - Milton Keynes UK (print on demand)

Legal Deposit

British Library, London (October 2024)
Bibliothèque Nationale de France (October 2024)

Milton Keynes UK
Ingram Content Group UK Ltd.
UKHW030910141024
449705UK00013B/624